Praise for Leigh Greenwood

"Leigh Greenwood continues to be a shining star of the genre!"

—*Literary Times*

"Leigh Greenwood remains one of the forces to be reckoned with in Americana romance."

—*Affaire de Coeur*

"Greenwood's books are bound to become classics."

—*Rendezvous*

"Leigh Greenwood is one of the best."

—*RT Book Reviews*

Someone Like You

"Greenwood never disappoints. His latest Night Riders romance is a tangle of lust, greed and betrayal. Continuous action, sharp intrigue, and well-rounded characters captivate."

—RT Book Reviews

"This is a love story that will keep your interest from the first sentence until the last page. Enjoy!"

—A Romance Review

Born To Love

"The characters are complex and add a rich element to this Western romance."

—RT Book Reviews

"[Greenwood] has a nice sense of place, and his ability to write interesting, flawed characters dealing with real issues is admirable."

—Rendezvous

Texas Pride

Texas Pride

A Night Riders Romance

Leigh Greenwood

sourcebooks
casablanca

Published by Sourcebooks Casablanca, an imprint of Sourcebooks, Inc.
P.O. Box 4410, Naperville, Illinois 60567-4410
(630) 961-3900
Fax: (630) 961-2168
www.sourcebooks.com

Printed and bound in Canada.
WC 10 9 8 7 6 5 4 3 2 1

Prologue

San Antonio, Texas, May 1870

"What are you doing here?" Ivan asked Laveau diViere. "Nate has vowed to kill you on sight. He's never forgiven you for his brother's death."

"He won't shoot me in the lobby of the Menger Hotel."

"After you stole my money, don't be too sure I won't shoot you."

Laveau's laugh infuriated him, but Ivan checked his anger. His boss wouldn't be happy if he started a brawl in a public hotel.

"Maybe I can make amends," Laveau offered.

"Nothing can make up for what you did. People died because of your betrayal."

"What if I gave you the chance to own half a ranch in a year?"

Ivan didn't believe Laveau owned even a piece of a ranch or that he would offer it to him if he did. "How did you get half a ranch?"

"I won it in a poker game, but as you've so thoughtfully pointed out, I'm not safe here. I need someone to run it in my absence."

Ivan couldn't trust Laveau, but the offer was tempting. He had always intended to go back to Poland and reclaim his position in the Nikolai family when he had enough money to keep from being dependent on his sister's Russian husband. "What is the catch?"

Laveau took an envelope from his pocket and held it out to Ivan. "There's a copy of my proposal inside. All you have to do is sign it."

Ivan opened the envelope and read the document. It seemed legitimate, but he'd show it to a lawyer to make sure. "Why are you doing this?" he asked.

"I feel bad about taking your money. This is a chance to repay you. At least go take a look at the place."

Ivan didn't believe Laveau ever felt bad about anything he'd done, but this was an opportunity he couldn't afford to ignore even though his friends might not understand. Since the war they'd been trying to bring Laveau to justice for his treason, but while Texas was under a Reconstruction government and Laveau was protected by the Union troops stationed in Texas, there wasn't much they could do without ending up before a firing squad. "I'll think about it. How would I get in touch with you?"

"There's a lawyer in Overlin named Lukey. Leave word with him."

And with that, Laveau walked off, leaving Ivan to wonder if he finally found his ticket home after all these years.

Chapter 1

CARLA REECE SCREAMED, CRIED, SHOUTED, HIT HER brother with all her strength, kicked furniture and walls, but none of it served to ward off the horrible realization that a stranger was coming to take possession of half her ranch. Just the thought caused nausea to well up at the back of her throat. How could this have happened? Danny was the best poker player in Overlin, Texas. He'd been playing for extra money ever since the older men started letting him sit in on friendly games.

"No one would let you play for stakes that high," Carla said to her brother. "They know what I'd do to them if they did." Carla liked a good time as much as anyone, but she never mixed business with pleasure, and anything having to do with the ranch or money was business.

"He was a stranger. Some guy named Laveau diViere."

"Did Ed know him? Frank? Lukey? Anybody?"

Danny shook his head.

"Then why did you play with him?"

"Nobody else wanted to play."

"How could you be stupid enough to play for that much money?"

"I didn't mean to, but I let him goad me into taking a drink."

"Why? You know you can't drink."

"He kept saying I didn't drink because I was too young, that my mama wouldn't let me, that I wasn't man enough to hold my liquor. I know that was dumb, but he was so cocksure, I wanted to take him down a notch. I was doing okay until I bet too much on a good hand."

"Why didn't you stop there?"

"Because he was such an arrogant son-of-a-bitch. I just wanted to wipe that awful smile off his face."

"Enough to risk your half of the ranch?"

"I had an unbeatable hand. A royal flush ace high."

"Nothing's unbeatable except four aces with jacks wild." She didn't play poker, but she knew the rules. "Did you sign anything? Was it witnessed?"

"He made me sign a paper before he would accept my bet. Lots of people saw me do it."

So there was no mistake, no miraculous way out of this nightmare. She'd have to share the ranch her parents carved out of the wilderness with a man she'd never seen and already despised for taking advantage of a beardless boy.

Over the following days she said a lot of things to Danny she regretted, or would come to regret once she was over the worst of the shock and outrage, but she wasn't there yet. Now it was more than a week later and still no sign of the villain who'd stolen half of their ranch. Each day that passed without his arrival wound Carla's nerves tighter. She awoke each morning dreading that it would be the day he would show up and went to bed each night relieved and anxious at the same time.

Insignificant noises annoyed her. The sound of an approaching horse caused her breath to catch in her throat. The slightest aggravation sent her temper spiraling out of control. She paced from one room to another, taking note of things to do, yet leaving most of the tasks unfinished. She felt imprisoned in the house, but she couldn't leave it. Her concentration was gone. Thoughts flew out of her head as quickly as they entered. She was hungry, but the smell of food caused her stomach to heave. She hated to be by herself but couldn't stand to have anybody around. She was slowly going crazy, each of the previous nine days being a little worse than the one before. It had gotten so bad Danny had moved into the bunkhouse.

Lukey, the only lawyer in Overlin, had told her Laveau diViere's claim was good, but she couldn't accept giving up any part of her ranch. Her father and mother had risked their lives to hold it against Indians, had worked themselves into early graves to make it successful. Danny loved the ranch as much as she did, so she couldn't understand how he could have risked it in a poker game.

She left the kitchen and walked through the wide hall to the sitting room, but her mind took in nothing about the room her mother had labored to make into a space that reflected her gentile upbringing. Not the velvet-covered settee or the brocade curtains pulled back by heavy sashes. White sheers filtered the Texas sunlight that flooded the room with warmth at variance with the chill that arced down her spine every time she thought of having to yield part of her ranch to a stranger. Her stomach heaved so violently, she put her hand over her mouth, but she refused to be overcome by the thought of the man who'd destroyed her peace of mind. She was going to get her ranch back. To have a stranger running it would be an affront to the memory of her parents.

Danny looked so much like their mother, Carla couldn't see him without thinking of what her mother would feel if she knew what happened. The ranch had been a job to their father, a way to make a living, but it had been life-changing to their mother. She had reveled in the freedom from the conventional restraints forced upon women in the little South Carolina town where she'd been born. She'd been excited when her husband suggested they try ranching in the new state of Texas. She had put up with hardship because she'd wanted Carla to grow up with freedoms she had never enjoyed. She had insisted that her husband buy their land. She didn't trust a system that allowed a rancher to claim land he didn't own. She hadn't understood ranching, but she'd liked it because it was different. She didn't understand Texans, either, but she loved them because they let her be herself no matter how unconventional or illogical.

Yet inside the house, her mother had preserved part of her former way of life. Never having lived in South Carolina, that was a side of her mother Carla never understood, yet she loved the house because her mother had loved it.

Carla straightened a doily, one of many her mother had crocheted during winter evenings. She ran her finger over the surface of a side table, but it left no trace. She already dusted it twice that day. She grunted in frustration. She couldn't stick with any task or keep her mind on any job as long as she was expecting this interloper any minute. Why didn't he come? Why did he *have* to come? Unable to stay cooped up in the house any longer she walked to the hall, opened the front door, and stepped out onto the porch.

The air was hot and still, but the sun was sinking on the horizon. It would soon be time to start supper. Her brother had to eat, whether or not she felt like cooking. Irritated at her inability to be still, she sat down in a chair, determined to remain there until it was time to go to the kitchen. But she barely settled her skirts around her when she noticed a horseman in the distance.

Her body went rigid, and her breath hitched. She shaded her eyes and squinted to see what detail she could make out. Was it someone she knew? Or was it *him*?

Her first impression was that he was bigger than her brother, who was easily over six feet tall. He rode easily in the saddle, his posture so erect you'd have thought he was in a military parade. His horse, a sorrel with dark mane and tail, was several inches taller than any horse on her ranch, but the most distinctive thing about him was his dress. Despite the heat and the dust, he wore a coat over a vest, white shirt, and tie. His flat-topped, wide-brimmed hat didn't disguise his fair skin or cover his almost-white, blond hair. His black pants clung to his muscled thighs, and his boots practically glistened. Sunlight glinted off the polished surface of his silver-studded saddle and bridle. For a moment she thought he might be trying to imitate a Spanish caballero, but as he drew closer, she sensed that his manner of dress was a reflection of something inside him rather than the other way around. He had an almost regal presence about him which put her back up.

He probably thought he was better than she was, better than anybody in Overlin, most likely better than anybody in Texas. He rode like he owned the world.

She told herself to relax. Danny had said Laveau diViere was dark and a native Texan of Spanish descent. It was unlikely he would have any connection to this blond giant. This man was probably lost. He certainly didn't know how to dress for Texas.

Yet as he drew closer, she found herself subjected to different feelings. He was so handsome no woman could look upon him and not be affected. There was a cool perfection about him that implied all feeling—mental, emotional, or physical—would be kept under tight control. She shivered despite the heat.

She got an unexpected surprise when he drew close enough to smile at her. All traces of disdain or cold cordiality fled, leaving her the recipient of a smile of incredible sweetness. Despite her usual reticence around strangers, it coaxed her to her feet and toward the steps. As he drew closer, she could see he was even more handsome than she first thought. What could such a man be doing wandering around Texas? He brought his horse to a stop, dismounted, and approached the bottom of the steps. He removed his hat and nodded in greeting.

"Good afternoon, miss. I am looking for Danny Reece." He spoke with an accent she couldn't quite place.

"I'm Carla Reece. Danny is my brother, but he's not here right now. Can I help you?"

"I am Ivan Nikolai. I have come to take over Laveau diViere's half of your ranch."

Chapter 2

CARLA'S WELCOMING SMILE FROZE, AND THE HEAT OF her long-smoldering anger and resentment burst into flame. It didn't matter that this man wasn't Laveau diViere. He was here for the same purpose, to take what didn't rightfully belong to him.

"You have no business here, Mr. Nikolai. You're not the man who cheated my brother of his inheritance."

"Laveau diViere contracted me to manage his share of the ranch."

"How do I know you're telling the truth? You could be trying to cheat diViere just like he cheated my brother."

"I do not know the means by which Laveau came into possession of half your ranch—"

"He didn't *come into possession* of it. He stole it!"

"—but I have a written contract which says I am to manage the property for a year."

That stopped her. "Why just a year? What does he plan to do then? Sell it? I will buy it if he'll give me time to find the money."

"If I stay for the year, the property will belong to me."

That was something she hadn't foreseen. "What will you do with it?"

"Sell it for the highest price I can get so I can go back to Poland."

Now she understood the origin of the accent, but the

situation was even worse. The Four Corners was the most successful ranch within six counties. They had the best grass and the best water. Several ranchers would jump at the chance to buy the land for more money than she could pay.

"What part of the land belongs to you, and what part belongs to Laveau?" Ivan asked.

"The ranch has never been divided. My brother and I own all of it equally."

Ivan smiled. She wished he hadn't. She found it harder to be angry at such a seemingly genuine smile. It had to be a trick, a ploy he used to make people think he was a nice person who would treat them fairly, when all the while he intended to rob them. Why else would he have anything to do with a man who would ply a boy with drink then cheat him out of his inheritance?

"That is good," Ivan said. "We will work together."

It was hard not to be distracted by his accent, by his smile, by his imposing stature, but she wasn't the kind of weak-minded female who would let that happen. "We will not *work together*," she told him. "I don't want you here. You have no right to be here."

"I have a contract—"

"Having a contract with a thief makes no difference. It just makes you a thief, too."

Ivan's reaction was immediate. He drew himself up, going from genial to imposing in an instant. "I am *not* a thief. I am of noble blood. To steal even the smallest thing would be an insult to my ancestors. My family has a long history in Poland. We—"

"I'm not interested in your family or its history." Not that she believed he was of noble blood. She wasn't even sure he was Polish. "My only concern is your attempt to take part of my ranch."

"I did not take it. Laveau diViere did. I am here to manage it until it can be mine."

"Why should he give it to you?" She'd been about to say something quite different, but that question had been at the back of her mind since he said the land would eventually become his.

"It is difficult to explain."

"I don't have to start supper for half an hour."

After Ivan's tangled explanation of theft, betrayal, and seven ex-confederate soldiers' five-year-long attempt to get revenge, Carla was even less inclined to believe anything he said. She wanted him off her ranch and out of her life as quickly as possible. She intended to bring her case before the circuit judge the moment he came to town. "Even if what you say is true, it doesn't make any difference. Laveau diViere won that card game by cheating. I don't want you here or anywhere near my ranch."

Carla expected an argument or flaring temper. Instead, Ivan continued to stand there looking at her like he hadn't heard a word she'd said.

"Didn't you hear me?" she asked when she couldn't stand the silence any longer.

"Of course, I did. I can hear very well."

"Then leave."

"Why should I do something so foolish?"

"Because you have no right to be here."

"I should show you my contract."

"I don't want to see your contract."

"It will tell you I have the right to be here."

"I don't care what your paper says."

"How can that be? In America one must have a paper for everything. It was so in Poland, too, but Russians do not care about papers. Are you Russian?"

Talking to this man was like throwing her words to the wind. "No, I'm not Russian, and I do care about papers. I just don't care about *your* paper."

Ivan looked at the document. "What do you not like about it? A lawyer who calls himself Lukey said it was a good paper. The writing is very pretty. The ink is good and strong." He snapped the paper to show its strength. "The paper is of good quality. Laveau would never write on anything cheap."

It was just her luck to be confronted by the most handsome and charming man she'd ever met only to find that he was an idiot. Or a conniving shyster. "I don't care about the penmanship or the quality of the ink and paper."

"But such things are important. There are many documents in my family that are hundreds of years old. If we could not read them, how would we know anything about our history?"

Texas was hardly thirty years old. Men ranched and farmed land they didn't own. Buffalo roamed over the western part of the state, and Indian raids were common. The state was run by a Reconstruction government that made its own rules and ignored any they didn't like. The idea that Ivan's paper would be of any interest hundreds of years from now was ridiculous. "Your paper has no value because I'm not going to share running my ranch with you."

"I am sorry you feel that way. I would be happy to work with a lady as pretty as you, but it is probably best to divide the ranch up now. That will make things easier when I get ready to sell my half. In Poland we have maps of all our ancestral lands. We mark everything—roads, farm tracks, fields, fences, stone walls, hedges, and even sheds."

Just thinking about anyone selling part of her ranch out from under her made Carla so angry she could hardly think, but she could think well enough to set this man straight. This was not Poland, and whatever they did there had nothing to do with Texas. "Let me make myself clear. I deny Laveau diViere's claim on my ranch. By extension, I deny your right to run any part of my ranch, own any part of my ranch, or sell any part of my ranch. Now I want you off my land immediately."

"I did not expect that I would stay in your house," Ivan said, "though it would have been gracious of you to make such an offer. I will stay in the bunkhouse."

"You can't stay in the bunkhouse either."

"Is the bunkhouse on your half of the ranch?"

"Yes," she said in hopes of simplifying the situation. "So are the corrals, the well, the chicken pen, and every building you see." That seemed to give Mr. Nikolai pause but not for long.

"That does not seem fair—I was told Texans were very concerned about fairness—but you are not happy about this. Am I right?"

Finally he seemed to understand something. "I'm *furious* about it. If I said half the things to you I've said to my brother, your ears would burn."

"I have very good ears. They never burn, not even in very hot weather. We do not have hot weather like this in Poland, but it gets very cold."

Carla shook her head so hard her vision blurred. But

when it cleared, Ivan Nikolai was still standing at the bottom her steps, so this insane conversation must really be taking place. Why would Laveau diViere hire such a man to manage his property? Either he was so stupid he was a danger to himself, or he was extremely clever. She decided he must have survived on his looks and a smile, which he didn't hesitate to use to his advantage. If he hadn't been trying to steal half of her ranch, she'd probably have been taken in. What woman could look at such a man without hoping he wasn't too good to be true?

"Mr. Nikolai, I don't want to be rude, but how can I make you understand that I don't want you on my ranch? Go back to town, go back to where you came from, go anywhere you want, but leave my ranch."

"I can see that my being here has upset you. That was to be expected. I do not hold it against you."

His smile was so understanding, so sympathetic, she wanted to slap him.

"I will not go. Your Mr. Lukey has said I have a right to be here, though he appeared to dislike it as much as you. I do not understand why you dislike me so much, but I do not want to make a woman as pretty as you upset. I will take care of myself."

She didn't know what he intended to do, but at least he understood she didn't want him here.

"It has been most pleasant to meet you. Now if you will permit, I will be going."

If she would permit! She'd been telling him to leave from the moment he arrived. But now that he was leaving, she felt a little sorry for him. He wasn't the villain. Laveau diViere was. Ivan was merely acting for him. Still, no matter how nice, handsome, or charming, he wanted to take half of her ranch, and she wouldn't allow anybody to do that. She watched as he replaced his hat, turned, and mounted his horse. He did so with the fluid motion of a man who's ridden all his life. She wondered where he did come from. It certainly wasn't any place she knew.

"It has been a delight to meet you," he said. "I look forward to our next meeting."

Rather than say something she didn't mean, she watched him ride away. Heaving a sigh of relief, she turned and entered the house. That was a lot easier than she expected. She still would talk to the judge, but it looked like the situation had resolved itself. All she had to do now was make Danny swear he would never play poker again.

Ivan didn't like this part of Texas. It was even less like the flat, lush plains of Poland than Cade's ranch below San Antonio. Wide stretches of open grassland reached into the distance, the horizon broken only by a scattering of trees and valley woodlands along streambeds that remained dry except during a downpour. The oppressive heat caused a thirst he couldn't quench. He could understand why Laveau didn't want to live on the ranch. He wasn't sure he did, either.

He didn't know if he'd done the right thing in accepting Laveau's offer, but it was done now. The other Night Riders might accuse him of being a traitor—at the very least that he'd backed out of his vow—but he was tired of working for someone else. He had been born Ivan Nikolai Augustus Stanislas, Prince of Poniatowski, a

distant descendant of the early kings of Poland. The
final partition of Poland in the late eighteenth century
had deprived his family of their ancestral lands. Rather
than be dependent on one of his Russian conquerors,
he'd chosen to seek his fortune in America. That he was
still a cowhand proved it hadn't worked out very well.

Despite the uninviting landscape, Ivan was satisfied with his campsite. He whistled to himself as he
washed the pot he'd used to cook his dinner. It would
have been nice to settle back with a nice cognac, but
that was for the future when he was back in Poland in
his rightful position. Until then, he had to save every
penny. He packed away his utensils and put the coffee
on to boil.

The sun was sinking over the horizon, causing bands
of dull yellow and vivid orange to splash across the darkening sky. The gravelly ground beneath his feet radiated
back the heat it had accumulated during the day, thus
insuring that the air would not cool off for many hours
yet. Small creatures that sought cover during the heat
of day came out to forage for food in the fading light.
After watering his horse, Ivan picketed him in the grass
alongside the stream. It surprised him to find the stream
still running so late in summer. It had to be spring fed.
No wonder Miss Reece was so determined to hold on to
her ranch. It was the only flowing stream he'd seen for
nearly a hundred miles.

Thinking about Carla Reece made him smile. She
was certainly a spirited young woman. Pretty, too. She
had backbone and intelligence, but she would never
fit in Poland. She wouldn't understand that a woman
of his class did not have the privileges and freedoms

she enjoyed in Texas. She wouldn't be allowed to own land, much less to tell a man to leave it. Nevertheless, he didn't hold it against her. She was fighting for her birthright. He understood that.

Deciding that his coffee was ready, he took the pot off the fire and kicked sand over the embers to put them out. Even though the sun had sunk out of sight, it was too hot for a fire. There was so much sand and quartz in the soil that it looked almost white in the moonlight. The reflected light threw the cactus, mesquite, and other brushy growth into silhouette. Soon it would be so dark that everything except the sky would fade into a bottomless blue black. In the stillness of the night, he would plan what to do next.

His coffee was hot and strong. No one in his family would swallow such a brew, but he'd come to like it during his five years of working on his friend's ranch. He chuckled. His mother wouldn't recognize half the dishes he'd learned to eat. She would say they weren't good enough for the servants. Only there had been no servants for his family after the Russians took their land. Reminded of the latest letter from his mother, he took it out of his pocket and read it once more.

> *...now that it has been ten years since you went away, Anika is saying her son should have your title and position. Since her husband has taken responsibility for the family, she says her son should have the position that goes with the obligation. Ludmila says her son should inherit because she's the older sister. They cannot meet without saying rude and hurtful things.*

*You must come home before the family is torn
apart.*

> *Your loving mother,*
> *Krystina Stanislas*
> *Princess Poniatowski*

Ivan folded the letter and returned it to his pocket.
His mother ended every letter with a plea that he come
home for the sake of the family. His two sisters had been
very close before Anika's marriage to a wealthy Russian
trumped Ludmila's marriage to an impoverished Polish
prince. Now every letter bore a tale of their increasingly
bitter estrangement, a state of affairs that could only be
remedied by his return. But he wouldn't go home when
he was even poorer than Ludmila's nobleman. He would
remain in exile forever before he would become Anika's
husband's pensioner.

But he didn't want to dwell on the past. It was the
present that needed his attention. He didn't know if he'd
done the right thing in letting Carla Reece believe he
was simpleminded, but it was easier to get the advantage of people when they underestimated you. He was
aware that women were attracted to him. Cade's wife
had encouraged him to become interested in one woman
after another. He never had because he had known he
was going back to Poland someday. Only then would he
look for a wife.

Still, he wouldn't mind spending time with Miss
Reece. She was spirited and prickly, but that didn't
bother him. He was the only one who could calm Cade's
Spanish grandmother-in-law. Compared to her, Carla
Reece was a lamb.

Not that she looked like a lamb. She looked more like an angel, albeit a thoroughly angry one. The lawyer told him Carla wasn't married and warned him not to get any ideas. The local citizens might have to tolerate his presence, but they wouldn't tolerate his attentions to Miss Reece. It was with a clear conscience that Ivan had assured him he had no intention of competing with any of the local gentlemen for Miss Reece's favors. Living on the ranch, seeing her every day, maybe even working with her, didn't constitute competing for her favor. It *did* look like an intriguing way to pass the next year.

At the sound of approaching footsteps, he looked up to see a young man emerging from the deepening gloom. "Who are you?"

"That's what I've come to ask you," the young man said as he drew near.

"I am Ivan Nikolai. I have a contract with Laveau diViere to manage his part of this ranch."

The boy dropped his head. "I'm Danny Reece, the fool who let diViere cheat him out of his half of the ranch."

Ivan sympathized with the boy and his sister, but he'd suffered at Laveau's hands as well. This was his chance to get something back.

"Why are you here instead of Mr. diViere?" Danny asked.

Ivan repeated what he'd told Danny's sister.

"That sounds fishy to me," the boy said.

"Fishy? What is this *fishy*? This place is like a desert. One does not speak of fish in a desert."

Danny's scowl disappeared, and a charming smile took its place. "Where are you from?"

"Poland."

"That would account for it. *Fishy* means something doesn't smell right, that something's wrong. How did you end up in Texas?"

Ivan knew he would have to tell his story sooner or later. He decided it was probably better to begin with someone who appeared to be sympathetic.

"My family lost its ancestral lands, so I came to America to make my fortune. I met Laveau when we fought together in the war. I became his friend because he could speak to me in French, but he was not *my* friend. He stole my money and betrayed our troop to the enemy. Most of my friends died in their sleep. At the end of the war, Cade Wheeler, my commanding officer, offered me a job on his ranch. I was there until I came here."

"Does Carla know that?" Danny asked when Ivan had finished.

"She was not interested in my history, only in my departure. She was very angry at me."

"Not half as angry as she is at me," Danny said. "But I deserve it. I don't know why I let diViere talk me into drinking or gambling so much. I've never done anything like that."

"Laveau has a way of convincing people to do what he wants."

"I can't blame him," Danny said. "I was cocky. Just because I can beat everybody in town at poker, I thought I could beat *anybody*." He paused, appeared to be thinking of something. He shook his head, as though ridding himself of a bad memory. "What are you doing out here?"

"I have to live somewhere. Your sister said the house and all the buildings were on her half of the ranch. Here

I have water, grass for my horse, shade from the sun, and level ground for sleeping. It is good."

"It's not good," Danny said. "Besides, we never divided the ranch. Everything is as much mine as it is hers."

"I thought that might be the way it was, but I decided it was best not to argue. Your sister is very fierce. I am afraid of her."

Danny laughed. "I don't think you're afraid of anybody." He gave Ivan a questioning glance. "She said you acted simpleminded, smiling like you didn't have good sense. You're not, are you?"

Now it was Ivan's turn to laugh. "No, but it is hard for a woman to do anything bad to a person of simple mind. I did not want your sister to dislike me. It will be hard to work with her if she is angry at me."

Danny had been standing of the far side of the remains of Ivan's fire. He dropped down and settled on the ground. He put his arms around his legs and drew his knees up under his chin. "There's no hope of Carla working with you. I'm her only brother, but she's so mad at me she can't stand to have me in the house. Did diViere really say he'd give you his part of the ranch after a year?"

"Yes."

"What will you do with it?"

"Sell it so I can return to Poland."

Danny sighed. "That's what Carla said."

"Why do you sound so sad?"

"Dividing the ranch would be hard no matter how we did it, but now it will be worse. Carla will want to keep the best parts, and you'll want the same parts so you can sell it for more money. Carla is determined to buy it back. We don't have that much money, but

Kesney Hardin does. He wants our ranch, and he wants to marry Carla."

"Who is this Kesney Hardin, and why does he want your ranch and your sister?"

Danny sighed again. "He came here after the war with lots of money and plans to buy up the whole county and marry the prettiest girl. He already owns the biggest ranch in the county. Now he considers himself practically engaged to Carla."

Ivan had no explanation for his instant animosity toward Kesney Hardin except that maybe he likened him to the Russians who had carved up Poland with the cooperation of Austria and Prussia. "Maybe this Kesney Hardin will give your sister the money to buy back your share of the ranch."

"That won't help me. I'll still be nothing more than a cowhand on what used to be my ranch."

Ivan would have been in the same position if he had stayed in Poland.

"You probably think I deserve what happened to me," Danny said.

"No one deserves bad luck."

"Carla says it was stupidity."

"We all make mistakes."

"Is that why you're here and not in Poland?"

"No. My ancestors made those mistakes."

"I have nobody to blame. I don't even know who my ancestors were."

"I can trace my family back more than five hundred years."

"Why would you want to do that? Those people have been dead so long their graves have disappeared."

"In Poland we do not lose the graves of kings and princes."

"Wow! After five hundred years, there must be a lot of them. Where do you put 'em?"

Ivan couldn't say why he laughed, but he liked Danny. The boy was just as disinherited as Ivan was when he left Poland. "The past is very important in my country. We take care of the graves of our ancestors. My family occupied the same castle for almost five hundred years." Ivan looked over his shoulder at the ranch house which could be seen in the distance. "We build with stone."

"You won't find any stone around here." Danny appeared to lose interest in the conversation. For a moment he looked like he wanted to go, but then he asked abruptly, "What do you plan to do now that you're here? I gotta tell you. Carla's going to put a spoke in your wheel every chance she gets."

Ivan didn't know what spokes and wheels had to do with the situation, but he figured Danny meant his sister was not going to be helpful. "You know the ranch better than I do. What do you think I should do?"

Danny grinned. "Leave before Carla poisons your coffee." He sobered quickly. "She thinks you left. She's going to be mad as a wet hen when she finds out you're still here."

Ivan couldn't understand why Danny would compare his sister to a wet chicken, but he'd learned to expect anything from Texans. "I think I should ride over the whole ranch. Then I will know what to do."

"Carla will be fit to be tied, but I'll ride with you."

Ivan thought he understood most American expressions, but Danny seemed to be speaking a different language. Not even Nate Dolan was so hard to understand, and he was from Arkansas. "Your sister does not like me. I will go alone."

"It won't be a problem if you get lost and end up on Kesney Hardin's range, but Wilbur Joiner or Frank Bass might shoot you."

"Why do they want to shoot me?"

"They don't like strangers on their land."

"Soon I will not be a stranger. Then they will not want to shoot me."

"Well, until you aren't a stranger, I'll ride with you."

"Why will you do that? Your sister will be angry."

Danny shrugged. "It's not your fault my sister hates you. Besides, you're a lot nicer than Mr. diViere."

"If you did not like him, why did you play poker with him?"

"It wasn't until I knew he was a cheater that I didn't like him."

"But you could not prove he cheated?"

Danny hung his head. "Nobody could."

"That is like Laveau. He earns your trust then betrays you."

"If you don't like him, why are you here?"

"It is a chance to earn money to return to Poland, but I do not trust him. Laveau never does anything good for anybody but himself."

"He certainly didn't do anything good for me." Danny got to his feet. "I'd better go. Carla will have breakfast ready at six o'clock. Don't be late."

"I will eat here."

"You can eat at the house with us."

"Not until your sister invites me."

"She'll never do that."

"Then I will never eat at the house."

"Suit yourself, but Carla is a great cook."

"I am too. During the war I had to eat what I cooked, so I learned."

"Well, good night. See you in the morning."

Ivan watched the boy walk away. He had accepted his misfortune while his sister hadn't. But he wasn't going to be driven away until he sold his share of the ranch. That meant he had to find a way to get along with Carla Reece for a whole year.

———

Carla always saddled her own horse, but today she was so angry and upset she was clumsy.

"Here. Let me," Danny said. "At this rate, you'll have your horse so worked up he's liable to throw you."

"I haven't been thrown since I was twelve."

"You haven't been this angry since you were ten and Forey Allen cut off your pigtail. And don't think you can do the same thing to Ivan you did to Forey. Ivan's twice your size."

"I don't plan to speak to the man."

"I don't see how you can avoid it since he owns half of the ranch. And don't start yelling at me again. Nothing either of us can do now will change anything."

"That's exactly the kind of attitude I can't stand. How can you just do nothing?"

"Because right now I can't think of anything that will change what happened."

"The judge—"

"That's a long shot, and you know it. I'm sure diViere

cheated, but unless we can prove it—and we can't—the judge will have no reason to throw out the bet." He finished tightening the cinch and stood back. "You ought to talk to Ivan. He seems like a nice man."

"I don't care if he's a saint. I'm not giving him half of our ranch. Give me a leg up."

Rather than let his sister step into his cupped hands, Danny picked her up and settled her in the saddle. She arranged her skirt round her then turned to her brother. "Keep an eye on him while I'm gone."

"What do you expect him to do?"

"I don't know. Just watch him."

She turned, and pressing her heels into her horse's side, rode off at a canter. She couldn't understand how Danny could like Ivan. It didn't matter what kind of person he was. He was trying to take half of their ranch. That was all that mattered.

It infuriated her that Ivan had set up camp along the trail to the house. She would have to pass him every time she went to town. It made him look like a vagabond, one she'd forced out into the cold. Only it was summer and not even the water in the well was cold. Still, it was the principle of the thing. What would people say? Nobody liked Danny being cheated out of his part of the ranch. Surely they wouldn't care that she'd forced this interloper to camp out by the creek. He wasn't a Texan. He wasn't *one of them*.

Her conscience niggled at her. Ivan wasn't the one who'd won the ranch by cheating. He was just taking advantage of a chance to earn money to return to his own country. She'd have been sympathetic if it wasn't her ranch he intended to sell. In any case, she had a year to figure out how to get it back. And she would. That's why she was going to town.

As she came around a bend in the trail, she saw where Ivan set up his camp. She wasn't sure it could really be called a camp, except that he was staying there. Or he had been. His bulging saddlebags were on his saddled horse, and he was in the process of tying his bedroll behind his saddle.

He was getting ready to leave.

Her initial relief was countered by worry that the next person diViere sent would be even worse. Or diViere might decide to sell his portion of the ranch to the first person who would buy it. Though she initially thought to pass Ivan without speaking, she changed her mind. "I hope you weren't too uncomfortable last night," she said when she brought her horse to a stop next to Ivan's.

"Not at all. I had a nice talk with your brother, and it was cool enough to sleep."

His smile was so dazzling she started feeling guilty for being so inhospitable. "I should apologize for the way I treated you, but I am still so angry at Mr. diViere I can't think straight."

"I understand. He has done worse to me and my friends."

She wanted to ask what could be more terrible than being cheated out of half of her ranch, but she didn't want to encourage him to linger. "I'm going into town, so I probably won't see you again. I hope you find a way to get the money you need to return to Poland."

Ivan looked puzzled. "Why will you not see me again? Do you not return to the ranch?"

"Of course I'll return, but it will be several hours from now. You'll be miles away."

"Why should I be miles away?"

"You're obviously getting ready to leave, and I can't see any reason why you would want to hang around town." There was that dazzling smile again. Why did he keep doing that? It made it harder to remember she never wanted to see him again.

"If I am going to live here by the stream, I need a tent and some supplies. I will ride to town with you, and you can tell me which are the best stores. Do you think I should build a cabin before winter?"

Chapter 3

It was a moment before Carla could speak. He couldn't be staying. She didn't *want* him to stay. "But you've got to leave," she sputtered.

"Why should I leave if I will have half of your ranch just for staying?"

"It's not divided in half."

"I will hire a surveyor when it is time to sell."

She felt like everything was closing in on her, but she refused to panic. She had a year to figure out how to get her ranch back. It would have been easier if she didn't have to do it with Ivan camped at the front door, but she didn't have to be seen with him or teach him where to shop.

"If you're determined to stay, I can't stop you, but I won't ride into town with you. I don't want anybody to think I'm happy about you being here."

"No one will think that."

Didn't the man know how to frown? Did he have to smile all the time? How was she supposed to think? At least she was still on her horse. Otherwise he would be towering over her and intimidating her further. She was used to men being taller—Danny loved being able to look down at her—but Ivan was a blond giant. "Why won't people think I want you here when they see me parading around town with you?"

"Every time you look at me, you frown like you smell

something bad. Since I do not smell bad, they will know you dislike me."

"I don't dislike *you*. I don't know anything about you. I just dislike what you're going to do."

"Then you will help me learn the best places to buy?"

None of this was really his fault, and she couldn't blame him for trying to take advantage of the situation that would enable him to return to his homeland. She knew how unhappy she'd be if she were forced to leave Texas. "Okay, you can ride with me, but you'll have to go shopping on your own. You also need to know I'm going to do everything I can to get this debt cancelled."

"That is expected," he said calmly.

Didn't the man ever get angry or upset? Was he too dim to realize not everything was going to work out the way he wanted just because he was too stubborn to leave? "Are you ready?" she asked. "I have a lot to do."

In answer to her question, he swung into his saddle and brought his horse alongside hers. "I am ready."

She felt like she was traveling in his shadow. Even his horse was bigger than hers. She didn't look forward to riding with him for the next hour. What do you say to a stranger you're hoping will leave and never come back? Apparently Ivan didn't have a problem. He asked about the grass, the trees, the bushes and the vines. He asked about the soil. What rancher knew anything about soil? It was just dirt. Texas was covered with it. At least she understood his concern about water.

"I have more than enough water," she told him. "The creek is fed by a spring that runs all year. We have a well for the house and a windmill that pumps water for the corrals."

"The soil is equally important," Ivan insisted. "It determines what kind of grasses grow, how nutritious they are, and how plentiful. All of that determines how many cows you can support per acre and how much they will weigh."

"I know that," Carla said, irritated he would think she was either ignorant or stupid. "If you'd wanted to know that, why did you ask about clay and loam and all that other stuff?"

"My family owned the same land for five hundred years. We had to take care of our soil, replenish it, so it would last year after year."

She couldn't imagine any ranch lasting five hundred years. Her father had had three different ones since coming to Texas. Once the Indians and the buffalo were gone, there would be millions of acres of new land available for settlement. No one thought about replenishing the soil. It was too poor to bother.

"Will you tell me about your family?" Ivan asked.

"Why do you want to know?" He was a stranger, a foreigner—an aristocrat if she could believe what he told Danny—who wouldn't understand anything as ordinary as a farmer's son who dreamed of owning his own ranch in what was considered the uncivilized West.

"Everything."

"That would take longer than it will take us to reach town."

"Then only as much as you want to tell me."

She didn't want to tell him anything, but his smile was doing awful things to her resistance. Why couldn't the sun be in her eyes? Then she wouldn't have to see him. "My parents came to Texas more than twenty years ago. They had to move twice, but they managed to increase their holdings despite three wars."

"My family lost everything in three wars."

It was hard to feel sorry for a family she didn't know, especially when the only member of that family she *did* know was determined to take half her ranch, but she could understand how Ivan felt. She just wished he could find another ranch to steal. "Maybe they'll get some of it back someday."

"My sister has. That's why I must return to Poland."

She was so busy being angry she'd forgotten that, but she supposed it wasn't important. It didn't matter *why* Ivan wanted to take half her ranch—just that he did.

"Tell me about Mr. diViere. Why are you working with him?"

"I used to think he was my friend. He repaid my trust by stealing my money."

"Didn't you try to stop him?"

"He took it when I was sleeping. I did not see him again for seven years. When I did, shooting him would have been doing a murder. I do not want to go to prison."

"But there must be some law, a judge, some court—"

"Laveau was the only one who knew I had money or where it was hidden. He has a way to charm even the most wary. He has even attempted murder."

"Then he can be arrested, tried in court."

"Laveau betrayed his troop to the Union army. Because of that, he is given the protection of the army here in Texas. Even the Reconstruction government protects him."

Another sin to be laid at the feet of the rascals who had taken over the capital in Austin. "Where is he now?"

"I don't know."

"When will you see him again?"

"Never. All the legal arrangements have been left in the hands of a lawyer called Lukey Gordon."

"Lukey would never do anything illegal."

"It's not illegal to transfer property from one person to another."

"It is when that person doesn't own the property."

"But Laveau does own that property. Your brother signed papers that make it legal."

She was going to see what she could do to convince a judge to change that. She couldn't let her brother lose his share of the ranch because of a moment of foolish overconfidence or his failure to spot a conniving and manipulative man. "Let's not talk about that. We'll never agree, and I'll only get angry again."

"It does not change the facts."

"The fact is diViere cheated, so that paper you have is worthless."

"Not until you can get a judge to say so."

"Don't think I won't." Carla struggled to control her temper. "In the meantime, it might be safer for you to move on. Once everybody knows what you're trying to do, they'll be just as anxious as I am to see you gone."

"I lived through a war with thousands of men with guns and cannons trying to kill me. I'm not afraid of a few Texans."

"Texans were better shots than Union soldiers. They hit what they aimed at the first time."

"You should give up trying to chase me away," Ivan said with one of his blinding smiles. "I will be here for the next year."

She didn't want to think about that. The man was

too friendly, too overwhelming, and too handsome for her to stay mad at him for a whole year. Besides, he seemed rather nice. He'd certainly been unfailingly pleasant despite her rough treatment. She had to stay away from him. She would never have believed it, but she found him attractive in a way she couldn't ignore. That was odd considering the attractive and eligible men she *could* ignore.

Kesney Hardin topped the list.

Kesney was mature, handsome, rich, and well-dressed as well as having charming manners. Despite being old enough to have a young daughter, Kesney was the most eligible man she'd ever met. Carla had been flattered by his interest. She had dreamed of marrying for love, but she'd never found any man who could ignite that spark. She had begun to wonder if she was capable of love. Her father said she thought like a man. Her mother said she was too practical. Her brother said she was a pain in the ass who always thought she knew better than he did. Fortunately, she *did* know better, but that didn't make Danny like it.

Then there was Maxwell Dodge, a businessman who'd recently arrived in Overlin. He'd quickly shown a decided partiality for Carla, something that Kesney hadn't liked at all. Neither had any other eligible bachelor in the area. Carla knew most of these men were as interested in her ownership of the most successful ranch in the area as they were in her, yet no one had attracted her the way Ivan's smile did. That was a danger sign, and she ought to have the good sense to talk herself out of thinking it was anything more than a tool Ivan used to get what he wanted.

"You are very quiet," Ivan said. "Did I say something to upset you?"

"Of course you did. You said you were going to be here for a year at the end of which you intend to sell half of my ranch to the man with the most money. Do you expect me to be happy about that?"

"No. My father lost the last of our land when I was six."

Great. He knew exactly how she felt because the same thing had happened to him. She hoped he wasn't expecting a show of sympathy. She was saving all she had for herself. And for Danny. As angry as she was at him, she knew he felt even worse because he'd failed her as well as himself. If she could get her hands on Laveau diViere, she'd like to strangle him. Instead, she had no one to direct her anger to except Ivan Nikolai. She needed to be thinking of reasons the judge could use to nullify the bet. She couldn't do that with Ivan looking over her shoulder all the time.

"Is that a neighbor of yours? She seems to be in trouble."

Carla followed the direction of Ivan's gaze. Some distance ahead, a buggy had come to a halt. It looked like a wheel had come off. A young woman was standing by the buggy, looking helpless and upset. "I don't recognize her," Carla said.

"We must help." With that announcement, Ivan urged his horse into a fast canter. Carla had no alternative but to follow. By the time she caught up with him, Ivan had dismounted and introduced himself.

"Her wheel has come off," he said to Carla as she dismounted. "I will put it back."

How could Ivan know how to fix a wheel? She couldn't imagine wagon repair had been part of his training to be a prince. She turned her attention to the young woman who seemed to be close to tears. "My name is Carla Reece," she said to her. "My brother and I own the Four Corners ranch a few miles from here. I don't remember seeing you before."

"I just got here," the young woman said, tears threatening to spill over her lower eyelid. "My name is Elizabeth Hardin, but everybody calls me Beth."

"Are you any relation to Kesney Hardin?" Kesney had a young daughter, but she was still in Kentucky.

"He's my father. He wanted me to wait until he could go to town with me, but I can drive by myself." She looked at the wheel, which Ivan had picked up from where it had rolled several yards away. "I had no idea the wheel was ready to come off."

Ivan was rolling the wheel toward them. "The problem is not your wheel. The lynchpin has come out."

"How could that happen?" Beth asked. "It looked fine when I left."

"It probably has become worn and worked its way out over the bumps. I will look for it." Ivan turned and started back down the trail.

"I'm so glad you and your husband came along," Beth said to Carla. "If my father found me like this, I'd never hear the end of it."

Carla was so startled Beth Hardin would think Ivan was her husband that she momentarily forgot her surprise that Kesney's daughter was in Texas rather than Kentucky. "We're not married," Carla said. "We're… ummm… neighbors… and are just riding to town together."

"I'll have to pay him for fixing my buggy. Where can my father find him?"

"Umm... you'll have to ask Ivan. I can't speak for him."

"He's very big." Beth said it in a way that told Carla the young woman found that attribute very appealing. "And he has a nice smile. Have you known him long?"

"No. He just moved here."

"Where is he staying?"

Carla didn't want to answer that question, but she couldn't think of an acceptable reason to refuse. "He's staying at my ranch until he can make other arrangements."

"Then I guess Papa will know where to find him."

Kesney had said his daughter was fifteen, much too young in Carla's mind to be allowed to drive herself to town. She was definitely too young to be casting her sights on a man like Ivan, who was probably twice her age. Besides, the child was beautiful. Carla could envision several of Overlin's young bucks getting into fights over the chance to hold a door for her or help her across the street.

"What is he doing?"

Carla turned to see Ivan had left the trail and was walking toward some bushy growth that grew alongside the creek. "I don't know. Maybe he couldn't find the lynchpin and is looking for something to replace it."

"He talks kinda funny, doesn't he?"

Carla didn't know why she resented that comment any more than why she was annoyed Beth thought Ivan was attractive. "He's from Poland. He says he was a prince." She didn't know why she added that, either. Considering the way Beth's eyes brightened, it was probably a bad idea. "He's going home as soon as he can." Why did she say that? To protect Ivan? He didn't appear to need protection from anyone, least of all her.

"Is he a prince now?"

"He may be, but it won't do him any good in Texas."

Beth looked to where Ivan was breaking a branch off a small tree. "What is he doing?"

"I'm not sure. I expect he'll tell us when he gets here."

Beth wiped a drop of perspiration from her forehead. "Is it always this hot here?"

"No. Sometimes it's hotter."

"I don't know why Papa wanted to move to Texas."

Carla had wondered the same thing. When she asked him, he said he was bored with Kentucky and Texas sounded like fun. "Did you want to leave Kentucky?" she asked Beth. "Your father didn't tell me you were coming."

"I couldn't wait to get away from those awful people. They treated Papa like a traitor just because he didn't fight the Yankees. How could he when we had the Union army all around us?"

Carla knew a lot of people were still angry about the war, but it was over, so it was time to stop fighting what couldn't be changed.

"I found your lynchpin," Ivan said to Beth when he returned. "But it is too worn. I will make a new one."

"How can you do that?"

"With a knife and this piece of wood."

Ivan went to his saddlebags and took out a small pouch from which he drew several tools. Both women watched with varying degrees of interest and confusion as he whittled, carved, and cut the branch until it looked like a duplicate of the worn lynchpin. After several trials, he slid it into the hole in the axle. He left one end of the lynchpin too large to go through the hole. "I will lift the buggy. If you ladies can roll the wheel to me, I will put in back on." Then he reached down, grasped the buggy's axle, and lifted it easily.

Beth was either unwilling to get her hands dirty or so impressed by Ivan's strength that she couldn't move. It was left for Carla to roll the wheel to Ivan. He fitted it on the axle. Once it was secure, he drove the new lynchpin into place with a small mallet he took from the pouch. Then using another tool, he split the small end of the lynchpin and inserted a metal wedge. "This will keep it from coming out," he said to Beth. "You must have it repaired as soon as you get to town."

"I don't know how to thank you," Beth said. "My father will pay you."

"It was nothing," Ivan insisted. "I will ride with you so the wheel will not come off again."

Beth practically beamed. "I'd be very grateful. My father will be grateful, too."

"I'll ride ahead." Carla hoped her voice didn't betray her irritation.

"Please ride with me," Beth begged. "I don't know anybody in Overlin. This will give us a chance to get acquainted."

Carla didn't want to ride with Beth, but she couldn't refuse without seeming rude. Besides, a girl Beth's age shouldn't be alone with any man, even one who seemed to be steeped in European gallantry.

"I just remembered," Beth said with a gush of excitement. "You must be the Carla Papa told me about. Now you've *got* to ride with me. I want to know all about you." She giggled. "Papa thinks you're beautiful."

Ivan had moved forward to help Carla dismount. "Of

course he does," he said to Beth. "That is obvious to anyone with eyes."

Carla looked down at Ivan in surprise.

"Do you not know that you are beautiful?" he asked.

"It's not something I think about," Carla said, unsettled by his question.

"In Poland, every woman who is beautiful *knows* she is beautiful. In America they pretend not to know or to think it is not important. I do not understand American women."

Beth giggled, a trait Carla was beginning to find annoying. "It's not that American women are unaware of their looks. It's just that it's not considered good manners to be overly concerned about them."

"That does not make sense. In Poland, a woman makes herself beautiful so she can marry the richest men. Why would you want to appear plain and marry someone with not much money?"

"In America, women prefer to marry the man they love."

Ivan shook his head as though unable to understand such a point of view. "My friends all marry women they love. Most often they have no money." Ivan flashed a grin. "We must start to town. I have much to do." With that, he helped Carla dismount. He then followed her over to the buggy and helped her in. After that, he helped Beth to her seat. "Do not drive fast. I will watch the wheel."

Beth took the reins and set her horse into a comfortable trot.

"When did you learn to drive?" Carla asked. "You do it very well."

"Thank you. Papa taught me from before I can remember. He said after Mama died, I was all he had, so he wanted to keep me with him all the time."

"That was sweet of him." Something Carla would not have expected—not that she didn't think Kesney was good-natured or thoughtful. She just never pictured him as the type to be interested in children, even his own, which just went to show how badly she could be mistaken when judging people she didn't know. She supposed the same could be said of Ivan—he did have some odd notions—but she hoped he wasn't going to be around long enough for her to know him better.

"Since Mama died, Papa has always said I was his one and only girl, but that changed when he moved to Overlin. He was eager for me to come to Texas so I could meet you."

Carla had had dinner with Kesney a few times and visited his ranch, none of which was sufficient as far as she was concerned, for Kesney to bring his daughter all the way from Kentucky to meet her. "How long will you be visiting?"

"I'm not visiting," Beth said with a trill of youthful laughter. "I'm going to live here with Papa." She winked. "Maybe soon it won't be just the two of us."

Carla wondered if Kesney was more interested in her as a potential wife, future business partner, or as a stepmother for his daughter. Whatever the reason, she had given him no reason to think he had a monopoly on her affections. She'd also been to dinner with Maxwell Dodge several times.

"Your father is a very nice man. I'm sure many women would consider themselves lucky to be his wife."

"Papa isn't interested in *many* women. From what he says to me, I'd say he was interested in only one."

Mercifully, Beth turned her attention to Ivan. With the artlessness of a girl not yet a woman, she didn't hesitate to ask him questions Carla would have considered inappropriate, even rude. Before long Carla knew almost as much about the history of Poland as she did about Texas. From the description Ivan gave of his ancestral home, she could understand why he wanted to return. She couldn't imagine living in a castle, but she could picture pastures knee-deep in grass stretching to the horizon. She could practically feel the cool breezes wafting down from tree-covered hillsides, but she couldn't fathom riding in a sleigh through a snow-covered countryside. She'd never seen snow, yet was sure she wouldn't like living in a country where you had to bundle up in furs to keep warm during the winter. As for fireplaces big enough to stand up in, well, that sounded wasteful and extravagant.

"It sounds wonderful," Beth said to Ivan. "Almost like living in a fairy tale."

"It can be wonderful if you have land and money. If you do not, it can be very hard." His description of peasant life was appalling. No wonder so many people wanted to come to America.

"I'm glad Papa has money," Beth said. "I wouldn't like being a peasant."

"You would never be a peasant," Ivan said. "Some handsome young nobleman would be overwhelmed by your beauty. He wouldn't care that your ancestors were not noble because he would see the nobility of your character."

This man's tongue was almost as dangerous as his smile. Beth was gazing at him like he was the most wonderful human ever created. Much more and she'd probably be so desperately in love with him, she'd die of a broken heart when her father refused to consider such a marriage.

"That definitely would be a fairy tale," Carla commented in what she hoped was a cool, sanity-inspiring voice. "Very much like Cinderella marrying the Prince."

"Don't you believe fairy tales are possible?" Beth asked.

Considering that her parents had died unexpectedly and her brother had gambled away half their inheritance, she felt more like Little Red Riding Hood trying to escape the big, blond wolf riding next to the buggy. "It's unwise to expect chance or luck to solve all our problems."

"I heard a saying once," Ivan chimed in. "Hope for the best but be prepared for the worst. Good advice, I think." She had always hoped for the best but hadn't been prepared for the worst. How could she have believed anything so terrible would happen? Her parents had always been so healthy, Danny excitable, but basically sensible. She felt more like the biblical Job than Cinderella. The conversation had gotten so unsettling she was relieved when Overlin came into view.

Overlin wasn't much of a town. It was more like a collection of buildings huddled together for mutual protection in the middle of an unfriendly terrain. The scrub land came right up to the edge of town, even swallowing up some of the outlying houses. The buildings were of weather-beaten wood, the paint gone or peeling from half of them. During the heat of the day, the sun beat down on the streets turning the dirt to dry, choking dust and driving everyone to seek shade no matter how meager. Horses stood motionless except for tails swishing at flies, their heads down, eyes half closed. Dogs lay panting in the shade of buildings or under porches. Pigs rooted for cooler earth in streambeds or in the occasional wooded grove.

Yet despite the heat and the lack of water, the town was vibrant, the people energetic and hopeful. Neither the horrors of Reconstruction nor the raids of Mexican bandits could dampen their belief that Texas was the greatest state in the country and that Overlin was the best place to live.

"It has been a pleasure to meet you," Carla said to Beth as soon as the young woman brought the buggy to a stop in front of the mercantile. "Please say hello to your father for me."

"You're not leaving." Beth seemed genuinely upset.

"I have quite a few errands to run before supper."

"But I don't know anything about Overlin. I guess Ivan will have to show me around," Beth said with what Carla could only characterize as a sly smile.

"I do not know Overlin either," Ivan said. "I was depending on Miss Reece to show me where to buy what I need."

Beth turned back to Carla. "You're much too kind to desert both of us when we need you so much. Papa would be most grateful," she added when Carla hesitated.

Carla was caught. What else could she do?

Chapter 4

CARLA DIDN'T KNOW WHETHER HER BRAIN WAS actual mush or if it just felt that way, but nothing about the morning had gone the way she wanted. Accompanying Ivan to town was bad, but shopping with Beth Hardin was worse. An hour spent with that young woman as she went through one store after another, rejecting everything she saw as inferior to what she was used to in Kentucky, turned the morning into a nightmare. Carla had never been so happy to see Kesney as when he showed up to collect his daughter. After using all her persuasive skills to refuse his invitation to continue shopping with them, she had felt obliged to promise to meet them for lunch.

As father and daughter walked away, Ivan turned to Carla and asked, "You do not like that young woman?"

He had postponed his own shopping to accompany her and Beth. Though she was reluctant to feel anything like approval for Ivan, her opinion of him had changed. He had proved remarkably adroit at finding ways to soften Beth's criticism, earning warm looks of appreciation from several store clerks. Ivan was a lot cleverer than he wanted to appear.

"It's not that. She says things that make me uncomfortable and that hurt other people's feelings."

"She is young and much indulged."

"Probably, but she'll have to change if she wants to

be happy here. People here may not have much, but they have their pride."

"Since you are so close to her papa, maybe you can help him teach her what she should say, what she should do."

Carla didn't know how it had come about that she was being forced to explain aspects of her personal life to a man she didn't even know existed twenty-four hours before, and it made her angry.

"Despite what Beth thinks, I'm not on such terms with her father."

"I believe it is not just Beth who thinks it. Mr. Hardin looked at you with a very special regard."

Carla was becoming more uncomfortable by the minute, and not just because standing in the middle of the Overlin boardwalk was not a good place to have such a conversation. She didn't want to have this conversation with Ivan at all. Determined to change the subject, she told Ivan, "I'll go with you only because Beth made me promise, but I don't have time to help you decide what to buy."

"I only asked that you show me the best places to buy. I do not want to be overcharged."

"What are you looking for?"

"Things I will need to live for a year by your creek."

She didn't know why she should keep feeling guilty. He was the one trying to steal her ranch. "Come on. I'll take you to the general supply store."

On entering the store, Carla had to pause a moment for her eyes to readjust from the bright sunlight of the street to the dim interior. While doing so, she inhaled the smell of new leather, cotton cloth, dried apples, and cinnamon that permeated the atmosphere. She always liked coming into this store because there was something earthy about the smell, something substantial. There was nothing frivolous here. People who came here were serious about life.

"There is a much bigger store in San Antonio," Ivan said.

"Then I suggest you go back there," Carla snapped.

Ivan flashed a wide-eyed innocent look. Carla would have to beware of that one. It was almost as dangerous as his smile.

"Is it not permitted to say what is true?"

"Sometimes it's better to leave the truth unsaid."

"I would never say such a thing to a clerk. I only say it to you because we are friends."

"We're not friends." Carla regretted the words as soon as they were out of her mouth. Ivan's hurt look was more unsettling than either his smile or his look of innocence. "Look, it's not that I dislike you. We don't know each other well enough to be friends."

Now he was giving her an earnest look, one that seemed so genuine it would be a sacrilege to distrust it.

"I am Danny's friend, as he is mine. It would make me very happy if you were my friend, too."

She had to get away from this man. He had come to Overlin planning to take her land and sell it, yet he had managed to make her feel guilty for not welcoming him with open arms. He was more dangerous than Beth and Kesney Hardin combined. Thankfully, Mr. Thompson, the owner of the store, came up to them just then. He was about fifty, gray, and of average height, but he was so thin he looked taller. Next to Ivan, he looked like an exclamation mark.

"Good morning, Miss Reece. What can I do for you?"

"Nothing today, Mr. Thompson. This is Ivan Nikolai. He wants to buy some supplies."

"What do you need?" Mr. Thompson asked Ivan.

"A tent."

"I don't carry tents," Mr. Thompson said. "We don't need them here."

"I will be living in a camp for the next year," Ivan explained.

Mr. Thompson looked puzzled. "Why do you want to live in a camp? We have a hotel and two rooming houses in town."

"I do not want to live in a camp, but Miss Reece says the house and the bunkhouse are on her half of the ranch. The corrals and the chicken pen, too."

Mr. Thompson turned to Carla with an inquiring look that made her wish she could sink through the floor... but not before giving Ivan a painful punch in the mouth. She was positive he'd said that just to embarrass her.

"Mr. Nikolai is here to take possession of the half of our ranch Danny lost in the card game." There was no need to say *which* card game. Everyone knew. "He knows I plan to dispute his claim as soon as the judge reaches Overlin. I suggested that he stay in town, but he insists upon staying at the ranch. Naturally I couldn't let him stay in the house. Frankly, I saw no need to allow him to stay in the bunkhouse, either."

Mr. Thompson turned to Ivan with a darkening expression, but Ivan's earnest expression was in full force.

"I understand Miss Reece's objection and would not think of causing her trouble," he told Mr. Thompson, "but I do not have much money. I am happy to camp by the creek where I have water and my horse can find grass. Danny will show me around the ranch so I will not get lost or stray onto the land of Wilbur Joiner or Frank Bass who he fears would shoot me. That would much distress my mother in Poland. She has not seen me since ten years."

That last was said with an expression of sadness that would have wrung the heart of a stone statue. In the space of fifteen seconds he'd changed her from a victim into a villain. Carla had never been prone to murderous rages, but she had the urge to strangle Ivan. She had watched the oily words out of his mouth melt Mr. Thompson's indignation until the man was dripping with sympathy. Maybe she'd kill both of them—Ivan for being the greatest flimflam artist she'd ever known, and Mr. Thompson for being stupid enough to believe him. Thompson turned to her clearly expecting an explanation.

"What do you expect me to do, welcome into my home the man who'd come to steal my ranch?"

"He's not the man who cheated Danny," Mr. Thompson pointed out.

"He's acting for him, so he might as well be." At least Mr. Thompson believed Danny had been cheated.

"Maybe I do not need a tent," Ivan said. "I can sleep under the bushes by the creek. It does not rain much here."

They all knew there was no reason for Ivan to sleep under a bush, but she was ready to cry uncle. It was obvious he could wring sympathy out of any situation, no matter how ridiculous.

"I'll ask around," Mr. Thompson said. "There must

be someone in Overlin with a tent they'd be willing to sell. If not, maybe I can locate one you can use until you can find one to buy."

"Thank you," Ivan said. "I have heard much about the kindness of Texans to strangers."

Ivan flashed a smile which caused Mr. Thompson to smile right back at him. Carla was so annoyed she wanted to slap both of them.

"What else can I do for you?" Mr. Thompson asked Ivan.

"Food. I need something to eat."

"I think you'll find everything you need, even eggs and milk." That last was accompanied by a disapproving glance in Carla's direction. "If you want, I can arrange for a regular delivery to your campsite."

Carla knew she wouldn't be able to hold her tongue or her temper if she stayed a minute longer. She would never have thought of Mr. Thompson as a traitor, but he'd gone over to Ivan's side without a fight. "I have a lot of errands to run," she said to Mr. Thompson. "I'm sure I can trust you to take care of Ivan."

"When will you go home?" Ivan asked. "I think you should not ride alone."

"I'm not sure." She didn't want Ivan's escort. She didn't expect that several hours of trying to invalidate his claim was going to improve her disposition toward him.

"It does not matter. I will wait for you."

Just what she needed, an oversized bundle of gallantry waiting on the street to escort her back to the ranch. That would have half the town imagining wedding bells before supper.

"That's not necessary. I'm sure you have things to do."

"I have nothing before I cook my supper and make my bed for the night."

Okay, it was time to admit defeat. She'd been outmaneuvered because she'd underestimated Ivan, but that wouldn't happen again. From now on she was going to fight dirty. She, too, had a killer smile. She just hadn't used it much since her parents died.

"There's nothing you can do about him being here until the judge arrives," Lukey Gordon advised Carla. "I'm sure diViere cheated, but no one knows how he did it. Believe me, if any of the men knew, they would have said. Everybody hates that Danny lost his share of the ranch."

"If everybody was so concerned, why didn't they stop him from drinking?" Carla demanded. "You know Danny doesn't drink."

"None of us realized he didn't drink because it went straight to his head."

Danny was so embarrassed by his inability to drink without getting drunk on fumes that he preferred to tell people he didn't drink at all.

"It was being told he didn't look old enough to drink watered down beer, much less play cards with grown men that got to him," Lukey said. "Danny hates that he still has a baby face. When he finally gets a few hairs on his upper lip, he'll be the happiest boy in Overlin."

Everybody said Danny was the best looking young man within a hundred miles. He could ride a horse or handle a rope as well as anybody, but even his friends teased him about being prettier than a girl. He'd been a lot less sensitive since his growth spurt had given him the body of a young man, but Carla could understand how needling by a man as sophisticated and worldly as diViere was reported to be would have made him feel like a little boy all over again. But understanding what happened, even being sympathetic for the reasons it happened, did nothing to change the facts.

"Until then, I can't see that you have any choice but to put up with this fella," Lukey told Carla. "If he gets to be a problem, you tell me, and I'll have the sheriff on him in a jiffy. Nobody in Overlin is going to put up with some stranger hassling you."

"You've met him, and you're still sympathetic with me?"

"Who wouldn't be?"

"Everybody else who's met him. It's like he puts a spell on people. In less than five minutes they're ready to believe every word out of his mouth. Even Danny."

"What did Danny do?"

"Fussed at me all through breakfast for not inviting Ivan to eat with us. He informed me he was going to show Ivan the ranch."

"Did you invite him in?"

"No, but he corralled me into riding into town with him and taking him over to the general supply store. He converted Mr. Thompson almost as quickly as Beth Hardin."

"Who's Beth Hardin?"

Carla realized she'd been so upset over Ivan she'd forgotten the biggest news to hit Overlin in a while. Lukey was just as surprised as she that Kesney's daughter was in Texas.

"Did he tell you she was coming?"

"No."

"I wonder why. Everybody in town is expecting him to ask you to marry him."

Carla knew people in Overlin knew nearly everything about everybody else, but she hadn't realized they believed a proposal was imminent. "I've seen Maxwell Dodge almost as often as I've seen Kesney."

"We're expecting him to propose to you, too. They're the two richest men in town, and you're the prettiest woman."

"Don't let your wife hear you say that."

"She's the one who told me. You don't think I keep up with this sort of thing, do you?"

Carla had to laugh.

"What's so funny?"

"I once told my father life here was so dull I could go to sleep and wake up ten years later and nothing would have changed. Now I've got a charming stranger trying to steal my land and the sympathy of my friends. And if gossip is to be believed, two rich and handsome men are on the verge of proposing to me. Actually none of this is funny. I wish things were as quiet as they used to be."

Lukey reached out to pat her hand. "Don't lose heart. Things will work out."

"Are you sure?" She knew he couldn't be, but it was nice to hear.

"Just wait until the judge arrives. Now I'd love to spend the rest of the morning talking to you, but I have to earn a living."

Carla got up. "I didn't mean to take up so much of your time. Thanks for listening."

"Anytime."

Moments later Carla was on the boardwalk mentally organizing her morning. The first place she decided to go was the mercantile. She entered to find a group of women with their heads together in animated conversation. Except for the now infamous card game, it had been months since anything of interest happened in Overlin so she hurried over, eager to learn what occurred to generate so much excitement. "I can't remember when I've seen you smile like this," a matronly woman said to Myrtle Jenkins, a widow well known for her severity.

"I haven't had reason until today," Myrtle explained, her customary frown returning momentarily.

"What happened?" Carla asked. People usually avoided Myrtle because of her habit of remembering their every failure.

"I was having some difficulty with the latch on my gate." Myrtle had gone to the considerable expense of fencing her yard to keep out ruffians and dangerous animals—children and their dogs. "A handsome young man with a charming accent asked me in the most polite way possible if he could be of assistance. You should have heard him say, *May I be of some assistance, ma'am?*" Myrtle quivered with inner ecstasy. "I nearly melted on the spot. In two shakes of a lamb's tail he had the latch working perfectly. He even explained to me how it got stuck and what to do if it happened again. And what do you think he did then?" she asked Carla.

"I don't know.'

"He fixed the slats that the horrid Croker boy broke last month."

"But he was a stranger, Myrtle," one of the women said. "How do you know you can trust him?"

"I can tell a gentleman when I see one," Myrtle said in a manner that suggested no one could doubt her judgment. "Besides, he was a foreigner and so handsome it was hard not to stare. I nearly had palpitations."

Then she did something completely out of character. She giggled. Myrtle had been known to laugh only once when Hobie Jackman got so drunk he went to sleep with some dried cow manure as a pillow.

"Who is he?"

"Where did he come from?"

"What's he doing here?"

"Is he staying?"

"Is he married?"

"He said his name was Ivan. I didn't understand his last name. It's something foreign. Naturally I didn't ask him any personal questions," Myrtle said in her usual superior manner. "I have better manners than that."

The sinking feeling in Carla's stomach hit bottom. Who would have believed Ivan could make a convert of Myrtle Jenkins, the most prickly, sour-tempered woman in Overlin? Not wanting to hear any more about Ivan's wonderful qualities, Carla turned away to look for some material for a new dress.

"Don't you want to hear what else happened?" Myrtle asked Carla.

Carla didn't, but she turned back to Myrtle.

"He said if there was anything else I needed fixing, he'd be more than glad to see to it next time he was in town." Myrtle practically swelled with pride. "He said it was a pleasure to know a lady such as myself lived in Overlin."

"He sounds like a very nice man." If Ivan thought Myrtle was a *pleasure*, he had a lot to learn. Carla started to turn back to the bolts of material stacked on a large table, but Myrtle wasn't done.

"He said he knew you, that you took him to the general supply store."

Myrtle was looking for information. If there was a hint of even the smallest snippet of gossip, she wouldn't rest until she had ferreted it out.

"He asked where he could buy supplies," Carla said. "We happened to be coming to town at the same time. That's how we met Beth Hardin. Did you know Kesney's daughter was here?"

Carla felt bad about pitching Kesney and his daughter into the gossip mill, but she didn't want Myrtle asking more questions about her and Ivan until she could convince him to leave or at least move into town. Having thrown out Beth Hardin's name, Carla was obliged to share what little information she had. Since she knew Beth planned to stay in Texas, she did her best to paint a favorable picture of the young woman. When she said she was going to meet Kesney and his daughter for lunch, the ladies rushed away after making plans to reassemble at the restaurant.

"You should be ashamed of yourself," the elderly clerk said to Carla as soon as the last woman left the store. "You might as well have loosed a hive of bees on the young woman."

"I know, but Beth is a nice girl, and Kesney can hold his own with any woman. Well, maybe not Myrtle."

"Apparently this Ivan fella did."

Carla decided to come clean. "His name is Ivan Nikolai. He's here to take over half of our ranch. I know everybody will find out before long, but I just couldn't handle all the questions this morning. And if Myrtle had started lecturing me again on the evils of strong liquor and the inherent wickedness of boys, I don't know that I could have held my tongue."

"Is he anything like Myrtle thinks?"

"I never saw him until yesterday so I don't know what he's really like, but he is handsome and has a smile that will blind any woman regardless of age. You don't need me to tell you he has more charm than a snake oil salesman. Any man who could give Myrtle palpitations has to be spilling over with it."

The clerk laughed. "I would have given a day's pay to see that."

"Just keep your eyes open. He's already charmed Danny, Beth Hardin, and Mr. Thompson."

The clerk's smile vanished. "But you don't like him."

"I wouldn't like anybody who's trying to take half my ranch."

"I guess not. What are you going to do?"

"I don't know, but I'll think of something. Now, could you help me pick out some material? I need a new dress for the dance."

"Who are you going with?"

"Depends on who asks me."

It hadn't taken Ivan long to finish his business with Mr. Thompson. Promising to pick up his purchases when he was ready to leave, he set out to look over the town. There wasn't a lot to see. It certainly didn't compare to San Antonio, but he decided it was a nice little town, and he liked it. Everybody was friendly,

especially the women. He wasn't so self-effacing
that he didn't know his size, looks, and accent had
a lot to do with that, but he also knew the value of
a good first impression. People weren't going to be
pleased when they found out why he was in Overlin.
He paused when he noticed a middle-aged woman
struggling with the door to a store. One very vigorous
pull resulted in the handle coming off in her hand. The
woman looked upset and angry enough to cry. "Can I
be of help, ma'am?"

The woman twisted around like she was afraid of
being attacked. "Don't come a step closer, or I'll scream.
People in this town don't put up with anybody messing
with their women."

Ivan found it hard to believe any man would be foolish enough to attempt to *mess* with this woman, but he
didn't say so. He just kept smiling and broadened his
accent a little. "I would never mistreat a lady. I was
wondering if you could use some help with that door. It
seems to be stuck."

Maybe it was his smile. Maybe it was his accent. It
might even have been that to look up at him the woman
had to shade her eyes against the sun. It was probably
because he was the only one who offered to help her.
Whatever the reason, some of her anger and distrust
faded to be replaced by a frustration born of helplessness.
"Gordon has promised to fix the door a dozen times,
but whenever I ask, he doesn't have time or his tools
aren't handy. It's really because he knows I don't have
the money to pay him."

"If he will lend me his tools, I will be happy to fix the
door for you."

A look of surprised hope bloomed in her eyes. "You will?"

"Of course. A gentleman should never hesitate to help a lady."

She eyed him suspiciously. "You're not from around here."

"No, ma'am. My name is Ivan Nikolai. I come from Poland."

"I never met anybody from Poland before. How do I know you can fix my door?"

"Doors stick in Poland, too."

That appeared to be all she needed to know. "I'm Sadie Lowell. Most folks call me Widow Lowell. I sell clothes and other fashionable items for ladies. I've got a customer coming by this morning who just about keeps me in business. I can't ask her to come in the back door."

"All I need is some tools."

She eyed the doorknob in her hand, a look of determination taking hold. "Gordon can't refuse to help me now." Beckoning Ivan to follow, she headed down the boardwalk.

Ivan estimated the Widow Lowell was probably about fifty. She was short, rotund, and looked every year of her age. She appeared to be a woman who had been content to leave everything to her husband. Widowhood had forced her to become independent, a change she still found uncomfortable. She turned and entered the store Ivan had left only a short while ago. She marched straight to the back where Mr. Thompson was talking to a young woman with two little boys clinging to her skirts. Widow Lowell waited until the young woman finished her business and left with her little boys begging for sticks of candy they saw under glass at the front of the store.

"Gordon," she said to Mr. Thompson, "this young man has offered to fix my door. He just needs to borrow your tools."

"Sadie, I told you I'd—"

"You're full of promises, Gordon, but you never keep them. I need help right now because I can't get the door open."

"I'd do it right now, but I can't leave the store."

"I don't want you to leave your precious store. I *do* want you to lend your tools to this young man so he can fix my door." She waved the doorknob at him. "This came off when I tried to open up."

Mr. Thompson wasn't happy with the widow, but he seemed to know he didn't have much choice. He led Ivan to a room at the back of the building, which he used for nearly every part of the business of the store he didn't want his customers to see. Boxes in the process of being unpacked vied with crates piled in corners and along walls. A desk was covered with a litter of paper. There was barely room to walk. They edged their way to a corner toward a large box of tools. "Sadie Lowell is a valued member of this community," he said to Ivan. "You'd better be able to do what you say you can."

"You are welcome to inspect my work." Ivan wasn't impressed by the condition of Mr. Thompson's tools. Having selected what he needed and placed everything in an empty box, Ivan headed back toward the store. "I should have everything back within an hour."

"How are you going to fix the door?" the widow asked as they walked back to her store.

"I will take the hinges off from inside," Ivan explained. "Maybe all I need to do is shave a little of the edge."

It was easy to remove the pins from the front door hinges. It was a lot harder to unstick the door from the frame, but he managed it after about ten minutes. "I will take it out back and shave it down a little."

He attracted the attention of three boys who were playing in the space behind the store. They asked a steady stream of questions as he worked.

"You can come over to my house," one boy said. "My ma says all the windows stick."

"Do you know how to build a clubhouse?" another asked.

"Can you fix a broken wagon?" the third boy wanted to know.

"My pa says no man worth his salt rides in a wagon."

"Your pa don't have a busted leg."

"He wouldn't have a busted leg if he'd got out of the way of that steer."

Ivan feared he was going to have to break up a fight, but the boys were diverted by the way the shavings curled as he planed the edge of the door. They collected each shaving and settled them over extended fingers.

"You going to make any more?" one boy asked when he stopped.

"No. I needed to take off just enough to keep the door from sticking."

The boys followed him inside the store and watched intently as he replaced the door on its hinges then opened and closed it to demonstrate to the widow that it didn't stick.

"Wait until I tell that useless Gordon Thompson it

didn't take you no time at all to fix that door," the widow said. "And he was making out that it would take him half the day, going on about having to redo the frame because the building had settled, or it had been put up wrong."

"My pa says Mr. Thompson talks a good story but don't deliver much," one of the boys remarked.

But the widow wasn't about to have Mr. Thompson maligned. "You tell your pa nobody has to shove Gordon Thompson out of bed so he can get his work done. Now you boys go on. A lady's dress store is no place for dirty brats."

"We ain't dirty. Our mamas make us take a bath every Sunday before we go to church."

"That was five days ago. You've had time to collect lots of dirt since then."

The boys sauntered away, then took off at a run once they were out of the store.

"Little ragamuffins," the widow said in a way that made Ivan think she regretted having no children of her own. She turned. "I'm sorry I can't pay you, but you come around to my house on Sunday, and I'll feed you all you can eat."

"That is not necessary," Ivan protested.

"One way or the other, I pay my debts, especially to strangers. Now you'd better get those tools back to Gordon before he comes looking for them."

Ivan was putting the tools back in the box when he heard the widow say, "You've got to meet the man who fixed my door. He even fixed the doorknob after it broke off in my hand."

Ivan turned to see Carla glaring at him with eyes that were far from friendly.

Chapter 5

CARLA WAS IN NO MOOD TO HEAR ANOTHER TALE about how wonderful Ivan was, but Sadie Lowell didn't stop until she poured the whole story into Carla's ears. And Ivan, the shameless wolf in sheep's clothing, didn't even have the decency to look embarrassed. Carla wanted to protest that he was a thief, that he'd come to Overlin to take land he'd stolen. Her land. So she smiled through every word Sadie said though the smile felt like a mask that weighed a hundred pounds. Her teeth came together in a painful clench. Even the muscles in the back of her neck grew stiff.

"Miss Reece does not wish to hear stories about me," Ivan said to Sadie. "I will return Mr. Thompson's tools and let you ladies do your shopping."

"Don't forget Sunday," Sadie said. "If you don't show up, I'll come after you."

"I am sure you are a wonderful cook."

Sadie blushed. "Not wonderful, but Mr. Lowell never pushed away from my table."

"You must miss him very much."

Sadie clutched her bosom and looked heartsick. "Every day."

Carla thought she would gag. It wasn't Ivan's fault that he didn't know a thing about Buddy Lowell, but she was surprised Sadie had the effrontery to act like that in front of anyone who'd known her husband. As far as Carla knew, Buddy had never hit Sadie, but he'd done just about everything else. Carla didn't know what it was about Ivan that seemed to affect people's brains so they ceased to function normally.

"Sadie Lowell," Carla exclaimed the moment the door closed behind Ivan, "how can you tell such a whopper?"

The transformation in Sadie was immediate. She dropped her hand to her side and marched behind her counter before turning to face Carla. "There was no need for that young man to know the truth. I won't have anybody feeling sorry for me." She turned her attention to three dresses she'd set aside. "I think you'll like one of these." She held up a dress of pale blue cotton with white trim.

"It's very pretty, but how about something with more color? Light blue looks faded on me." She didn't like a yellow dress or the gingham any better. She caught sight of a red dress lying across a table in the back room. "Why didn't you bring out that one?"

Sadie's face was a study in dismay. "I don't… it didn't seem… it never occurred to me… it's not exactly…"

"What are you trying to say?"

Sadie seemed finally to gather her thoughts. "Don't you think it's a bit too bold for an unmarried lady?"

"I can't tell until I see what it looks like on me."

Sadie reluctantly handed the dress to Carla. It was a simple frock with a flared skirt. The neckline wasn't low enough to be considered daring. If she wore a shawl to guard against the chill, she would be quite modestly dressed. She was holding it up in front of her and looking at herself in the mirror when the door opened and Ivan returned.

"That dress looks very nice on you," he said. "You should buy it."

The look in his eye said so much more. Carla felt the heat of embarrassment rise along the back of her neck. "I thought you went to Mr. Thompson's?" It was all she could think to say.

"I came back to fix Mrs. Lowell's back door. It is so loose it barely locks."

"Bless your soul!" Sadie exclaimed. "I don't know what kind Providence sent you to Overlin, but I hope you never leave. I've been worried sick about that door."

"It is not hard to fix," Ivan said. "All I have to do is put some shims behind the hinges." He held up two thin pieces of wood for her inspection.

"Is that all it takes?"

"Yes, ma'am."

"I could kill Gordon," Sadie fumed. "He said there was nothing I could do but buy a new door. From him." She harrumphed in a manner that didn't bode well for Mr. Thompson. "You'll have to come to lunch two Sundays," Sadie said to Ivan. "Maybe three."

"One is enough. Now I fix your door."

Ivan disappeared through the back, and Sadie turned to Carla, a look of sheer adoration on her face. "That young man is an angel. I wonder if he has a place to stay. Do you think I should offer him a room?"

"You never saw him before today," Carla exclaimed. "You don't know what kind of person he might be."

"I know all I need to know," Sadie declared. "He doesn't know me, but he's done more for me in the last hour than anybody in this town has done in the last year. I'll probably have to force him to eat more than a couple of mouthfuls. Poor boy. I wonder where he eats. Do you know anything about him?"

Carla was caught. She couldn't say she didn't know Ivan, but if she told Sadie the entire story, it would be all over town by the day's end.

Carla was saved by the arrival of Myrtle Jenkins. Never one to wait her turn, Myrtle barged right in and proceeded to relate to Sadie everything she'd told Carla earlier that morning. Before long, both women were trying to outdo the other in praise of Ivan. Carla considered herself a Christian woman, but there were limits to what she could endure.

"I'll take the red dress," she told Sadie when the two women paused for breath.

Myrtle's disapproval was obvious. "Why would you buy such a dress?"

"I want something new to wear to the dance."

Myrtle's frown deepened. "I don't approve of dancing. It leads to lewd behavior."

"Only if you want to behave lewdly," Carla responded, "which I don't and never have."

"I wasn't speaking of you, my dear," Myrtle said with a grimace that was anything but endearing. "I was speaking of the men who would attend the dance. You know they all have only *one thing in mind*." Myrtle whispered the last words even though she had been married twice. Both husbands had been well thought of by the community; both had died young leaving Myrtle without the need to marry again.

"Danny is capable of providing all the protection I might need," Carla said.

"He's so young," Myrtle said. "And there was that

time when he got drunk and…" Myrtle let the sentence trail off, but Carla knew she was referring to the card game with Laveau diViere.

"I would be happy to provide Miss Reece with any protection she might need."

Carla didn't have to turn to know Ivan had reentered the shop. She didn't even need to hear his voice. The transformation in Myrtle and Sadie was more than enough.

"I appreciate your offer," Carla said to Ivan in what she hoped was an even voice. "But there's no one in Overlin I need protecting from. And if I did," she added when Sadie started to speak, "there are at least half a dozen men who would come to my aid."

"I'm sure there are more than that." Myrtle's expression went sour when she turned to Carla. "But it's better to be safe than sorry."

"What do you mean?"

"You should allow this young man to escort you. With *him* by your side, no one would dare to take liberties."

"That's a brilliant idea," Sadie exclaimed.

"It might be if I didn't already have a choice of escorts."

Myrtle's sour expression was back in full force. "If I had a daughter, I wouldn't trust her with Kesney Hardin or Maxwell Dodge."

"What's wrong with them?" Sadie asked.

"They're outsiders," Myrtle said. "I never trust people when I don't know where they came from."

"You don't know Ivan," Carla pointed out.

"He comes from Poland," Myrtle said. "I once spent a week in a town of Polish immigrants. They were good people. I'm sure Ivan is just as nice."

"I will escort Miss Reece from the ranch to the dance

and back," Ivan told Myrtle. "I am staying at her ranch, so that will cause me no trouble."

Looking surprised as well as affronted that Carla should have kept such an interesting piece of information from them, both women turned to Carla. "What does he mean?" Myrtle demanded.

Carla couldn't think of a thing to say.

"I am talking with Miss Reece and her brother about a business proposition," Ivan said. "We have told no one but you kind ladies. It would be appreciated if you would not speak of it until we come to some agreement."

"Certainly not," Sadie said. "I wouldn't think of it."

"You certainly would think of it," Myrtle contradicted, "but you won't *do* it, will you?"

Sadie drew herself up. "I said I wouldn't."

"Everybody knows you're a hopeless gossip," Myrtle said.

"I feel certain Mrs. Lowell is a woman of her word," Ivan said.

Myrtle looked skeptical, but she didn't correct Ivan.

"I need to be going," Carla said, eager to get away from Myrtle's crushing disapproval.

"It won't take a minute to wrap up your dress." Sadie took the dress and disappeared into the back room.

Carla watched in amazement as Ivan talked Myrtle out of her attitude of stern disapproval to a humor that could pass for that of a doting grandparent. Carla needed to tell Danny to pay close attention to Ivan so he could learn his secret.

Sadie came back with a bundle wrapped in brown paper and tied with string. "Here's your dress. I hope you have a good time at the dance."

"You make sure you stay close to her," Myrtle said to Ivan. "No telling what will happen if she wears that dress."

"She will be as safe as if you were watching her yourself."

The image of Myrtle Jenkins scowling her way around a country dance wasn't something Carla was eager to picture. She'd have pretty much the same effect on everybody's spirits as an unexpected cloudburst.

"I'm sure she will be," Myrtle said to Ivan. "It's very good of you to offer to watch out for her. I don't trust those two men she seems to favor."

Carla had had it with Myrtle and her candid opinions. Having paid Sadie for the dress, she accepted the bundle and turned for the door.

"Let me carry that for you," Ivan offered.

She wanted to refuse, but she could tell from their expressions that doing so wouldn't sit well with Myrtle or Sadie. She handed the bundle to Ivan, said good-bye to the two women, and fled the shop. Ivan caught up with her a little later.

"You will *not* escort me to the dance," she said, her gaze straight ahead. "I *will* choose who I go to the dance with."

"Of course," Ivan said. "I only offered to ride with you to keep you company."

Carla stopped and turned on Ivan. "That's not what you told Myrtle."

"What would you want me to tell her? That you are a stubborn woman who refuses to obey the law? That you will not even let me enter your home? That you would throw me off your land if you could? That you ignore every effort I make to be friendly?"

Carla practically sputtered with indignation. "You wouldn't dare!"

"You have no idea how much I would dare. I am not a coward, but you would be the one to suffer. I am a gentleman. I would not treat any woman that way."

Carla swallowed her exasperation, though it didn't go down easily. It was hard to remember Ivan hadn't created the mess she was in. Laveau diViere and her brother were the culprits. But Laveau wasn't here, and she loved her brother even if she wanted to strangle him from time to time. Ivan was the only one on whom she could vent her wrath. It was even more difficult to hold her tongue when he charmed women who'd been critical of her since her parents died.

"I know I'm not treating you fairly, but I can't help it. And seeing you oozing charm just makes it harder."

He remained silent.

"I've spent my whole life on that ranch. My parents died on that ranch. It's everything I know, holds everything I love. I know what Danny did was stupid, but I can't just hand over my inheritance." Carla struggled to hold back tears. She was stronger than this. If only Ivan wasn't so nice. The look on his face was genuinely sympathetic. "It's only worse when everyone in town takes your side."

"So you think I should not fix the widow's doors?"

"It's not that. I—"

"Then I should not fix Miss Myrtle's gate?"

"That's not what I meant."

"Should I tell her I will not escort you even though we will be coming to town at the same time?"

"You know what I'm talking about!" She hadn't

meant to raise her voice enough to attract attention. "Now see what you've made me do?"

"I merely asked what you would have me do. Why should that make you angry?"

He looked so genuine, so truly concerned, she wanted to tell him to stop acting, to save it for sentimental widows like Sadie. "I don't want you following me around," she said from between clenched teeth. "I don't want you offering to escort me to town. And I don't want you carrying a package that's so light I'd hardly notice I was carrying it."

"I'm not carrying it for you. I'm carrying it because that's what Miss Myrtle wanted."

Ivan's response almost took her breath away. She didn't think she was vain, but no man had ever said anything like that to her. "You shouldn't let people take advantage of your kindness." It didn't seem like the right thing to say, but it was all she could think of.

"I see no reason to withhold kindness when it costs so little."

He hadn't been constantly criticized by Myrtle Jenkins. His judgment hadn't been questioned just as often by Sadie Lowell. He wasn't a young woman trying to be taken seriously in a town controlled by men. He'd never been told not to worry his pretty head about anything as serious as the best kind of rope to use for lassos. But that didn't change the fact that Ivan was right. She let out a big sigh. "I just can't seem to hold my temper around you. That card game changed everything."

"Maybe you can buy the ranch back."

"I don't have that much money."

"Maybe you will marry one of those rich men, and he will buy it for you."

Carla glanced up so quickly, she nearly ran into a boy weaving his way through traffic at a run. Ivan pulled her aside just in time to avoid impact. She momentarily lost her balance and fell into his chest. His arm came around her waist to steady her. And in a flash, Carla knew she'd never felt a connection like this with Kesney or Maxwell. With that one touch, she suddenly felt… safe.

Before she could think on it any further, Ivan pulled away, leaving her oddly bereft. While she wasn't one to allow liberties, Carla hadn't reached the age of nineteen without having been embraced more than once. She'd even allowed a small number of chaste kisses, yet none of them had affected her as strongly as Ivan's touch. Even after he'd stepped back, she felt as if his hands were still on her, like he'd left an invisible handprint on her skin, like he was saying she belonged to him.

She didn't understand that. Ivan hadn't said or done anything to give rise to such a feeling. Why should a few polite gestures have this effect on her? Everything weighed against him, so why did she feel his touch was the first to reach beyond the surface of her skin?

"Would you do something for me, and for you, too?" he asked.

"What?" she asked, trying not to sound as breathless as she felt.

"Go with me to see Lukey Gordon."

The ranch. Of course. She couldn't forget for one second what Ivan was really after. "Why would I do that?"

"We need to be clear that my claim to half of your ranch is valid."

"I've already told you Laveau cheated."

"You said no one knows how he did it."

"He also used undue influence to get my brother drunk. I intend to ask the judge to cancel the wager."

"Just because your brother had something to drink?"

"Danny is only seventeen, too young to make a binding wager of such magnitude."

"You have a right to take your case to a judge. But until then, I want it clear that I have a valid claim."

Carla had no desire to have Lukey tell her again that Danny had lost his share of the ranch. Nor did she have any desire to be seen walking through town with Ivan. There would be rumors before noon that she found a new romantic interest. "Okay, but I don't have much time before I have to meet Beth and her father for lunch."

"This will not take long."

Nor did it. Ivan had a document which stated clearly that he was to manage the property for Laveau diViere for one year, and that at the end of that year he would receive title to the property as compensation for his custodianship. It contained all the proper signatures and dates.

"This contract is legal and binding," Lukey told Ivan. "However, a question remains as to whether the card game can be accepted as a legal and binding agreement. You should understand Miss Reece intends to place the case before the circuit judge when he comes to Overlin."

"That could be weeks, even months," Ivan pointed out. "Until then, Miss Reece and her brother should divide the ranch in half. If they do not want to do that, then I should be included in decisions affecting the whole ranch."

Carla didn't know how it was possible for a man to make such brutal demands and still look like butter wouldn't melt in his mouth. What did they teach people in Poland? "Do I have to?" she asked Lukey.

"You don't *have* to do anything, but if you don't, Mr. Nikolai may ask the sheriff to force you. And it would look better to the judge if you at least *try* to compromise."

Carla was about to explode with impotent rage. Rather than say something that she would later regret, she rose to her feet. "I promised to meet Kesney and his daughter for lunch. If I don't leave now, I'll be late. I won't divide the ranch, but I will agree to allow Mr. Nikolai a voice in any decisions Danny and I make. Will that satisfy you?" she asked Ivan.

There was that damned smile again. It either made her want to slap him or kiss him. Just the thought of the latter caused her to think she must be losing her mind.

"It is a good beginning."

She didn't want to know what he meant by that, so she said good-bye to Lukey. Before she could leave his office, Ivan asked, "When will you be ready to go back to the ranch?"

She had been hoping she could think of a way to avoid riding back with him, but it looked like she was out of luck. "In about an hour."

"Where should I meet you?"

"How about meeting here?" Lukey offered.

"Thank you." At least she would be spared waiting for Ivan on the street.

―⁓―

"I was telling Papa about meeting you and that nice man on the way into town," Beth said as soon as Carla was seated at the table. "Do you know where he went?"

"He had several things to do."

"Will he be at the dance?"

"Beth hasn't stopped talking about the dance ever since I mentioned it," Kesney said. "You'd think she'd never been to one before."

"I've never been to a dance in Texas." Beth made a face. "The ones back home were so boring." She brightened. "Papa says here I can dance with anyone who asks me. Back home anyone who wanted to dance with me had to put his name on my dance card. If my chaperone didn't approve of him, she wouldn't let him sign the card."

Carla had never been told who she could and couldn't dance with. Her parents had given her credit for having enough sense to choose her own partners. Since their deaths, she sometimes fell afoul of the scrutiny of matrons like Myrtle and Sadie, but she didn't let their censure affect her. As an independent ranch owner, she considered herself on a par with anyone in town, even if they didn't return her esteem.

"Not every man is a good choice, even for a dance partner, but most of the time there's no problem as long as you stay on the dance floor."

"She won't have any trouble while I'm around," Kesney said. "Now how about some lunch? I can hear my stomach growling."

Carla was still too agitated to be hungry. She listened to Beth attempt to talk her father into letting her try some of the hottest dishes on the menu.

"You can't have jalapeno chilies until you get used to some that aren't so hot," Kesney told his daughter. "I don't want you drinking so much water you get sick."

Giving in to Kesney's insistence that she eat something, Carla ordered chicken salad. Beth opened her mouth to say something—from her expression she intended to protest against such a tame choice—but ended up uttering a sound similar to that of someone choking.

"Are you all right?" her father asked.

"There he is."

"There who is?" Kesney wanted to know.

"That man with the strange name Carla said was from some foreign country"

Carla turned to see that Ivan had entered the restaurant. She should have guessed that in a town as small as Overlin there was a good chance they'd end up in the same restaurant. She wanted to hide under the table until he found a place to sit, but it was too late. Beth was waving at him, drawing his attention.

"He's the one who fixed my wagon when the wheel came off," she told her father. "May I invite him to eat with us?"

Chapter 6

IVAN RECOGNIZED BETH AT THE SAME MOMENT SHE spotted him. Despite her frantic beckoning and broad grin making it clear she wanted him to join them, he smiled and nodded in her direction before resuming his search for an empty table. He didn't have to be a mind reader to know Carla was cringing at the possibility. Her posture was rigid, and she didn't look in his direction. He barely settled into his chair at an empty table in a corner when Beth came running up.

"Come eat with us. We have plenty of room at our table."

"It will be an intrusion."

"I told my father all about you. He wants to meet you."

"I can meet him after your meal."

"He wants to meet you now. He said he didn't get a chance to thank you properly this morning. He sent me to get you."

From what Ivan saw, Beth didn't take time to speak to her father before she bounded out of her chair and came over to where he was sitting, but it was apparent from her father's expression that he was in agreement with his daughter. Ivan intentionally stayed talking to Lukey for several minutes to give Carla a head start so they wouldn't run into each other. Giving in to Beth would undo both their plans, but he didn't see a polite way to get out of it. Bowing to the inevitable, he got up. "I will stay only a minute."

Beth took him by the hand, apparently fearing he would get away if she didn't. "I want you to have lunch with us. You and Carla are my best friends here."

Ivan had a sinking feeling Beth had more than *friendship* in mind, but he was certain her father had no intention of letting his daughter develop an attachment to a penniless foreigner. Kesney stood to greet Ivan with a broad, welcoming smile.

"I didn't have a chance earlier to thank you properly for rescuing my daughter." His handshake was firm, his smile relaxed and genuine. "She should have waited for me to bring her to town." He smiled fondly at his daughter. "The little puss is too strong-minded for her own good."

"How was I to know your buggy was falling apart?" Beth countered. "Why didn't you tell me the wheel was about to come off?"

"I didn't know," her father replied. "I always ride."

"If *I* could ride, it wouldn't matter if both wheels were ready to fall off."

"I knew this would somehow end up being my fault." From the look Kesney gave his daughter, Ivan guessed she could do no wrong in his eyes. "Won't you join us? A lunch is the least I can do to thank you."

"That is not necessary," Ivan protested. "I would do the same for any young woman."

"I'm sure you would," Kesney said, "but you did it for my daughter, and I would like to express my thanks."

Ivan cast a quick glance at Carla. She still hadn't looked at him. "You already have a guest."

"You don't mind, do you, Carla?"

"Of course not." If Kesney hadn't been so preoccupied

with his daughter or had been more perceptive, he might have seen it took all of Carla's self-control to pretend to be welcoming. But after her smiling acceptance, there was nothing Ivan could do but accept the invitation graciously. The only chair available was between Beth and Carla. Ivan took it reluctantly.

"How did your morning go?" Carla asked. "Did you find everything you need?"

"Let me know if there's anything you can't find," Kesney offered. "I'll make sure you get it."

"Thank you, but I have all I need for now."

"Where are you staying?"

Ivan glanced at Carla. "I have not decided yet, so I have a camp."

"You mean you're sleeping outside?" Beth asked.

Ivan laughed. "I slept outside during the war. I do not mind."

"Where are you camping?" Kesney asked.

"It doesn't matter where," Beth declared. "You can't sleep outside. What if it rains? You have to stay with us until you have a place."

Ivan guessed from Kesney's stiffening expression that his thankfulness didn't extend that far. "I have a nice spot by a creek on Miss Reece's ranch," Ivan told Beth. "I have shade, water, and my horse has grass. I do not need anything else."

"Tell him he has to stay with us, Papa," Beth begged her father.

"You can't tell a man what he *has* to do," Kesney said to his daughter before turning back to Ivan. "I'm sure Carla will let him use her bunkhouse if the weather turns bad."

"He can't stay in a bunkhouse," Beth protested. "He's not a common cowhand. Carla said he's a prince or something wherever he comes from."

"I *am* a common cowhand," Ivan told Beth. "I left my title behind when I left Poland."

A waitress came to ask Ivan what he wanted to eat. Despite having been in Texas for five years, he occasionally longed for the food he'd grown up eating. Of all the choices the waitress gave him, Carla's chicken salad looked closest, so he ordered that.

"Why don't you tell us what your life was like in Poland?" Kesney asked. "My mother's family came from Prussia."

Ivan resisted the temptation to tell him Prussia was one of the countries that destroyed Poland and was responsible for his family losing their estates. Kesney might be interested in what it was like to live in Poland, but Beth had already heard it so he made it quick and unglamourous.

"You don't miss it?" Kesney asked.

"I miss it very much."

"Ivan plans to go back to Poland," Carla said. "His family has regained some of their lost property."

"When are you leaving?" Beth asked.

"Not for a year."

Beth's frown vanished. "Anything can happen in a year. You might find a reason to want to stay. Are you going to the dance?"

"I have not been invited to any dance. Naturally I will not go."

"You don't have to be invited," Beth exclaimed. "Anyone can go."

Ivan turned to Carla. "This is true?"

"All of our dances are open to anyone who wants to come."

"You will come, won't you?" Beth asked. "You can dance with me if you like."

"I do not know Texas dances," Ivan said. "They are not like in Poland."

"I'll teach you. We have a piano."

"You can't play the piano and teach him at the same time," Beth's father pointed out.

Beth turned to Carla. "Can you play the piano?"

"Yes, but—"

"Then you can play for us. I know all the most popular dances," Beth assured Ivan.

"Not so fast," Kesney said to his daughter. "Ivan may not want to go to the dance. And you can't just commandeer Carla's time. She has a ranch to run."

Beth looked properly contrite and made all the appropriate apologies, but when her smile peeped out, Ivan could tell she was used to getting her way. It was confirmed when her father winked, and she broke into a bright smile.

"Ask Carla properly," her father said.

Ivan didn't like having Carla put in the position of having to play the piano, but he intended to go to the dance, not just escort Carla there and back. He wanted a chance to spend more time with her. If, in order to do that, he had to allow Beth to teach him to dance, then he would. He had been an accomplished dancer back in Poland. There was no dance he'd seen while working at Cade's ranch that he felt he couldn't learn.

"Can we start tonight?" Beth asked. "We need to begin right away in case Ivan needs more than one lesson."

Ivan liked that suggestion. He didn't look forward to an evening of listening to his horse munch grass. He turned to Carla. "Is that good for you?"

It didn't appear that it was, but she said, "It's fine. What time?"

"Why don't you both have supper with us?" Kesney suggested.

Beth clapped her hands in delight. "That would be perfect!"

When their food arrived, Ivan and Kesney began eating, while Beth listed for Carla all the dances she knew. "It doesn't matter if you don't know all of them," Beth said when Carla said for the second time that she didn't know a certain tune. "I brought all my music."

"Stop plaguing Carla and eat your lunch," Kesney told his daughter.

"But I haven't asked—"

"Not another word until you've eaten," her father said. "Ivan and I are done. You haven't touched your food, and Carla has barely had a chance to eat for all your chatter." Beth was clearly unhappy when her father turned to Ivan and asked, "What did you do during the war?"

Ivan grinned. "I studied to be an engineer, so they put me in a cavalry unit."

Kesney returned his grin. "Ah, you know the army— why assign you to where you can use your talent? Did you at least know how to ride?"

"I learned as a boy." He would have been a disgrace to his family if he hadn't been an expert rider by the time he started school. "We mounted night raids against

Union supply lines and anything else that might slow them down."

"How did you end up in Texas?"

"My commanding officer needed help with his ranch. It seemed a good thing to do."

"So now you're ready for a ranch of your own?"

"I think more of a partnership."

"Do you have someone in mind?"

"Yes."

"But you're not ready to divulge their name?" Kesney added when Ivan said no more.

"Now is not a good time."

"Negotiations still underway?"

"Yes."

Kesney laughed. "Clearly a man who likes to keep his cards close to his vest."

Ivan wasn't sure what that meant, but there was an edge to Kesney's laugh. Apparently he expected to be told more.

"I'm through eating," Beth announced.

"Then we should be on our way," Kesney said to his daughter. "We have to prepare for company this evening. That's an unusual event for me." Ignoring Ivan's protests that he should pay for his own lunch, he put money on the table to cover all four meals. "I invited you to be my guest. We will see both of you tonight."

As soon as Kesney and his daughter left the table, Ivan turned to Carla. "I did not mean for this to happen."

Carla's shoulders slumped. "It's time I stop trying to pretend you're not here to take half our ranch. Everybody already knows about the card game."

"What will you say?"

"Nothing until they ask."

"When they do, you can say we are discussing it. That will explain why I camp by your creek."

Carla pushed back her chair. "For the ladies you've charmed with your smile and your determination to fix anything that's broken, nothing will explain why I haven't invited you into my home and given you the best bedroom."

"I would not take it."

"And I won't offer it." Ivan held her chair while she stood. "But I'll still be blamed."

"It does seem unfair that you should be blamed for what your brother did."

Once outside, they paused to allow their eyes time to adjust to the bright sunlight. "And for what *I* didn't do."

"What was that?"

"Marry and let my husband take care of everything."

"Are you in love with anyone?"

"No."

"Then you were right not to marry."

"I thought in Poland every girl married young."

"Yes, but they do not marry for love. They marry for money and position. They look elsewhere for love."

"Would you do that?"

"I have neither money nor position."

Carla shaded her eyes from the sun so she could see Ivan better. "I mean marry for money and position and look for love elsewhere."

Ivan didn't hesitate to answer. "No."

"Why not?" They had to move aside to allow people to pass.

"Are you ready to go home?"

"Yes."

"Then let us go."

"You haven't answered my question," Carla reminded him as they headed toward the livery stable where they had left their horses.

"I have American friends who married for love. I have seen the happiness that has brought them. I want that for myself."

"But when you go back to Poland, won't you be expected to marry for money and position?"

"A father with money and position does not want his daughter to marry a man who has neither."

"But you're handsome and charming." Carla suddenly blushed and directed her gaze to where she was about to step. "A-a-and you have a way with older women."

Ivan chuckled. "You should not blush and stammer when you give a man a compliment. It makes him doubt whether you mean it."

Carla looked up at him, impatience writ on her countenance. "You know what I say is true. You trade on it."

"I do not know what you mean by *I trade on it*, but I help people because I can. Everyone has been good to me since I came to this country."

"Do you call having to fight in the war being treated well?"

"The war left me with friends who gave me a home where I am welcome to stay or go as I wish. If I need help, I would not have to ask."

Conversation ceased while they crossed the dusty street. Avoiding horses and their droppings didn't allow for a lapse in concentration. Holding her skirts to keep them out of the dirt, Carla allowed Ivan to take her elbow. Once they reached the opposite boardwalk, Carla stamped her feet to shake off the dust.

"Do you have packages to pick up?" Ivan asked.

"Only the dress I left at Lukey's office."

They retrieved the dress and their purchases at the general store and started back to the ranch. They didn't talk much. There would be plenty of time ahead for that.

"Well, what do you think of him?" Danny pounced on his sister the minute she got back from town. He was impressed that Ivan had insisted on unsaddling her horse.

Carla's temper didn't improved during the ride home. It wasn't anything that Ivan did. Or rather, it wasn't *anything else*. She realized the damage was done before she got up from the lunch table. Probably even before that. She was attracted to Ivan. She tried to deny it, but after she realized she was jealous she would be playing the piano while Beth danced with Ivan, there was no point. Being thoroughly put out with herself, she was in no mood to endure Danny's curiosity. "It's not a question of whether Ivan is nice, charming, or even honest," Carla snapped, virtually snatching her wrapped dress from her brother's hands. "It's what he's here to do."

"Better him than Laveau diViere," Danny said.

"Better no one at all." Carla refrained from saying that neither would have been there if Danny hadn't been so foolish. They'd been over that ground too often to warrant plowing it again. She dropped her package on the kitchen table, pulled out a chair, sat down, and allowed Danny to help her take off her boots.

"He could have sent someone worse."

Carla sighed. "I'm sure he could, but they'd be doing the same thing."

"At least he's not trying to push his way in here. I suppose he could rightfully claim half the house. Half the bunkhouse, half the wagons, half the horses, half the—"

"I get your point." Carla stood, picked up her boots, and set them near the back door. She reached for the shoes she wore indoors. "You should talk to Myrtle Jackson."

"Why?"

"Because she adores Ivan as much as you do."

"I don't adore… Myrtle doesn't adore anybody, and she hates strangers."

Carla put on her shoes and stood. "She doesn't hate Ivan. To hear her talk, he's the most wonderful man she's ever met. Sadie is nearly as bad." Carla wasn't pleased when Danny broke out laughing. "You wouldn't think it was so funny if you'd been in my shoes this morning."

"What did he do to pull the wool over that old dragon's eyes?"

"He fixed the latch on Myrtle's fence then replaced some missing slats. After that he fixed both doors on Sadie's shop."

"There's nothing special about that."

"Maybe not, but no other man in town has done it. And he did it with a smile that would blind the sun."

Danny laughed even harder. "If this weren't all my

fault, I'd shake his hand in welcome." Danny followed his sister out of the kitchen and down the hall toward her bedroom. "Why hasn't he worked his magic on you? You're not nearly so hard to please as Myrtle or Sadie."

"I'm not as easily taken in by a smile and a good deed. But I did promise Lukey I'd work with him, include him in all decisions concerning the ranch." She shrugged out of the light wrapper she wore to keep the dust off when she went to town. "But he's from Poland and was trained as an engineer. What can he know about ranches? I'm depending on you to back me up if he wants to do something crazy."

"He doesn't strike me as a man to do anything foolish. First he got Sadie and Myrtle singing his praises. Now he has Kesney inviting him to dinner and his daughter teaching him to dance. "

Carla turned so Danny could unbutton the back of her dress before she changed back into her ranch clothes. "Do you think he's underhanded?"

"I'm sure he's as nice as he seems, but I think he's a lot smarter than either of us suspected. All of those things might have been coincidence, but he saw them as opportunities to do something nice for someone else. I'm afraid people are going to think badly of you for making him camp out."

"They already do. Beth even asked her father if he could stay with them until he found a place to stay."

Danny burst out laughing. That irritated Carla at first, but then she saw the humor. "You should have seen Kesney's eyes. I give him credit for remarkable control, but he was definitely startled." She stepped out of her dress, laid it across the bed, and picked up the skirt and blouse she wore around the house.

"What's his daughter like? Is she pretty?" Danny picked up his sister's discarded dress and hung it in the wardrobe. "Why don't you and I put our heads together? You marry Kesney, and I'll marry his daughter. He'll buy back my half of the ranch for you. It won't do for his daughter to be married to a poor man, so he'll find a nice job for me."

They both laughed. "That might work for me, but I think Beth has her sights set on Ivan."

"How old is his daughter?"

"She can't be a day more than sixteen."

"She's too young for Ivan, but just right for me."

"Don't get your hopes up. I'm sure Kesney won't allow his daughter to throw herself away on a penniless cowboy, not even one who's an ex-Polish prince. You'll be on your own for supper tonight. Try not to burn anything when you heat it up."

—∿∿—

"They dance well together, don't they?"

"Yes, they do." Kesney stood next to the piano most of the evening. He said he needed to be there so he could turn the pages, but he ended up making Carla feel like they were an older couple chaperoning the youngsters. Since she was probably ten years younger than Ivan, she resented being made to feel old.

"Ivan is a quick learner."

Carla had a feeling Ivan knew more about dancing than Beth, that he allowed her to believe she was the teacher and he the student. Beth—young and inexperienced despite her veneer of sophistication—didn't appear to realize that Ivan was leading and she was following. She beamed with happiness and pride.

"You're marvelous," she told Ivan for what had to be the twentieth time. "I've never known anyone to learn to dance so quickly and so well."

"We have dances in Poland," Ivan said.

"Your dances can't be anything like ours," Beth insisted. "Everybody is always so proper."

"Not all the time."

Ivan accompanied that statement with one of his blinding smiles, which appeared to send Beth's mind reeling. That only made Carla more annoyed. What was he doing? She was certain Kesney would never consider allowing Beth to marry anyone like Ivan, but he seemed as captivated by Ivan as his daughter. What was wrong with everybody? Ivan was just a man. Okay, he was tall and muscled, handsome, and spoke with a charming accent. He had wonderful manners and a smile that should be outlawed. But he was still just a man, and one without money. Americans didn't put much value on titles or position in society. They wanted land, livestock, and cash. She didn't see how being a prince back in Poland could compensate for that.

Watching Kesney beam at his daughter as she danced in Ivan's arms, Carla wondered why she couldn't see what everybody else saw. Even Lukey, her staunchest ally, had thawed considerably toward Ivan. Was there something wrong with her?

Whatever it might be, it didn't stop her from being attracted to him. Contrary to local opinion, she didn't consider herself an old maid at nineteen. She was independent and the owner to half a ranch. She didn't feel that her chances for marriage were passing her by, not with the two wealthiest bachelors in town paying court to her. Setting all that aside, no sensible young woman would let herself become enamored of a penniless stranger who numbered traitors among his friends and who was planning to return to Poland as soon as possible.

A horribly wrong chord wrenched her out of her abstraction. "Sorry," she said to Beth, who looked at her in shock and Ivan who regarded her with an inscrutable raised eyebrow. "I wasn't paying attention."

"That's because you're tired," Kesney said. "I blame myself for letting Beth keep you tied to the piano for so long. That's enough dancing for tonight."

"But I haven't taught Ivan all the dances," Beth objected.

"He seems to need very little teaching," Kesney said. "I expect all he has to do is watch a dance one time, and he'll have it."

"He is a marvelous dancer," Beth said.

"Thank you," Ivan said. "My dancing master would be pleased to hear you say that."

"You had a dance master? Of all the tricks," Beth exclaimed. "And I thought you couldn't dance at all."

"I exaggerate a little," Ivan admitted. "I learned from my mother who learned from *her* mother who did have a dance master. By the time I was born, we could no longer afford such luxuries. It was thought best to spend what little money I had on education."

"A wise decision," Kesney said. "It will stand you in good stead."

"So far I have only had a chance to use it to install indoor plumbing for my friend's wife."

"I would like to hear more about that when we have time," Kesney said, "but I think it's time I escort Carla home."

"That is not necessary," Ivan said. "I can make sure she arrives safely."

Chapter 7

KESNEY STIFFENED PERCEPTIBLY. "IT'S A LONG RIDE, it's getting dark, and she hardly knows you."

"I'll be perfectly safe with Ivan," Carla said.

"I would not allow anything to happen to you," Ivan declared. "To do so would bring dishonor to me and my family."

"Is that because you are a prince?" Beth asked.

"I am a prince no longer. It is because of my honor as a gentleman."

Beth's brow furrowed in confusion. "I didn't think you could stop being a prince. Aren't you born one?"

"Only in Poland," Ivan said, "but I am not in Poland."

"But if you go back, will you be a prince again?"

"Yes, but I will not be a rich prince, so the title will not be important."

Carla wasn't surprised to find Poland was like the rest of the world. Ivan must love his country a great deal to face going back without being able to take his former place in society.

"I need to be going," she said to Kesney. "Danny will expect breakfast at the same time even if I get to bed late." She could tell Kesney was unhappy, but it was ridiculous to worry when he was unconcerned that Ivan had been her only protection on the ride to his ranch. Kesney accompanied them to the door and waited for her outside while one of the hands brought her buggy around. Ivan insisted upon fetching his own horse.

"Are you certain you will be safe?" Kesney asked again.

"Of course she will," Beth assured her father. "Ivan is a wonderful dancer."

Carla had no idea what dancing had to do with a man's character, but she was too tired to ask. "If you want a character reference for Ivan, ask Myrtle Jenkins or Sadie Lowell. Or three grubby little boys he's invited to visit my ranch whenever the notion strikes them."

She almost laughed at Kesney's confusion. Once she explained, they both laughed, which upset Beth.

"I think Ivan's wonderful," she declared. "You shouldn't laugh at him or those old women. Someday you'll be old like them."

It amused Carla that Beth didn't appear to think that she, too, would be old someday, but the thought of being treated as everyone treated Myrtle and Sadie was sobering. The two women could be annoying, but so could everyone. Carla knew she annoyed people from time to time, but she was treated well because she was young, attractive, and part owner of a successful ranch. Would she, sometime in the future, find herself in a similar position as these two women?

"We're not laughing at these two ladies," Kesney assured his daughter, "just at their reaction to Ivan."

Beth wasn't mollified by her father's explanation. "It looks like the same thing to me."

Carla had to agree with Beth. "You're right. I've allowed their criticism to make me think unkindly of them."

"They're probably just jealous they were never as

beautiful as you," Beth said before looking up at her father with an impish grin. "I doubt they ever had every eligible man in town competing for their attention."

The arrival of Ivan with his horse and a cowhand with her buggy relieved Carla of having to respond to that embarrassing statement. She thanked Kesney for dinner, managed to avoid giving Beth a definite date for a second dance lesson, and told Kesney once again he didn't need to see her home. As she drove from the ranch house yard, she could feel the muscles in her back and shoulders start to relax. The evening had been uncomfortable, but until then she didn't realize just how much so

As lengthening shadows heralded the approach of night, the earth began releasing the heat that accumulated during the day. It rose from the ground like long-tailed minnows swimming in a crystal clear lake. Carla could feel the competing currents of air on her skin.

"That was a nice evening," Ivan said. "It was kind of Beth to offer to teach me to dance." Carla had rejected Ivan's offer to drive her buggy, so he rode alongside.

"And underhanded of you to hide that you know more about dancing than she does." Her eyes having adjusted to the night, she could see Ivan's look of surprise despite the shadows.

"Of what do you disapprove?"

She wasn't sure *disapprove* was the right word. It sounded too parental or old-maidish, and Carla didn't feel at all like either. "I didn't say I disapproved, but I do think you misled a young girl who probably has a crush on you."

"What is this *crush*? I do not think we have such a thing in Poland."

Carla didn't know how Ivan could have been in America so long and still not understand common expressions. "It means she likes you, is infatuated with you, maybe even dazzled by you."

"I do not like this *dazzle*. It sounds like you think I have cast a spell over her. I do not cast spells. We do not approve of witchcraft in Poland."

Talking to Ivan was like trying to ride through a prairie dog town without stepping into a hole. "I mean you should have told her that you already knew how to dance."

Ivan regarded her with a questioning look that contained a strong element of disapproval. "Have you always disliked making people happy?"

Carla was so stunned by his question she didn't know how to answer him. "I've never been against making people happy."

"You do not like that I helped Myrtle Jenkins or Widow Lowell."

"I never said you shouldn't have helped them."

Ivan ignored her protest. "Now you think I should tell Beth I will not let her teach me to dance."

"That's not what I said!" She hadn't meant to raise her voice, but something about Ivan made it nearly impossible to behave normally. "I said you shouldn't have let her think you didn't know how to dance."

"I have never done these Texas dances."

"Now you're quibbling?"

"What is this *quibbling?* Why do you not speak the same words as everybody else?"

Carla couldn't explain the perverse impulse that caused her to burst out laughing rather than blister Ivan with a scalding retort. What was it about this man that infuriated her at the same time it charmed her? She wanted to be furious at him, and she was, but he made her laugh. She wanted to ignore him, forget he existed, yet Fate seemed determined to keep her aware of everything he did. She wanted to make him understand that what he was doing was a subtle kind of dishonesty, yet she was the only person who wasn't thrilled with him. Something was grievously wrong with this situation. When she got home, she intended to give it some serious thought, but right now she had to try to explain the meaning of quibbling. "It means splitting hairs, avoiding the issue, equivocation."

Ivan's expression cleared. "In Poland we have a saying—"

"I'm sure you do, but I won't understand it any better than you understand me." Ivan's blinding smile bloomed, and she lost all desire to bring him to an understanding of why it was wrong to make everybody believe he was the most wonderful man they'd ever met. "I don't mean to pick at you all the time, but I think you should have told Beth you knew how to dance even if you didn't know the specific dances she was going to teach you."

Ivan's brow furrowed again. "I understand that you do not like why I am here. I do not understand why you must dislike me as well. Do I do awful things to you or your brother? Do I say bad things about you to your friends?"

"I don't dislike you." That was part of the problem. It would have been easier if she did. "I know you haven't said anything unkind about me or Danny. I think it was kind of you to help Myrtle and Sadie. I don't think you should encourage Beth's interest in you, but I admit it's hard to say no to her. Her father doesn't even try."

Ivan looked puzzled. "Why do you say I encourage her to like me? She is a child. I do not like children in that way."

"She doesn't think she's a child. And she's looking for a man."

"I am too old. Why would she look at me?"

"You don't see yourself the way Beth does. You're better looking than any man in Overlin except Danny. You have a charming accent, an exotic background, a smile that should be declared illegal, and you practically fall over yourself helping anybody you can."

Amusement tinged Ivan's voice. "You like my smile? You think I am handsome?" His expression faltered. "But surely you do not like my accent. It does not sound like Texas."

"That's part of your charm. I'm about the only person in Overlin who doesn't think you walk on water." The puzzled expression warned her that she'd wandered into territory foreign to him. "It means I'm about the only person who doesn't think you're perfect. Where have you been hiding in the ten years you've been in America?" she asked, exasperated. "Don't people talk to you? Don't you listen to them?"

"One does not need to talk to chase cows."

"What about during the war?"

"We rode at night in secret. Even whispering was dangerous."

Carla wanted to ask him about the secret rides at night, but she noticed several riders coming toward them. It would not have been so unusual to see half a dozen riders coming from the direction of Overlin—this was ranch country where cowhands had to be up early—but they were coming from the direction of the Rio Grande. She didn't know every cowhand in the county, but when they drew near, she realized she had never seen any of them. She started to drive past, but the lead rider signaled that he wanted her to stop.

"Howdy, ma'am," the man said when Carla brought her buggy to a stop.

"Good evening," Carla replied. "Can I help you?"

"Maybe I'd better ask your husband."

Carla started to explain that Ivan was just a friend but was stopped by an almost imperceptible shake of Ivan's head. His wary expression said he was on the lookout for possible danger. It surprised her that he was so ready to defend her. It made her feel like a heel for having treated him so harshly. She'd have to find a way to apologize. "He's new to this area," Carla told the man. "I'm probably better able to help you."

The man hesitated but reluctantly turned his gaze to Carla. "We're trying to find Laveau diViere's ranch. We were told it was somewhere around here."

A jumble of words jammed in Carla's throat. Before she could untangle them, Ivan answered.

"I manage Mr. diViere's property. He never said I was to expect anyone. I do not need so many new hands."

The man looked affronted that Ivan would take him for a cowhand.

"We're not here to chase cows," one man in the group called out. "We're here to—"

The man who appeared to be the leader interrupted. "We're here to stop the raids from across the Mexican border. There's been a lot of trouble since the war, especially in the southern counties."

"And the Reconstruction government has done nothing about it," Carla said.

"That's about to change," the man said. "The governor is setting up operations all along the Rio Grande."

"How does that involve diViere?" Ivan asked.

"He's given us permission to set up a camp on his land. We'll need access to grass and water for our horses, but we don't want to get in your way. An out-of-the-way spot would be good."

"Do you have some proof of what you say?" Ivan asked.

Carla was irritated at being practically shoved aside in this conversation, but Ivan was asking the right questions. The man reached into his vest pocket and drew out some papers, which he handed to Ivan.

"Here's a letter from Mr. diViere and one from the governor authorizing me to organize a patrol."

Carla wouldn't have thought there was enough light to read the papers, but apparently Ivan could see in the dark. That shouldn't surprise her. He could do everything else. He read slowly, appeared to read both papers twice. From his expression, he appeared to think the letters were legitimate. She could also tell he wasn't happy about it.

"I need to keep these until the morning," Ivan told the man. "DiViere owns only half of the ranch. Miss Reece owns the other part. The ranch has not been divided, so she is as much involved as I am."

"How do we know you'll give 'em back?" the malcontent in the rear demanded.

"Why would I keep them?" Ivan asked. "I do not want to set up a camp to catch rustlers. If a man steals cows from me, I do not need permission to get them back."

"Ignore Bricker," the leader said to Ivan. "We've

been in the saddle for several days, and we're tired. All we need is directions to a place we can camp."

"It is late," Ivan said. "You could not see even if I knew how to give directions. Miss Reece's brother is to ride over the ranch with me tomorrow. You can bed down near the creek for tonight and ride with us."

The man appeared to hesitate before reluctantly agreeing. "My name is William Riley." He extended his hand to Ivan. "I hope we won't be too much trouble."

"How can we be too much trouble if we're sleeping out?" Bricker asked.

Riley ignored Bricker. "We have our own supplies, ma'am," he said, directing his remarks to Carla, "so we won't be expecting you to cook for us."

Not knowing the best response, and being certain the sharp retort hovering on her tongue wasn't it, Carla just nodded before she put her horse into an easy canter. Ivan rode alongside while Riley and his men followed at a distance.

"Did you know anything about this?" Carla asked.

"I said I did not."

"I don't mean about those men," Carla said. "I mean about the governor trying to stop rustlers from Mexico."

"No, but my friends have been complaining about it for years. I hear Richard King has lost thousands of cows."

Lawless bands from across the border had been raiding cattle ranches ever since the war had deprived Texas of most of its fighting men, and neither the army nor the Reconstruction government did anything to stop it. She hoped the arrival of these men signaled a change in official attitude, but Ivan wasn't happy. "Do you think these men are telling the truth?" she asked.

"I do not know. Governor Davis has passed laws that give him the right to do almost anything he wants. The militia and state police are under his personal control. One of the papers says Riley has his authority directly from the governor."

"What about the other one?"

"It gives Riley the right to use any part of the ranch he needs."

Carla hadn't gotten used to the idea that someone else owned part of her ranch. How could she accept that strangers had the right to use part of it any way they wanted? "He can't do that."

"Laveau has done it," Ivan said.

"I don't mean just Mr. diViere," Carla said. "I mean all of them. This is my ranch. No one can just come in and do what they want."

Even in the gathering darkness, Ivan's frown was easy to see. "That's what happened in Poland."

"But this is America. I intend to be at Lukey's office the minute he opens in the morning. I want you to go with me. Danny can show them around." Ivan showed surprised at her request. "It concerns you as much as me."

"*More* since I'm the reason they're here."

"If those papers are real, they could have come anytime they want."

"Maybe, but I think I should ride with them tomorrow. I may learn more than we have tonight."

Carla didn't understand why she was unhappy that Ivan wouldn't be with her. He was her foe, but with the appearance of these men, she found herself thinking of him as an ally. "Do you think they're going to do what they say?"

"They must, or we will have reason to tell them to leave."

"But if they have authority from the governor?"

"I will write my friends. Maybe they will know something we do not."

"But if they're really here to stop rustlers from Mexico, we ought to give them all the help we can. The bandits only want cows or horses, but they kill anybody who tries to stop them."

"If they do what they say, I will help them."

Now that Carla had gotten over the shock of someone else demanding some part of her ranch, she was feeling hopeful about the situation. "Riley seems honest. I don't like Bricker, but I guess only rough men would be willing to go after the bandits."

Carla looked over her shoulder at the men following about fifty yards behind. Bricker was talking—he seemed angry about something—but Riley wasn't answering him. She hoped Riley could control his men. Bricker was the kind of hothead who could cause trouble in a little town like Overlin.

She was surprised when they reached the lane leading to her ranch house to find Ivan's campsite empty.

"Where is everything?" she asked.

"How can I know? I have been with you all evening. Maybe it is a good thing. Your husband would not sleep outside."

"I know, but—"

Riley and his men were getting too close for Carla to say more. "I'll meet you at the house," she said to Ivan before driving on.

Ivan showed the men to where he'd slept the night

before. It didn't take long for the six men to set up camp. Seeing there was nothing else he could do, Ivan bade them good night and headed for the house. Danny came running up before he could bring his horse to a stop.

"Carla told me about those men," he said. "It's a good thing I moved your stuff to the bunkhouse." He broke out laughing. "I wish I could have seen Carla's face when Riley called you her husband." He slapped his thigh. "I bet she almost had a fit."

Ivan dismounted. "Your sister could be an actress. No one could guess we were not married."

"I've already decided she's going to be an old maid. She's been courted by lots of men, and she's never seemed interested in marrying any of them. I think she likes this ranch better than she likes men." His face fell. "That's why she's so mad at me for losing half of it."

"Why did you move my stuff to the bunkhouse? You know Carla does not want me here."

"She told me she'd agreed to discuss everything about the ranch with you. She can't do that with you always down by the creek." He shuffled his feet and looked down at the ground. "Besides, it's not neighborly to make you camp out. If anybody should be banished to the creek, it's me."

"Carla would never do that. She loves you."

Danny's head came up with a snap, his eyes filled with laughter. "You should have seen her when I told her. I've still got bruises where she hit me. You can probably find scratches on the furniture and marks on the wall. For a while, nothing was safe."

"It was the shock."

"She looks like Ma, but she's got Pa's temper. I'm

built like Pa, but I got Ma's temperament. Carla should have been the boy, not me."

Ivan thought that would have been a tragedy, but he didn't say so.

"Do you think those men are on the level? I hope so," Danny said before Ivan could respond. "Our ranch has never been hit, but bandits have been a nuisance for years. They don't come this way much because the land is so dry the cows are really spread out, but they raided Kesney's place a month back. They didn't get anything, though, because he'd been warned."

"Who warned him?" That struck Ivan as an unusual piece of luck.

"Don't know that he said. In any case, he hired some extra men. Sent the bandits back across the Rio Grande with their tails between their legs."

"I need to talk to your sister," Ivan said. "Since you have decided I should sleep in the bunkhouse, you can put my horse in the corral."

"Sure." Danny pointed to Ivan's bunk. "Your feet will hang off the end. Nobody around here is as tall as you."

Ivan got the feeling Danny was a little unhappy that Ivan's size had made his recent growth seem less impressive. "You will be this tall in a few years."

Danny's expression remained glum. "That won't do much good as long as everybody thinks I'm prettier than half the girls in Overlin."

"When the right girl comes along, she will think you are perfect. I have seen it happen to my friends. It will happen to you. Now I need to talk to your sister."

Ivan didn't know what to say to Carla, but he knew somewhere something was wrong. New laws gave the governor nearly absolute power over the state, but Ivan doubted there was anything anybody could do. People had been complaining about the army and the state government for years, and nothing had been done. If Laveau hadn't been involved, Ivan would have been willing to take Riley at his word. The man seemed genuine, but Ivan had never known Laveau to do anything that didn't benefit him in a manner that was nearly always to someone's disadvantage. Laveau was up to something. And Ivan was determined to find out what and put a stop to it. Carla and her brother had suffered enough at Laveau's hands.

———— ⁓ ————

Carla took the pan of biscuits from the oven and placed them in a bowl before covering them with a cloth to keep them warm. "I don't know what you eat for breakfast in Poland," Carla said to Ivan, "but I hope you like ham and eggs, potatoes with gravy, and hot biscuits."

"We usually have grits," Danny told Ivan, "but Carla said you probably never heard of them."

Ivan stood in the doorway, apparently waiting for Carla to invite him in. "Sometimes during the war, grits and gravy was all we had to eat."

"Well, don't stand there looking like a bashful beau," Danny said. "Carla only looks like she'll take a chunk out of your hide. She's really a pretty decent sister."

"Which is not easy with you for a brother. Come sit down," she said to Ivan as she placed the biscuits on the table and turned to find the butter. "Eat before everything gets cold."

"You can sit across from me," Danny offered. "That way you won't have to face Carla's scowls."

Carla returned with the butter, which she placed in front of Danny. "I'm not scowling, but I will be if you won't be quiet."

Danny grinned at Ivan, put his finger to his lips to indicate Ivan was to be quiet, and motioned him to take a seat at the table.

"Much more of your nonsense, Danny Reece, and you'll be fixing your own breakfast over an open fire. Do sit," she said to Ivan when he seemed reluctant to come to the table. "I'm sure Mr. Riley and his men will be here soon."

Carla didn't like that having Ivan at her table made her nervous. Or maybe it was just that she was jittery. She was irritated that Danny had taken it upon himself to move Ivan's belongings to the bunkhouse and invite him in for breakfast without asking her first. She drew the line when Danny said it was necessary to continue pretending she and Ivan were married.

The fact that Ivan looked more handsome than usual did nothing to ease her discomfort. She didn't know if it was sleeping in a bunk instead of on the ground, but he looked fresh and eager. He had a unique ability to be part of Danny's silliness without losing his innate gravitas. He could be reluctant to come to the table without losing the aura of assurance that seemed to fit him so comfortably. It wasn't fair that he could do all of this without appearing to be aware of it. She wondered if that came from being born into a family with a five-hundred-year history of wealth and privilege as well as a lineage that included kings. She couldn't imagine what it would be like to be surrounded by portraits of her ancestors. She had no idea what her grandparents looked like.

"Are you still too mad at me to answer?"

Gathering her wandering thoughts, Carla turned to Danny. "Sorry. I was thinking. What did you ask?"

"I was saying I'd clear up after breakfast if you wanted to start to town early."

"I've changed my mind. I'm going with you and Ivan."

Chapter 8

CARLA DIDN'T KNOW WHAT SHE WAS GOING TO SAY until the words came out of her mouth, but she knew immediately she'd made the right decision to go with Ivan and Danny on a tour of the ranch.

"I thought you were going to see Lukey," Danny said.

"I told Lukey I'd include Ivan in all decisions concerning the ranch. I can't do that if I'm not with you."

"I'm not making any decisions, just showing Ivan around."

"I'm talking about Riley and his men."

"They only want a place to set up a temporary camp."

"It will be on our land so I want to know about it."

Danny glanced at Ivan before turning back to his sister. "They asked to camp on Laveau's part of the ranch."

"We've never divided the ranch. Until then, I consider every part of it as ours."

"You've never ridden over the whole the ranch," Danny reminded his sister.

"That was a mistake. Maybe that's the reason everyone wants to talk to you instead of me."

"You know that's not it," Danny said. "It's because you're not a man."

"And you're a man because you're old enough to gamble away your part of the ranch?"

Danny hung his head. "You know that's not what I meant."

Carla didn't mean to let her temper run away with her, but the whole situation—from trying to convince everyone she was capable of managing the ranch to coping with the results of Danny's gambling—had stretched her patience to the breaking point. Having to deal with this unexpected attraction to Ivan was about to push her over the edge. She wanted to go into her room, close the door, and not come out until he was gone. She couldn't because she wasn't a coward. In any case, she wanted to know what he was doing, where he was going, even what he was thinking.

"Finding a place for Riley's camp is a decision for everyone to make," Ivan said. "If his men will be riding back and forth to the border, it will be best to find a place where they will not upset the cows."

"I know a couple of good spots," Danny said, "but it's a long ride, Sis."

"I'll manage." Carla wasn't as sure as she sounded. Though she was the nominal head of the ranch, she wasn't used to full days in the saddle.

"Do you have a good horse?" Ivan asked.

"We have lots of good horses." Danny sounded irked that Ivan would question the quality of their riding stock.

"I mean do you have a good riding horse for your sister. A bad horse can make a short ride miserable just as a good horse can make a long ride less tiring."

"Any of them would do," Danny told him.

"In Poland we give horses the work best suited to them. Our horses are expected to do just one thing but do it very well."

"Our horses have to do everything," Danny insisted.

"Do you use the same horses to catch cows that Carla uses for her buggy?"

"No, but—"

"That is what I mean. Now finish eating. We must have time to choose carefully."

Carla listened as Danny quizzed Ivan on what he looked for in a riding horse. She wasn't as interested in what he said as she was that Ivan would take the time to choose a horse especially for her. Not even her father had done that. As far as she knew, the only quality men looked for in a woman's mount was that the horse be so slow they wouldn't fall off. From what Ivan was explaining to Danny, Ivan would look for a horse with the ability to do everything his own horse could do. The difference would be in the manner, comfort, and temperament.

Ivan acted like what he was doing was nothing out of the ordinary, but that was far from the truth. If a woman dared venture out of the house, Texas men expected her to do everything a man could the same way a man would do it. That such an expectation was impossible was their rationale for feeling women should do little beyond keep house and occasionally teach school or run a shop. It would never occur to most men to look for ways to make it more comfortable for women to do their work. As for working side by side with them, well, that was out of the question.

Ivan drank the last of his coffee and pushed back from the table. "Are you ready?" he asked Danny.

"He can't go yet," Carla said. "He has to help me clean up and put away the food. I want you to show me how you choose a horse."

—m—

Carla and Danny talked together while resting their horses in the sparse shade of a mesquite that grew alongside the creek. Riley and his men were taking a rest about fifty yards away in the windward side of a towering thicket of catclaw and several types of acacias. Being no fan of thorns, Ivan chose to dismount next to a young cottonwood. In a few years the tree would provide even more shade than the pecan trees that forested some of the creek bottoms on Cade's ranch.

The day provided more information than Ivan had anticipated. At first, his attention was directed to the ranch itself. The land was drier than he expected. According to Danny, they had more rain than usual during the winter and spring, but the summer had been dry. The new growth was already showing signs of dying back. The Reece herd benefited from the ever-flowing creek and the more plentiful food along its banks, but the water from the creek didn't reach most of the thousands of acres it took to support their herd. While there were areas where trees grew in groves or vines formed nearly impenetrable tangles, many acres were treeless with little grass to hold the soil from wind and rain or shade its roots from the baking heat of the sun. The land was so poor it took about ten acres to support one cow. That same openness limited Riley to a few choices for his base camp.

Riley was as personable as he seemed the night before. He was so approachable, Danny peppered him with questions. Riley answered all of them, but it didn't take Ivan long to realize he wasn't giving out much information. The other five men were also friendly, even Bricker. Apparently Riley convinced them it was important to build good relationships with the people in the county. Everybody would be on his side if he could protect them from the bandits, but Ivan learned during the war that it never hurt to build extra layers of goodwill. There would be times when the power of authority wasn't enough to hold people's loyalty.

The day went so well that Ivan was finding it difficult to harbor suspicions against Riley. Riley didn't provide much information, but it was the first time the government mounted an organized attempt to deal with the bandits who raided across the Rio Grande River from Mexico. With only a few men to patrol the border, Riley said he expected to be away from camp for long periods of time. Other than buying supplies, he didn't anticipate having much contact with the townspeople. He said he would do his best to stay out of Ivan's way.

Still, Ivan couldn't banish that lingering shred of doubt. Laveau diViere was evil. So was everything he touched, regardless of how straightforward it might appear on the surface. Ivan tried to convince himself that Laveau had nothing to do with Riley, that his commission had come from the state government, but the new governor was already getting a reputation for using his office to fill his pockets and those of his friends, exactly the kind of person who would associate with Laveau. Riley left his companions and walked over to Ivan.

"The land around here is really open," he said. "Nowhere to hide stolen cows. It makes you wonder how the bandits can take so many herds without anyone knowing."

"Not many people to watch them do it." Towns were

few, small, and far apart. Ranches were huge, and herds were left on their own except for branding and roundup.

"Not many good places for a concealed camp, either."

"What about the spot Danny pointed out?" He had shown Riley an area on the far edge of their ranch where a large semicircle of chaparral provided a natural screen.

"It's not ideal, but it looks like the best spot. I'd expected to have more trees."

Ivan wondered why the government sent a man who knew so little about South Texas that he expected forests substantial enough to provide cover for a camp of several men, their horses, and equipment.

Carla and Danny walked over to join them. Danny approached with his open smile and unquestioning honesty. Carla was more circumspect, but Ivan believed her reticence was based upon her reluctance to have strangers on her land rather than any distrust of their stated reason for being there.

"Is this place okay," Danny asked, "or do you want to keep looking?"

"If you want to be close to the border," Carla said, "you should talk to Kesney Hardin. His ranch runs down to the Rio Grande."

"Maybe I'll do that once I figure out what works best," Riley said. "For now, I'll stick with my agreement with Mr. diViere. He said we could use his land as long as we want."

Carla started to speak. Afraid she might tell Riley about his agreement with Laveau, Ivan cut her off by saying, "Everyone hopes you can stop the raids in a few months."

"So do we," Riley said.

"As long as you spend money in Overlin, nobody will care how long it takes," Danny said.

While Danny and Riley were talking, Ivan whispered that he didn't want her to say anything about his agreement with Laveau. She looked bewildered, even a little annoyed, but she nodded her acceptance.

"If you have no objection," Riley said to the three of them, "we'll start setting up camp."

Carla gave her permission. Danny even offered to help.

"I will come around in a day or two to see if you need anything," Ivan offered.

"Don't bother," Riley said. "We'll be on patrol by then." He turned down Danny's repeated offer to help before going back to his men.

"I wish he'd talk to Kesney about setting up camp on his land," Carla said.

"I don't," Danny said. "It's exciting having them here. They might even let me ride with them sometime."

"You've got enough to do here," Carla said.

Danny's expression darkened quickly. "I've got nothing here, or have you forgotten how many times you've reminded me of that?"

"That's not what I meant," his sister said. "This will always be your home."

"No, it won't. If you marry Kesney and Ivan sells his half of the ranch, I'll be nothing more than a cowhand. Hell, that's all I am now."

Ivan didn't try to help Carla convince Danny the ranch would always be his home. When you didn't own the land, you were just there as long as someone else let you stay. Even when you did own the land, there were no guarantees. The Russians had taken his family's land in Poland. Cade's grandfather had taken his neighbor's land in Texas. Power trumped right, something Ivan would never forget.

Cutting off his sister's argument with a colorful oath, Danny stalked off, mounted his horse, and rode away. Carla started after him.

"I would leave him alone," Ivan advised. "I know how he feels. Words will not change anything."

"But he's got to know I'd never desert my own brother."

"I expect he is thinking about when you marry. Your husband may not think of him as part of the family."

"I wouldn't marry any man who would do that to my brother."

"What about when *he* wants to marry? What does he have to offer a wife?"

"I'd give him my half of the ranch," Carla said.

"Maybe he has too much pride to accept such a sacrifice."

"How do you know what he'll think?"

"I never said I know what he thinks or what he will do, but I do know he has a lot of pride. He is like you in that."

Carla's reaction showed her surprise. "You think I'm full of pride?"

"I said you have pride, not that it controls your thinking. Pride is a good thing. It is something we all need."

"Do you think I have too much pride?"

Ivan was surprised Carla would care what he thought. "I do not know you well enough to answer that question."

Carla gave him a skeptical look. "I think you're avoiding the question."

"Why would you care if I am? You do not like me, you do not want me here, and you will be happy when I leave."

Carla's gaze flickered before returning to him. "It's true I don't want you here, but I don't dislike you. I don't want you to leave until I can buy back Danny's half of the ranch."

"I thought you were hoping the judge would agree that Laveau cheated. I am sure he did." Laveau seemed to like doing things the wrong way. Ivan believed he got a perverse kind of pleasure from it.

"Of course I hope the judge will invalidate the wager. Even if Mr. diViero didn't cheat, he took unfair advantage of Danny by goading him to drink until he was drunk."

"Then you will get your ranch back and be rid of me at the same time. That will make you happy, no?"

This time when Carla's gaze flickered, it didn't return to Ivan. It focused instead on Danny as he disappeared into the distance. "I don't dislike you. I just dislike what has happened."

"Then we can work together? I can stay in the bunkhouse, and you will let me eat with you and Danny?"

Carla didn't look at Ivan. "Danny has already invited you. You don't need my permission."

"But I do. The bunkhouse is on your half of the ranch. The house is also."

Carla's gaze zeroed in on him. "Are you making fun of me?"

"Would I do something like that?"

Carla's brow creased. "I don't know. I misjudged you in the beginning. I really don't know you at all. Sometimes I think you're just trying to confuse me by smiling like that."

Ivan laughed. "I do not try to confuse you."

"Well, you have."

"Ask me any question, and I will answer it. But first we should start back to the ranch. It is a long way. And you must have time to make your dress for the dance."

"That's what I mean," Carla said after they had mounted up and set their horses into a slow canter. "You offer to answer any question I ask then try to turn my attention to something else. You know I've decided to wear the dress I bought from Sadie Lowell. I'll save the material for another time."

"It is very nice material. It will make a very pretty dress."

"I caught you!" Carla declared, something between laughter and anger in her eyes. "You haven't seen the material I bought."

"I saw it when Mr. Thompson showed it to the widow Lowell."

"Why should he show it to Sadie?"

"She said you were coming to her store to buy a dress for the dance. Mr. Thompson said that could not be true because you had already bought some material. When the widow Lowell did not believe him, Mr. Thompson took out the bolt and showed her. I thought it was very nice material and would make a beautiful dress, but I did not feel it was my place to say so."

"You've never been slow to offer your opinion before," Carla snapped. "Why should I believe you are now?" She burst into unexpected laughter. "What a fool I am. You've found a way to give your opinion even while protesting you didn't have the right." She shook her head. "If the rest of your family is like you, I'm surprised they haven't hornswoggled the Russians out of everything but their underwear."

"What is this *hornswoggle*? I think you make up words to confuse me."

Carla chuckled. "It means to swindle, to cheat."

"A Stanislas does not cheat. It would violate our honor."

Carla gave him a sharp look. "You said your name was Ivan Nikolai."

Ivan drew himself up. "I was born Ivan Nikolai Augustus Stanislas. At my father's death, I became Prince Poniatowski. When I came to America, I decided to shorten my name. I do not want anything I do to reflect badly on my family."

They rode for a few moments in silence. The sun was already three quarters of the way across the horizon, but it beat down on their backs with undiminished intensity. They crossed an arroyo, which would stay dry except during the heaviest rainstorm. Their horses avoided cactuses without needing guidance. The stock they passed appeared well-fed despite the withering heat and extended dryness.

"Your family means a lot to you." It was a statement rather than a question.

"Just as your family means a lot to you," Ivan replied.

"It's not the same," Carla said. "I love Danny and my parents because they were part of my life. You love people you've never seen, people who've been dead hundreds of years."

"It is not love I feel for those people so long dead. It is respect for what they have done that I value. They have done much for the good of Poland."

"My family hasn't done anything for anybody but themselves." Carla seemed to say that more to herself than Ivan.

"They have helped develop this country. They built a ranch where none was before."

"And Danny lost half of it because he gambled when he was drunk."

"There have been drunks and gamblers in my family as well." Ivan had heard many stories about the sad endings of those who had besmirched the family name. They had been turned into cautionary tales to scare younger family members into a making sure such a fate didn't overtake them.

"He doesn't drink because he knows what it will do to him, but your friend Mr. diViere knew just how to needle him. Danny has been teased about his looks his whole life. Even girls do it. They don't mean anything by it, but it hurts him."

"Laveau is not my friend."

"Then why did he give you his half of the ranch?"

"Laveau is not safe in Texas. He has many enemies."

"Why didn't he just sell? Somebody would buy half a ranch, especially if it was being sold cheaply."

"Laveau has enough money to live well, but he likes to make trouble. I think he is angry at me for surviving his treachery. He is most angry at Cade for marrying his sister and making successful a ranch Laveau would have driven into ruin."

"Do you think he's trying to cause trouble by letting Riley set up his camp here?"

"I have no reason to distrust Riley. I will never trust Laveau again."

Their aristocratic backgrounds had made them outsiders in a troop made up of farmers, ranchers, and a few misfits. In a group that slept in concealment by day and rode in silence by night, there was little chance to develop friendships. It had been Laveau's ability to speak French, the only language Ivan knew besides Polish, that had been the real basis for the bond between them. Because it had been so difficult to learn English, Ivan had depended heavily on Laveau.

"I don't trust Mr. diViere or the Reconstruction government," Carla said, "but if Riley can stop the bandits, he can use any part of my ranch he wants. As soon as the other ranchers find out, they'll probably offer him the use of their land as well."

"Perhaps you should mention it to Mr. Hardin."

"Why?" Carla looked suspicious.

"You said his land was closer to the border."

"You don't trust Riley, do you?"

"I would like it better if his camp was not on our ranch."

"It's not *our* ranch," Carla reminded him. "As far as I'm concerned, every foot of it still belongs to me and Danny."

Ivan figured that was how she would react. He just wanted to make sure. "What are you going to do if the judge does not rule in your favor, and you do not have the money to buy Laveau's half at the end of a year?"

"I'll worry about that when the time comes."

"You could always marry Mr. Hardin. I am sure he would give you the money."

Carla reacted like he'd slapped her. "I would never marry Kesney—or any other man for that matter—just for the money to buy back the land Mr. diViere won by cheating."

"I did not think you would."

"Then why did you ask?"

Angry with him, Carla kicked her horse into a fast

canter and left him behind. That didn't bother Ivan. In fact, he smiled. He found out what he *really* wanted to know. Carla wasn't in love with Kesney Hardin.

"Laveau's letter looks valid to me," Lukey said to Carla two days later. "Even if it wasn't, Governor Davis has the power to do just about anything he wants. Do you have any reason to think something is wrong?"

Carla glanced at Ivan. "He can explain better than I can."

Lukey looked slightly baffled. "You two seem to be getting along a lot better. What happened?"

Carla felt the heat rise in her neck. She resolutely refused to blush. "I'm still angry about why Ivan's here, but he's given me no reason to dislike him personally."

"Myrtle is still singing his praises," Lukey said with a chuckle. "Half the town thinks she's set her sights on him. But give her time. She'll soon find something to dislike. But that's not answering your question about Riley. Is he bothering you in any way?"

"No."

"People in town are glad to have him here. We've been lucky to lose so few cows, but even a few cows can make a big difference for some ranchers."

"I know that, but Ivan has known Mr. diViere for a long time. He says he can't be trusted."

"What does he have to do with Riley's troop?" Lukey asked Ivan.

"That is what I do not know," Ivan said. "Laveau diViere is a very bad man. If he can do a thing in a way to hurt someone, he will."

"Maybe," Lukey said, "but I don't see how he can have anything to do with Riley going after Mexican bandits."

"Laveau never does anything without expecting a profit in return."

"Maybe he's being paid for the use of his land."

"*My* land," Carla corrected.

"That is possible," Ivan said, "but I do not think so. It is too respectable."

"I don't like diViere any more than you do," Lukey said. "Even if he was involved in Riley's operation, there's nothing I could do. I doubt a judge would say any different. Riley has his authorization directly from the governor."

"That's pretty much what I figured Lukey would say," Carla told Ivan when they were outside once again. "Maybe diViere is charging Riley rent for the use of my land."

"Maybe," Ivan agreed, "but it is not like Laveau to be honest, even in small things."

"Stop worrying until you have something to worry about," Carla advised. "Now I need to buy some extra supplies if I'm going to be feeding you."

"I can feed myself."

"You'll be working with me and Danny. It only makes sense for all of us to eat together."

It felt like she was telling a lie. She wasn't. She just wasn't telling the whole truth. She hadn't realized, when she had watched Ivan dance with Beth, that her attraction was more than physical. She'd ignored the feeling at first, deciding it was irritation at being forced to play the piano for his dance lesson. After she had allowed Ivan to handle the situation with Riley, a concession she wouldn't have allowed Danny, she couldn't pretend any longer.

She still couldn't say why she'd done it. She didn't trust Ivan's judgment more than she trusted her own. She hadn't conceded that Laveau owned half of her ranch or that Ivan had the right to decide what happened on it. Ever since her parents died, she'd vigorously maintained her independence in managing the ranch as well as her personal life. She'd tried to make it clear to everyone in Overlin that neither Kesney Hardin nor any other man had a claim on her. So why had she allowed Riley to think Ivan was her husband? Why was she treating Ivan differently? Being forced to accept him temporarily may have been what brought them together, but it was no reason for her growing feeling that Ivan was unlike any man she'd ever known, a difference she found more appealing than she would have ever believed.

And it wasn't his charming accent, his devastating smile, or his amusing, yet frustrating, trouble with the English language. If she hadn't been able to come up with a satisfactory answer last night even though she'd lain in bed for at least an hour trying to do so, she couldn't reasonably expect to do so in the short walk from Lukey's office to the mercantile.

"I wonder if Mr. Thompson found a tent for you," she said to Ivan.

"I should tell him I have no need of it now," Ivan said. "I will do that when we finish your shopping."

"I can do that myself."

"You will need me to carry everything to the buggy."

Carla laughed. "Ivan, I did the shopping by myself before you came."

"But I am here now."

That seemed as good an answer as she was going to get. Ivan was here now, and everything was different. She wondered if every man in Poland was like Ivan. Her attention was drawn to a man galloping into town. No one rode a horse at a gallop down Overlin's narrow, often crowded streets.

"I wonder what's happened to Wilbur," Carla said to Ivan.

"He seems upset," Ivan said.

"I hope nothing has happened to Laurie or the children." She moved to the edge of the boardwalk intending to call out to Wilbur, but he shouted to her as he rode past.

"Bandits! I'm wiped out."

Chapter 9

DANNY AND IVAN RODE DOWN A DRY WASH, LINED with chaparral thickets, that stretched hundreds of feet on each side. The soft sand absorbed the force of each step with a muffled whoosh. The afternoon sun boiled down on them, causing perspiration to run down their backs and soak through their shirts. Danny had tied his bandana around his forehead to keep the sweat out of his eyes.

"I don't know why you're so reluctant for me to contact Riley," Danny said to Ivan. "Chasing down bandits and finding stolen cows is why he's here."

Ivan had given up trying to justify his distrust of Riley's stated reason for setting up a camp on Reece land. Not everyone believed Laveau had cheated, but Ivan knew him as no one in Overlin did. The man took pleasure in causing pain and suffering, especially to the survivors of his treason and those they loved. Ivan didn't know how Riley having a camp on Carla's land could hurt him, but he'd been suspicious from the moment Laveau promised him ownership of the land after one year. Laveau didn't give anything away without expecting more in return.

"I'm going to ask Riley to let me ride with him," Danny said.

Ivan had been afraid of that. Danny was restless, eager for a way to restore his pride. "He already has his troop."

"There's only six of them. I'm sure he could use an extra man."

"Have you told your sister?"

"I told her when we were looking for a place for his camp."

"What did she say?"

"Exactly what you'd expect. I'm too young, too inexperienced. That it'll be too dangerous."

All of which was true. "What about your work on the ranch?"

"What work? I don't have any land anymore."

"That is not a reason to desert your sister."

Danny drove his horse out of the streambed through a break in the chaparral. The soft sand gave way to a crusty surface that supported a thin crop of curly mesquite grass. Cactus and yucca dotted the open plain between clumps of huisache. Each plant seemed to be holding its breath, conserving every precious drop of moisture until the fall rains started. On this blazingly hot day, that seemed very far off.

"I'm not deserting her. I probably won't be gone more than a day or two. Besides, doing this will help protect the ranch. If the bandits know they can't steal from us without us taking the cows right back, they'll stop bothering us."

There was some logic in what Danny said, but Ivan was certain his sister wouldn't care about that.

Danny patted his saddlebags and pointed to his rifle in its scabbard. "I came prepared. I can show Riley the quickest and easiest way to Wilbur's ranch. Time is important."

Ivan knew that better than Danny. During the war,

their ability to get far away quickly had been their best defense against reprisals.

"Why don't you come with us?" Danny asked.

"Someone has to stay here."

"Well, it won't be me. Carla likes you better than she likes me just now."

"I hope Carla has come to think of me as a friend, but she loves you."

Danny chuckled. "And I have the bruises to prove it."

Ivan advanced several more arguments during the time it took to reach Riley's camp, but he was unable to change Danny's mind.

Riley's camp was compact and tightly organized. It was almost completely enclosed by the chaparral thicket. The horses were picketed a distance away so they could graze when they weren't needed. Riley came out of his tent to meet them.

"Come to check up on me?" he asked Ivan.

"No," Danny answered. "We've come to tell you bandits hit Wilbur Joiner's ranch last night and drove off nearly every cow he owned."

Riley turned to face the small cluster of tents. "Fall out," he shouted. "Be ready to ride in ten minutes."

Five men burst from their tents and headed off at a run.

"How can they be ready that fast?" Danny asked.

Riley favored Danny with a fatherly smile. "We're always ready to ride at a minute's notice. It's the only way to catch bandits before they get so far south it's too dangerous to go after them."

"I want to ride with you," Danny said.

Riley looked hesitant.

"Wilbur is going," Danny said. "I don't see why I can't."

"We don't usually take civilians with us," Riley said.

"If you think you're riding without Wilbur, you don't know him," Danny said. "Those were his cows. He'd go all the way to Mexico City to get them back."

"We don't have time for you to get ready," Riley said.

Danny grinned broadly. "I figured that, so I came ready to go." He pointed to his saddlebags. "I even brought my own grub."

"Will you come, too?" Riley asked Ivan.

"No."

"I could use a man with your experience."

"My experience is needed here."

"Suit yourself," Riley said before turning to Danny. "We really do ride out in ten minutes. Now I have to get ready."

"Be careful," Ivan said to Danny. "Going after men who will try to kill you is a serious business."

"I know that," Danny said, impatiently. "I'm not stupid."

"I know, but you have never done anything like this. I have."

"I'm tired of being the only one who's *never done anything like this*," Danny complained. "I'm seventeen, but everybody acts like I'm twelve. It's time everybody started treating me like a man."

Ivan could understand Danny's frustration. His family had acted the same way when he decided to come to America. Danny had to have his chance to prove he had grown up, that he was worthy of the responsibilities of a man. Ivan just hoped he could make his sister understand.

—◊◊◊—

"Why didn't you stop him?" Carla demanded. "He doesn't know anything about chasing bandits."

"I am not his father," Ivan said. "I cannot tell him what to do."

"You're bigger than he is."

"So you think I should have tied him up and returned him to his sister? Is that the kind of humiliation you wish for your brother?"

"Of course not," Carla shot back, "but I don't want him returned to me across his horse's saddle."

Carla had been about to start supper when Ivan returned. She'd greeted him with a smile so warm, so welcoming that he wished he could have found a way to put off telling her about Danny. He would have enjoyed, even for a few minutes, being treated as a friend rather than as a hostile invader. But he couldn't wait for her to ask why Danny would miss supper.

Carla thrust the last piece of wood into the stove and slammed the door. "I can't believe he would leave without saying anything to me."

"He said he mentioned yesterday that he wanted to ride with Riley."

Carla took a match out of a box but didn't strike it. "Saying he wanted to ride with Riley and actually doing it are two different things." She looked around, appeared not to find what she was looking for, and put the match back in the box with a hiss of irritation. "Didn't you even *try* to stop him?"

Ivan related his several arguments.

"I don't know why I thought he would listen to you," she said when he had finished. "He probably wouldn't have listened to me, either."

"Riley tried to discourage him, but he would not change his mind."

Carla moved to the table and dropped into a chair. "I don't understand why he was so determined to go."

Ivan hesitated a moment before joining Carla at the table. "He said everybody still treats him as a child. He wants to prove he is now a man."

"That's stupid! Nobody treats him like a child."

"Did you not hit him when he lost the ranch? I think you kicked him, too. I know you shouted at him because you told me. Is that what you would have done to Lukey?"

"If Lukey had done anything that stupid, I'd have shot him!" Carla declared.

"See. You do not treat Danny as a man. You did not try to shoot him."

Carla choked off a spurt of laughter. "I wouldn't shoot my brother no matter what he had done."

"No, but you should have tried."

Carla lost all desire to laugh. "You can't be serious."

"I know you would not shoot Danny. He would take the gun away, or you would only threaten, but by threatening to shoot him, you face him with a man's punishment. Hitting him is what you would do to a misbehaving child."

Carla stared at Ivan. "Either you're crazy, or I am."

Ivan laughed. "You have never been a young boy trying to become a man. Because he is so handsome and so nice, everybody has treated him like a pet. You make decisions for him. You do not let him do things you expect other boys to do. You protect him from danger."

"He's my little brother. What would you expect me to do?"

"He is not such a little brother. Maybe it is time you let him protect *you*."

Carla started to say something. Instead, she cast Ivan an angry look then turned away. "I have my father's temper," she said in a subdued voice. "I also have his certainty that I'm the only one who can make the right decisions." She raised her gaze to Ivan. "After what Danny did, do you think I could trust him to make any important decision?"

"You could invite him to make decisions *with* you. That way he could learn why you think as you do."

"I've tried, but Danny doesn't want to make decisions. He just wants to ride his horse and play cards."

"I think losing his part of the ranch has changed him."

"I should hope so," Carla said emphatically. "It certainly has changed me."

"How?" Maybe he shouldn't have asked that question, but he wanted to know what Carla was really like. The longer he was around her, the stronger his attraction to her grew. She had a temper and didn't try to hide it. She was brusque, opinionated, and strong-willed. She was as ready to spend a day in the saddle as she was to cook a supper of bacon, beans, and cornbread. She considered herself the equal of any man and disdained the use of the usual feminine arts to make herself more attractive. She was about as different as possible from the women he knew growing up in Poland.

Despite all that, she possessed a feminine allure that nothing could disguise.

"I thought good would always triumph over bad," Carla said. "Silly of me, wasn't it?"

"No."

Carla got up, walked over to the window above her working area, and looked out. "I never used to be afraid of tomorrow. Now it scares me silly."

"Why?"

Carla just shook her head then turned away from the window. "I'd better get started on supper before you starve."

Even though Carla wasn't like the women he'd known growing up, Ivan had been around Cade's wife long enough to know that a strong woman occasionally needed comforting. He rose from his chair and intercepted Carla on her way to the stove. When he took her hands in his, she tried to pull away but stopped resisting when he wouldn't release her. "What frightens you?"

She shook her head and refused to meet Ivan's gaze.

"You can tell me. I will help."

Carla pulled her hands from Ivan's grasp and turned away from him. "How can you help when you're part of the problem?"

"I do not understand."

"As soon as you get what you want, you're going back to Poland."

"Do you care that I go to Poland?"

"Of course not. You can go now for all I care. In fact, it would be better if you leave now."

"Why? I would not have any money."

"Men!" Carla exclaimed. "Why are you all so stupid?"

"You think I am stupid?"

"You can fix all the doors and gate latches you want, but you don't know a thing about people."

"What people?"

"Me!"

Before Ivan could think of a response, Carla turned and ran from the kitchen. A moment later he heard the door to her bedroom close. He stood there, poised between hope and despair. Was she upset with him because he had let Danny ride off with Riley, or was she upset with him because she liked him and didn't want him to leave? He was certain it was the first, but he hoped that didn't mean the second was impossible. Once he sold his land, he didn't mean to stay in Texas a minute longer than it took to pack his saddlebags. He hoped Carla would be able to find the money to buy back Danny's half. Breaking up her ranch would take a lot of the pleasure out of going home.

He looked at the room around him. It was completely different from the way a Polish prince would live. In Poland he would never see the inside of a kitchen. Food was brought by servants to the family dining room that could seat a dozen. A dining room that could seat fifty was used for special occasions. Their home was built of stone and marble, not logs and rough-hewn timbers. Rooms were measured in meters rather than feet. Walls were covered with hand-painted wallpaper and intricately carved wood. Life-sized portraits of ancestors long dead lined the halls and galleries. Women wore silks and satins, a fortune in jewels around their necks and in their powdered hair. They spoke French. And no one *worked*. That was left to the lower classes.

Much to his surprise, that world seemed more foreign to him than Carla's kitchen with its wood-burning stove, rough-topped table, and wooden cupboard. The plain food she prepared each day was as satisfying as anything that could be prepared by the three chefs his family used to employ. Getting dressed and undressed here was a matter of minutes, not hours. Here no one criticized what he wore or valued him according to their estimate of his wealth. Here he didn't have to spend his days in unproductive activity and his evenings in search of entertainment.

But life here was foreign to him. The language was a continual mystery. Before he came to Texas, he wouldn't have believed humans could survive such heat. And that didn't take into account the insects or the snakes. Or Longhorns that would rather gore you than be branded and driven to market. And only Texans could drink what commonly passed for whiskey without ending up dead, or nearly so. Just about the worst thing he could do would be to develop feelings for Carla.

She might not actually dislike him, but she came close enough. In any case, no matter how she felt about him, she would never forgive him for selling half her ranch. There was no chance she would consider going back to Poland with him—or that he would ask her. Just thinking about the reaction of his family and friends to her independent ways would be enough to give him nightmares. They'd probably be ostracized. Even if he wasn't miserable, Carla would be.

What was wrong with him? Thinking of such a thing was madness. He shook his head to dislodge the thoughts. He was becoming too involved with this family. Carla was more than capable of taking care of the ranch and herself. She had at least two men ready to marry her who appeared capable of providing her with a life of comfort. Danny was young, but this trouble was causing him to take a more serious look at his life. In a year or two, he'd probably be as mature as his sister. Age would also alter his looks, making him look more like a handsome young man than a beautiful boy. Once that happened, there wouldn't be a girl in all of Texas with the desire to tease him.

―⁓―

"What are you doing?" Carla asked Ivan when she returned to the kitchen.

"Frying ham."

"I can see that."

"Then why did you ask?"

"Cooking supper is my job. Besides, you can't eat just ham."

"I have some sweet potatoes in the oven. Pilar taught me how to cook them."

"Who's Pilar?"

"Cade Wheeler's wife. He was my commander during the war. When it was over, he invited me to Texas to work on his ranch. That's where I learned all I know about ranching."

Carla moved to a cabinet and took out two plates. "Is that where you learned to cook?"

"We had to do all our own cooking during the war."

"We can't have just ham and sweet potatoes. I'll fix some—"

"I made a pan of cornbread."

Carla stared at him. "Is there anything you *can't* do?"

"I cannot make coffee like you. We did not drink it in Poland."

Carla moved to the can where she kept the freshly ground coffee. "What did you drink?"

"The women drank cocoa for breakfast and fruit-flavored drinks or tea until dinner. The men drank beer or mead made from honey. After wine at dinner, we might have brandy or a heavy wine, but most of the time we had vodka."

"Didn't you ever drink water?"

"It is not safe." Odd that Poland had lots of water nobody drank while Texas had very little water that everybody drank. He finished cooking the ham and transferred it to a plate. He took the sweet potatoes out of the oven where they'd been staying warm. He took both to the table.

"The coffee isn't ready," Carla said.

He grinned. "Then we will drink some of your Texas water."

Carla's grin was weak, but it felt like a reward.

He cut a piece of ham and placed it on Carla's plate. He did the same with the sweet potatoes and cornbread, but she just sat there looking at her food.

"Do you not like it?" He took a bite of ham and chewed. "It is good."

"I'm sure it is," Carla said. "It's just that this is the first meal I've eaten in this house since my mother got sick that I didn't cook myself. It will probably be the *only* meal I'll ever eat that was cooked by a man."

"In Poland all the best chefs are men."

Carla's smile was slow to grow, but it finally bloomed. "No matter how many meals a Texas man might cook for himself, once he gets married, he'll never set foot in the kitchen except to eat. What you have just done would destroy his manhood."

"I do not always understand Americans. It's even harder to understand Texans. You do not act like everyone else."

"Neither do you."

"Is that a bad thing?"

Carla concentrated on the sweet potato until she had removed its skin. Finally she raised her gaze to his. "I don't know."

They ate the rest of the meal in silence.

Carla dried the last dish and put it away. Ivan had offered to help her, but she insisted on doing it herself. She needed something to keep her occupied so her thoughts wouldn't drive her crazy. She didn't know what got into her earlier. She never ran from a room feeling like she was about to burst out crying. She wasn't completely sure why she had been on the verge of tears. She was attracted to Ivan, but that was no reason to feel teary-eyed. She liked Kesney Hardin and Maxwell Dodge, yet she'd never come close to shedding a tear over either of them.

It probably wasn't Ivan at all. Or if it was, it was Ivan combined with all the other things that had happened recently. Having Danny go off with Riley was just one thing too many. She heard that women often cried when they were worried or were under terrible strain, but she'd never felt like that. Problems were more likely to annoy her than upset her. What good did crying do? You'd waste time, embarrass yourself, and still have the problem. No, it was better to go about finding a solution.

Only she didn't have a solution this time. She had

no idea what she would do if the judge decided diViere had won the card game fairly. She had no idea what she would do if something happened to Danny. She had no idea where she would find the money to buy back the other half of their ranch a year from now. She had no idea why she couldn't work up any enthusiasm about marrying Maxwell or Kesney. Most of all, she had no idea how to put an end to her attraction to Ivan.

She foolishly let herself be overly impressed by his gallantry. Considering how most men in Texas thought of women, that was understandable. Even Kesney Hardin, the most gallant and gentlemanly man in Overlin, couldn't compare to Ivan. Maybe it was something a man could acquire only by growing up in Poland. Maybe it was characteristic of aristocrats whose families had been rich and influential for five hundred years, something that was bred so deeply into them they didn't realize they had it.

Maybe, but she didn't think so. Whatever it was, she believed it came from inside Ivan rather than from the world into which he had been born. There was goodness in him that couldn't be taught. And she had to admit his size was comforting. It was easy to believe nothing could happen to her when he was around. It was stupid, but she couldn't put it out of her mind. Maybe she shouldn't have been so hard on Danny. He wasn't the only one acting like the Texas sun had fried his brain.

She closed the cabinet and poured herself a cup of fresh coffee. Despite the heat, it always seemed to help her think. She moved to the front porch to take advantage of the breeze. It would be nice to be able to sit outside for a spell.

The wind was cooler and stronger than she expected. It had the smell of rain in it. They could certainly use it. Her cows were doing well, but Kesney had been complaining that the grass on his range was drying up.

The wind was picking up. The trees along the creek that passed less than a hundred feet from the house swayed in the wind. A limb broke off a cottonwood, twisting end over end as it was flung about twenty yards away. A young ash bent so far in the wind she was certain it would break. A soapberry thicket rustled like two steers were inside fighting to get out. A shiver ran through her body.

A gust blew across the porch that caused Carla's skirt to wrap around her legs nearly throwing her off balance. Dismayed at the thought of Ivan finding her lying flat on her back, she chose a chair out of the wind. She didn't know why Ivan should be the first person to come to mind, but a lot of things she didn't understand had been happening since that man showed up.

She wondered what he was doing. Was he getting ready for bed? Was he already asleep? How could a man who'd spent his adult life as a soldier and cowhand, both jobs that required a great deal of strength and stamina as well as necessitated considerable physical discomfort, adjust to the life of an indolent aristocrat? Despite his proved proficiency as a dancer, she couldn't see him spending his days eating and drinking and his nights dancing with women who spent their days trying to make themselves as beautiful as possible. She didn't know much about Ivan, but she did know he wasn't idle of mind or body.

A particularly strong gust of wind whipped the supple

limbs of the cottonwood about so fiercely that its leaves were ripped off and sent rocketing into the darkening sky like battered and tattered green butterflies. Two big drops of rain, driven by the fierce wind, landed on her skirt. Deciding it was time to go in, she was about to rise to her feet when Ivan burst from inside the house.

"A tornado's coming. We must hide."

Chapter 10

CARLA REMEMBERED HER FATHER TALKING ABOUT A tornado that struck their farm when he was a boy, but she'd never seen one. "How do you know?"

Instead of answering her, Ivan pulled her up from her chair so abruptly her coffee cup went flying. It hit the wall before falling to the porch floor. Scooping her up in his arms, he catapulted down the steps and headed around the house at a run.

"Put me down!" she shouted, but the wind must have swallowed her words because he didn't slow down. "Where are you taking me?"

Ivan rounded the corner of the house and headed for an open area to the north of the bunkhouse.

"I want to go back to the house."

He didn't respond. She was about to hit him with her fist to force him to listen when she saw a huge funnel sweeping toward them, twisting and squirming like it had something indigestible inside. It reminded her of a great, brown worm barreling across the plain. At times the bottom would withdraw into the upper portion, and it would skim above the ground before touching down again.

Ivan headed for a spot where a dry wash passed about fifty yards away between a small rise and the bunkhouse. Without pausing to put her down, he leapt into the wash, virtually threw her flat on the ground, and dropped on top of her. She was too shocked to utter any of the protests that crowded her mind. She couldn't have in any case. His weight had knocked the breath out of her.

Despite her shock at Ivan's behavior, her attention was riveted by a roar unlike anything she'd ever heard, unlike anything she'd ever imagined. It was so big, so enormous, the earth seemed to tremble. What could a thing this big and terrible do? Would they survive? She'd never seen Ivan even mildly upset. Tonight she'd seen fear in his eyes. He'd always treated her with utmost care and respect. Tonight he'd handled her with less care than he would a sack of grain.

Most astonishing of all, he'd covered her body with his.

Despite the shock, the fear, her racing thoughts, Carla was acutely aware of his body pressing against her. She could feel his groin jammed against hers thigh and felt heat suffuse her face. But her attention was torn from their physical closeness by the roar that grew so loud it threatened to burst her eardrums. They were being pelted with debris flung at them from all directions. Dirt. Leaves. Bits of wood. Branches. She heard Ivan grunt, but he didn't move. Then, nearly as quickly as it came, the roar faded away.

In its aftermath, a cold, pelting, heavy rain seemed hardly more than a whisper.

She expected Ivan to move. Instead, he remained motionless. "Get off. You're squeezing the breath out of me."

The danger had passed. She couldn't understand why he didn't get up. She pushed against him, but he was too heavy to lift. *Maybe he didn't move because he couldn't.* The rain made it impossible to tell if he was still breathing. Fueled by fear that he might be seriously hurt, she summoned the strength to wiggle out from under him. Even in the dark, she could tell his hair was soaked with blood.

Was he dead? Had he sacrificed his life to protect her? He groaned, and her relief was so great she felt weak.

"Don't move," she said. "You've been hit on the head."

"We *must* move," he muttered as he rolled over. "This wash will soon fill with water." He sat up and put his hand to the back of his head. It came away bloody.

"You have a gash in your head. You need to see a doctor."

Ivan got to his feet. "I was hurt worse in the war. I hope the tornado didn't hit your house. You need to get out of this rain."

So much had happened so quickly, Carla hadn't thought of what damage the tornado might have done to her home, the bunkhouse, or any other part of the ranch. Ivan lifted her out of the wash then climbed out himself.

At first glance, it appeared nothing had changed. The buildings and corrals were undamaged, but the trees along the creek looked like they'd been attacked by a huge animal with razor-sharp claws that ravaged their branches and stripped them of their leaves. The ground was cluttered with pieces of limbs, torn branches, and shredded leaves which had begun to float away as the rainwater puddled and ran in rivulets toward the stream.

"Go inside," Ivan said. "I will see if there is any damage."

"Let me do something about that cut in your head first."

"You must put on dry clothes. Open the back door when you are ready for me."

Carla wanted to protest that his head was more important than her wet clothes, but she was certain he would put her modesty before his welfare. She wondered if his eagerness to get away from her stemmed from embarrassment at their being thrown so closely together. Just thinking about it caused her to flush with warmth.

"I'll hurry," she said as she turned toward the house.

Ivan checked out every building on the ranch, but his mind wasn't on what he was seeing. He couldn't forget what it had felt like to lie atop Carla, their bodies pushed against each other. He'd done what he had to do, but he should have tried harder to find an alternative. He had never seen a tornado, but Nate Dolan's description of them had been so vivid, his tales of the terrible damage they could do so graphic, that Ivan hadn't hesitated to do what Nate had said was the only way to survive. If you don't have an underground cellar, lie flat in the bottom of the deepest ditch you can find.

Fortunately, the tornado hadn't touched down here. There was a lot of wind damage, but nothing that couldn't be fixed. Including his head. A glance in the direction of the house told him the back door was open. He headed toward the light.

"You've got to get out of those clothes," Carla said the moment he stepped inside. "You're dripping wet."

He showed her a bundle wrapped in his rain slick. "I got dry clothes from the bunkhouse." He put the bundle on the table. "I could find no damage, but I can see better in the morning."

"Forget about that for now. You have to change."

His teeth chattered involuntarily.

"You're cold."

"Not much."

"I'll light a fire."

"No."

"Don't argue because I won't listen. As soon as I get the fire going, I'll leave so you can change. Don't dawdle. I need to look at that cut in your head."

His puzzled look told her she'd stumbled into another hole in his English vocabulary.

"Dawdle means be slow, take your time, drag your feet." She wasn't sure whether she'd cleared up his confusion or made it worse, but it would have to do for now. She lit the fire quickly, poured some water into a basin on the stove, and left the kitchen.

During the war and at Cade's ranch, Ivan had been in almost exclusively male company. He felt awkward undressing, knowing Carla was on the other side of the door. He hurriedly peeled off his wet clothes. He wasn't sure of the meaning of all Carla's words, but he was sure she meant she wouldn't be gone long. He wanted to be fully dressed before she came back. He pulled on dry pants and wrapped his wet clothes in his rain slick.

"Are you dressed?" Carla asked from the other side of the closed door.

"Almost." He grabbed a shirt, slipped his arms in, and quickly buttoned it.

"I'm coming in."

Ivan barely managed to stuff his shirttails into his pants before Carla entered the room with an armload of enough stuff to perform a major operation.

"Now let me look at your head."

"It is not bad."

"You don't know because you can't see it. Pull a chair next to the stove." She put everything down on the table then reached for the basin of water. She drew up a chair in front of Ivan and sat the basin on it. "Lower your head. I need to wash the cut first."

Soaking a cloth, Carla squeezed it out over Ivan's head. The water in the basin turned red.

"With so much blood, I thought the cut would be bigger," Carla said.

"Head wounds bleed a lot." Ivan had had plenty of chance to observe that during the war. Ivan raised his hand to feel the cut. It was hardly half an inch long. "It is not bad. I will be okay."

Carla moved so she could look him in the eye. "You shielded me with your body. The least I can do is bandage it until the cut heals."

Ivan didn't need a bandage, but he didn't object because he enjoyed having all of Carla's attention, especially since she wasn't trying to drive him off or blame him for ruining her life. A bandage would be a small price to pay for this change.

"Okay. You can make a bandage for me."

The results weren't what he expected. The wound was on the top of his head. In order to secure the bandage, Carla had to tie it under his chin. He couldn't see himself, but he imagined he looked like he was suffering from a toothache. Carla's grin, when she stood back to study the results, confirmed his suspicions.

"I know it isn't very comfortable, but don't take it off until morning."

"How can I sleep like this? I can hardly talk."

She turned businesslike. "Danny is gone so you don't have any reason to talk." She gave him a stern look. "I'll know if you take it off when you reach the bunkhouse then put it on again in the morning."

Ivan was certain she would. Women seemed to know the one thing men didn't want them to know. Her bearing changed abruptly from stern to embarrassed, even upset.

"Thank you for protecting me." Her gaze didn't leave his face for an instant, didn't waver or flicker. "I haven't been very nice to you, and you still risked your life for me. I promise I will stop blaming you for what Laveau diViere did."

"I would rather you be angry at me than at Danny."

Carla sighed. "I'll love Danny no matter what, but gambling away his half of the ranch was stupid. What kind of future does he have now?"

Ivan couldn't answer that. Since the shock wore off, his head hurt so badly he could hardly hold onto a thought. All he was able to focus on was that Carla was no longer angry at him.

"Leave your clothes," Carla said. "I'll wash them when I wash Danny's."

Ivan reached for the bundle. "I can wash them."

Carla got to them first. "Don't be ridiculous. It will take twice the wood to heat two fires. Now go to bed. I'm sure your head feels like it's fit to burst."

Ivan was coming to the conclusion he should have spoken less French with Pilar and her grandmother, and more English with Cade and the others. Texans spoke a form of English all their own. But his head hurt too much to worry about that now. He'd think about it tomorrow.

Or the day after that. Right now all he wanted to do was sink into his bed and dream of Carla's promise to treat him differently.

—⁓—

"Wake up."

Ivan's dream shattered like so much glass. He fought against the voice trying to force its way into his consciousness, against the shove that caused his head to throb.

"Wake up."

Ivan forced his eyes open to see Danny leaning over him.

"Man, you look stupid," the boy said. "What happened to you?"

"I got hit by a piece of wood," Ivan mumbled. "What are you doing here?"

"We got back before dawn. The bandits didn't get far. I can't believe they didn't head for the border as fast as they could. Anyway, when we took the cows back, we saw the tornado had hit part of Overlin. You should see it. One building's the same as always, and the one next to it smashed flat."

Ivan sat up too quickly. It felt like a spike had been driven into his head. He waited a moment for the pain to subside.

"Are you all right?" Danny asked.

"I am fine."

"Carla said you were hurt pretty bad, that you protected her." Danny grinned. "I'd sure like to have seen that. Kesney will be mad as a roped steer if he finds out he didn't get to be the hero."

"You will not tell anyone," Ivan managed to say. "It is not good to hurt your sister's reputation."

"Hell, nobody would care. They'll consider you a hero."

"In Poland, a hero does not disgrace a woman."

"Well, you're in Texas now, and protecting a woman is not a disgrace." Danny's brow creased. "I don't know why you're so fired up to go back to Poland. It sounds like a damned uncomfortable place."

"It is my home."

"It hasn't been for ten years. If I was you, I'd give some thought to staying here. I sure would like it if you did."

"Why? I would have your half of the ranch."

"Better you than somebody I wouldn't like." Danny's eyes suddenly grew wide, and he started to laugh. "You could marry Carla and keep it in the family." Apparently Danny found the idea very amusing because he couldn't stop laughing.

"You think I would be such a bad husband that you laugh?" Ivan demanded.

"I think you'd make a great husband," Danny said between outbursts. "But I think Carla would make a terrible wife." He dropped down on his bunk. "She'd be arguing and telling you what to do until you'd go off chasing cows to get some peace and quiet."

"You do not want a wife like that?"

"Hell no! I want a sweet young beauty who will think I know everything."

"Then *you* should go to Poland. There, beautiful women are brought up to obey their husbands in everything."

Danny's mood changed quickly. "No beautiful woman is going to marry a man who doesn't have any money. No woman, beautiful or not, is going to obey a man who was stupid enough to lose everything he had in a card game."

The pain in Ivan's head had receded enough for him to get dressed. He reached for his pants. "Why did you wake me?"

"Carla said she wants to go into Overlin to see if she can help clean up after the storm. She has breakfast ready."

Ivan stepped into his pants and reached for his shirt "I will go, too."

"Why?"

"To help. What about you?"

Danny yawned. "I'm going to bed. I was in the saddle all night."

Ivan's head hurt so badly he'd forgotten about the bandits. "Did you have much trouble? Did anyone get hurt?"

"Naw." Danny sounded disgusted. "They took a few shots at us then turned tail and ran. Can't imagine how they found the guts to steal the cows in the first place. They didn't even have enough sense to hide the herd. They were bedded down in the open."

"Maybe that is how they do things in Mexico."

"I never chased bandits before so I don't know." Danny flopped back on his bed, apparently losing interest. "Riley said I could ride with him again. He said some ranchers pay a reward for getting their cows back. He said I'd get a share. If we find enough cows, maybe I can earn enough money to buy back my half of the ranch."

"I thought the government was supposed to pay to get the cows back."

Danny shrugged. "Maybe they don't pay enough. I don't know." He yawned again. "I'm really tired. You'd better head to the house before Carla comes after you."

By the time Ivan had put on his boots, the boy was asleep, but his comments had started Ivan thinking. Thieves didn't give up that easily. Nor were they so stupid. Anyone desperate or lawless enough to steal was prepared to fight to keep what they took. The whole country had just fought a war over an ideal, a principle. How much more would people be willing to fight for food? If that was true, why were the bandits so easily foiled when they tried to raid Kesney's herd? He could accept one instance of inept bandits but not two. He couldn't get it out of his mind that there was something wrong here, but his head hurt too much to worry about that now. It was more important to see what he could do to help people in Overlin.

"Overlin has two heroes today," Maxwell Dodge declared. "William Riley for returning Wilbur Joiner's stolen cows, and Ivan Nikolai for practically putting Overlin back together by himself."

"Everybody is a hero," Ivan said. "Every citizen of Overlin did what they could."

Carla smiled to herself at Ivan's efforts to refuse any credit for the work that had been done that day, but he couldn't deny that he'd singlehandedly lifted the beam that had kept Sally Wynn pinned for hours. Nor could he deny that he'd inspected every house that was damaged, assessed what could be saved and what couldn't, and told people how to make the best use of what they had left. They'd never had an engineer in Overlin. If he accepted all the jobs that were being offered him, all at more pay than he could make riding herd, Ivan would be spending most of his time in Overlin. Carla didn't pretend to be enthusiastic about that.

She was even less pleased when Eve Lawrence latched on to Ivan like she was drowning, and he was the only one who could save her. Eve had lost her clothes that had been hanging out to dry. Unfortunately, that hadn't included any of the scandalous dresses she wore when she worked in the One Horse Saloon.

"That is the Texas spirit," Maxwell Dodge was saying. "Let it not be said that anyone in Overlin suffered and the rest of us stood aside."

"I don't know why Maxwell is taking it upon himself to act like the mayor and speak for all of us," Myrtle Jenkins said to Carla. "He's no more a Texan than Ivan."

"He's not half as nice," Sadie Lowell added.

"I doubt there's a man in Texas with Ivan's manners," Myrtle declared. "He is an example to us all."

Carla was pretty impressed by Ivan herself, but she was having a hard time listening to people turn him into a larger than life hero. Everybody had worked hard all day. Men, women, and children. Young and old. Ivan was just bigger, stronger, and smarter than anybody else. And the only one who never seemed to lose patience.

Whether dealing with someone suffering from shock, despair, anger, or frustration, Ivan never got upset, never became impatient, was never at a loss to know what to say to give reassurance, offer hope. And he did it all with an accent that brought a smile to many faces that were streaked with tears.

"I offered to fix anything he'd like to eat," Myrtle said, "but he insisted I feed the children." Myrtle looked like she couldn't decide whether her admiration for Ivan was greater than her dislike of children.

"That Eve woman is running around telling everybody all he's eaten today is a piece of chicken she gave him." Sadie snorted in disgust. "Like she knows how to do anything in a kitchen harder than boil water."

"You can tell Eve she doesn't have to worry about Ivan," Carla said. "He had a good breakfast, and he'll get a good supper tonight."

"I have nothing to do with women like Eve," Myrtle said.

"I don't like her, either," Sadie said, "but she's a customer."

"If I had a dress shop, she wouldn't be a customer of mine."

"She would if you hadn't had two husbands die and leave you more money than anybody else in town."

The two women considered themselves the leaders of Overlin society. Since neither could establish a position of leadership above the other, they'd joined in an antagonistic alliance against all newcomers. Carla was the only woman willing to stand up to either of them. "What are you two fixing for the supper tonight?" Carla asked before the women could get at daggers drawn.

"I'm fixing chicken," Sadie said. "The tornado knocked over my coop and killed several of my hens."

"I've got a roast on right now," Myrtle said. "I'm also bringing potatoes and gravy. With all the work they have to do, the men need something that will stick to their ribs. What are you doing?"

"I'm not fixing anything. Ivan has invited Sally Wynn and her boys to stay with us until her house can be fixed. I've never cooked for so many."

Inviting the Wynn family to stay at the ranch hadn't been Ivan's idea. It had been the idea of Sally's two sons. They were two of the boys who'd been fascinated by Ivan when he fixed Sadie's doors. They remembered his invitation to visit whenever they wanted. They'd asked if they could come until their house was fixed. Naturally Ivan had said they could. Which meant Carla had to convince Sally Wynn it really was all right for them to stay, that she wasn't saying that just because her boys had asked.

"I'm willing to do my part," Myrtle said, "but I could never endure having two boys in my house."

"I offered to let Sally stay with me," Sadie said, "but she said she couldn't leave Carla alone with her two hellions."

"I should think not," Myrtle declared. "Put them in the bunkhouse," she told Carla, "and feed them outside."

"I don't think they're that bad."

"They're boys, aren't they?" Myrtle said. "You were raised with a brother. You ought to know what they're like."

Until the card game, Carla had always defended Danny against Myrtle's attacks. Now it was easier to ignore them. "I'd better head back if I'm going to have everything ready by the time Ivan gets home."

"Don't let those boys eat you out for house and home," Myrtle advised.

"They're only seven and eight. How much can they eat?"

"Wait and see," Myrtle cautioned. "Wait and see."

"It was so kind of you to invite us to stay with you," Sally Wynn said to Carla. "I don't know what I would have done. I hope it's not too much trouble."

"Not at all," Carla said. "It'll be nice to have a woman to talk to."

Sally's husband had been killed in one of the last battles of the war. She had a job in the bank, and everybody helped look after her boys.

"I don't know what would have happened to my boys if Ivan hadn't lifted that beam off me." Sally teared up as she did every time she mentioned Ivan. "It's bad enough not having a father. I can't bear to think of them as orphans."

"Then don't," Carla said. "You're fine, the boys are happy as larks being with Ivan and Danny, and supper is almost done. Why don't you tell them to get ready?"

"Thank you so much. Everybody has been so good to us since Tom was killed."

"That's because everybody loves you and the boys. Now call the boys to supper. I expect they're starving by now."

Carla didn't mind giving Sally and her boys a place to stay until their house was fixed, but she was uncomfortable with the repeated thanks and expressions of gratitude. Most of all she disliked the tears. Why did women have to cry so often? And what was wrong with her that she never felt like that? Well, there was that one time, but it was an exception.

Before Sally could call the men, a knock sounded at the door, and a little boy's voice asked, "May we come in?"

Thinking this might be a game of Danny's invention, Carla replied, "What's the password?"

"Ivan didn't say nothing about no password, and I'm hungry." The boy sounded miffed.

Carla opened the door immediately. Tim, Sally's older son, was standing on the steps. Lew was behind him between Danny and Ivan. "*I'm hungry* will always work for a password at suppertime," Carla told the boy. "Now come in and find a chair."

Rather than dash in and take the first chairs they came to, the boys walked in, moved to the chairs Ivan indicated, and waited.

"Ivan said we had to wait for the ladies to be seated," Lew announced. "He said that meant Mama, too."

"He made us wash," Tim said, holding up his hands for his mother to see.

"He said where he grew up he had to put on special clothes before he could eat supper." Lew looked up at Ivan with adoration in his eyes. "He said we didn't have to because the wind blew ours away."

Between the tornado and the rain, there wasn't much Sally could salvage from her home. Carla took her seat. Sally was quick to follow.

"Can we sit down now?" Tim asked Ivan.

"Yes." As soon as the boys were seated, he asked, "What would you like your mother to pass to you?"

Lew looked over a table laden with food, and his eyes grew wide with excitement. "Can we have some of everything?"

"Of course," Carla said. "Your mother and I fixed it for you."

Carla watched as Ivan guided the boys through the

meal in a manner she was certain they'd never experienced. Even more amazing, the boys seemed to like it. Even Danny behaved better. Much to her surprise, Carla found her eyes watering. Ivan was going to make a perfect father. But where in a country filled with insipid women concerned only with their looks was he going to find a wife worthy of him? Just then, Lew opened his mouth and asked a question that nearly floored Carla.

"Mama, would you marry Ivan?"

Chapter 11

DANNY SPUTTERED WITH LAUGHTER, THEN SENT Carla a look that was so impudent she itched to slap him.

Flushed with embarrassment, Sally asked her son, "Why ever would you ask that?"

"I want Ivan to live with us. Danny says you would have to marry him, or old Myrtle would fall down in a fit."

"I don't like old Myrtle," Tim announced. "I hope she has a big fit."

That was too much for Danny. He burst into full-blown laughter.

"If you can't behave any better, you can leave the table," Carla told her brother.

"And miss what these two brats might say next? You've got to be kidding."

"It is very nice of you to want me to live with you," Ivan said to Lew, "but I have to live here with Danny and Miss Carla."

Carla could feel what was coming next just as clearly as if it had been written on the wall.

"Are you married to Miss Carla?"

"No."

"Does that mean old Myrtle is going to have a fit?"

"Can I watch?" Tim asked. "I've never seen anybody have a fit."

"You can watch me," declared Carla. "I'm just about to have a fit and beat my brother to death."

Despite her irritation, Carla couldn't suppress a laugh at Lew's open-mouth stare. Since Danny was already in the grip of helpless laughter, it needed only Ivan's grin to encourage Sally's laughter. The children, not sure why everybody was laughing, joined nevertheless. That served to clear the air of tension.

"Now that's over, you'd better eat your supper so you can get to bed early," Carla said to the boys. "Ivan is going back to Overlin tomorrow. He'll take you with him if it's okay with your mother."

"I'm going, too," Sally said. "I can't let other people work on my house and me not be there."

"I'll help," Carla volunteered.

"I'll help Ivan," Danny said.

"Somebody has to stay here," his sister said.

"I was here yesterday."

"And spent nearly all of it in bed."

"I would stay," Ivan said, "but I can be more useful in town."

"Mr. Dodge said Ivan was a hero," Tim announced.

"He said the men who found Mr. Joiner's herd were heroes, too," Ivan reminded the boy.

"When I get big, I'm going to chase bandits," Lew declared.

"I hope there won't be any more bandits by the time you're grown," Carla said.

Her hopes were not shared by the boys.

It turned out to be one of those rare days people remember years later. A mixture of clouds and cool breezes from a distant thunderstorm brought the temperature down twenty degrees below average. The welcome rain that followed the tornado had invigorated people as much as it refreshed the earth. Plants and trees, washing clean of the dust and grit that had covered them for the last month, waved proudly in the breeze. Flower buds that had threatened to wither in the heat had burst open in bright color. Honeybees and fluttering butterflies hurried to harvest the gifts from the flowers before the heat withered their brilliance.

Yet Earth's newly polished beauty was badly tarnished by the debris left in the storm's wake. Broken boards lay scattered between buildings, across the open prairie, even caught in branches of trees. Household items and pieces of clothing had been tossed in all directions, some snagged on the thorns of cactuses, others deposited in depressions or streambeds, some broken into bits, others apparently unharmed.

The children ranged far and wide, returning with arms and wagons loaded with mounds of life's necessities to be sorted through by families that had lost part or most of their possessions. Men and boys labored to clear away debris, throw out what couldn't be fixed, and start the process of rebuilding. Women and girls labored to feed everyone in-between who were struggling to restore some order to badly shattered lives. Those fortunate enough to have been out of the path of the storm shared with their neighbors, knowing that only chance had kept them from being among the less fortunate.

"I've never seen people so happy with each other," Sadie said to Carla. Food was set out on a series of tables. People stopped to eat when they had a few minutes. Carla and Sadie had been designated to replenish the empty bowls and plates.

"Trouble brings out either the best or worst in people. Today it was the best."

"I think most people are just glad it wasn't their house that was scattered from here to the Rio Grande."

Carla handed Sadie a plate that had been emptied of fried chicken and picked up a bowl with only a few spoonfuls of succotash left. "Don't be so cynical. Even Riley and his men are helping."

Riley's men had been turned into carpenters and handymen. Everyone was so grateful for the quick return of Wilbur Joiner's herd that they gave his men the easiest jobs, the choicest pieces of meat, the best places in the shade, and generally showered them with so many compliments even Bricker managed to smile. It didn't hurt that several young women, having learned the men were unmarried, favored them with special attention. Sadie cast a glance at one young woman who'd been concentrating her attention on the youngest and most attractive of Riley's men.

"Look at that! The foolish girl can't have any respect for herself, not with throwing herself at a man that way."

"You can't blame Sueanne for trying to draw attention to herself," Carla said. "There aren't many single men in the county."

"Drawing attention to yourself is one thing. Practically throwing yourself at a man is another. If she's got to make a spectacle of herself, she could at least direct her attentions to Ivan. Now that's a man worth having."

Carla kept an eye on Ivan throughout the day. Nearly every man in Overlin had some experience in building, but none of them had Ivan's training. In a short time he'd been promoted to supervising all the building projects. During the course of the day, nearly every woman found at least one opportunity to consult his opinion on everything from how to pipe water into a kitchen to what to do about a skinned knee. It infuriated Carla that he treated every question with equal gravity.

"Not every single man is looking to get married," Carla told Sadie. "Everybody might as well know Ivan means to go back to Poland."

"Why ever would he want to do that?"

"Because that's where he was born, where his family is. He's a prince there."

"I thought that was a silly tale Beth Kesney had made up. Everyone knows she's been after Ivan ever since she set eyes on him. You mean it's true?"

"His family has been important in Poland for more than five hundred years. They've got castles, and I don't know what else. His sister married a very rich man so he'll be an important person when he goes back. I'm sure he'll expect his wife to have an equally impressive background."

"Golly," Sadie gushed. "A prince. Wait 'til I tell Myrtle. She'll be furious that I knew before her."

Carla probably shouldn't have told Sadie about Ivan. Sadie would repeat it to everyone she met as quickly as she could, probably with embellishments, but people might as well know Ivan didn't mean to stay in Texas. He would treat every woman with flattering graciousness then head off to Poland like nothing had happened.

Carla was in the habit of being honest with herself so she had to admit she wasn't doing this for unselfish reasons. She didn't like that she was jealous of the attention Ivan showered on other women. For some reason she couldn't understand—or didn't *want* to understand—she felt he belonged to her. Every time she saw a woman approach Ivan, she wanted to push her away. Every time he smiled at them, she wanted to tell him to stop. If he wasn't going to focus on helping people rebuild their homes, he ought to be back at the ranch with Danny. If he intended to take ownership of the land in a year, the least he could do was work for it.

She was nearly as annoyed with herself as she was with Ivan for coming into her life and confusing her. Never before had she had been unsure of what to do. Everything went back to Mr. diViere. If he hadn't come to Overlin, Danny wouldn't have lost half the ranch. If diViere hadn't found himself with half of a ranch, he wouldn't have told Ivan he could have it if he worked it for a year. Without that offer, Ivan would never have come to Overlin. If Ivan hadn't come to Overlin, her life wouldn't be in such turmoil.

If she ever met diViere, she'd be sorely tempted to put a bullet in him.

"I wonder if Sueanne knows Ivan's going back to Poland," Sadie said. "It's not like her to ignore a handsome man."

"She didn't ignore him earlier," Myrtle said. "And what's this about Ivan going to Poland?"

Within minutes, Sadie had poured out the whole story, turning to Carla for corroboration or elaboration. Myrtle's response was unexpected.

"We can't let him go back to Poland," Myrtle said to Carla. "You've got to marry him and keep him here."

Carla was bereft of speech.

"Don't gape at me like a landed fish," Myrtle snapped. "I know you like him. Any woman with sense would, and you've got plenty of sense. He's worth two of your Kesney Hardin. Probably three or four of that grandstanding Maxwell Dodge."

"I don't know what you're talking about," Carla managed to sputter.

"Don't play dumb with me," Myrtle said. "I've seen you watching him all morning. I've also seen how you act when one of those silly women sidles up to him, grinning like a saphead, and asking her half-witted question."

"I'm sure you're mistaken."

Myrtle ignored her interruption. "I was afraid for a time you were going to fall for Kesney's flash and money. I wouldn't blame another girl for being taken in, but I always knew you had too much sense."

"Thank you. I think," Carla managed to say.

Myrtle lost patience. "Don't give me any pretense. If you don't yet like him enough to want to marry him, get going and do it. It's not going to be easy to convince him to stay in this godforsaken corner of the world rather than some fancy palace filled with painted women falling over themselves to do what you won't." Myrtle was notorious for plain speaking, but today she was breaking new ground.

"I think Ivan likes me, but he's not interested in me that way."

"Then make him. You're a beautiful woman, and you're smart. I managed to get two husbands without half your looks or money. He's worth more than both my husbands together."

"I didn't know you liked Ivan," Sadie said to Carla, her expression one of surprise mixed with confusion.

"I don't. I mean, not the way Myrtle thinks."

"I don't *think*," Myrtle said. "I *know*."

Sadie brightened. "Well, I think you ought to do what Myrtle says." Her expression darkened. "He'd be better off with you than that flighty daughter of Kesney."

"He's not interested in children," Myrtle declared. "Ivan is a man who needs a woman."

Carla was tempted to tell Myrtle there were few men who'd turn their backs on a pretty child bride who was rich into the bargain, but she was too busy trying to grapple with the maelstrom of emotions Myrtle's suggestion had set off.

"Does he like being a rancher?" Sadie asked. "I never knew a rancher who liked being cooped up indoors."

"Princes don't stay cooped up," Myrtle said. "They have huge estates and spend all day on horseback chasing foxes and deer."

Carla didn't know how Myrtle could know anything about Polish aristocracy, but she was relieved when one of the cooks shouted she had a plate of barbecued beef ready for the table. Another called that she had a bowl of potatoes ready.

"Don't forget what I said," Myrtle called to Carla as she rushed away. "The whole town is depending on you."

Carla didn't know how Myrtle should think that. Nor did she know how she'd come up with the idea that Carla should marry Ivan. Myrtle didn't know much about Ivan if she thought he could be swayed so easily. If Ivan said he was going back to Poland, that's what he was going to do.

Even if Carla *did* decide she wanted to marry him.

———⁓———

Danny took one look at his sister and whistled through his teeth. "Damn, Sis, you look great. There won't be a female at the dance who can come within a mile of you tonight."

After a week of hard work, houses damaged by the tornado had been repaired, furnishings had been found, borrowed, or rebuilt, and clothes had been retrieved, washed, and put back in wardrobes. Families were sleeping in their own beds, and children were playing in yards free of debris. Life was so nearly back to normal it was hard to believe a tornado had passed through just eight days ago.

The dance that had been postponed was on again. Maxwell Dodge had taken it upon himself to declare that this time it would be a victory dance to celebrate the recovery of the town. He'd topped that by saying it would be a chance for the ladies to thank the men for working so hard by making sure they had partners for every dance. Myrtle had asked why it wasn't equally important for the men to thank the women. Carla had said she thought Myrtle had made a good point, but Maxwell had ignored both of them.

This would be the biggest dance in Overlin's short history. People would come from miles around. Some would come in wagons with their whole families and stay for a day or two. Single cowhands would ride as much as twenty-five miles just for the chance of dancing with a pretty girl. There would be food and drink for everyone. The musicians would play as long as anyone wanted to dance. Everyone, from the youngest to the oldest, would attempt to pack as much fun as possible in a few hours.

"I hope you've got lots of energy," Danny said to his sister. "Every man there is going to want to dance with you."

Carla blushed with pleasure. "I don't want to stand out that much."

"Then take off that red dress." Danny shook his head and grinned broadly. "I can't believe Widow Lowell would have something like that in her shop."

"She didn't want to sell it to me."

"Who did she expect to buy it? She probably got it by mistake. I bet it gave her heart palpitations."

Carla laughed at her brother's nonsense. He was so handsome he would be surrounded by giggling girls from the minute he arrived. "I doubt everybody will be begging me for dances. Wait until you see Kesney's daughter."

Danny frowned. "I don't need another person who thinks I'm too pretty to be a man."

"Who would say such a thing?"

Carla hadn't heard the kitchen door open and was surprised to see Ivan had entered the room. "Danny thinks Kesney's daughter won't like him." But Ivan wasn't looking at Danny. He was looking at Carla in a way she found unnerving and unexpected.

Myrtle's having practically ordered Carla to marry Ivan had forced to her realize her feelings toward him were more than mere liking. She wasn't in love with him, but every time she tried to pin down her feelings, they eluded her grasp. Ivan was no help. He was such a gentleman, his manner so practiced and easy, it was almost impossible to guess what his feelings might be.

"How could anyone not like a young man with such a beautiful sister," Ivan said before turning to Carla and saying, "but you should not wear that dress."

"Why?" Ivan had never been critical before.

Danny was quick to defend his sister. "I think she looks beautiful."

"She is more than beautiful," Ivan said. "No one will be able to see anyone but her."

Carla's breath caught in her throat. The look Ivan was giving her had nothing to do with polished manners or gentlemanly behavior. It was the look of a man who sees a woman he desires. It was a look that would have cut across a crowded room or through a haze of smoke to reach her. It was a look that caused heat to rise from somewhere deep inside her body. It was a look that told her Ivan was susceptible, that the castle walls were not built so high that they couldn't be breached.

Yet she wasn't so taken with Ivan's flattery that she hadn't noticed Danny's mischievous smirk.

"Carla says everyone will be too busy looking at Kesney's daughter to pay her any attention."

"Your sister does not have very good judgment when it comes to people."

Carla didn't like to be criticized, but the sensual undertone of that look was powerful enough to blunt even the sharpest barb. What Ivan's code of conduct would never allow him to say with words, he said with his eyes. Carla wanted to know if he really did harbor warm feelings toward her, but she wasn't sure she was ready to find out.

Danny's grin reached from ear to ear. "Why would you say that?" he asked Ivan.

"I have seen Kesney's daughter. I have danced with her and had lunch with her. I have spent a morning shopping with her. At no time did I ever think she was more beautiful than your sister."

Danny laughed. "So why do you think Carla shouldn't wear her new red dress?"

"She will break many hearts." Ivan shook his head sadly. "It is not good to see a man waste away until he has no will to live."

When Ivan said things like that, it made Carla wonder if she knew anything at all about him. He was too serious to make jokes like Danny, but he certainly couldn't believe a man could waste away because of a broken heart. She knew Myrtle would say they couldn't because Myrtle was certain men didn't have hearts.

"Stop it, both of you. I don't think this is funny, Danny. And as for you, you Polish prince in exile, I don't think it reflects well on your family to tell such whoppers."

"I do not know about these *whoppers* you say I speak, but I do not shame my family. You are truly more beautiful than Miss Kesney ever could be."

The sincerity in Ivan's voice caused Carla to blush deeply."It's time we started for the dance," she said to both men. "We don't want to be the last to arrive."

Danny's mischievous grin was back. "Yes, it would be terrible to see all the men leave their partners standing the moment they slapped eyes on you."

Carla decided it was better not to respond. Her brother liked few things better than teasing.

On the way into town, Danny ran through a list of nearly everyone within twenty miles of Overlin, wondering if they would be at the dance, who they would bring, what they would wear. Carla knew that would be very helpful to Ivan, but she wasn't sure he was paying much attention to Danny. She had insisted on driving her buggy while Danny and Ivan rode. She needed time to think, and she hoped Danny and Ivan riding together would give her the opportunity.

It didn't work out quite as she planned. Even though Danny talked almost nonstop, and even though Ivan appeared to be paying polite attention, he still managed to direct several glances laden with meaning her way. Ivan was as far from indifferent to her as she was from being uninterested in him. It was in that unsettled frame of mind that she arrived at the dance.

Overlin wasn't a large town, but it was too big to hold a major social event indoors. In preparation for the dance, lanterns had been strung from ropes tied to poles that formed a big square. A platform had been set up for a band of a fiddle, two banjos, and a drum. A couple of tables off to one side offered drinks, lemonade for free, and beer and whiskey for a quarter. There was also food for those who had traveled so far or fast they hadn't taken time for supper. Wagons, buggies, and horses were parked out of the range of the lanterns. Though they had arrived a few minutes before starting time, there was already a crowd gathered, which forced Carla to park her buggy farther from the dance area than she wanted. She hoped her shoes wouldn't be covered with dust before the first dance.

As they wound their way between the parked

vehicles, the sound of the fiddle tuning up caused her worries about Ivan to fade. This was an evening for having fun, for visiting with friends, for flirting, for catching up on gossip, for doing all the things people who lived in semi- isolation did when they got together. Some would drink too much. Others would laugh too loud or say things they would regret the next day. There would probably be a fight or two. It seemed it was impossible to gather men, women, and liquor in the same place without somebody taking a poke at somebody else. But even that was part of the exuberant high spirits that characterized these gatherings.

"Want some lemonade?" Danny asked his sister.

"No."

"How about you?" he asked Ivan.

"None for me."

Danny grinned. "I expect you want something stronger than lemonade."

"I drink nothing stronger than water as long as I am responsible for your sister."

"Glad I'm not you. I'm parched so I'm off to get something to drink."

Danny took two steps in the direction of the lemonade and came to an abrupt stop. "Who is that?" he asked in an awed whisper.

Chapter 12

IVAN TURNED TO FOLLOW THE DIRECTION OF DANNY'S gaze. He wasn't surprised Danny was staring at Beth Hardin standing with her father under one of the lanterns. The young girl looked lovely in a simple white dress with a white flower in her dark brown hair. Her animation, her high spirits, were reflected in her smile and girlish laughter.

Carla grinned at her brother. "That's Beth Hardin. She's the girl you said you didn't want to meet, remember?"

"I was a fool," Danny mumbled in nearly reverent tones. "I have to meet her."

"Wait until you've had time to get that stunned look off your face. She's liable to think you're half-witted."

"Why don't you get us all some lemonade?" Ivan suggested.

Too dazed to remember Ivan and his sister had only moments earlier refused his offer of refreshment, Danny wandered off toward the drink table.

"Did you see the look on his face?" Carla asked Ivan with a laugh. "I've never seen him bowled over by a young woman. Usually they're gaping at him, and he can't wait to get away."

"I wish it were that way now."

"Why?" Carla sounded surprised.

"Danny is young. If this is his first infatuation, being refused will hurt very much."

"Why should Beth refuse to dance with him?"

"I do not refer to dancing. I refer to love."

Carla frowned. "Don't be ridiculous. Danny's just set eyes on the girl. He doesn't know anything about her. He can't be in love with her."

"What he sees when he looks at Beth is his idea of perfection. She is the girl he has dreamed of but has never met. It is knowing nothing more about her that makes it so easy to fall in love."

Carla looked at him as though he was losing his mind. "Why do you say this? Danny's no silly, idealistic boy. He's seventeen. He's been a working cowhand practically since he could ride."

"When I was eighteen, I, too, had worked for many years, but my heart was like that of an innocent child. Then one day I saw a woman of great beauty such as I had not thought possible. My heart was lost before I knew what had happened. I did not care that she was Russian or that her father owned many estates. I loved her as only one who loves for the first time can. It would have been better if she had not shared my passion, but she felt as I did. I dreamed of a life of such happiness as can only be imagined."

"What happened?"

"What anyone but a lovesick fool would have known would. Her father could not allow his daughter to marry a penniless Pole, even one who would become a prince. She was immediately engaged, and soon married, to an equally wealthy Russian. I learned later that she'd agreed only on the condition that her father send me to school."

"She sacrificed her happiness for yours?"

"I did not think so at the time. I was bitter. I studied hard, determined to become a great engineer, grow very rich, and get my revenge by finding an even more beautiful and wealthy bride. Only gradually did I realize she must have known a love such as ours could not long endure."

"It was better to break it off while it was still alive and wonderful, rather than hang on while it withered and died."

"I am sure it was best, but it was years before the pain went away. Even now it hurts to remember."

"Why did you tell me this story if it's so painful?"

"Because I do not think Kesney will welcome Danny's interest in his daughter."

Carla bristled impatiently. "For goodness sakes, Ivan, Danny has just clapped eyes on Beth. Let another pretty girl show up, and he might forget all about her. Even if he didn't, there's no reason to think Beth will have a similar interest in him."

"Have you been watching her?"

"No. I was listening to you."

Carla's gaze followed Ivan's when he turned toward Beth. She was still standing next to her father, but her gaze was locked on Danny. Beth tugged on her father's sleeve and spoke without taking her eyes off Danny.

"I believe she asked her father for his name," Ivan said.

Carla was no lip reader, but it was easy to see Kesney had said *Danny Reece*. Carla couldn't tell what Beth said in response, but when she looked to where she and Ivan were standing, she could guess. Speaking once more to her father, both of them started in their direction.

"They are coming here," Ivan said.

"I can see that. What should we do?"

"Nothing. If Danny had not stayed at the ranch all week, they would have met before now."

Danny was concentrating so hard on not spilling the three glasses of lemonade he didn't see Beth until she had almost reached them. If Ivan hadn't taken the lemonade from him, he'd have dropped all three glasses.

"I was wondering when you would get here."

Beth's remarks appeared to be meant for Carla, but her gaze remained locked on Danny. Her expression was so close to the dumbfounded look on Danny's face Carla's heart sank. Kesney, too, seemed worried.

"I want to see if Ivan remembers his lessons." Beth's gaze didn't leave Danny.

"I'm sure he does," her father said. "Would you like something to drink? You're not looking quite yourself."

"Here. Have my lemonade."

Danny practically shoved his glass at Beth. Looking as though she had been offered something akin to the holy grail, Beth reached for the glass. Their hands touched for so long Carla was certain Kesney would say something, but he seemed unaware of the true nature of his daughter's affliction. When the fiddle stuck up the first tune of the evening, he looked even more worried.

"I don't think you ought to dance just yet," Kesney said to his daughter. "Why won't you sit for a while?"

"I'll sit with her," Danny said to Kesney. "I'm Danny, Carla's brother," he said to Beth.

"This is my daughter, Beth," Kesney said to Danny. "She's only been in Texas a short while. I don't think she's used to the heat yet."

"Maybe the lemonade will help," Danny said to Beth.

"But now you don't have any."

"He can have mine." Ivan had to place his glass in Danny's hands because the boy couldn't take his eyes off Beth.

"I'd offer to dance," Kesney said to Carla, "but I don't want to leave Beth until I'm sure she's all right."

"That's okay," Carla said. "I don't want to dance a jig anytime tonight, certainly not the first dance."

"And not in that dress." Kesney hadn't been so concerned for his daughter that he had failed to take notice of Carla's dress. "Half the good ladies of Overlin would probably faint."

Vaguely annoyed by his comment, Carla said, "I bought it from Sadie."

"I'm surprised it didn't burn down the store."

"Ivan said I shouldn't wear it." She didn't know why she said that. She knew Kesney didn't think Ivan had the right to have any opinion in regard to her.

"He was wrong."

"He said it would attract too much attention."

The look Kesney cast Ivan wasn't friendly. "He's right about that. If anybody tries to get fresh, just let me know. I'll set them right."

"No one will take liberties with Carla as long as she is with me," Ivan announced.

Carla wasn't worried about anybody taking liberties, but the tension between the two men was uncomfortable. It was flattering to have two handsome men squaring off over her, but having it come out in the middle of a dance was not good timing. "I want to say hello to some of the ladies," she told Kesney. "And Maxwell wants to talk to Ivan about digging a deep well for the town."

"I know nothing about a proposed well," Ivan said to Carla as they walked away.

"Neither do I, but the town could use one."

"So why did you say—"

"I wanted to get you away from Kesney. It won't improve the atmosphere to have you two glaring at each other."

"I do not glare."

"Maybe not, but you have that look of an aristocrat about to squash a bug."

"I am not an aristocrat. I am a cowhand. And cowhands do not squash bugs. We swat them."

Carla laughed. "I'm glad to know you're catching on to English."

"It is an impossible language. I do not understand—"

"Carla Reece! That dress is a disgrace."

Carla turned to see Myrtle elbowing her way through the crowd, a look of outrage on her deeply lined countenance.

"I will hold her if you want to run." The twinkle in Ivan's eye caused Carla to smile.

"If I had any sense, I'd take you up on your offer, but she'd probably follow me."

Having reached Carla, Myrtle declared, "Where did you find that... that... that abomination? No place in Overlin, I'm sure."

"I bought it in Sadie's shop." It wasn't an abomination. It merely showed part of her shoulders, her upper chest, and her arms below the elbow. Myrtle thought every unmarried woman's dress should be made out of gingham and button at the wrists and under the chin.

"Sadie Lowell is a foolish woman, but she would never allow such a dress through her doors."

"In her defense, she didn't want to sell it to me."

"I should think not. I don't know why Ivan let you out of the house. I'm sure there's not a dress like that in the whole of Poland."

The twinkle in Ivan's eyes grew more pronounced. "I told her she should not wear it."

"Just the kind of excellent advice I would expect from a man of your caliber. Why didn't you follow it?" she demanded of Carla.

Carla was as annoyed with Myrtle's public censure as she was with the gathering crowd of amused onlookers. She wasn't shy about taking a public stand that women should be treated equally with men when it came to business, but she didn't feel the same about a public debate on her clothes.

"I chose this dress because I thought it would be fun," she told Myrtle.

"It's fun for me," some male wag in the gathering commented.

"Me too," said another.

"See." Myrtle waved a finger in the direction of one of the voices. "Do you want that kind of attention?"

Carla was grateful Kesney was too worried about his daughter to notice what Myrtle was saying.

"This is a dance," Carla told Myrtle. "People are here for fun. After all the hard work they put in this last week, it's time to let loose a little—just for tonight. Nobody will expect me to take Eve Lawrence's place in the saloon."

"You couldn't blame them if they did." Myrtle removed her wrap and handed it to Ivan. "Put this around her shoulders. So much bare skin is bound to stir up already inflamed sensibilities."

"What about your shoulders?" Carla asked, even though Myrtle's dress had long sleeves and a collar that buttoned under her chin.

"No one would look at my shoulders even if I were so lost to all decorum as to wear such a shocking outfit. Take her home before all the whiskey is gone." Having said that, Myrtle turned and made her way through the amused crowd.

"Take your wrap," Carla called after her.

Acting as though she hadn't heard, Myrtle didn't look back.

"Let me put it around your shoulders," Ivan said.

"I don't want it."

"I think you should wear it now. You can take it off later."

Carla looked at the people who were drifting away from her and Ivan. "It will look like I'm giving in to Myrtle's bullying."

"Myrtle is not bullying you. She cares about you."

Carla felt like Ivan had pulled the stuffing out of her indignation. "I know, but I get so tired of her criticism."

"She does it out of love."

"Myrtle doesn't love anybody except maybe you. You ought to hear what she says about everybody in Overlin. She won't even talk to anybody under fifty."

"Yet she talks to you. Why?"

"I've never been quite sure."

"I think she sees in you the person she wishes she could have been. I think she wants for you the things she never had."

"She's probably the richest person in Overlin."

"And probably the most unhappy."

Carla had to admit that while she often took issue with what Myrtle did, she admired her spirit. She would face down the most powerful man in Overlin with the same ferocity she turned on the boys who delighted in breaking her fence.

"Give me the wrap. I'm not sure you're right, but I'll use it just in case." She let Ivan drape it over her shoulders. "Now I want to dance."

The twinkle was back in Ivan's eye. "I know I can dance because Beth has taught me, but I do not know if you can dance. Will my toes be in danger?"

"If I wasn't sure it would cause almost as big a commotion as Myrtle, I'd punch you in the stomach," Carla threatened.

"I was told that fights would not start until later. And that drunk men would be the fighters."

She didn't know whether to laugh or to punch him anyway. The red dress gave her courage, and she settled on the punch that merely caused Ivan to laugh so loud half the people gathered turned in their direction.

"Stop it," she hissed. "You have everybody looking at us."

"After the red dress and Myrtle, there was no hope people would look at anyone else. Did I not say you were the most beautiful woman in Overlin?"

"And you are the most impossible man. Come on. I'll prove to you I can dance just as well as Beth."

Under ordinary circumstances, she probably could dance better than Beth, but being in Ivan's arms transformed her. He was such a marvelous dancer he made her better. They seemed to float over the floor, their bodies perfectly synchronized. She could understand how Beth had been so excited when she danced with Ivan. It was like suddenly finding she had winged feet, that every movement was perfectly executed without effort or thought. The music of the squawking fiddle and twanging banjos changed into a sound that was as soft and alluring as the night air. The light from the dozens of lanterns turned luminous, their softened rays finding only the best parts of the tired, weathered faces that surrounded them.

Carla wondered if Ivan had ever had the chance to dance with that young girl when he was eighteen. If so, how would he compare Carla to her? She knew he liked her. She knew he wanted her. She *didn't* know if his heart had been so wounded he could never love again. If so, it would be a great tragedy. Ivan was a wonderful man. The way he dealt with Sally's boys showed he would be a wonderful father. The way he treated all women gave every indication that he would be the kind of husband women only dream of.

The end of the song came as an unpleasant jolt. Carla was so wrapped up in the magic of being in Ivan's arms that she wanted it to go on forever. She didn't come out of her trance until they'd walked back to where Beth and Danny were sitting, both looking as though they had a touch of the fever.

"I don't like the way Beth looks," Kesney said as soon as Carla reached them. "I think I ought to take her home."

"I'm fine, Papa," Beth protested.

"You don't look fine to me. What you do think, Carla?"

"Tell Papa I'm not sick," Beth begged. "This is the first dance I've been to in months. If I have to go home, I *will* be sick."

"Move over," Carla said to her brother. "I want to sit next to Beth."

Since there wasn't room for both of them on the bench, Danny had to stand, which is exactly what Carla intended. "Why don't you and Ivan bring us some lemonade?" she said to her brother.

Beth glanced up at Danny then back at her hands, which she was twisting in her lap. "I'm not thirsty."

"Danny will bring you some lemonade just in case you change your mind."

Danny looked as reluctant to leave as Beth was to have him go, so Carla leveled a steady look at Ivan, hoping he would understand she wanted him to take Danny away. Accurately interpreting her plea, Ivan gripped Danny by the shoulders and propelled him toward the lemonade table.

"Why don't you stretch your legs?" Carla said to Kesney.

"I'm too worried to leave Beth."

"She'll be fine, but worrying about *you* worrying about *her* isn't helping. Maybe you'd like something stronger than lemonade."

Kesney shuddered. "What man in his right mind wouldn't?"

"Go," she encouraged when Kesney hesitated. "I'll take care of Beth."

Beth seemed to breathe a sigh of relief when her father left. She cast one glance at Danny's back before he was swallowed by the crowd. She turned back to Carla. "I'm really not sick."

"I know," Carla said. "He's quite handsome, isn't he? If he weren't my brother, I'd be angry with him. No man should be more beautiful than his sister."

Beth buried her gaze in her lap. "I don't know what you're talking about."

"If you have any hope of convincing your father you're well enough to stay here and dance with Danny, which any idiot but a doting father could see is what you're longing to do, you have to be honest with me."

Beth seemed to be struggling with herself.

"You needn't be afraid to admit your feelings. Danny feels the same about you."

Beth jerked her head up and looked at Carla with anguished eyes. "Do you really think so?"

"I've watched him through every infatuation, but I've never seen him stare at a female like he was a half-wit."

"I'm the one staring at him," Beth protested. "He's gorgeous."

"I agree. Just don't tell him he's beautiful enough to be a girl. He's heard that too many times."

Beth was indignant. "I don't think he looks like a girl. What an awful thing for his friends to say."

"It was the girls who said it."

"Then they're all blind and stupid," Beth declared heatedly. "He's more handsome than Ivan, and one of these days he's going to be almost as big. Then they'll be sorry they teased him."

"I agree with you, but what you have to do right now is convince your father you're sufficiently recovered from a momentary indisposition to stay. Maybe you can blame it on something you ate."

Beth made a face. "That won't be hard. We had some beans the cook said he fried twice. I can't imagine why anyone would want to eat them even if they were fried only once."

Carla laughed. "I guess it's an acquired taste."

"I have no intention of acquiring it."

"Never mind. It ought to be enough reason to ease your father's mind. Now I want to talk about your infatuation with Danny."

Carla got a stubborn look. "Don't try to tell me I'm too young to know my feelings."

"Who told you that?"

"My father."

"I didn't think he knew how you felt about Danny."

"He was talking about Ivan."

Carla felt a stab of emotion that was uncomfortably like jealous anger. She was surprised and a little frightened at how difficult it was to get under control. "Why would he say that about Ivan?"

Beth delivered herself of a dismissive sniff. "He said I was acting like a little girl who was infatuated by a handsome older man. I was saying how handsome Ivan was, how beautifully he danced, what exquisite manners he had. I *think* I said I wished I could grow up really fast so he would marry me. *Maybe* I said he wasn't too old for me. I don't remember what I said, but Daddy acted liked I'd said we were engaged and the wedding was next week. He didn't shout at me, but I'd have liked that better than some of the things he said."

It was amusing as well as a little sad to think of Kesney acting like a parent who didn't realize his little girl was almost grown. Maybe he didn't want her to grow up yet because he knew that would mean he would lose her. She was probably already more grown up than her father thought. Carla was as impressed by Beth's ability to put her feelings into the proper perspective as she was unhappy with her own reaction. She was three years older. There was no excuse for her. She had to get her feelings under control. And soon!

"Fathers always have trouble realizing their little girls are growing up. They're much more protective than they are with boys. Which leads me to your interest in Danny."

"Don't *you* tell me I don't know what I feel."

"I won't, but I will tell you that you don't know Danny. I don't know that anybody does."

"It's not just his looks," Beth insisted. "That's what caught my attention at first, but it's not what held it. You only have to look into his eyes to know he's honest and gentle. His smile shows he's sweet-tempered and kind. In spite of being so handsome he took my breath away, he's strong and manly. He's perfect."

Carla almost snorted. "No one is perfect. Least of all my brother."

"I know you'll say I don't know him, that it's not possible to fall in love with a man you've never seen before, but that's how I feel. Besides, he's your brother, and I really like you, so it's kinda like I already know him a little bit."

Carla could have listed a dozen ways she and Danny were different, but she didn't think Beth was ready to hear them. "Whether I agree with you isn't important," she said. "You need to convince your father you have recovered enough to stay here. Then you need to get to know Danny better. Your father may not approve— there are a lot of reasons why he might feel that way," she said when Beth started to object. "But don't try to hide your feelings from your father."

"Maybe he won't disapprove of Danny. Why should he?"

"Because Danny is only seventeen, and you're very young."

"I just turned sixteen," Beth declared. "I know lots of girls my age who are married."

"Danny has no money and no property. I doubt your father will see him as a suitable husband for you. Since he knows Danny gambled away his half of the ranch, I'm certain of it."

"How did that happen?"

Beth listened attentively while Carla recounted the story. "It was all that Mr. diViere's fault," Beth stated when Carla finished.

"I agree, but your father may see it differently. Now they're coming back. You've got to look like you're completely recovered. It might be better if you didn't stare at Danny all the time."

Beth had a stubborn jut to her chin. Carla was certain Kesney had overindulged his daughter after her mother's death, but she doubted his lenience would go so far as accepting Danny as a future son-in-law. She was relieved when Beth's mulish look faded.

"I will do what you say," Beth said, "but none of this would matter if you marry Daddy. Then he couldn't object to my marrying Danny."

Carla could have given her plenty of reasons why she was mistaken—the first being that Kesney hadn't asked her to marry him—but Danny and Ivan were back. Danny looked like he'd recovered. He was smiling brightly, acting much more like his old self. She wondered if Ivan had had a talk with him.

"Here's your lemonade," he said, handing the glass to Beth.

"Thank you, but I don't want it yet."

"Why don't you dance?" Danny asked. "That will make you thirsty, and you'll want it then."

"Are you asking me to dance?" Beth acted coquettish but not besotted.

"I guess I am."

"Since Papa isn't here, I'll have to ask Carla's permission."

"You don't need anybody's permission to dance," Danny argued.

"It's clear *you* didn't grow up in Kentucky."

"You can tell me about it while we dance."

"Go on," Carla said. "I'm sure your father won't mind."

Carla watched her brother lead Beth to the dance area. In a way it was touching to watch the two young people so focused on each other they might as well have been the only couple at the dance. At least they'd managed to get the love-struck looks off their faces.

"What do you think her father will say?" Ivan asked.

"I hope he'll say it's nice to see the youngsters having fun."

"Is that what you really think?"

Carla turned to him. "What do you think?"

"What I think does not matter. I am not her father."

"Well, here he comes."

"Maybe you should dance with him to take his mind off Beth."

Carla had expected she would dance with Kesney more than once before the evening was over, but she hadn't expected Ivan would be the one encouraging her to do it. *Did he care if she danced with Kesney?* Now she was the one acting like a love-struck fool. She was sure Ivan was only trying to help defuse the situation. He had already danced with her and showed no interest in dancing with anyone else. She had to get her emotions under control before she did something to expose herself as a jealous and slightly irrational female.

"Where's Beth?" Kesney asked.

"Dancing with Danny," Ivan told him.

"Are you sure she's all right?"

"She's fine now," Carla said. "She thinks something she had for supper upset her stomach."

"I don't think she likes Texas food," Kesney said. "Maybe I should take her home."

"I think you should dance with Carla," Ivan said. "Then you can watch Beth more closely and see for yourself that she is fine."

Kesney turned to Carla and smiled. "That's the best suggestion I've heard all evening." He extended his hand to Carla. "Would you like to dance?"

"I'd be honored." Maybe she shouldn't have said that. It might give Kesney the impression he meant more to her than he really did, but it was too late to retract her words.

The dance turned out to be even less satisfactory than she expected. Not only did Kesney pay more attention to Beth than he paid to her, he couldn't dance nearly as well as Ivan. He stepped on her toes twice. It didn't make matters any better that he apologized by saying he was busy watching Beth. Carla wasn't used to having a man pay attention to someone else when she was dancing with him. She tried to tell herself she should be pleased Kesney was so concerned about his daughter, but it didn't work. She supposed she was nothing more than a vain woman who thought so much of herself she got upset when a father paid more attention to his daughter than to her.

That was a humiliating admission to make. What was wrong with her? She really wasn't like that. At least she never had been before. What had changed? She wasn't even in love with Kesney.

"Beth really does look fine now, doesn't she?" Kesney asked.

"She looks more than fine," Carla said. "She's beaming with happiness. I'm sure part of her feeling upset was excitement. This is her first dance. It's hard for a young girl to be marooned on a ranch. She must miss her friends back in Kentucky."

"She's glad to be away from Kentucky," Kesney said. "She says she likes the freedom unmarried women like you have. That would never happen in Kentucky."

Carla wasn't sure whether that sounded like a compliment or complaint, but Kesney had always approved of her independent spirit so she supposed it was support. Their conversation settled into easy channels with his attention more focused on her, but she was still relieved when the dance ended.

Over the next two hours, Carla danced with Kesney once more, Ivan twice, Maxwell Dodge, Lukey Gordon, and a few older men from Overlin. She also danced with several young cowhands who had ridden in from outlying ranches. Most hesitated before coming toward her, hat in hand, bashfully asking if they could have that dance. Some couldn't have danced if their lives had depended on it, but most managed to spare her toes any serious damage. The more vigorous the dance, the more they liked it. When one particularly clumsy fella who'd done serious damage to several sets of toes approached her, Carla decided she needed a rest. She was grateful for the seat Ivan had saved for her. She was equally grateful for the glass of lemonade he handed her.

"I don't think I've ever been so tired," she told Ivan.

"I see several other men looking hopefully in this direction."

One of them detached himself from the crowd and came toward Carla. She felt a sudden stiffening of the muscles in the back of her neck when she recognized one of Riley's men. Bricker. Because of their success in recapturing Wilbur Joiner's cows, Riley and his men had been welcomed to the dance and were never without partners. Carla had danced with one named Tom, but she was not happy when Bricker stopped in front of her, smiled, and executed what he probably thought was a bow. He'd been drinking. She could smell it as well as see the effect on his balance.

"Can I have this dance?" he asked.

"Thank you, but I need a moment to rest."

In a flash, Bricker's smile was transformed into an ugly sneer. "You danced with half the cowhands this side of the Rio Grande. What makes you think you're too good to dance with me?"

The abrupt change in mood was as much of a surprise as his ugly accusation. "I don't think I'm too good to dance with you." Carla was used to having to fight for respect when it came to handling the ranch business, but no one had ever attacked her in such a personal manner. Not even Myrtle's most pointed criticisms had left her this angry and insulted. "I won't dance with you now or at any other time when you've been drinking," Carla declared.

With a growl that sounded more like a snarl, Bricker reached out to grab Carla. Instead he found himself facing Ivan's considerable presence.

"Miss Reece has said she does not want to dance with you."

"I don't give a damn what she says. She's going to dance with me." Bricker pulled a knife. "And no one's going to stop me."

Chapter 13

IVAN HAD EXPECTED THERE WOULD BE TROUBLE BEFORE the night was over, but he hadn't expected it to embroil him or Carla, and he hadn't expected it to involve weapons. Everyone had been told to leave their guns at home or in their wagons or saddlebags. Apparently no one had thought to mention knives. Hoping to attract no attention, Ivan spoke quietly to Bricker.

"Put away your knife."

"I'll put it up when you get out of my way," Bricker snarled.

"You and Riley were sent here to protect the people of Overlin, not harm them."

Apparently Bricker didn't believe in talking through situations. Without warning, he threw himself at Ivan.

Ivan wasn't expecting an unprovoked attack, and he didn't move fast enough to keep Bricker's knife from making an ugly gash in his forearm. The pain was searing, but its most profound effect was on Ivan's outraged code of behavior. No man with even a modicum of self-respect would behave like this in public. When one did, it was up to others to show him the error of his ways.

With a roar that was almost primeval, Ivan attacked Bricker with such ferocity it managed to penetrate the drunken rage that filled the man's brain. He attempted to back away, but Ivan's iron grip had closed around Bricker's wrist. With a sharp snap, he broke it. The startled man screamed and dropped the knife. That didn't stop Ivan from lifting him off the ground by his belt and shirt collar and tossing him halfway across the dance floor.

The whole episode took only a few seconds, but everyone around them fell silent, some of the dancers freezing in position as though turned into wax effigies. One woman uttered a small shriek when Bricker's body passed within inches of her head. He hit the ground hard and lay still. In the background, the band continued to play a lively rendition of "Sourwood Mountain."

Into this void stepped Myrtle Jenkins. "That man belongs in jail." She pointed to two husky young men. "Carry him there immediately."

So dreaded was Myrtle's disfavor that the young men would probably have picked Bicker up and obediently hauled him off to jail if Riley hadn't emerged from the crowd. "What happened?" he wanted to know.

Without giving anyone else a chance to speak, Myrtle strode up to Riley. "Carla said she was too tired to dance, but the drunken fool tried to force her. When Ivan stepped between them, he attacked Ivan with a knife. Unfortunately Ivan broke his wrist rather than his neck."

"I'm sorry," Riley apologized to Carla. "Bricker is a good man, but he has trouble holding his temper."

"He can't hold his liquor, either," Myrtle added. "Now take him away. You don't want to ruin these good people's celebration."

Offering apologies all around, Riley and two of his men got Bricker to his feet.

"Take off your coat. I need to see your arm."

It took Ivan a moment before he could calm the rage still boiling through his veins to understand that Carla was speaking to him.

"Don't stand there bleeding all over yourself," Myrtle ordered. "Do as Carla says."

Ivan looked up at the circle of people surrounding him. Their expressions ranged from horror and shocked surprise to approval and admiration. Bricker's knife had cut through the sleeve of Ivan's coat. The pain in his forearm still burned, but only a little blood had soaked through his clothes. "It is not much," he said.

Danny and Beth came running up. "What happened?" Danny asked.

Beth caught sight of the blood on Ivan's sleeve and shrieked, "You're bleeding!" One woman offered to tear strips off her petticoat to bind Ivan's arm.

Kesney pushed his way through the crowd, closely followed by Maxwell Dodge. "What's going on here?" Dodge asked in his officious manner.

There was no shortage of people ready to answer.

"Bring him to my house," Myrtle said to Carla. "He can't receive proper attention in the middle of this crowd."

"I'm coming, too," Beth declared.

"Only if you have enough sense to keep out of the way," Myrtle said.

Beth's startled look implied she wasn't used to being spoken to so directly.

"It would be better if you stayed here with your father and Danny," Carla said. "You don't want to miss the dance. It'll probably be a long time before we have another."

"Carla will take good care of Ivan," Danny assured Beth. "She's patched me up many times."

"I'll take your horse and Carla's buggy over to Myrtle's," Kesney offered. "I doubt you'll be coming back to the dance."

Ivan was relieved to be away from the gaping crowd. He didn't like being the focus of attention. Everyone in his troop had suffered worse injuries during the war, but none of them expected sympathy. They patched themselves up and were back in the saddle the next night.

"How are you feeling?" Carla asked once they were away from the crowd and the lights.

"It hurts, but it hardly bleeds."

"You can't tell that in the dark," Myrtle said. "Wait until we get inside."

Ivan had never expected to be invited inside Myrtle's home. He wasn't surprised when Myrtle took off her shoes and handed Carla a pair of slippers. Certain Myrtle had no male visitors and therefore had no slippers large enough for his feet, Ivan took off his shoes and walked in his socks.

Myrtle's house wasn't at all like he'd supposed it would be.

Hand-knotted rugs were scattered over floors that virtually gleamed with wax polish. The walls were covered with wallpaper. Whether in the hall or in one of the rooms, the theme was flowers, large and small, bright or subdued, in bunches or strung together like a daisy chain. Chairs were covered with festive slipcovers and adorned with crocheted doilies stiff with starch. Her pictures were unremarkable, but nearly every tabletop and cabinet shelf was covered with a wide variety of colored glass vessels and painted porcelain figures. The busy-ness of the room was only partially relieved by plain, white curtains with a gathered ruffle.

"Take him to the kitchen," Myrtle said to Carla. "I don't want him bleeding all over the furniture."

So much for his worry that Myrtle would fuss over him.

The kitchen was nearly as highly decorated as the rest of the house, spotlessly clean and everything in its place.

"Sit down at the table, and take off your coat," Myrtle said to Ivan. "Your shirt, too. I'll have none of this nonsense of being embarrassed to undress in front of a woman. Carla may turn pink about the ears, but you won't bother me. I've seen more of men than I want." Myrtle rummaged in her cabinets gathering things needed to care for Ivan's wound, but she turned to face him. "None of them were as handsome as you. If they had been, I might have felt different."

Ivan felt himself growing warm under his collar. It didn't help that Carla nearly burst out laughing.

Myrtle turned her attention to Carla. "You can fold up that tablecloth before he bleeds on it. I'm too old to do a lot of washing."

From the looks of the house, Myrtle must have spent most of each day cleaning, dusting, and washing. Rather than risk more of Myrtle's caustic tongue, Ivan allowed Carla to help him out of his coat.

"It's ruined," Carla said.

"No, it's not," Myrtle said. "Leave it with me. I'll sew it up."

"It is not necessary," Ivan said.

"I like to sew," Myrtle declared. "Are you going to deny an old lady her harmless pleasures?"

"No," Ivan said. "I will leave you my shirt, too."

He was quick to learn that while Myrtle might volunteer her services, she would balk if anyone appeared to be taking them for granted. "I didn't say a word about your shirt," Myrtle informed him. "What do you think I am, your personal servant?"

Ivan assured Myrtle that thought had never crossed his mind.

"Now you see what I mean," Carla whispered in his ear.

"I'll have no whispering in my house," Myrtle declared. "If you have anything to say, you say it where all can hear."

"I said *now you see what I mean*," Carla said. "You've been so kind to Ivan he had trouble believing you could be brutal to the rest of us."

"I'm not kind or brutal," Myrtle declared. "I just tell the truth as I see it. And that red dress is still a scandal."

Moving quickly to forestall a storm that threatened to break around him, Ivan said, "It is as I said." He pointed to his wound. "It is not much."

The cut was about three inches long but only a quarter of an inch deep. The blood that had dried on his shirt had stopped the bleeding. Now that his arm was bare, the wound started bleeding sluggishly.

"It's not enough to put you in your grave," Myrtle said, "but it will keep you out of the saddle for a few days."

Ivan had ridden with more serious wounds, but he decided not to tell Myrtle. It amused him to watch Myrtle tell Carla exactly what to do then show her how to do it. He gained considerable respect for Carla's ability to keep a tight rein on her temper despite Myrtle repeatedly telling her she was doing everything wrong.

She criticized Carla, a woman she'd known for years, often and severely, while she rarely had anything except praise for Ivan, a man she'd met for the first time only a few days ago. But Carla couldn't see that Myrtle was deeply fond of her. It was unfortunate that her fondness for Carla found its expression in criticism, but that didn't mean her affection wasn't genuine. Ivan could only guess at the reason.

Maybe she sympathized with a young woman left alone to run the family ranch. Maybe she admired Carla for being determined to be taken seriously by the businessmen of Overlin. Maybe she didn't want Carla to think her looks entitled her to more consideration than others. It was probable that she felt all those things, but Ivan sensed it was more personal than that. She believed Carla was capable of being the leader of society as well as a successful rancher, an example and an inspiration to all women. Because of this, Myrtle was determined to make sure Carla measured up to Myrtle's standards.

Ivan felt sorry for both women. Despite Carla's annoyance at Myrtle's frequent criticism, she appeared to have a genuine liking for the old woman. What could have been a mutually supportive and friendly relationship never rose above mere tolerance. He'd never thought of himself as a diplomat, but maybe he could do something to help them around this impasse.

"I think that's all we need to do," Myrtle declared to Carla when the last strip of bandage had been pinned into place. "Now you take him home, and make sure he gets plenty of rest. Bring him back in two days, and I'll change the bandage."

"Shouldn't he see the doctor?" Carla asked.

"I know as much about taking care of cuts as any doctor in Texas. And I don't charge a sinfully large fee to do it." Myrtle walked over to a cabinet, opened it, and took out a bottle filled with a dark liquid. "Give him a spoonful of this each morning," she said to Carla. "It tastes terrible, but it'll build him up after the loss of so much blood."

Ivan didn't think he'd lost much blood, but he didn't want to argue with Myrtle. Nor did he want to take her tonic.

"Tie your horse behind Carla's buggy and let her drive," Myrtle instructed Ivan. "I don't want you straining that arm."

Ivan agreed. He was certain Carla would have made the same demand. "Thank you," Ivan said to Myrtle as he got to his feet. "My own mother could not have taken better care of me."

For a moment he thought his comments might have embarrassed Myrtle, but if so, she recovered quickly.

"If you had stayed in Poland, you wouldn't have escorted Carla and her red dress to a dance where a drunk could start a knife fight."

Much worse had happened in Poland many times over, but he decided to let Myrtle keep her rosy picture of his homeland. "Had I stayed in Poland, I would never have met you."

"Young man, I am not swayed by empty flattery."

"It is not flattery," Ivan stated with as much of an innocent look as he could manage. "It is a mere statement of fact."

What might have been a ghost of a smile raced across Myrtle's face. "Take him home," she instructed Carla, "before he utters any more foolishness. I have come to think highly of him. I'd hate to be proved wrong."

Myrtle followed them outside and waited until they'd tied Ivan's horse behind the buggy, and Carla had taken the reins in her hands. She waved as they drove away.

"How do you like getting the rough side of Myrtle's tongue?" Carla asked when they'd cleared the edge of town.

"She said and did everything that was kind."

"She ordered you about like an errant child."

"Because she likes me."

"I know that." Carla sounded disgusted. "You must be the only man allowed inside since her second husband died. I wish she liked me half as much as she likes you."

"She likes you more."

Even in the darkness, Ivan could see Carla roll her eyes. "You've heard some of the things she's said to me. Why just tonight she raked me over the coals about my dress."

"I think Myrtle admires you."

Carla gave Ivan a long look. "I know Bricker didn't hit you on the head, so it can't be that. The wound hasn't had time to give you a fever, so it can't be that, either. The only possible reason for thinking that is you're insane. You'd have to be to think Myrtle sees herself in me." She urged her horse into a faster canter. "I'd better get you home before you get worse."

Ivan laughed. It had been a strange evening. Danny and Beth had fallen in love at first sight. Kesney was so concerned about his daughter's behavior he forgot to treat Carla with his usual fawning attention. No straight-forward operation would employ a man of Bricker's character thereby proving in Ivan's mind that there was something underhanded behind Riley's presence in Overlin. Lastly, he'd discovered that Myrtle had a soft side no one else seemed to see.

"Don't you dare laugh at me, Ivan Nikolai. You're the one who pushed his way into my life. Nothing has been the same since."

"Laveau did that. I'm just trying to make things better."

"How is selling my land to anyone with the right price and running back to Poland going to make things better?"

He couldn't answer that question now. Maybe not ever. Events had been set in motion over which he had no control. It was no longer just a question of selling the land. It was about seeing Danny grow into a man. There was Kesney's interest in Carla, and Myrtle's interest in everybody. There was also Riley's presence in Overlin. Most important of all was the question of Carla's happiness.

He could not leave for Poland while all these threads were still knotted.

— ∿ —

"Why didn't you tell me about her when you first met her?" Danny demanded of his sister.

"If I'd had any notion you'd start acting like a love-crazed fool, I'd have asked Kesney to send her back to Kentucky."

Carla was frying sausage to go along with a breakfast

of eggs, grits with gravy, and hot biscuits. For much of the morning she had had her back to Ivan, but he found his view entrancing. The heat from the cast iron stove had caused her to push up the sleeves of her blouse, affording him the rare sight of her arms from elbow to fingertips. He didn't understand why American women insisted on wearing dresses with sleeves down to the wrists and collars that buttoned under chins. Polish women were not reluctant to wear gowns that exposed their arms from the shoulder, a generous portion of their bosoms, and the glorious columns of their necks. Ivan thought it was a custom American women should emulate, especially a woman like Carla. He wondered what she would look like in one of the gowns he remembered seeing wealthy women wear when they went to parties. Just thinking about it caused a physical reaction he knew Carla wouldn't appreciate, especially at the breakfast table.

"I'm not love-crazed," Danny objected, "but how could any man clap eyes on Beth and not think she's the most beautiful creature in the world?"

"Ivan managed it."

"I am not seventeen," Ivan said.

"You're not dead, either," Danny shot back.

Ivan was fascinated by the relationship between Danny and Carla. They could yell at each other, even say things that were hurtful, yet it didn't change their love for each other. He wondered if that kind of love was possible for him. His family had been raised to follow strict codes of behavior that made it nearly impossible to know what another person was thinking or feeling. He liked this American passion for getting things out in the open. It allowed a person to live without pretense, without dependence on rank, social position, or wealth.

It was something he would have to give up when he went back to Poland.

Carla put the sausage on a plate and brought it to the table. Danny was drinking milk, but Carla and Ivan preferred coffee.

"Look, Danny," his sister said. "I have no objection to your liking Beth, but you've got to be realistic. You're only seventeen. Beth has just turned sixteen. Both of you are too young to start thinking of anything permanent."

"Just because you're a cold fish doesn't mean I am."

Carla stopped in the midst of serving herself some eggs. "What do you mean that I'm a *cold fish*?"

"You've had practically every man in Overlin hanging out after you, but you're not interested in any of them."

"You don't know that." Carla's gaze flew to Ivan and back to her brother. "I don't tell you everything."

Danny was too consumed by his own situation to see the faint tinge of color that bloomed in his sister's cheeks, but Ivan didn't fail to notice it. Or the quick glance in his direction. Did that mean Carla was attracted to him? Did it mean she liked him? That was hard to believe considering the way she acted when he arrived, but a lot had changed since then. He was no longer a stranger. She may not have realized it, but she had started to include him in her thinking, whether it was about the ranch or something else. Ivan was both pleased and bothered because the same thing had happened to him.

"You said Maxwell Dodge leaves you cold," Danny

said to his sister, "even though he's better looking than Kesney and probably as rich."

"A woman may marry for money, but she doesn't fall in love with it. Fortunately, I don't have to make that sacrifice."

"I don't care about Beth's money, and she doesn't care that I don't have any."

Carla finished chewing and swallowing a piece of sausage. "I expect her father cares a great deal. And at her age, what Kesney thinks matters. Now eat your breakfast. You and Ivan have work to do."

Danny attacked his food, stuffing it in his mouth, chewing, and swallowing as quickly as possible.

"Don't choke yourself," Carla said. "I don't want Beth crying her eyes out over your dead body."

"That's not funny!" Danny practically shouted.

"Sorry, but you're stretching this whole situation out of proportion. You just met Beth last night. You were the best-looking young people at the dance. It was natural you would be drawn to each other, but that has nothing to do with the kind of love that matures into a permanent commitment."

"How would you know? You've never been in love. You've never even really liked anybody."

Carla kept her gaze firmly on her plate. "I haven't been in love, but I know what it's like to be strongly attracted to someone and know it's impossible for anything to come of it."

"Who said it's impossible for…" Danny stopped in mid-sentence. "You never told me you were attracted to anybody. Who is it?"

Carla refilled her coffee cup. "It's not important."

"It can't be Dodge or Kesney," Danny said. "Both of them would marry you at the drop of a hat."

"Don't be ridiculous. They haven't asked—"

Danny didn't let his sister finish. "Not if you mean neither one got down on his knees and begged, but you can't deny they've been chasing after you ever since they came to Overlin."

"I don't know why we're even talking about me." Carla sounded annoyed. "You're the one who's about to die from love."

"I am not," Danny contradicted. "I just want you to accept that I'm not too young to be in love. I mean *really* in love."

"Okay, I can accept that," his sister said, "but you have to accept that there are two major barriers to this relationship even if Beth feels the same way about you."

"I know she does."

Carla ignored that comment. "Both of you are too young to start thinking about marriage. Even if you weren't, you have no way to support a wife. Or did you expect Kesney to support both of you?"

Danny jammed a piece of sausage into his mouth. "I haven't thought that far," he said through his food, "but Kesney could make me his foreman. He said he was looking for a new one. Pete Forrester decided to join Riley."

That caught Ivan's interest. He stopped eating and turned to Danny. "Why would he do that? Working for Kesney is a good job."

"Riley said they were going to be looking for cows that had been stolen from ranches farther north. He said ranchers were willing to pay to get their herds back. All the men will share the money." Danny glanced over at his sister before turning back to Ivan. "I'm thinking about working for him, too."

"No." The one word was short and unequivocal.

Danny turned to his sister. "I'm old enough to decide what I'm going to do."

"With Ivan injured, you have enough here to keep you busy."

"I don't have anything here. I lost it in a card game, remember?"

"I know that, but—"

Danny jumped up from his chair. "There's no *but*! You just said I couldn't support a wife. I'm going to do something to change that. I'd rather work for Kesney, but if it means I have to work for Riley, I'll do it."

Without giving his sister a chance for a rebuttal, Danny grabbed his hat, jammed it on his head, and went out the door. Carla had turned toward the doorway through which her brother disappeared. "I used to get upset when girls teased Danny about being so pretty. I never thought I'd be upset when one actually liked the way he looks."

Ivan didn't know what to say, so he drank some of his coffee and waited for Carla to continue.

"He talked about Beth like he couldn't think of living a day without her."

"In Poland young people often become over-wrought when they fall in love the first time. Are they so different here?"

"Is that how you felt when you fell in love for the first time?"

"I was sure I could never love anyone else."

"Have you?"

Was she asking whether he had fallen in love since then, or was she asking if he loved her? He was certain he'd been successful in masking his attraction, but it was getting harder. There was also something about her expression, the look in her eyes, and the set of her mouth that convinced him she wasn't asking out of idle curiosity. His answer would be important to her. "No, but I know I can with the right person."

"How can you tell when you've found the right person?"

Everything about her had become more intense, more focused. She reminded him of a cat hunting its prey, her gaze unwavering, her motionless body virtually crackling with potentially explosive energy. She was willing the right answer out of him. But what was the right answer? Her attitude toward him had changed from rage to tolerance. At times she seemed happy to work with him, even willing to depend on him or listen to his suggestions, but that was a long way from being attracted to him or wanting a personal relationship. How would she react if he said he was attracted to her? What if she was the *right person*? Would it matter since he was going back to Poland in a year?

"I cannot say how I know, only that I do."

She seemed to turn to stone in front of him. "Are you saying you're in love now?"

She had misunderstood him. He had meant to say that he *would* know when it happened, not that it had already happened. "I do not mean that. I tried to say—"

He was interrupted by the door bursting open and Danny striding into the kitchen, his face twisted in anger. "Kesney is here. He has something he wants to say to both of us."

Chapter 14

IVAN COULDN'T DECIDE WHETHER HE WAS MORE relieved at being prevented from attempting to answer Carla's question, or disappointed in Kesney for thinking he had to say what he surely must have guessed Carla had already said to her brother. Danny took up a position at the end of the table close to Ivan, his arms folded across his chest, his mouth set in a hard line, his eyes hooded and smoldering.

"Morning, Kesney," Carla said. "What's so important that it brings you out before breakfast?"

Carla's voice and expression were so unencouraging Kesney seemed to hesitate. Maybe he wasn't completely insensitive.

"I'm not sure whether I should say anything."

"If you are not sure, why not wait until you are?" Ivan asked.

"I would if I thought my daughter would listen to me. Since she won't, I'm hoping Danny will."

Danny's demeanor changed immediately. "What did you do to Beth?"

"Nothing like what you're thinking."

Kesney was so obviously uncomfortable Ivan started to feel sorry for him. It had to be difficult for a father to a raise a daughter alone, especially when brought into conflict with a young girl's idealistic vision of love and happiness. Ivan wasn't prepared to say Kesney had spoiled his daughter, but he had protected her from the realities of life and let her have her way most of the time. As much as Ivan liked Danny and was confident he would grow into a fine, dependable adult in a few years, he wasn't yet the kind of man Ivan would have wanted for his daughter.

"What did you do to her?" Danny asked again.

"For an hour I listened to her tell me how wonderful you are. When she could finally stop talking about your looks, she read me a list of enough sterling qualities and faultless character traits to qualify you for sainthood. When she reached the point of planning her wedding, reducing the number of rooms in *my* house that would be left to my use to two, and how I had to find you a job immediately, I finally spoke up."

Ivan was surprised he'd waited that long.

"If you made her cry, I'll—"

"He can't answer your question if you keep interrupting, Danny," Carla said.

Ivan was relieved Carla had stopped her brother from making a foolish threat. Once words were spoken, it was hard to forget them.

"I told her she was too young to be thinking of weddings and marriage," Kesney told Danny. "She's just sixteen."

Kesney looked to Carla as often as Danny, making Ivan wonder if the reason for his mild approach to Danny was to keep from doing anything that would prevent Carla from marrying him.

"What do you want us to do?"

Carla's expression hadn't softened. Ivan hoped Kesney was clever enough to figure out that while Carla might criticize her brother, she wouldn't allow anyone else to do it.

"I want you to continue being her friend." Kesney smiled briefly at Carla. "She likes you and thinks you're very courageous to have worn that red dress, but I want Danny to stay away from her."

Danny looked like he was about to explode, but he held it in when Carla said, "Let Kesney finish."

"I like you," Kesney said to Danny, "but you're too young. Even if you weren't, you have no way to support a wife. I know I've spoiled Beth, probably given her more than I should since her mother died, but she would be miserable married to a cowhand. She's never fixed a meal, sown a stitch, or cleaned a room."

As Kesney reeled off a dozen other things Beth had never done, Ivan could see Danny gradually deflate. No matter how all-consuming his infatuation with Beth might be, he couldn't help but see that marrying her would force her into a life that was completely alien to her.

"Like I said," Kesney continued, "she's only sixteen. I want to see her enjoy being young. I want her to go to parties, dance with lots of boys, and think picking out a pretty dress is more important than planting a garden. She's not like Carla, capable of taking over the ranch when your parents died."

"I don't know how you expect me to be friends with her yet never let her see Danny," Carla said. "Even if he weren't my brother, she's bound to meet him in Overlin. It's not a large town."

Danny's posture had continued to wilt—his gaze falling to the floor—until he looked like he was trying to become invisible. Kesney had made him see the reality of the situation in ways that his sister hadn't. Now he raised his head and looked straight at Kesney.

"I can make sure she never sees me."

"How?" Kesney asked.

"Never mind that. I just want you to know that I love Beth. I'd never do anything to hurt her."

"I'm sure you wouldn't. It's just—"

But Danny had turned and walked into the part of the house that led to his bedroom.

Kesney turned to Carla. "What's he going to do?"

"I don't know, but you don't have to worry about it. He's given you what you came for. Now you'd better get back to your daughter."

Kesney went from protective father to unhappy suitor.

"I didn't want to do this," he said to Carla. "I really like Danny, but I can't have Beth thinking of marriage at her age."

Carla's gaze remained fixed, her eyes cold. "I don't know that you can stop her from thinking of it, but neither Danny nor I will do anything to encourage her. Now I have to clear away breakfast and change the dressing on Ivan's arm to make sure it's not infected."

As though reminded of an oversight, Kesney turned to Ivan. "Thank you for protecting Carla from that drunk. I've been upset with myself for leaving her, but I was worried about Beth."

"No need to thank me. Any man would have done what I did." Ivan didn't like the way Kesney intimated he had some ownership of Carla. From the change in her expression, Carla didn't like it, either.

"I'm sure Beth is chewing her nails worrying about what you're saying to Danny," Carla said. "You'd better get home and reassure her that there was no fight and that all will be well in the end."

Kesney tried to apologize. "I'm sorry about this."

Carla stopped him by standing up and moving to the door. "There's no need. I understand completely. Now you'd better go."

There wasn't much else Kesney could do but leave. He did so reluctantly.

"He has some nerve," Carla said once she closed the door behind him.

"That went better than I expected," Ivan said. "From the way Danny looked, I thought Kesney would come in shouting and making threats."

"I wasn't talking about that," Carla said. "He talked like he owned me, like it was *his* responsibility to protect me."

Ivan knew it was stupid to be happy that Carla was irritated with a man who seemed to truly like her and who could give her a comfortable life. If he were really interested in what was best for Carla, he'd encourage her to fall in love with Kesney rather than develop an interest in him. There was no future in such a relationship, but he couldn't stop himself from feeling happy he'd gained a little in Carla's regard.

"I'll set him straight next time I see him." Apparently feeling that she had dealt with the issue, Carla turned her attention to Ivan. "How is your arm? You didn't roll over on it during the night and start it bleeding again, did you?"

"My arm is fine. I told Danny I would ride with him."

"Let me look at it first."

Ivan was used to Cade's wife giving orders to the cowhands when it came to taking care of them, but it felt especially nice to have Carla do it. He warned himself not to get used to it. Nothing had changed. He was still there to take half of Carla's ranch. Carla removed the bandage. After assuring herself that his wound really was better, she covered it with a salve she said her mother had taught her to make then bandaged it up again.

"I know I can't stop you from getting in the saddle today. You may be Polish, but you're just as stubborn as any Texan."

Whatever else she might have said was cut off when they heard footsteps leading to the front door followed by the door slamming.

"I've got to see what Danny's doing."

"Let me," Ivan said. "He has no reason to be angry with me."

"But I'm his sister."

"The sister who just told him he could not have the woman he wants."

"Woman! Beth is still a girl." Carla struggled with herself for a moment. "Okay, but you've got to tell me everything he says."

"When a boy gets to be seventeen, there are some things a sister should not know."

"Don't you dare keep anything from me. He's my brother. I'm responsible for him."

Ivan got to his feet and walked toward Carla. "I have to go before Danny rides away without me."

"Ivan Nikolai, if you dare—"

The kiss Ivan dropped on her forehead caused her to break off without finishing her sentence. "Stop worrying. I will do what I can."

"What can you do? You hardly know him."

Ivan shrugged. He didn't know, but he wouldn't find

out standing there arguing with Carla. He gave her a quick smile and left the house.

He found Danny leaving the bunkhouse, his saddle-bags over his shoulder.

"Where are you going?"

Danny kept walking toward the corral where he kept his horse. "To join Riley," he said. "Any hope I had of asking Kesney for the foreman's job just got blasted to kingdom come."

Ivan wondered why Texans couldn't speak a language that could be understood by ordinary people. "What about Carla?"

"What about her?" Danny tossed his saddlebags to the ground, picked up a rope, and entered the corral.

"She's depending on you to take care of the ranch."

Danny cut his favorite horse out of the herd. "She doesn't need me. She's got you. I'm not even sure she wants me."

"You know better than that."

Danny's lasso settled over the head of his horse which came to him willingly. "I guess so, but I seem to mess up everything I touch. Maybe it's better for everyone if I disappear for a while."

"How will working for Riley make you a suitable candidate for Beth's hand?"

Danny laughed as he brought his horse over to the corral fence to saddle him. "*Suitable candidate for Beth's hand*," he mimicked. "You sound like a Polish prince when you talk like that."

"And you sound like a Texan when you talk about blasting things to kingdom come."

Danny placed the saddlecloth on his horse and smoothed out the wrinkles. "It means I don't have a chance."

"Riley will not pay you much money. How will that help?"

Danny placed his saddle on his horse and started to tighten the girth. "Riley's men don't just go after herds stolen from around Overlin. They also look for cows that have been stolen from ranches in other parts of Texas. He says ranchers will pay to have their herds returned to him. Everybody in his group gets a share."

Riley was here to protect Texas ranchers, but from the first Ivan had been certain he had found a way to profit from it as well.

Danny finished strapping his saddlebags into position. "You've got to stay here to take care of Carla," he said to Ivan. "You're the only man who didn't become half-witted the minute he clapped eyes on her. If you weren't set on going back to Poland, I'd try to talk you into marrying her."

Ivan's stomach seemed to rise up in his chest making him short of breath. "Why would you do that?"

"Because you'd be the kind of husband she needs." Danny swung into the saddle. "She'll probably marry Kesney and lead him around by the nose."

Ivan despaired of ever understanding half of what was said to him. "I am not the husband for your sister."

"No. She's too bossy." He rode his horse out of the corral. Ivan put the rails up behind him.

"When will you be back?" Ivan asked. "What can I tell Carla?"

"Nothing except I'll take care of myself."

"You must. She has no one but you."

Danny leveled a measuring look at Ivan. "I'm not so sure."

Ivan watched the boy ride away, his thoughts divided between what Danny meant by that last remark, and worry that Danny was about to get involved in something that was not what it seemed.

—₩—

It had been Carla's worst day since she learned Danny had lost his half of the ranch. Every time she heard a sound, even those she knew had nothing to do with a horse, she would rush to a window to see if Danny had returned. In between, she'd wandered about the house, starting one task after another. Half the time she would forget what she had intended to do. Other times she would decide the task could wait until later. She gave up trying to cook. Her concentration was so shattered she wasn't able to remember whether she'd used one egg or two... or any eggs at all. She wanted someone to talk to, had even started to dress for a ride into town, but didn't know what she'd do when she got there.

To keep herself from pacing senselessly from one room to another, she settled on the sofa in the front room. She needed to dust—one always needed to dust in Texas—but she would do that later. Maybe.

After telling her what Danny intended to do, Ivan had offered to stay with her. She was sorely tempted, but this was something she had to deal with alone. She had been brokenhearted when her parents died, but taking over management of the ranch had helped her get through her grief. She resented the struggle to get everybody in Overlin to stop thinking of her as a girl and start thinking of her as a woman capable of managing a successful ranch, but she had known what she wanted and how to get it. She even had two handsome and successful men courting her.

Then Danny lost that card game, and everything changed.

Now her life was filled with things she couldn't control. To make matters worse, she was no longer sure of what she wanted. She was falling in love with a man who didn't love her and was planning to sell half of her ranch so he could go back to Poland. She had tried to deny that she was doing anything so foolish, but she found herself turning to Ivan, certain he could make everything right, wanting him to be there to do the same thing in the future. She'd sent him away when what she really wanted to do was lean against his broad chest and cry in frustration.

She knew what she would have answered if either Kesney Hardin or Maxwell Dodge had asked to marry her. She could see herself being the wife of either man, but she felt no desire to change her situation. She was only nineteen, and she liked her freedom.

Then Ivan Nikolai had entered her life, and she started doing things she'd never dreamed she would do. From being furious at him and trying to drive him away, it was only a few days before she'd progressed to wanting him to take her in his arms and tell her everything was going to be all right.

Too restless and irritable to stay seated, she got to her feet intending to go to the kitchen for a glass of water. As she turned, she glanced out the front window and caught a glimpse of a rider approaching at a fast gallop. Her curiosity aroused, she opened the front door and stepped out on the porch.

"I think it's Beth Hardin," Ivan said.

Startled, Carla turned to see Ivan seated in a chair on the far corner of the porch. "I thought you were working on your plan to pipe water into the house."

"I've done all I can without going inside. I didn't want to bother you."

It touched her to know he'd respected her wish to be alone yet had remained close. "I can't stay in hiding forever." She looked toward the rapidly approaching rider who she now could see was indeed Beth Hardin. "I wish I didn't have to face Beth just yet. I have no idea what to tell her."

"Do you want me to talk to her?"

She wondered what it was about this man that caused him to be willing, even eager, to help anyone he could. He was like some large, benevolent presence ready to fix whatever was wrong, but this was something she had to do. Danny was her brother.

"I'll talk to her."

Ivan nodded, but she was relieved when he didn't leave. Beth was close enough for Carla to see she had been crying. Her tears had left wet trails down her cheeks that glistened in the sun. Carla hoped she wasn't hysterical. She'd never had to deal with a woman in that state and wouldn't know what to do. She wasn't given much time to consider the problem. Beth brought her horse to a stop at the base of the steps. Nearly blinded by her tears, she stumbled up the steps and threw herself into Carla's arms. It was several minutes before Beth was calm enough to speak.

"Where is Danny? I've got to see him."

"Let's go inside," Carla suggested. "It's hot out here."

Beth's dark brown eyes were filled with desperation. "I don't care how hot it is. I don't care about *anything*. I just want Danny."

"Have you talked to your father?"

"I no longer have a father. He turned into a monster determined to ruin my life."

Despite her protests, Beth allowed Carla to lead her to the kitchen where she washed Beth's tear-stained cheeks. After she drank some water, Carla led her to the table. When they were all seated, Carla said, "Now tell me what happened."

Beth's story was accompanied by fresh bouts of tears. When she told her father about her feelings for Danny, her thoughts crowded with visions of a blissful future, she had expected him to be glad for her. She had never believed he would say she was too young to start courting, refuse to consider marriage in anything but the distant future. She had been so upset, she'd fled to her room, determined to stay there until he could see reason. She would never have done that if she'd realized he meant to find Danny and tell him to stay away from her. She nearly fainted when he told her what he'd done.

"I guess I went crazy. I started screaming. I don't remember half the things I said, but I'm sure it was terrible. I know I said I hated him."

"I'm sure he knows you don't," Carla said.

"I hit him and threw things at him. He finally locked me in my room and said I couldn't come out until I got hold of myself."

"Does he know you're here?"

"No. I crawled out my window. I knew if I didn't see Danny I'd truly go crazy. Where is he?"

"He's not here."

"Has he gone to see Papa? If Papa is cruel to him, I'll never forgive him."

"I don't know where he's gone, but I do know he didn't go to see your father."

Some of the wildness left Beth's eyes to be replaced by a fear that made her look older than her sixteen years. "Has he run away?"

Carla supposed that was the easiest explanation. "He was very upset when your father said he wouldn't allow Danny to see you."

"He can't stop me," Beth declared, the wildness back in her eyes. "I'll find Danny, and we'll run away together."

"Danny would never do that."

"Of course he will. He loves me." She stopped, the fear back. "He does love me, doesn't he?"

"Danny feels about you the way you feel about him, but he is too honorable to talk you into running away."

"I'll go willingly."

"Danny loves you too much to ruin your life," Carla said.

"Not being with him is ruining my life," Beth declared.

"Danny has no job, no money, no way to support a wife. That is not the kind of life he would want for you."

"I don't care. I'll live in a tent."

"No, you won't because Danny won't let you," Carla said.

"He will. I know he will. Where is he? I know you know. Did Papa tell you to keep him from me?"

Carla didn't see any reason to keep Beth in the dark. "He's headed to Mexico with Riley. I don't know when they'll get back."

"Why did he go? Because Papa said he told him to stay away from me," she said, answering her own question. Then she covered her face with her hands and broke into tears.

"You and Danny only met last night," Carla said. "Your father thinks you need time to get to know each other."

Beth dropped her hands. Tears rolled down her cheeks. "You agree with him, don't you?"

"I think both you and Danny are too young to be thinking about marriage."

"In Kentucky lots of girls were married by my age."

"I'm not ready to be married yet, and I'm older than you."

"I don't want to be an old maid."

"I don't want to be an old maid, either."

"Then why have you turned down everybody who's asked you?"

Carla was so shocked she couldn't stop herself from asking, "Where did you hear that?"

"Everybody says you want to run this ranch more than you want a husband."

Carla wasn't sure how this conversation had suddenly become about her, but she wasn't willing to discuss her personal life with a hysterical girl who could be trusted to repeat everything she heard.

"Someone is coming." Ivan rose and went to the front room.

Beth stopped crying with a hiccup. "It's my father." She looked like a scared rabbit. "I've got to hide."

"You'll do no such thing. If it is your father, it wouldn't do any good to hide with your horse out front."

Ivan came back into the kitchen. "It is Kesney. I will wait for him."

"Pull yourself together," Carla said to Beth as Ivan left. "Your father loves you. He wouldn't do anything to hurt you."

"Yes, he would. He won't let me see Danny."

Carla didn't answer. Having no one to argue with, Beth's hysterics quickly ran out of steam. She leaned on the table, a dejected figure whose crying had dwindled into an occasional sniff. She didn't look up when her father entered the kitchen.

"Why did you run away?" Kesney asked his daughter.

"She came looking for Danny," Carla explained when Beth didn't answer. She gestured to Beth who was looking more like a child than a rapidly maturing teenager. "She's calmer now, so maybe she'll listen to what you have to say. Take as long as you need."

Carla left the kitchen. Rather than look for Ivan or wait in the front room for Kesney to finish his conversation with his daughter, she headed out the back door. Beth's words had shaken her down to her foundation. Why did everyone think she was determined to be an old maid, or that she wanted to run her ranch more than she wanted a husband?

It was still morning, but the sun was so hot, she immediately sought shade in the grove of trees her father had planted. The shade was sparse because the trees were young, and there was nothing to sit on but a chair with a broken back, but anything was better than staying in the house.

She didn't consider herself old, and she did want to have a family so why did everyone think she wanted to run the ranch more than have a husband? Why didn't they think it was possible to do both?

She had turned down some proposals, but she hadn't turned down Kesney or Dodge because they hadn't proposed. Surely people would realize that if she'd refused them, they wouldn't still be courting her. She'd made it very clear when they first expressed interest in her that she enjoyed their company but wasn't ready to get married. They had accepted her limitations so readily that at times she'd wondered if either man was *really* interested in more than pleasant company for an occasional dinner.

She expected to feel insulted, at least annoyed, thus she was unprepared to realize she didn't care what either man thought about her. There was, however, one man whose opinion was important to her.

Ivan.

How could she be so stupid as to allow herself to become emotionally involved with a man who announced when he arrived that he was leaving in a year? He was constantly in her thoughts. It was as though she'd been waiting for him for her life to start.

That thought so disgusted Carla she got to her feet. She was *not* a weak, mindless female who had to lean on some man before she could think. In fact, Ivan had the opposite effect on her. She'd noticed a tendency not to think at all when she was with him. Ignoring the sun bearing down on her bare head, she turned toward an old, lightning-scarred cottonwood that grew alongside the dry wash a short distance from the house. Ever since her family moved to this ranch, it had been where she would go when she wanted to be alone. Maybe it was the isolation, or maybe it was the size. Or it could be the tree having survived one crisis after another that gave her comfort?

Today had confronted her with more questions than answers. Ivan didn't love her. He was going back to Poland. What was she going to do when she found herself separated from the man she loved by four thousand miles, five hundred years of history, and an impossible language? Would she go with him to Poland if he asked?

That question so startled her she was beginning to think the heat had affected her brain despite the shade of the venerable tree. Its leaves hung in the dead air, motionless and dust-covered. In one sense she felt the same, her life motionless, hemmed in by problems not of her making, unable to find solutions even as the difficulties seemed to grow and multiply around her.

On the other hand, she simmered with compressed energy. She wanted to go, to do, to be, but where to go, what to do, who to be? Somewhere in this Gordian knot that was her life there had to be a thread that, when pulled, would make sense of everything, but she had no idea what that thread might be.

She became aware of the sound of approaching footsteps on the rough, rocky soil. Using her hands to shade her eyes against the glare of the sun, she looked into the face of the man who'd somehow captured her heart.

Chapter 15

IVAN HAD BEEN TROUBLED WHEN CARLA DIDN'T COME in search of him after she left Kesney and his daughter. She hadn't been behaving like herself recently. She didn't grind her teeth when she saw him. She didn't scowl and turn her back when he entered the house. She didn't treat him like he was Laveau diViere in a different skin. She was acting as though she actually *liked* him. She listened to him, occasionally even sought his advice. They'd shared the conversation with Beth like they were equally involved. Either she was too devastated by Danny's leaving to think properly, or she was coming down with something.

When he saw she'd taken refuge under the cottonwood, he didn't know whether to join her or leave her to adjust to the fact that Danny had reached the point in his life where he was starting to make his own decisions. The devastated look on her face when she looked up and saw him ended his hesitation.

"I wondered where you went," he said when he reached her.

For a moment, she looked at him as though he was a stranger. He couldn't decide what he saw in her eyes. This was so unlike Carla he was starting to grow worried. She almost flinched when he reached out to her. He couldn't understand what had happened to bring about such a drastic change in her. She'd never been afraid of him. Was she that angry at him for not stopping Danny? Should he have said something different to Beth or her father? He couldn't think of anything to say except, "You should not be outside in this heat."

His words seemed to bring her back to an awareness of herself and her surroundings. The baffled look disappeared, but it didn't appear to bring any relief from whatever had made her look at him so strangely.

"I wanted to give Kesney and Beth plenty of privacy."

Something else was bothering her, and he didn't believe he was Danny. "You are troubled?"

"Of course I'm *troubled*," she said. "With all the things that have happened recently, who wouldn't be?"

He was relieved to have back the Carla he knew, even if it meant she was angry at him again. "Something new seems to worry you."

She turned away from him. "There's nothing new. Why do you ask?"

"You do not look at me. Have I done something to hurt you?"

"How could you when Myrtle has declared you're the most nearly perfect man in Texas?"

He wasn't very good at understanding women, but he understood enough to recognize sarcasm. Carla sounded jealous. Upset. Angry. He wondered why it should be that the only woman he'd been seriously attracted to in America should dislike him so. "I am not nearly perfect."

"I know, but why am I the only one who can see it? And even then, I can't bring myself to dislike you as I should."

Seeing Carla caught in the toils of misery, he wanted to take her in his arms and comfort her. He wanted more than that. He wanted to kiss her. This wasn't the hot flame of passion he'd experienced twelve years ago. Rather it was steadily growing warmth that embraced him instead of throwing him off balance with its suddenness and ferocity. It might have been its gradualness that had caused him to underestimate its strength. But now, it could no longer be denied.

Yet even as his body leaned in her direction, he reminded himself he was going back to Poland. He couldn't imagine never seeing his home again, yet it could never be Carla's home. Poland wouldn't be any more comfortable with her than she would be with it. So why did he find it hard to think of his life without Carla in it?

"I am glad that you cannot dislike me because I like you," Ivan said.

The news didn't appear to make Carla any happier. "Wonderful. We can be friends. That will make Myrtle happy."

"I do not like you to make Myrtle happy. I like you because it makes *me* happy."

Carla's gaze narrowed. "What are you trying to say?"

"That I like you."

Carla relaxed, or did she deflate? "You like Danny, Beth, Myrtle, and Sadie. You like practically everybody."

"Not in the same way I like you." He moved his hand to her waist. "I like you in the way a man likes a woman." He shouldn't have said that. He shouldn't have touched her. He shouldn't have started this whole conversation, but he couldn't stop himself. It was important to know she didn't hate him. But rather than lend a sense of relief, he was suddenly filled with nearly unbearable tension. This wasn't enough. He had to know more. Feelings he had worked hard to suppress burst their bonds. He was losing control, and he couldn't do anything about it. Without warning, he leaned forward and kissed Carla on the lips.

Carla jumped back, eyes wide with surprise and bright with accusation. "Why did you do that?" It was a cry of protest rather than a question. "You're going back to Poland. I'm staying in Texas. What good is starting something we know can never last?"

He shouldn't have done it. It went against his personal code of behavior, but he couldn't control the impulse. It was something he had to do, even if he could only do it once. "I just want to be with you. It makes me happy. I would like to make you happy."

"Why? So you could have more memories of a tragic love affair to take back to Poland?"

Until now Ivan hadn't allowed himself to think too much about a future for him and Carla. She'd been so clear in her disdain for him, it hadn't seemed possible. But he couldn't spend the next eleven months seeing her every day and say nothing. "If we have feelings for each other, they will come out."

"They don't have to." He reached for her when she turned away, but she took a step back.

"Could you face the next eleven months knowing you loved me but were unable to say anything?" Ivan asked.

"It would be easier than falling in love despite knowing you were going to leave."

"Can you control whether you love somebody?"

"Can't you?"

"No. And I do not want to. Being in love is the most wonderful feeling in the world."

"Is that the way you felt when that girl's father told you you could never see her again?"

"I thought there was no reason to go on living."

"So why would it be different this time?"

"I am not eighteen. I am not burning up with the fever of love."

For the first time Carla didn't seem to be trying to get away from him. "What are you feeling?"

Did he know? Was it clear enough in his mind to put it into words she could understand? He'd never tried to explain something like this because he'd never felt like this. "It is a lot of little things. I like being with you. I like making you smile. I like thinking of you when we are apart. I like doing things for you when you let me."

"You sound like a Good Samaritan rather than a star-crossed lover."

Another confusing expression, but his mother had made sure he knew lots of Bible stories. "Rather than leave you in the care of the innkeeper, I would stay by your side until you were well."

"But you aren't going to stay by my side. You're going to leave."

"Not for a long time yet."

Carla's gaze locked on him and didn't waver. He didn't have to wonder what thoughts were going through her mind. She was trying to talk herself out of saying anything. Inbred chivalry said he ought to step back and give her time to make up her own mind, but he had already broken through that restraint. Even if she never spoke of it again, he had to know if she felt about him the way he felt about her. He stepped forward and took her hands in his. She tried to pull away, but he wouldn't release her.

"Let me go."

"Not until you answer my question."

"You won't like my answer."

"I want it nonetheless."

She refused to meet his gaze. "I don't love you. I don't want to marry you. I wish you'd never come here."

"Look at me. Look at me!" he repeated when she didn't heed him. When she did look at him, he had his answer, but it was necessary for her to say the words. "Now tell me that you wish I had never come here."

"I wish you had never come here." The words were monotone with no emotion behind them whatsoever. No venom. No spark. "Then I'd never have been so foolish to fall for a man who was going to sell half my ranch and leave me in the bargain."

She tried to pull away, but when Ivan managed to get his arms around her, her resistance collapsed, and she fell into his embrace. No sooner had she done that then she burst into tears. Ivan had always thought himself a stalwart man, steady in battle, dependable in all things, but he had no idea what to do when it came to a woman in tears. How could he tell her how happy it made him when it made her so miserable?

He couldn't, so he wrapped both arms around her and pulled her close. Inexplicably, that made her cry harder. He kissed the top of her head, but Carla pounded on his chest and kept on crying. Yielding to what he'd wanted to do all along, he put his hand under her chin, raised her face to his, and kissed her. This wasn't a soft brushing of lips or a quick kiss before stepping back. It was the kind of kiss that claimed her as his own, the kind that asked her to let go of all her doubts and listen to her heart. It was the kind of kiss he'd always dreamed of sharing with the woman he loved. Deep... searing... demanding... an outward expression of his inner capacity and desire to love and be loved.

Carla gulped, hiccupped, stopped crying, and kissed him back.

It had been so long since Ivan had kissed a woman and had a woman kiss him back, he'd forgotten its emotional force. He felt neither stalwart nor steadfast. His knees didn't buckle, but they felt like they might. His heart hammered so wildly he felt breathless. His strength seemed to drain away at the same time a wave of energy coursed through his body. His brain was spinning so fast it was all he could do to hold on to one complete thought. *Kissing Carla was more incredible than any kiss he experienced twelve years ago*. When Carla broke their kiss and turned away, it was like having all his underpinnings yanked away.

"I hope you're satisfied," she said softly.

"How can a man in love be satisfied with a single kiss? Can a starving man be nourished with scarcely more than a crumb? Can a man know joy if his heart beats only once? I want you! *All of you*. All the time." Falling in love with Carla had awakened a longing that made him disregard everything he'd been taught about how a gentleman should treat a woman, especially the woman he loved. He wanted to crush her in his embrace, make scorching love to her, and claim her as his forever. He couldn't back away now. He could only go forward. He pulled Carla back into his arms.

"Both of us have tried to deny our feelings," Ivan said. "It is time to bring them out in the open and discover their true nature."

"Let me go." Carla didn't struggle, just asked to be released.

Ivan was reluctant. It felt good to have his arms around her. In the aftermath of the devastation of his first love, he'd devoted himself to his studies and avoided any emotional relationship. When he came to America, he'd been too busy fighting a war, which gave him virtually no opportunity to meet the same woman twice. After he moved to Texas, Cade's ranch was too far from San Antonio for anything except occasional visits. Coming to Overlin was the first chance in ten years he'd had to get to know a woman who wasn't married or a grandmother.

Despite the nearly overwhelming need to follow his own desires rather than Carla's wishes, he could feel his training beginning to reassert its hold on him. He could indulge his own needs when he was sure that's what Carla really wanted. When it wasn't, he had to step back.

When he dropped his arms to his side, Carla moved away from him, straightening her clothes, which didn't need straightening, and patting her hair, which wasn't disarranged. Once she was satisfied that all traces of her momentary indulgence had been erased, she turned to Ivan.

"We don't need to *bring things out in the open*. We need to forget this ever happened."

"How can I forget what it felt like to hold you in my arms, to kiss you, to feel your heart beating against mine?"

"The same way I'm going to forget it. By putting it out of my mind."

Ivan took Carla's hands. He didn't let go until she

looked at him. "That will not work. I will think of this moment, feel it... yearn for it, whenever I see you. I will dream of it every night. You will do the same."

Carla reclaimed her hands and moved a step back, but she didn't look away. "I won't let myself do any of that," she declared. "To do so would be foolishly indulgent as well as ignoring common sense."

"You would not think like that if you were Polish. You would embrace love with all you possess. You would take it in your two hands and hold it fast for fear you would miss a single moment. You would nurture it for fear it would grow weak from neglect. You would think of it, talk of it, sing of it."

"And Danny would have me locked away in a home for the insane."

"You are not being serious."

"You're the one who's not being serious. The way you're talking, I could think you were younger than Beth. At least she didn't talk about *singing* about love."

"Do most Americans have no hearts, or does something happen to them when they get older?"

"Stop talking nonsense. We have hearts like everybody else, even like people in Poland."

"If that were true, you would not be afraid of love."

Carla acted like he'd insulted her. "I'm not afraid of love, you, or anything."

"If that were true, you would kiss me again."

"Why would I do anything as stupid as that?"

"Because you want it, but you are afraid you will like it too much."

"Of all the conceited, egotistical comments I've ever heard, that takes the cake."

Ignoring another phrase that made no sense, Ivan said, "I only say what I feel to be true."

"Then put this in your pipe and smoke it. You can forget my feelings for you. Whatever they are, I'm not going to let them lead me into making the biggest mistake of my life. You're a fascinating man spilling over with charm and a devastating smile, which you don't hesitate to use. However, you're going back to Poland as soon as you can. From what you've told me about it, I'd be foolish to consider marrying and going back with you."

"You have thought of doing that?" He was shocked.

Carla ignored his question. "You need a wife who understands your customs, your history, preferably one who's rich so you can go back to being a prince."

"I place no value in that title."

Carla shook her head. "You can't not value it because everyone else in your country does. It would be the same as saying Kesney doesn't value the money that makes him the richest and most influential man in Overlin."

"A title can't buy anything. Money can."

"A title gives you social position money could never buy. Now it's time to put an end to this conversation. I shouldn't have let you kiss me, but my feelings are out in the open as you wanted. Now we won't speak of them again because that's what I want. Are you sure your arm is well enough for you to ride? I'm going into town. I need to hire someone to help you until Danny comes back."

Ivan didn't want to turn his back on their conversation. He didn't know what to do about his feelings for Carla, but he didn't want to pretend they didn't exist.

Yet he could tell from Carla's compressed lips that she would stop talking to him if he persisted. "I will finish working on the pipes to bring the water into the house."

"That'll be even harder on your arm."

"I can manage."

"Do you want to interview any man I might hire?"

"No. I trust your judgment."

Carla lingered, apparently trying to decide whether to say something more. Finally, with a shrug, she turned and walked away.

Ivan felt like she was pulling something out of him, that each step separating them added to his emptiness. He didn't understand how his feelings for her could have developed so deeply so suddenly, but there was no point in denying that they had. How could he figure out what to do when Carla refused to talk about it? He thought he could get her to change her mind, but was that fair? Could he, in good conscience, encourage her to explore her feelings for him when he knew he was leaving and there was no chance she would go with him?

He knew the answer to that question, but he didn't know whether he could stop himself from falling even more deeply in love. It had been so long, he'd forgotten that falling in love wasn't something you did out of choice. It was something that happened whether or not you were ready. He was ready. It was the time and situation that were all wrong.

Carla poured the peaches out of the jar into a bowl and placed it on the table. She checked the biscuits and stirred the beef stew. She placed the butter on the table and reached for the bucket to get water before remembering she never had to go to the well again. Ivan had installed a pump inside the kitchen. He'd promised to build a water tower before he left, so all she had to do was turn a knob, and water would flow into her kitchen on its own. He also said something about an indoor bathroom, but she couldn't imagine that such a contraption as he described could work.

She stopped pacing to rub her hands on her apron. Her palms were sweating but not from the heat. Ivan would soon come in for supper. It would be the first time she'd faced him since that morning. Just thinking about it made her want to hide. She'd almost hired an unsatisfactory cowhand just to have someone to keep her from being alone with Ivan. Fortunately she wasn't that much of a coward. At least not yet.

She was kidding herself if she thought she could put Ivan out of her mind. She *might* have succeeded before she knew the nature of his feelings. Now that was all she could think of. She found herself comparing every potential cowhand to him. Even Kesney and Maxwell Dodge slipped a few notches. When it came to Ivan, objectivity, logic, even common sense, flew out the window. That's what had her so upset. She'd never acted like this. Her thinking had always been methodical and logical, never clouded by her feelings. But ever since Ivan had arrived, she was a bundle of emotions, all out of control.

Making a determined effort to calm her nerves, she checked the biscuits. They were almost ready so she went to the door and opened it. Ivan was sitting in a chair in a tiny band of shade cast by the house and drawing on a piece of paper. He looked up when he heard the door open, smiled when he saw her. It didn't seem to matter how many times he smiled at her. It affected her just as powerfully as the first time. It erased any desire to behave rationally or think unemotionally. In that moment, nothing mattered but that he loved her. It wasn't logical, and it wasn't rational, but she didn't care.

"It's time to eat," she said. "I'm taking the biscuits out." She didn't give him time to respond before she went back inside. If merely seeing him could affect her so strongly, it was going to take every bit of her self-control to get through supper without throwing herself into his arms. As satisfying as that would be… it would only make things worse.

She didn't realize how badly his smile had flustered her until she burned her hand taking out the biscuits. She had done that hundreds of times. How could she have been so clumsy?

"What's wrong?"

She hardly realized she'd uttered an expletive she'd picked up from Danny until Ivan spoke. "I just burned my hand." She dumped the biscuits into the waiting bowl, but Ivan stepped between her and the table, took the bowl out of her hands.

"Let me see."

"It's nothing."

"Let me see." He spoke softly, even respectfully of her right to refuse, but he was like a large boulder, a force that could not be deflected. He seemed to surround her, to encompass her, to absorb any desire to refuse. The small burn was on the side of her thumb, a single line where her skin had brushed against the biscuit pan, but it stung. It was red, a blister already forming. She held out her hand.

He took it in his. His hand was so much larger, the fingers so much longer and broader, that her hand looked like that of a child. She felt embarrassed, somehow inferior. His touch was gentle, but his skin was rough from working without gloves.

"We need some ice."

Did he really ask for ice? She felt like she was in some kind of daze, maybe suspended animation. Thoughts floated through her head with the sluggish movement of clouds on a hot summer afternoon, their meaning often staying just beyond her grasp. "This is south Texas. We don't have ice, not even in the winter."

"Then cold water will have to do. I will find some." He flashed a quick smile then it was gone.

When he walked out the door, she felt like the air had been sucked out of her lungs, the strength out of her body. She felt so weak she was tempted to sit down, but she wasn't going to give in to weakness no matter how enervating. She was not a silly girl even if she sometimes felt like it. He didn't need to leave when supper was on the table and getting cold. She didn't need cold water. Anyway, where could he find cold water when it was like an inferno outside?

She put her mouth on the burn. The moisture made it feel better. Her reflection in the window surprised a laugh out of her. She looked like she was sucking her thumb, something her mother said she'd never done even as a baby. With a shake of her head, she took her thumb out of her mouth and walked to her place at the table. She wondered how long it would be before Ivan returned. She wondered if she should put everything back on the stove to keep warm, or if she should begin without waiting for him. She had a strong dislike of cold stew, even in summer. She heard Ivan's footsteps before he opened the kitchen door. He carried the water in a large jug.

"If this is creek water, it'll be as hot as if I had heated it on this stove," she said.

"This did not come from the creek. It came from a spring that is below water level except when the creek falls to almost nothing. I found it when I was building the water line to the kitchen. Put your hand in."

Carla was prepared for slightly cool water, but the liquid in the jug felt icy cold. "It feels like ice."

"You would not say that if you had grown up in Poland. Some winters are so cold ice will burn your skin."

Carla didn't understand how that could happen, but she wasn't interested in the explanation. Ivan was looking at her in a way that made everything else seem insignificant—even her burned thumb. Her mother had once told her a fairy tale about a little girl who stared too long into the eyes of an evil serpent and became hypnotized. That's how she felt now, as though she was slowly losing touch with reality, that nothing existed except Ivan. She fought off the feeling with a determined shake of her head. "My hand feels better now. We should eat before everything gets cold."

"Let me see."

Ivan lifted her hand out of the water and patted it dry with the tail of his shirt. He turned it one way in the light and then the other. He touched the small blister with his fingertip. "Does that hurt?"

"No." It probably did, but she couldn't feel anything. Her whole body was numb.

He lifted her hand to his lips and blew gently on her blistered thumb. "Does this make it feel better?"

Carla was sure she was either going to faint or suffer some kind of stroke. Her whole body was feeling out of sorts. Hot and cold chased each other through her veins. Her nerve endings were so inflamed Ivan's fingers felt like hot coils pressed against her skin. Her pulse thrummed in her temples, yet she felt like the blood was draining away from her brain. She felt unable to breathe.

"Are you all right?"

She answered without conscious thought. "Of course. Why do you ask?"

"You look a little pale."

"It's just the heat."

"Are you sure?"

She wasn't sure of anything, least of all why she should look pale when her face felt flushed with heat. She couldn't think when her hand was clasped in Ivan's, when he was so close she could feel his breath on her cheek, when the urge to move closer, to reach up and pull him down into a kiss, was so powerful it obliterated nearly everything else. She had been prepared to face him across the supper table. She wasn't prepared for this. Any of it.

"You should sit down."

"No." She didn't know why she said that. Ivan would have let go of her hand, and she would have been able to regain her senses, but she couldn't make herself say the words because she didn't want to be released.

Ivan must have understood what she was thinking,

what she was feeling, because his hold on her hand grew firmer. His look of concern turned to something quite different. Carla had seen that look in the eyes of many men and learned to be wary of it, but she felt none of that with Ivan. Rather it reached out to kindle a similar feeling inside her.

She had granted only a few men the privilege of a chaste kiss and a quick hug. The moments she'd spent in Ivan's arms earlier that morning had proved she would accept a lot more from him, that she *wanted* more. That fact that their relationship was impossible didn't change that. She willingly moved into Ivan's embrace. She welcomed his arms as they embraced her. She breathed in his nearness. She forgot her burned finger. She didn't care if supper got cold. All that mattered was that she was in his arms, that in the next moment he would kiss her.

A series of loud knocks on the front door shattered the moment.

Chapter 16

CARLA DIDN'T KNOW A WORD OF POLISH, BUT SHE WAS certain the words Ivan uttered were profane. She felt much the same way, but the knock on the door had the effect of restoring her to her senses. She extricated herself from Ivan's embrace. "I'd better see who's at the door."

"Send them away. Your supper is getting cold."

She was surprised he remembered food was on the table. She hadn't, and she'd cooked it. She was not pleased to open the door and find Beth standing on her porch.

"Is Danny back?" Beth marched inside without waiting to be invited.

"No. He's not."

"When do you expect him?"

"I have no idea when Riley plans to leave, where he'll go, or when he might return."

Beth appeared on the verge of tears. "I've got to talk to him," she said, wringing her hands.

"Is anything wrong?"

"No. I just have to talk to him."

For an instant, Carla wondered if Beth might be pregnant, but the only time she and Danny had been together was at the dance. "You'll have to wait for him to come back just like I do. Does your father know where you are?"

"I told him I was coming to see you." Beth turned to Ivan. "Do you know where he's gone?"

"Nobody knows except Riley."

"Can you take me to his camp? Papa said it's on your land."

"You can't go there now," Carla said. "It's nearly dark, and their camp is hours away."

"Will you take me tomorrow?" Beth asked Ivan.

"I will not take you," Ivan told her, "but I will ride there tomorrow and see if I can find Danny."

"Why haven't you asked your father to take you?" Carla asked.

"You know he doesn't want Danny and me to be together."

"You can't expect Ivan to help you do something your father has forbidden," Carla said. "He would have every right to be furious with us."

"I don't care. I want to see Danny." With that, she flopped into the nearest chair and burst into tears.

Carla was on the verge of making a sharp retort when she looked at Ivan. He looked so flummoxed she nearly burst out laughing. "She's overemotional," she whispered. "She'll be okay once she has a good cry."

"Are you sure?"

"If she's not, you can get her father and let him deal with her."

Beth stopped crying abruptly. "I don't want to see my father. He's cruel and heartless. He doesn't understand what it means to be in love."

"He loved your mother very much," Carla said. "I doubt he's forgotten that."

"If he remembered, he wouldn't try to keep Danny and me apart."

Carla realized it was useless to attempt to reason

with Beth until she calmed down. "We were about to sit down to supper. Why don't you join us? You'll feel better after you eat something."

"I couldn't eat a thing," Beth proclaimed.

"Then sit with me while Ivan eats. I'm sure he's about to starve."

Beth got up with a pettish flounce. "My father can eat no matter what happens. I don't know how men can be so insensitive."

Carla winked at Ivan. "I don't know either, but it's a cross all women have to bear."

"Danny is not insensitive," Beth declared. "He understands my feelings exactly."

Carla knew Danny was just as insensitive to women's whims and moods as any other man, but that was something she would leave Beth to discover for herself.

It amused her that not only was Beth quick to take a seat at the table, but once she had placed food on Beth's plate despite her protests, the young woman managed to overcome her momentary distress sufficiently to eat a substantial meal. In-between chewing and swallowing, she treated them to a virtual sermon on Danny's virtues and how he was so different from other inferior men.

"You should be getting home," Carla said when Beth swallowed the last of her second buttered biscuit. "I'm sure your father is worried about you."

"He won't be home until late. He went into Overlin on some business."

"I will ride with you," Ivan offered.

"I can ride by myself. I'm not a baby."

"It is not safe for a young lady to ride alone at night."

"Why not?"

"We have rustlers," Carla said. "Have you forgotten they tried to run off your father's herd a while ago?"

"If they're after cows, they won't bother me."

"What they want is money," Ivan said. "You are worth far more to your father than his cows."

Apparently Beth hadn't thought of it in that light. "Okay, but you've got to tell me as soon as you find Danny."

"I don't expect to hear from him for several days. Maybe even a week."

"I'm sorry you got caught up in this," Carla whispered to Ivan. "I hate to think of you riding out to Riley's camp for nothing."

Rather than say anything, Ivan gave her hands a gentle squeeze.

"Time to go," he said to Beth. "If I have to be up early to look for Danny, I have to go to bed early."

While Ivan went to saddle his horse, Beth told Carla one more time that she had to tell her the instant they found Danny. She put forward several plans for relaying the information as quickly as possible, none of which took into consideration the time and effort these plans required of other people. Carla listened and nodded, aware that in Beth's present mood, she wasn't capable of thinking of other people. She felt sorry for Ivan. She was certain Beth would go over all her plans on their ride home and try to drag a whole string of promises from him. But Ivan would likely know exactly what to say to mollify her.

Carla wondered how Ivan managed to hold to his own principles without angering people who didn't agree with him. She'd always considered herself a reasonable woman, but nearly everybody had been angry with her at one time or another. Everybody seemed to adore Ivan. Even Lukey had started to trust him. It made her feel good that such a special man had fallen in love with her. Unfortunately, it was a love that couldn't have a happy ending.

―⁓―

Several days later, Carla was sitting at the kitchen table, grateful she'd gotten through another morning without yielding to her desire for Ivan and planning how to present her case against Laveau diViere to the judge in two days. The kitchen door opened without a warning knock. All thoughts of Laveau flew out of her head, and her heart leapt in anticipation. Had Ivan come back?

But it was Danny who strode through the door. Caught between disappointment that Ivan was still behaving as a gentleman and the shock of Danny's unexpected return, Carla couldn't move.

"I know I said some terrible things before I left," Danny told his sister, "but I never thought Ivan would be happier to see me than my sister."

The sound of his voice having released her from her paralysis, Carla jumped up from her chair, ran to her brother, and threw her arms around his neck. The force of her attack threw him backward against Ivan.

"I'm glad you're happy to see me," Danny said with a laugh, "but you don't have to knock me down."

Carla gave her brother a hard hug before she released him and stood back. "You deserve to be knocked down and stomped on for leaving me without a word of where you were going or when you were coming back."

"I told Ivan."

"Ivan's not your family. I am."

Danny glanced back at Ivan standing in the doorway who gave him a supportive smile. "I was feeling you were more like my mother," Danny said to his sister. "Ivan never lectures me."

Carla was too glad to see Danny home safely to start a brother-sister argument. "Come in, and tell me where you've been and what you've done. Are you hungry? It won't take a minute to heat something up." She was relieved he looked healthy and appeared to be in good spirits.

"I'm not hungry, and I can't stay long. I just came to tell you what I've been doing."

It was against Carla's instincts to allow anyone to sit down at the table without at least a cup of coffee, but she was too eager to learn what her brother had been doing. "Why did you go to Ivan first?"

Danny laughed and dropped into his usual seat at the table. "Apparently you've forgotten what happened just before I left."

"Don't be an idiot," Carla said without heat. "If I could still love you after losing half the ranch, I could love you despite falling in love with a mere child." She knew she'd said the wrong thing before the last words were out of her mouth. "Forget I said that. Tell me what you've been doing."

Danny's smile struggled before making a full recovery. "Making money," he said.

"How?"

"Finding herds that have been stolen and returning them to their owners."

"I thought Riley's men were supposed to do that for free."

"Lots of herds are stolen from other places from owners we can't identify. We bring them back and turn them over to people who find the real owners."

"And you get money for this?" Ivan asked.

"Yes."

"How much?" Carla asked.

"I didn't get a lot because I'm still learning," Danny said, "but I'll get more when I can help more."

"How will you do that?" Ivan asked.

Carla had been so elated about Danny's return she didn't want to interrupt him to ask Ivan why he was looking particularly solemn.

"When we go into Mexico, we don't all go as one group," Danny said. "We pair up and go in different directions. In a couple of days we meet at an appointed place. If we've found a stolen herd, we bring it back."

"This has to be dangerous," Carla said. "You're trying to reclaim cows from rustlers and thieves who won't hesitate to shoot you."

"That's why we get paid," Danny said. "Texas has no official authority in Mexico. The government can't go after these herds, but we can."

"Who do you deliver the herds to?" Ivan asked.

"I don't know. That's Riley's business. Have you seen Beth since I left?" Danny asked his sister.

"She comes by every day wanting to know if you're back. Have you tried to see her?"

Danny looked downcast. "I went there first, but her father wouldn't let me near the house. Will you invite her for supper?"

"Sorry, Danny, but I'm not going behind Kesney's back. Besides, if he knows you're home, he probably wouldn't let her out of the house."

"No point in staying then."

"You could stay because I'm your sister, and you haven't seen me in three days."

"Beth's father won't let her marry a pauper, and I can't make any money staying here." Danny got up and gave his sister a hug. "Don't worry about me. I'll be back in a few days."

"I can't help worrying when I know people are shooting at you."

"We go in at night. It's a lot easier than I thought. Why don't you go with me?" he said to Ivan. "You can make more money than you can taking care of Carla's cows."

"He has to take care of my cows because *you* won't," Carla told her brother.

"I can make a month's wages in a couple of days. By the time Beth is old enough for her father to let her marry me I'll have enough money to buy my own ranch."

Carla couldn't imagine her impulsive brother settling down and waiting the two or three years before Kesney thought Beth was old enough to marry, but she wasn't going to discourage him from thinking about the future rather than the next five minutes. She just wished he had found a less dangerous way to earn the money. "Do you need anything?" she asked. "Clothes, food, a new bedroll?"

"I've got everything I need. Now I'd better go." He gave Carla a peck on the cheek. "Take care of her," he said to Ivan. "She's not as strong as she thinks."

Carla stifled an impulse to take issue with that statement. She didn't want them to part on an angry note again. "Come see me as soon as you get back," she said. "I won't sleep soundly until you do."

"If you're going to lie awake, spend the time thinking about Ivan instead of me." He winked at Ivan. "I can't marry you."

Carla felt heat rush up the back of her neck. "Don't talk nonsense."

Danny laughed and disappeared through the door. Carla turned to Ivan, but he seemed to be deep in thought. "What's wrong? Do you think Danny is in some danger he didn't tell us about?"

"I do not know."

"Then what are you frowning about?"

"Have you ever heard of a rancher paying to have his herd returned from Mexico?"

"No."

"Neither have I."

"Is that all the evidence you have to set before me?" the judge asked.

"What more do you need?" Carla asked.

Her chance to place her case before the judge had finally arrived. Because Overlin was so small, the only available place for the judge to hold court was in the largest of the town's saloons. One advantage was that it allowed the judge to eat his meals while he held court. A disadvantage to the owner was that for the few hours a day that the judge spent listening to cases, everyone wanting beer or whiskey had to go to another saloon.

To compensate, everyone bringing a case had to pay a small fee to the saloon owner. Carla had no objection to paying the fee when there was a chance she could get her ranch back. The judge, however, didn't appear anxious to do that.

"What I need is real *evidence*," the judge said. "Not opinion, not hearsay, and especially not supposition about what might have happened."

"There's no supposition involved," Carla insisted. "Danny is only seventeen. He's not old enough to sign legal documents without adult approval. There is also no supposition that Mr. diViere got Danny drunk. You've heard several men testify to that."

Lukey and two others in the saloon nodded in agreement.

"What I haven't heard is testimony that Mr. diViere restrained your brother and poured the whiskey down his throat."

"Of course he didn't," Carla said, irritably. "No one would have stood for that."

"Then how can you say Mr. diViere got your brother drunk?"

"Everybody knows Danny doesn't drink because it goes straight to his head. Mr. diViere used that to question his manhood. In Texas, if a man can't drink, he's not considered a man. Danny already gets teased for looking so young. Mr. diViere played on all of Danny's insecurities to induce him to drink."

"That's not very sportsmanlike," the judge agreed, "but it's not against the law. What makes you think Mr. diViere would do such a thing? Do you know him?"

"No, Your Honor."

"Does anybody here know him?"

"Ivan knows him," Carla said. "He's known him for ten years."

"Which one of you is Ivan?" the judge asked.

"I am," Ivan responded.

"What's your full name?"

"Ivan Nikolai Augustus Stanislas."

The judge blinked. "You're a foreigner, aren't you?"

"I was born in Poland."

"Then how do you know this Mr. diViere?"

"We served in the same troop during the war."

"You fought for the Confederacy? Why?"

"I like to ride horses."

Apparently accepting this as a reasonable answer, the judge asked, "Can you speak to his character?"

"Yes."

"Then do so."

"Laveau diViere is a traitor and a thief. He betrayed his troop during the war and stole my money. Since then he has been involved in murder, blackmail, rustling, and bribery. He is wanted in California for trying to kill a woman."

The judge lost interest in the papers he'd been shuffling while listening to Ivan. "Can you prove this?"

"There are many witnesses to these things," Ivan said.

"Why hasn't he been brought to justice?"

"He betrayed his troop to the Union army, which still protects him."

"Texas is under a Reconstruction government. The army no longer has control."

"He is still protected."

The judge pursed his lips, sat in thought for a few

moments. Finally he frowned and shook his head. "Your brother has undoubtedly been the victim of an unscrupulous man," he said to Carla, "but I can't set aside the bet."

"Why not?" Carla asked before the judge could continue.

"First, neither your brother nor Mr. diViere is present. I have heard from others who were there," he said before Carla could protest, "but I haven't heard from the two people most directly involved. Though Mr.—" The judge struggled with Ivan's names before giving up. "Ivan has given a very damaging account of Mr. diViere's character, it hasn't been corroborated by anyone else. I only have a sister's account of how Mr. diViere's remarks *probably* affected her brother."

"My brother is out helping a group authorized by the governor to return stolen cows to their rightful owners," Carla said. "No one knows where to find Mr. diViere."

"I understand your dilemma, Miss Reece, but my hands are tied. People make unwise decisions all the time, but it's not up to the courts to try to put right their mistakes. Intervening in a situation like this would set a dangerous precedent. If, when I return to Overlin, I am able to talk to your brother and question additional witnesses to Mr. diViere's character, I will reconsider the case. Until then, I must let the results stand. Who's next?"

Carla felt as though she'd been thrown down to the ground so hard she had difficulty breathing. She hadn't known until then just how much she was depending on the judge to throw out the results of the card game. "I've got to get out of here," she said to Ivan.

"Come to my office," Lukey offered. "From the way you look right now, you're not ready to drive back to the ranch."

Carla's thoughts were so chaotic she was only vaguely aware the streets were unusually quiet. She was struggling to accept the probability that Danny would never get back his half of the ranch. She didn't know how she could endure knowing that for the next two years or more he'd be putting his life on the line every time he went into Mexico. She would have to talk to Kesney. Surely there was something he could do.

However, it was the second realization that came close to robbing her legs of their strength. She had been hoping the judge would throw out the bet so Ivan wouldn't have any property to sell. Without money, he wouldn't be able to return to Poland. If he stayed in Texas, he could marry her. She was horrified at herself. That was practically the same as trying to trap him into marriage. She would never have believed such a devious plan would have entered her mind. Not only had it entered her mind, she'd been depending on it. Her only consolation, small as it was, was that Ivan would never know.

She was relieved to reach the relative coolness of Lukey's office. She wished she'd been alone so she could shout, kick a few pieces of furniture, or even borrow a few of Danny's less colorful curses as she struggled to absorb the dual consequences of this defeat. As it was, she had to try to appear mature, calm, and pragmatic. Maybe she was more like Danny than she thought. At least she didn't drink, gamble, and fall in love with children.

"Are you okay?" Ivan asked after settling her into a comfortable armchair.

"No, I'm not."

"That's the verdict I expected," Lukey said. "He really couldn't do anything else under the circumstances."

"There ought to be something he could do," Carla said, "*especially* under the circumstances."

"He can't set aside a gambling debt. If he did, he wouldn't have time to do anything else. Nobody wants to lose."

Carla knew what Lukey was saying was logical, but she was in no mood for logic. She needed someone to be the object of her anger. Mr. diViere wasn't here. Neither was Danny, nor the judge. That left Ivan. "If you hadn't come to Overlin, everything would have been different."

"How would that get Danny's land back?"

"Maybe diViere would have gotten tired of looking for someone to take care of it and just left it."

"You would not think that if you knew Laveau as I do," Ivan said. "I have thought from the beginning he came to Overlin for a reason."

"He couldn't have come just to beat Danny at poker."

"When the game was over, he left without even looking at what he had won. Why?"

"I've wondered about that," Lukey said. "He had me write up that document right after the game, and then he left."

"But what would be the purpose of getting Danny's land if he didn't plan to sell it for himself?" Carla asked.

"I do not know, but Laveau never does anything without a reason," Ivan said. "That is why it worries me that he gave Riley permission to set up his camp on his land."

"But Riley is here to prevent rustling," Carla said.

"And spend money in town," Lukey added. "He and his men are very popular with the merchants."

"Riley gave Danny a job even though he's only seventeen," Carla said to Ivan. "You only distrust him because you know Mr. diViere is such a terrible person."

"I distrust anyone who deals with Laveau," Ivan stated.

"Lukey said, "You won't find anyone in town who—"

He broke off at the sound of gunshots from the street. Ivan was closer to the door so he got there before Carla. She edged past him until she had a clear view of the street where a large number of frightened women and crying children were surrounded by a group of men brandishing rifles.

Chapter 17

MORE THAN A DOZEN MEN WERE USING THE WOMEN and children as shields.

Lukey had gone to his desk to get his gun. "What's going on?" he asked. "Is anybody hurt?"

"I don't know" Carla said, "but it looks like most of the women and children in Overlin are being held hostage." Lukey's wife and children where among the captives.

Lukey rushed from behind his desk to the window.

"The shots were not meant to hurt," Ivan said to Lukey. "They were meant to get our attention. They want to tell us why they have come."

"They could have done that without putting a gun to my wife's head." Lukey rushed to fill his pockets with bullets. "I'll kill the sons of bitches."

Ivan blocked Lukey's attempt to rush into the street. "They have gathered up the women and children so that will not happen. We must find out what they want."

Accepting that Ivan wasn't going to release him until he calmed down, Lukey stopped struggling, but his face didn't show less anger. The street was already filling with men, all brandishing weapons. No one attempted a shot for fear of hitting one of the women or children. They were scared—some of the children were crying—but it didn't appear that anyone was hurt.

"What do they want?" Lukey asked.

"It looks like Mr. Dodge is going to ask them," Ivan said.

Once Ivan was sure Lukey had gotten his anger under control, they moved out of the office and down the boardwalk.

"They're speaking in Spanish," Lukey said when one of the men started to speak. "Maxwell doesn't know enough Spanish to order his own food."

"You should interpret for him. Leave your gun," Ivan said when Lukey started forward. "They want something very badly, but they do not what to hurt anyone. Carla should go with you."

"Why?"

"If your wife is with you, it will reassure them that you do not intend to shoot."

"My wife is out there."

"They cannot know that."

Lukey paused, but Carla didn't hesitate. "Come on."

They joined Maxwell Dodge who was yelling ineffectually at the intruders. Ivan listened anxiously as Lukey talked to one of the Mexicans. The man's explanation was long and accompanied by many angry gestures. Rather than be equally angry, Lukey seemed to go from startled to insulted to determined.

"What did he say?" Maxwell Dodge demanded.

"They were warned rustlers would try to steal their cattle two nights ago, so the men were with their herds, waiting to ambush the rustlers. While they were away, some Americans rode into their town. They stole all the gold and silver from the churches and anything of value they could find in the homes."

"Why are they here?" Maxwell asked. "We didn't steal anything."

"They followed the bandits into Texas before losing their trail. Overlin is the closest town, so they believe the men came from here."

"Tell them we had nothing to do with the theft."

"I've already told them that."

"Then why haven't they released our women and children?"

"They don't believe me."

"They think I would lie?" Maxwell looked so indignant Ivan couldn't repress a smile.

"Americans stole from them and roughed up their families," Lukey told him. "You can't blame them for not believing us."

"Of course I can." Maxwell started to say something to the Mexicans but turned back to Lukey. "Did they say what they wanted?"

"They want to search the town for what was stolen."

That request caused an uproar. The men waved guns and shouted threats. Out of the corner of his eye, Ivan saw a man start toward the circle of hostages. If he got too close, one of the Mexicans would shoot. If that happened, there would be carnage in the street. Without hesitation, Ivan threw himself into the man's path, wrestled him to the ground, and took his gun.

"Do you want people to be killed?" Ivan inquired angrily.

The man struggled to get away, but Ivan was too big and too strong. "No one is going to search my house."

"Do you have anything to hide?"

"No."

"So even though you have stolen nothing, you do not hesitate to start a fight, which will get many people killed? You are a fool. So are the rest of you if you provoke a confrontation," Ivan said to the crowd. "Some Americans have lied to them, stolen from them, and mistreated their families. All they want it proof that you did not do it."

"It's an insult," someone shouted. "I won't stand for it."

"So what will you do? Shoot somebody who will shoot back at you?"

"They should take our word for it," someone said.

"Would we take theirs?"

"They're Mexicans," someone said.

"And we're thieving Americans who defile churches and steal from women," Carla said. "Which do you think is worse?"

The crowd wasn't any less angry, but they seemed more willing to listen.

"If we cooperate," Carla said, "they will be more likely to believe us in the future."

"Why should we care about that?" one asked.

"Because the bad men will steal from another town and another town after that," Ivan told them. "Overlin is the closest town to the border. You will always be the first to be suspected. The next time they may not be willing to talk first."

The leader of the Mexicans conferred briefly with Lukey.

"What is he saying?" Maxwell Dodge asked, irritated at being bypassed.

"He wants Ivan to search along with them."

"Why? He's not one of us."

"He believes Ivan can be trusted not to shoot anyone in the back. He wants me to go, too."

"Well, he can't have what he wants."

"Why not?" Carla asked.

"We can't have Mexicans coming in here telling us what to do."

"Don't be an idiot, Maxwell. They've been lied to, robbed, and their families mistreated. What they're asking isn't half as bad."

"I won't have any foreigners going through my house," one man said.

"Then I don't suppose you mind if they take your wife and daughters back to Mexico with them," Carla said.

Ivan listened in silence while Carla and Lukey argued with the angry crowd. After a time they reached a compromise. They would search the public buildings first. If that went without incident, they would turn their attention to the individual homes.

It ended up being the most unusual day Ivan had lived through. Once they worked out a procedure that everyone could accept—that took more than an hour itself—they started with the churches, moved to the saloons and restaurants, and finally to the individual businesses and offices. Ivan was relieved when each search turned up nothing that had been stolen. Since neither side truly trusted the other, he did most of the searching. It embarrassed him to know so much about people's private business. Because of that, he decided there should be a change when the search moved to the individual homes.

"You should take my place," he said to Carla when the search of Sadie Lowell's shop was completed.

"Why?" Carla had stayed with the women and children, a willing guarantee of everyone's good behavior.

"There are many things these ladies would not like a man to know, especially one who is a stranger."

One woman spoke up. "I'd prefer a stranger. I don't want a man I know looking through my bureau."

Another woman said, "I don't want *any* man messing with my things."

Since a Mexican had to be present to verify that no stolen items had been found, they were at a momentary impasse until Ivan asked, "Would you agree to let Carla and Myrtle Jenkins make the search?"

Myrtle had not made many friends. Some objections were quite loud.

"Somebody has to do it, so make up your minds," Carla said.

The crowd was getting upset and angry again, so Ivan decided to go to Myrtle himself. She had been watching the confrontation from her front window.

"I thought I would be better if I didn't go into the streets," she explained.

"How did they miss you?" Ivan asked.

"They didn't, but I keep my doors locked. I don't trust little boys."

"We need your help."

"Why?"

Ivan quickly explained what had happened and that they were at an impasse.

"Are you certain no one in Overlin is involved?"

"Yes."

"Do you know who the thieves are?"

"I have an idea, but I need you to help us right now."

Myrtle looked him in the eye. "I won't protect a thief, even if he has a wife and children."

"We must hurry before someone does something stupid."

"There are men involved," Myrtle stated. "Of course someone will do something stupid."

Thinking it best not to comment, Ivan waited until Myrtle had retrieved her parasol.

"I refuse to be baked by the sun for anyone. What am I supposed to do?" she asked as they left her house and turned toward the main street of Overlin.

"Reassure the women that strange men are not handling their personal belongings, while you convince the Mexicans you haven't found any of the stolen items."

"That sounds like a job for King Solomon."

Considering that churches had been stripped of their plates and ornaments, maybe Myrtle was right.

When Myrtle arrived, everyone seemed determined to talk at once. She stood quietly, eyeing them like a queen on her throne until the talking gradually faded. When everyone had fallen silent, she turned to the Mexican and spoke to him in fluent Spanish. He responded at some length. When he finished, Myrtle turned to the gathered men.

"I have been told what was stolen. Carla and I will search the bedrooms and kitchens. Ivan will search the rest of the house and any outbuildings. If I find anything that seems to fit the description of something they lost, I will show it to them. Otherwise, they will see nothing."

"Will they believe you?" a woman asked.

"Do I look like a woman who would lie?"

Ivan guessed their silence indicated that many had been scarred by the sharp blade of Myrtle's honesty.

"Let's get on with it," Maxwell Dodge said. "The sooner we get our wives and children home safely, the better."

"You don't have a wife or children," Myrtle said.

Maxwell looked irritated that anyone would talk back to him. "I was speaking for the whole town."

Myrtle's harrumph was more eloquent than words. "Let's begin," she said, turning to Carla. "If I have supper too late, it keeps me up."

The search of the houses didn't go smoothly. If a wife or daughter got upset at having her possessions questioned, her husband and neighbors got upset. If it hadn't been for Myrtle's brusque dismissal of their objections as being too foolish to deserve her attention, there might have been serious trouble. A few items were subjected to detailed examination, but when the search was over, the Mexicans were satisfied that none of the stolen items were in Overlin. That, however, didn't assuage the anger of the townspeople. In fact, it made some of them angrier at being accused of something they hadn't done.

"I will ride out of town with them," Ivan said to Carla.

"That's a good idea," Myrtle said. "I wouldn't put it past some of these idiots to try to dry gulch them."

Another term Ivan didn't know, but he figured it wasn't a good thing.

"Get between them and the rest of the townspeople before they release the women and children," Myrtle advised. "I'll walk with you to the edge of town."

"I'll ride with you," Carla offered. "They wouldn't dare shoot at me."

"I'll go too," Lukey volunteered. "I want to know more about those Americans."

Once they were released, the hostages rushed to their loved ones. While the men were busy reassuring themselves that their families hadn't been harmed, Ivan started the Mexicans on their way home.

Lukey caught up with them after making sure his wife and children were okay. He peppered the leader with questions, but Myrtle turned to Ivan, "I want to hear more about your idea of who might be behind this. You may come to supper tomorrow. I go to bed early, so be at my house at five o'clock sharp."

When they reached the edge of town, Lukey was still asking questions. "Ride from here as fast as you can," Ivan advised the men. "If you are quick, you should be away before anyone has time to saddle up and follow."

"I didn't find out what I needed to know," Lukey objected as the men took Ivan's advice and put their horses into a gallop.

"It is more important that they get away safely. If even one of them is shot, they will come back shooting."

"From what they said, the thieves could have been anybody," Lukey said.

It could have been, but Ivan was sure he knew who to blame. Laveau diViere never did anything without a reason, and that reason always had to do with personal gain.

"You have no proof it's Riley and his men," Lukey said.

Ivan had been reluctant to reveal his suspicions, but if he was to find out who was behind the thefts, he needed support. Myrtle had prepared a supper of fried chicken, fresh corn, and pecan pie. Ivan thought it was too hot for coffee, but everybody drank it like it was natural. Myrtle offered him a glass of her homemade wine, which he discovered was surprisingly good, even though he found it to be too sweet.

"We know Mr. diViere is involved," Carla said, "and he's a crook."

"Do you think Danny would be involved in anything like that?" Lukey asked.

"No," Myrtle stated with singular forcefulness. "Danny is just as foolish as any other boy his age, maybe more so because everyone has spoiled him disgracefully, but he has an honest backbone, which he wouldn't bend for anyone."

Ivan was surprised at the vehemence of Myrtle's support for Danny, but Carla seemed stunned into speechlessness.

"Don't stare at me like a landed fish," Myrtle scolded. "I don't have to approve of everything Danny does to know he's a young man with very strong principles." She gave Carla a particularly stern look. "I'd say the same of you in spite of that red dress, if you had the good sense to get yourself a proper husband." She sniffed deprecatingly. "I don't know why you haven't when he's practically shoved himself under your nose."

Ivan felt the heat rise in his neck. He thought he'd kept his feelings for Carla under control, but he wasn't really surprised Myrtle had sensed them. Or that she knew Carla shared his feelings. For a woman who swore she wanted nothing to do with people, Myrtle knew a great deal about them.

"We've wandered from the subject," Lukey said,

glancing anxiously around the room. "If Riley's men are doing the stealing, we'll need proof before the sheriff will do anything. They're popular with the merchants because they spend a lot of money."

"And our sheriff prefers to spend his day in the saloon drinking rather than doing his job," Myrtle added.

"Maybe we do not need to wait for proof," Ivan said. "Maybe all I have to do is tell him he must leave our ranch." He didn't realize until the word was out that he'd said *our* ranch. He turned to Carla who was looking at him in a way he didn't quite understand. It wasn't angry or upset. She looked puzzled.

"Do you think he'll go?" Lukey asked. "He has Mr. diViere's permission, and he's the one who owns the land."

"If he refuses, the sheriff will have to light a fire under him," Myrtle said. "It's about time he did something to earn his pay."

Light a fire under him! Ivan shook his head at some of the strange things Americans said. "I will ride out to his camp tomorrow," Ivan said.

"I'll go, too," Carla said.

"I'll come and bring the sheriff," Lukey said.

"With that crowd, you won't need me," Myrtle said.

Carla and Lukey looked surprised at Myrtle's remark, but Ivan could see a mischievous twinkle in her eye. It amazed him that people who thought they knew her so well didn't know her at all.

Lukey got to his feet. "I'd better get home. Ida is still nervous about being in the house by herself."

"We should be going, too," Carla said to Myrtle. "Let me help you clean up."

"Nonsense. I'll be in my bed before you reach your ranch."

Ivan took his wineglass and Carla's cup to the kitchen, while Carla went to fetch her wrap.

"You take care of that girl," Myrtle said to Ivan when they reached the kitchen. "She's real smart when it comes to running that ranch, but she hasn't got a grain of sense when it comes to her own life."

"She is smarter than you know."

"Then why hasn't she agreed to marry you?"

"Because I have not asked her."

"And why is that?"

"Because I am going back to Poland."

"Have you asked her if she'll go with you?"

"She would never be happy in Poland."

"Shouldn't that decision be up to her?"

"Are you two talking secrets?" Carla was standing in the doorway, grinning broadly. "I never saw a man who could captivate women like Ivan."

"All the more reason you should get him before a preacher quick as you can. If I were thirty years younger, I'd cut you out without a second thought."

Carla colored, and her smile faltered before making a brave recovery. "I don't know what you're talking about. Ivan's going back to Poland as soon as he sells his part of the ranch."

"If babies can learn to speak Polish, adults can, too."

Carla looked completely flustered. "I'm sure they can," she replied, "but I have no reason to learn Polish. Now we'd better start home. We have a long ride tomorrow."

Ivan had never thought she would consider going to Poland, but it was clear from the degree of her embarrassment that she had. It was a shock because it changed everything.

The next several minutes were taken up setting a time to leave tomorrow and making arrangements to meet Lukey and the sheriff. Yet he could see Carla visibly stiffen when he climbed into the buggy next to her.

"You do not have to be afraid of me," he said. "I never expected you would move to Poland with me."

Carla kept her gaze straight ahead. "I'm not afraid of you, but how would you know whether I would move to Poland?"

"I did not ask because I did not think you could be happy in Poland. Would you consider it?"

"I would *consider* anything. What I would *do*, however, might be entirely different."

It was clear from Carla's set frown that she was unhappy with him. Had he been too much of a gentleman? Did American women expect men to whisk them off to strange lands? In Poland, a woman expected to know exactly what her future would be down to the size of her allowance, the number of servants, even the kinds of carriages and riding horses. But women of his class in Poland didn't own ranches. Nor did they cook their own meals or clean their own homes. Before marriage, their fathers made decisions for them. After they were married, their husbands did it. But Carla was used to making her own decisions. She would probably expect to keep doing it after she was married.

Though he'd fallen in love with Carla, Ivan had never considered *marrying* a woman like Carla. After his desperate affair so many years ago, he decided love and marriage were two different things that shouldn't be looked for in the same place. He felt that held true for him despite seeing Cade and Pilar manage both day after day. Was he still locked into the pattern of thinking like a traditional Polish nobleman? If so, did he *want* to be a captive of that social environment? It offered many advantages, but one could never be an individual. One had to fit in. One had to support the social order by being a good representative of one's class. One had to live by the rules. He hadn't lived by them for a long time. Was he sure he wanted to go back?

"You've been very quiet," Carla said. "Don't tell me I shocked you."

"Not a shock exactly, but it was a surprise."

"Why should it be? I assume you've considered staying in Texas."

"Yes, but out of necessity rather than choice."

The purpose of coming to America had been to make his fortune so he could return to Poland and the society into which he'd been born. He liked his American friends, but they were not family. Members of Polish families were bound by strong ties beyond that of a parent's love of children and children's love and respect for their parents. There was history, a common heritage, age-old customs, and a religion that was nearly two thousand years old. There was a strong sense of community in the extended family of grandparents, aunts and uncles, and cousins, regardless of how many times removed. The strong defended the weak, the wealthy provided for the less fortunate, the beautiful never lost sight of those less favored.

"Would it be so terrible?" Carla asked.

How could he explain what it was like to be in exile

from his own country, his society, his family? After being in America for ten years, he still felt like an outsider.

"Many people leave their country because they want a life they cannot find there. That was not true for me. I have a place. I only lacked the means to support that life."

"And you will have the means when you sell your part of the ranch."

"Yes." That's the only reason he accepted Laveau's offer. Otherwise, he would have had nothing to do with a man who'd proved over and over again that he preferred evil over good.

"And you haven't changed your mind?"

Carla had always insisted that she handle the reins whenever they used the buggy. Ivan hadn't objected, but tonight he wished he had because she was using that as an excuse to avoid looking at him. It was hard to figure out what she might be thinking when he couldn't see her eyes or her expression.

"Things have happened too quickly for me to think about all the possibilities."

She flicked the whip to put the horse into a brisk trot. "You'll have almost a year to make up your mind. Do you think that will be enough?"

―⁓―

"Why did they have to choose a spot so damned far away?" the sheriff asked.

He'd been complaining from the moment he showed up at the ranch that he didn't like having his morning routine interrupted.

"He and his men are away a lot," Ivan explained, "so he wanted a place not just anyone could find."

"I still say you're making a mistake," the sheriff said. "That man is here to see nobody steals our cattle. Why would he be involved in stealing?"

"We don't know that he is," Carla said, "but if he leaves, that will spare everybody in Overlin of being suspected of the thefts."

"I don't see how."

"Maybe the thefts will stop."

"Maybe they'll move elsewhere," was Lukey's hope.

"If Laveau is behind them," Ivan said, "they will not stop."

"I know why Carla hates Laveau," the sheriff said, "but what's your beef with him?"

Ivan didn't want his personal history to become common knowledge, but the sheriff was owed some explanation. "He stole from me and betrayed our troop during the war."

The sheriff might be lax about his duties, but his loyalties were never in doubt. "Why didn't one of you shoot the bastard?"

"He has been protected by the Union army and the Reconstruction government."

"Hell, shoot him anyway."

That's what Nate had wanted, but Cade said it would make them as bad as Laveau. Nate argued that Cade only felt that way because he had married Laveau's sister, but the others had agreed with Cade. Besides, Laveau had made it known that if anything happened to him, the authorities should look first to the members of his old troop. Since five of the seven surviving members were married, some with children, there were other people to be considered. Because all of them had served in the

Confederate army, none would stand much of a chance in a Reconstruction court.

"Mr. diViere is not the issue here," Lukey said. "It's Riley and his crew."

"I don't think you've got a good reason to run him off," the sheriff said to Carla, "but it's your land."

"I never wanted him here," Carla said.

Ivan knew that, but he also knew Carla wouldn't have suspected Riley's men or considered asking him to leave if it hadn't been for him. There was nothing concrete to tie Riley to the robbery, but Ivan didn't need more than to know Riley was connected with Laveau. The evil inside Laveau was in everything he did, and he infected everyone who worked with him. Ivan had wanted nothing to do with Laveau, but he couldn't turn his back on a chance to return to Poland. He should have followed his instincts, but he was glad he was here to see that nothing happened to Carla. Laveau didn't care that the things he did could destroy lives. He actually seemed to enjoy it. It gave him a sense of power that was as intoxicating as it was dangerous.

"You can tell Riley your suspicions to his face," the sheriff said to Carla. "It seems he's in camp."

Chapter 18

IT APPEARED THAT RILEY'S WHOLE CREW WAS IN CAMP. From the number of men moving around and the numerous tents set up, Carla guessed Danny and Kesney's foreman weren't the only new recruits. Whatever he was doing apparently paid well.

"There he is," the sheriff said to Carla when Riley emerged from one of the tents. "Go tell him."

"His arrangement is with Laveau," Ivan pointed out. "I should tell him."

"I don't think he's going to take kindly to a foreigner telling him to clear out," the sheriff said before turning back to Carla. "Or a woman, either. You better do it, Lukey."

"This was Reece land long before Mr. diViere ever set foot in Overlin," Carla said. "I'll tell him."

She spurred her horse forward. Ivan moved quickly to stay at her side. Lukey and the sheriff followed.

Riley didn't appear happy to see the delegation. "What brings you all the way out here?" he asked when Carla brought her mount to a stop. When Carla dismounted, Ivan did as well.

"We've had some trouble in town," Carla said.

"What kind? We've been gone for several days." Riley's face gave away nothing. Either he didn't know about the trouble, or he was a good actor.

"Hey, Sis. What are you doing here?"

"We had about twenty men from a town in Mexico come into Overlin yesterday," Carla said to Riley. "They were looking for Americans who robbed them and stripped the churches of their gold and silver. They held most of our women and children hostage until we allowed them to search the entire town. They only left when they couldn't find anything that had been stolen."

"Where did they come from?" Danny asked. "We can go after them tonight."

"There's no need to go after them," Carla told her brother.

"Why not?"

"They didn't take anything or hurt anybody."

"We still can't have foreigners coming into Overlin with guns," Danny insisted.

"What do you want us to do?" Riley asked.

"We're not accusing you and your men of anything," Carla said, "but they thought Overlin was involved because your men are camped here. Since they know you're going into Mexico, and since you're Americans—"

Apparently impatient with Carla's diplomatic effort, the sheriff interrupted her. "They want to you pull out and set up camp someplace else."

"Why would you want that?" Danny asked.

"As long as they suspect anyone in this area, the women and children are in danger," Ivan explained.

"If Riley's men were not here," Carla added, "there wouldn't be anyone they could suspect of stealing from them, and they'd have to look somewhere else."

"That's not fair," Danny protested.

"Was it fair to have our women and children terrorized for a day and half the night?" Lukey hadn't spoken

yet, but his sense of outrage forced him to break his
silence. "My wife and daughter were held hostage. I
ready to hunt down the thieves myself."

"Our taking back stolen cattle has angered
tlers," Riley said. "This camp on your ranch i
keeping them from coming back. Since y
largest herd, you'd be the first target."

"How do you know this?" the sheriff a

"We hear things when we go into vill
always someone willing to share information

"Maybe they're just angry at you, not us,
proposed.

"We have nothing for them to steal. You do."

"Maybe they're more interested in getting even with
you than stealing more cows," Lukey suggested hopefully.

"We can take care of ourselves, but can the ranchers protect their herds? How many hands to you have?"
Riley asked Carla.

Carla was too embarrassed to say she had only one.
"Not enough."

"We're concerned about our cows," Lukey said, "but
we're more concerned about our families. We can always
buy more cows."

Carla had been wavering until Lukey put everything into perspective. "I think Lukey speaks for
everyone," she said. "We're willing to risk our herds
but not our families."

"He doesn't speak for me," Danny objected.

"That doesn't matter," the sheriff said. "You don't
have any cows or a ranch."

Flashing an angry look around the circle, Danny muttered a curse and stalked off.

"If you're sure you want us to leave," Riley said to ▓a after an awkward pause, "we'll clear out today."

▓ink it's best."

▓u have any place to go?" the sheriff asked.

▓f ranchers would be happy to give us a place ▓st have to decide which would be better for ▓eed to send some of the men into Overlin

▓ trying to keep you out of town," the ▓ "They're just trying to keep the women ▓s from being shot up. As far as I'm concerned, you can stay here as long as you want, but this ain't my land. Anybody got anything else to say?" When no one answered, he turned and mounted his horse. "I'm headed back to town. I suggest y'all do the same, and let this man get about his business."

"Thank you for being so understanding," Carla said to Riley. "This has got everybody in town really upset."

Riley's measured expression never changed, but Carla couldn't escape the feeling there was rage in the back of his eyes. She was relieved when they rode out of the camp.

"Glad you kept your trap shut," the sheriff said to Ivan. "People around here don't take to foreigners giving them orders."

"It is my land," Ivan said. "I have the right to give the orders."

"Maybe, but people around here have the right to wish you was back where you came from."

It surprised Carla that the sheriff disliked Ivan. Maybe he was jealous that after the way Ivan managed the search of the town, people trusted Ivan more than him.

"Nobody wishes Ivan was back in Poland," Lukey told the sheriff. "If you have any doubts, just ask Myrtle Jenkins, or any man who had family held hostage."

"I'm not asking Myrtle Jenkins anything," the sheriff declared. "Just knowing she likes this foreign fella is all I need to distrust him."

Carla grinned to herself. Yes, the sheriff was jealous. He had to know if the election for sheriff were to be held the next day, Ivan would probably win.

Carla wondered if something like that could induce Ivan to stay in Texas. She had considered the possibility of going to Poland if Ivan should ask her, but she was sure she would be miserable. She once met a Polish woman when her parents took her to San Antonio. The woman, who was a servant in a wealthy household, had left Poland to escape a life of servitude. At the time, Carla had been too dazzled by the descriptions of houses, clothes, jewels, and fabulous parties to pay attention to the woman's description of her mistress's life. When combined with what she'd learned from Ivan, Carla realized a Polish nobleman's wife was expected to be a beautiful possession who had no thoughts of her own and did only what her husband wished. She loved Ivan, but she wasn't sure her love could survive such a life.

She had nearly a year to convince Ivan to change his mind, but would he be any happier staying in Texas when she would be going to Poland? Would a part of him always feel she had kept him from taking his natural place in society? He was a prince, for goodness sake. It might not mean anything in Texas, but it put him in a privileged class in Poland. With his family's connection to some of the most powerful men in Polish history, he would be an important person. He might even be given a position of power and influence. In Texas he'd just be another rancher struggling to keep his cows safe from drought, disease, and rustlers.

She had always been a sensible woman, logical and unemotional, not prone to daydreams or flights of fancy. She saw every situation as a puzzle to be solved with pragmatic thinking. Why should falling in love have caused her to abandon every one of those habits?

~~~

… Why do I not hear from you? Do you not understand that your sisters fight every day? Their husbands will not be in the same room. Now my beloved grandsons, the two sweetest boys in the world, eye each other like barnyard roosters. Ludmila insists that precedents must be followed and that her son is heir after you. Anika argues that no one will respect a prince without money. Both are right. It is your obligation to come home and take up your title. Only you can restore harmony in this family.

> *Your loving mother,*
> *Krystina Stanislas*
> *Princess Poniatowski*

~~~

"Do you want anything else?"

"No."

"You haven't eaten much."

"How can one be hungry when it is so hot?"

But Carla knew the issue wasn't the heat. It was that

they had admitted they were in love with each other. It had been wonderful and glorious at first. For a few days it was all she could think about. She had awakened in the morning feeling life finally made sense, relieved she hadn't been denied the chance to experience the love every woman wanted. She couldn't wait for Ivan to come in for breakfast, to see his smile, to feel his touch. They planned the day together, rode together, made decisions together. When the day was done, the last chore completed, the last dish washed and put away, they would sit on the porch talking quietly until the stars came out, and it was time to go to bed. For a short time, she was sure everything would somehow resolve itself, and they could enjoy a life of happiness beyond her expectations.

Now it was the burden of those expectations that constricted their conversation, clouded their vision, and blunted hope whenever it dared to show its face. The letter from Ivan's mother just added more weight to the growing constraint between them. Even before he told her about it, she knew its purpose. It annoyed her that his mother should place the responsibility of resolving his sisters' quarrel on him, but she was sure that was due to her own selfish interests.

"You have to eat to keep up your strength. You're in the saddle all day."

"You are as well, and you ate less than I did."

She wanted to talk about what was really bothering them, but they already had. There was nothing to be gained by going over it again. She kept telling herself things could change before a year was up, but she had no assurance they would change the way she wanted. She didn't know how she could leave Texas for Poland. Why could she expect Ivan to do what she couldn't?

Myrtle lost no opportunity to remind Carla of Ivan's good qualities. When she told Myrtle that Ivan hadn't asked her, Myrtle said she should ask him, that it was stupid to let such a good man get away. Myrtle couldn't understand why Carla wouldn't do everything she possibly could to convince Ivan to stay in Texas. She said such a man would be wasted on the silly European aristocracy, that he could only realize his full potential in a free society like Texas.

Carla agreed with Myrtle, but she refused to try to talk Ivan out of going back to Poland. That had been his goal from the moment he came to America. As much as she loved him, she knew he was the only one who could make the decision that what he found in Texas was more important to him than what he'd left behind.

She picked up Ivan's empty plate and turned toward the sink. "I'd hoped to hear from Danny by now. I wonder if Riley has found a place to set up his camp."

"I doubt he will have trouble. Many ranchers would be glad to give to him all the space he wants."

She rinsed the plate before dropping it into hot, soapy water. It seemed a miracle to have running water inside the house. "Do you think we made a mistake telling him to leave?"

"As soon as I knew he was connected with Laveau, I never wanted him here."

"Rustlers have been stealing cows for years."

"Laveau is evil. Everything he touches is evil."

"Then why did you come here if you were sure something was wrong?"

"Because it was the only way I saw to go back to Poland. By putting my desire to return home above all else, I have stained my honor. Now I cannot leave until I have cleared it."

Carla told herself she should be ashamed of hoping he would never feel it was clear enough to leave. If she truly loved him, she wouldn't want him to stay on those terms. "You haven't done anything to be ashamed of. I can't set foot in Overlin without someone singing your praises."

"I should never have come."

"If you hadn't, Mr. diViere would have sent someone as dishonest as he is. Do you think rustlers really are planning to steal my herd like Riley said?"

"If anyone is planning to steal your herd, it is Riley."

"Why would he do that?"

"So he could bring it back and be a hero. I believe Riley is responsible for the thefts. Now that Overlin is free of suspicion, what better place could he want? Here he is safe but close to the border. He can steal herds in Mexico to sell to ranchers in Texas and rob them at the same time."

"Why didn't you say this before?"

"Because nobody will believe me."

"I believe you."

"Why do you believe me?"

Carla started to say because she loved him, but she realized Ivan needed a concrete reason, not a statement of blind faith.

"If anybody can figure out what's going on, you can. You've known Mr. diViere ever since you came to America. You've given me more than enough reason to believe he's evil. Besides, it makes sense. Everybody knows the Reconstruction government has never done anything to stop the rustling. Why should they suddenly change unless it's to their advantage?"

"That is all?"

"No. You have a deeper, stronger, clearer sense of honesty than any man I know. If you believe something is wrong, I'm willing to trust your instincts."

She was about to put the clean plates in the cabinet. Ivan took the plates from her hands, placed them on the shelf, and then turned back to her. "How can you believe that of me? I came in the place of Laveau. I could be as terrible as he."

Carla looked into his eyes because it was important that he believe what she was about to say. "I could never have fallen in love with you if you were."

"You wanted not to love me. Why did you?"

She averted her gaze. She couldn't think clearly when she looked into his eyes. "The moment I met you, I felt something different. I was too angry at first to believe it was anything more than an attraction to a handsome man with a charming accent and a smile that would cause any woman's heart to beat faster. But I was letting my anger at Mr. diViere keep me from seeing you as the person you are." She raised her head until their eyes met. "Once I did that, I realized I was already half in love with you. By the time I got over my shock, I was too deeply in love to pull back."

"But I must return to Poland."

"You could be going to Egypt or China. It wouldn't make any difference. *You* fell in love with *me* even though you know you weren't going to stay. Why?"

Ivan hung his head. "I could not help myself."

Carla took his right hand and clasped it tightly. "No matter what happens, I'm glad we love each other. It would be terrible if I loved you, but you didn't love me in return. I don't think I could stand it."

Ivan took her hands in his. "I love you more than I thought possible. Never can I love anyone else this way."

"I can't, either."

Ivan's gaze bored into her. "But you must. You must marry. You must have children."

"How can I marry another man when the only children I want are yours?" She hadn't meant to say such a thing. She hadn't even thought it until the words popped out of her mouth. Yet she knew it was the truth. She would never marry Kesney, certainly not Maxwell Dodge.

Ivan gripped her by the shoulders, his face a study in love wrapped in agony. "You must marry. Myrtle insists on it."

"Myrtle thinks I should marry you."

"To do that, you would have to go to Poland with me."

It was painful to see him twisting in the grip of two loves he believed were mutually exclusive. She didn't know all the ties that held him to Poland—she doubted she could have understood them if she had—but she knew they were so important he was suffering from being caught between them and his love for her. She couldn't stand seeing him suffer. She locked her gaze with his. "That's not impossible."

Ivan seemed to turn rigid. "What are you saying?"

She hesitated. It would be cruel to raise his hopes if she couldn't honestly consider going to Poland.

She didn't want to think of what her life would be like, but she couldn't imagine life without him. "I can't imagine living in Poland, but I can't refuse to consider the possibility."

"To be a Polish wife is wrong for you."

"Why is it so wrong?" She was sure she wouldn't like it, but why was Ivan so emphatic that she shouldn't even consider it?

"The wife of a prince, even a poor one, must follow many rules. She can have no money except what her husband gives her. She can have no opinions that do not agree with his. She must see to his comfort, have his children, and on no account do anything that would bring dishonor on his name."

"It wouldn't be that bad if I was married to you."

"There is more. You cannot go out without someone from the family to accompany you. If you ride at all, it can never be faster than a canter. You cannot leave the house or see visitors from the time you know you are expecting a baby until months afterward. You will rarely see your children. They will be cared for by servants. About the only decisions you will make for yourself are what we will eat and what you will wear. You would have none of the freedom you have here."

Carla had tried to tell herself things wouldn't be as bad as that Polish woman had told her. Now Ivan was telling her they would be worse. "You wouldn't hem me in like that. I know you wouldn't."

"The worst would be how others would treat you, even my mother and sisters. You are not Polish. You were not born into their class. In their eyes, I might as well have married a peasant."

Carla was shocked by the crushing weight of disappointment that hit her like a physical blow. By allowing herself to believe there was a way to work things out, she'd let herself be swallowed up by her love for Ivan. She'd given in to it with all the abandon of a woman who'd never known love and had unexpectedly stumbled on it in its purest form. She hadn't merely accepted love. She'd run toward it, embraced it, had developed a thirst for it, which could never be quenched.

Now Fate seemed poised to take it away from her, but she couldn't let go. Not yet. Not then. She would hold on longer. She didn't know how long that would be, but it would be as long as she could. If Fate had decreed her time with Ivan would be brief, then she would savor everything love had to offer. It would have to last her for the rest of her life. As soon as the resolve formed in her mind, she knew that's what she wanted. She looked up into Ivan's eyes.

"Will you make love to me?"

Chapter 19

ALL EXPRESSION FADED FROM IVAN'S FACE. HIS BODY seemed to stiffen, to withdraw from her, even though he didn't move so much as a muscle.

"Do you know what you are asking?" he finally managed to say.

Carla swallowed her doubts. "Yes."

"To do what you ask could make you believe in promises I cannot make."

Carla took both his hands and clasped them to her bosom. "I understand why you must return to Poland. It is your family, your home, your heritage. I understand," she said when he started to protest, "because I feel that way about this country, Texas, and Danny. But I've come to realize I love you more. I know it won't be easy, but I want to be with you. Always. I don't see why I can't go to Poland with you. Danny can have my half of the ranch so he won't have to work for someone else."

"You do not know what you will be up against."

"You didn't know what you would face when you left Poland, but you learned first to be a soldier then a cowhand."

"It is easier for a man."

She wasn't going to let him undervalue his accomplishment. "It couldn't have been easy, especially when you didn't know English." She laughed. "I've seen you look puzzled at some of the things we say, but you figure it out and keep going. I can do that as long as you're there to help me."

"Women are not treated the same in Poland as they are in this country."

"We're not treated especially well here. Being unmarried at my age practically shouts there's something wrong with me and no man will have me. I might as well level at the moon as try to convince the men in Overlin I know as much about running a ranch as they do." Ivan tried to pull away, but she wouldn't let him. "I love you. I want to be with you because I can't stand the thought of having you for a year then having to say good-bye. It would drive me crazy."

Ivan tore his hand from her tight grip and wrapped her in a fierce embrace. He was losing ground in his battle to stifle the need that was roaring through him like a brush fire consuming dry tender. He'd dreamed of making love to Carla so many times he could almost feel it happening. Standing with his arms around her, her body pressed against his, made it almost impossible to think of anything else.

"You are a strong woman," he said. "You can endure anything."

Carla looked up at him. "What's the use of enduring misery if you don't have to?"

Ivan had tried to block the thought of a future without Carla from his mind. He'd fallen into the habit of telling himself he had almost a year to spend with her, that he wouldn't have to worry about figuring out how to leave her until then. He knew that was cowardly, that he should have kept his emotional distance, but it had been impossible to ignore his feelings. Now she had solved the whole problem by promising to go to Poland with him.

Somewhere in the back of his head a voice whispered that her love was stronger than his, that he should have been the one to turn his back on his country. But that voice was swept away by the impact of Carla's decision. He had thought it was impossible to love her more, but now he knew he was wrong.

"Everything I know about life in Poland pushes on me to urge you to change your mind, but the thought of leaving you has been haunting me. You will face many hardships."

"We will face them together."

He knew it wouldn't be that easy, but he let himself be overborne by her enthusiasm. What if she was right, and he lost the chance to spend his life with her? The thought was too terrible to contemplate. "How will Danny manage the ranch without you?"

She put her finger over his lips to stop his words. "We have plenty of time to figure that out. All we have to think about now is us."

It was easy to give in because it was what he wanted to do. For the first time he could think of his love without the threat of separation hanging over his head. He could think of making love to her without feeling guilt or remorse. She would be his wife. They would be married here then married again when they reached Poland. He would convince his sister to throw a lavish celebration. After all, he was a prince, the titular head of the family. His mother and sisters would be there. Aunts, uncles, cousins, friends from childhood, and friends of the family. It would be a huge celebration that would last for days during which everybody would come to love Carla as much for her character as for her beauty. A few might be slow to accept her, but with the family standing behind him, their objections would soon be swept away.

"Are you sure you can leave Texas?"

"I don't want to, but I can be happy as long as I'm with you. Besides, how many Texas girls get to be a princess?"

He could see the doubt in the back of her eyes, but he could also see the courage which she would depend on to carry her through the rough times that undoubtedly lay ahead. He marveled that it was possible to love someone as much as he loved Carla. What he felt twelve years ago was only a fraction of the love that flowed from him in ever increasing waves. He was the luckiest man in the world.

"Stop worrying," Carla said, "and kiss me. I'm starting to wonder if you love me as much as you say you do."

Ivan had undertaken many tasks in his life, but he had committed to none more readily than convincing Carla his love for her reached well beyond her expectations.

Their first kisses were driven by such heat, such passionate need for each other, that Ivan feared he would bruise her lips. When he tried to ease back, Carla clasped both hands behind his head, trapping him in a kiss so fiery he didn't understand why they weren't scorched by it. He loved the feel of her mouth against his. It was so soft, yet so firm. He couldn't seem to get enough of her. He relegated the kisses in his past to mere touching of the lips, the embraces to languid entanglements. Everything was familiar, but nothing was the same.

Carla broke the kiss, leaned back so she could look into his eyes. "Why haven't you kissed me like this before?"

"I did not let myself for fear I would not be able to leave when the time came."

"I want you to kiss me the way you've always wanted to kiss me."

Ivan had dreamed of a thousand ways to kiss Carla, far too many to fit into a single evening. He wanted to smother her mouth in wild kisses. He wanted to tease it with a soft brushing of the lips. He wanted to explore every part of her mouth, to taste its sweetness, to linger over her lower lip, to tease her upper lip with the tip of his tongue.

He could have spent hours seeking new ways to kiss her if the awareness of her body pressing hard against his own hadn't diverted his thoughts. He was so swollen with desire it was impossible for Carla to be unaware of it, yet she didn't pull back or stiffen with surprise. It seemed, instead, to fuel the fire burning within her. Her kisses grew more insistent. She pressed against him as though trying to get inside his skin.

Almost without being aware of it, Ivan's fingers started unbuttoning the back of Carla's dress. She continued to scatter kisses over his face as though she wanted to map its surface. Realizing he'd passed the point of no return, Ivan swept Carla up in his arms and headed for her bedroom.

Carla felt a surge of triumph when Ivan carried her to her bedroom. She had been afraid his rigid code of behavior might force him to change his mind. It was a testament to how much he needed her that he could sweep aside all his reservations. She had trembled at the feel of his fingers on her back as he worked the buttons loose, but that was only a prelude to the euphoria when he swept her into his arms and carried her to the bedroom as though her weight was a mere bagatelle. His strength acted on her as an aphrodisiac. She gloried in the power of his arms, the breadth of his shoulders, the sheer size of him. He could employ the charm of a high bred nobleman when he chose, but tonight he was in the toils of a need that was as old as man himself, a need that took no cognizance of social station or heritage.

He was just a man who desperately needed to make love to the woman he loved.

Ivan set her on her feet with great tenderness. The grey evening light coming through the window meant his expression was barely visible, but she didn't need light to feel the warmth of his touch, to sense the heat that rolled off him in waves. She was so impatient to be fully against him, that she undid the last few buttons herself. A quick pull on the tie that held her chemise in place, and he was able to lay her shoulders open to the assault of his mouth and fingertips.

The touch of his lips on her bare skin sent so many shock waves arcing through her body that she could barely keep a thought in her head. Almost from the day she met Ivan, she had tried to imagine what it would be like to have him make love to her, but she had never thought it would be like this. She was losing control. Their need for each other had seized command of their minds and bodies. She offered no resistance when he slipped her dress and undergarments off her shoulders, allowed them to slide down her body and pool at her feet.

She felt awkward standing naked before him while he was still fully dressed. She reached out to undo the buttons of his shirt but forgot what she had started to do when he cupped her breasts with his hands. It felt like lightning was striking in a dozen different places at once. The storm grew more intense when he gently rubbed her nipples with his thumbs. It became a torrent when he bent down and took her nipple in his mouth. He teased it with his lips, his tongue, his teeth, until she was certain she would pass out. It was with a sense of relief that she sank down onto the bed.

"You have to undress, too," she said when he started to join her.

He looked startled, so absorbed in making love to her he'd forgotten about himself. Once he wrestled his boots off, the rest of his clothes practically disappeared from his body. She might have been impressed at the speed with which he could undress if her first look at a naked male body in full erection hadn't given birth to a tickle of fear. It was hard to believe he could fit inside her without pain.

Ivan lay down next to her and gathered her in his arms. "I will not hurt you."

"I know." But fear still lurked in the corners of her mind.

Ivan began rubbing her back as he kissed her lips. He made slow movements up the spine and massaged her shoulders before doing it all over again, murmuring softly in her ear. In Polish. She had no idea what he was saying, but she didn't care. They sounded like the words of a man deeply in love, and that sounded wonderful even in Polish.

After a few moments, he turned his attention to her breasts once more. She was so caught up in what he was doing she almost failed to notice his hand had left her back and moved along her side to her hip and a little way along her leg before moving back to her hip. Once again his mouth on her breasts so distracted her that she didn't realize he had parted her legs, until she felt him enter her with his hand.

As his fingers slowly moved inside her, she found herself responding to him, rising to meet him, falling away, and rising again. It was quite pleasant until he touched something inside her that made everything that preceded it pale in comparison. She heard herself cry out.

Ivan froze. "Did I hurt you?"

She shook her head. "Again," she managed to whisper. "Please."

Within moments she was in the grip of a feeling she would have had difficulty describing even if she hadn't been too deeply in its toils to think at all. She felt she would rise right off the bed. She was sure she would explode. Any moment her brain would stop working altogether.

When she did explode, it was from a force so powerful she was certain she wouldn't survive. How could she have anticipated anything like this? Before the waves had receded and the exploding lights faded to mere dots, Ivan rose above her. Before fear had a chance to settle in, he had entered her.

It seemed natural to move in rhythm with him. It wasn't something she needed to think about. It just happened. Within minutes, the feeling that had washed over her moments ago returned. Wrapping its tentacles around her, it encompassed her so completely she was only vaguely aware that Ivan's breath was beginning to come in snatches. Instinctively she clung to him, moved with him, breathed with him. Together they rode a wave that increased in power with each surge, ascended higher each time it broke over them, clasping them ever more firmly in its grasp. They approached the precipice only to retreat before plunging over. But each retreat was shorter, each advance bringing them closer to the edge until—with the feeling of having been propelled from a powerful gun—they catapulted over the edge and into the abyss.

The explosion was more powerful the second time, shattering in fireworks that were beyond description. It was hard to think, but she had to try. There was something she needed to acknowledge, to put into words, to remember. Then when she feared it was beyond her grasp, it suddenly became clear.

At last they were one.

Carla awoke with a delicious feeling of well-being. An overnight rain had lowered the temperature enough to make sleeping delightfully comfortable. The chill in the air coming through the open window felt good on her skin. She had never slept naked before, but with Ivan sharing her bed, she might never wear a nightgown again. It wasn't until she stretched and felt an unusual tenderness that the events of the previous night came flooding back. She bolted upright. Ivan had made love to her. They'd gone to sleep wrapped in each other's arms, but Ivan wasn't in the bed, and his clothes were gone.

She laid back, a smile on her face. It worried her that she'd promised to go to Poland with him, but that was outweighed by the anticipation of spending the rest of her life as his wife. It wouldn't be easy, but he'd be there to help her.

Streams of pale yellow light coming through the window told her it was well past time to be up. Ivan should have had his breakfast an hour ago. Throwing her legs over the side of the bed, she reached for her shift, which Ivan had placed over the chair next to the bed. A few minutes later, having dressed, washed her face, and combed her hair, she left her room.

The mingled smells of coffee and bacon greeted her before she went three steps. She hurried to the kitchen believing Danny was back, but it was Ivan she found standing at the stove.

"I was just about to wake you," he said. "The bacon is fried, the coffee is boiling, and the eggs are almost ready. I wanted to make biscuits, but Cade says my biscuits are not fit for even the dogs."

"Why am I always surprised you can cook?" Why did she ask that when all she wanted to know was if he still loved her, if he regretted making love to her, and if he would do it again?

"Soldiers and cowhands learn to cook, or they starve." He patted his stomach and flashed the smile that told her everything was right in their world. "I do not like to starve."

Carla walked up behind him and put her arms around his waist. "I should be the one fixing your breakfast. Why didn't you wake me?"

"You were sleeping so peacefully I could not make myself disturb you."

Carla released Ivan and moved to pour the coffee. "I

don't want you to spoil me. I intend to carry my weight around here."

Ivan turned and tipped her chin up so he could kiss her. "I like to spoil you, but I do not like to cook. And I like it when I can have biscuits with jam."

Carla laughed. "I promise you biscuits for supper. Now what do we need to do today?"

As they ate breakfast and planned their day, Carla realized she'd never felt such contentment. It didn't matter where she lived. As long as she could be with Ivan, nothing else was truly important.

—⁓—

"You knew people in town were going to be angry with you," Kesney said to Carla. "Riley and his men spend a lot of money."

"It's not just that," Maxwell Dodge added. "They felt they should have been consulted. Riley was guarding their herds, too."

Six of them were having lunch in Maxwell's favorite restaurant. He had sent a message out to the ranch that they needed to discuss the simmering anger in Overlin over what Carla had done.

"Are money and cows more important than their wives and children?" Ivan asked.

"Of course not," Maxwell said. "But their wives and children are safe now, so they can afford to think of cows and money."

Every time Carla had come into town during the last week, she'd been accosted by at least one person who was angry she'd told Riley and his men to leave. Ivan tried to make it clear it had been his decision, that they had been camped on the part of the ranch that was his responsibility, but the sheriff had already told everyone it was Carla's doing.

"Some of it is driven by jealousy and fear," Myrtle said. Having learned the purpose of the meeting by the mysterious communication system that exists in every small town, she had insisted that both she and Lukey be present.

"How is that possible?" Carla asked.

"Some of the men are angry that you've been allowed to run your ranch without any male advice. They're even more upset that you've succeeded. You've got them worried their wives may start to think they can accomplish similar things on their own."

"The sheriff's annoyed he wasn't here when the Mexicans came," Lukey added. "Everybody's been telling him how well Ivan handled the confrontation and search. There's even some talk about him running for sheriff next year."

"I will not be here next year," Ivan said.

"That's an excellent idea," Myrtle exclaimed, ignoring Ivan's objection. "I'm ashamed I didn't think of it myself. It's about time Overlin had a sheriff who thought more of his duty than his breakfast."

Maxwell cleared his throat twice, an ineffectual method of curtailing the discussion as it turned out.

"You can stop that silly noise right now, Maxwell," Myrtle scolded. "Everyone knows the only reason that man is sheriff is that he's the only one who will make even a pretense of going after rustlers. Ivan is not such a coward."

"How do you know?" Kesney challenged.

"He fought in the war," Myrtle said, "which is more than can be said for either of you."

Carla found it amusing that Ivan's growing reputation should cause both men to be so defensive. Myrtle had said it didn't surprise her for any fool could see Ivan was more of a man than either Kesney or Maxwell.

"I'm sure Ivan's everything you say he is," Maxwell said to Myrtle, "but the people of Overlin would feel more comfortable with one of their own as sheriff."

"I wasn't proposing that he be appointed," Myrtle said. "Have him run against the sheriff, and let the town decide who they prefer."

"That's not why we're here," Kesney said. "We need to decide what to do about Riley and his men."

"Where are they?" Ivan asked.

"No one seems quite sure," Maxwell said. "I guess he hasn't found a place he likes well enough to ask about it."

"He is still here," Ivan said.

"How do you know?"

"He came here with a purpose. He will not leave until it is accomplished."

"Since you know so much," Maxwell sneered, "maybe you can share his purpose with us."

"To make as much money as possible."

"That's ridiculous." Maxwell insisted.

"Why?" Myrtle asked. "That's what everybody tries to do. Why should Riley be any different?"

"He was sent here by the governor."

"Who's as big a thief as anyone in Texas," Carla stated.

"Don't try to deny it," Myrtle told Maxwell. "Every honest man in Texas knows it."

"That still doesn't answer the question of—" He broke off, suddenly aware of an uproar in the street.

"Something's wrong." Maxwell pushed away from the table in preparation for getting up. "I'd better go see about it."

"Stay where you are," Myrtle commanded. "We still have a sheriff even if he is nearly worthless."

"The people depend upon me to—"

"The people put up with you because you're harmless," Myrtle said. "Now be quiet. I expect they'll find us soon enough if we're needed."

Myrtle had hardly finished speaking when a man rushed into the restaurant, looked around until he spotted them, then rushed over to their table.

"It's rustlers!" he shouted. "They stole from every ranch around here." He pointed an accusing finger at Carla, his face twisting with rage. "All except your ranch. Some people are saying you really didn't get rid of Riley at all, that you only pretended, so he could steal our cows and split the money with you. What have you got to say to that?"

Chapter 20

CARLA DIDN'T KNOW WHAT SHOCKED HER MORE: that rustlers had stolen from every ranch except hers, or that people she had known most of her life believed she could be dishonest. She had angered several men in the community by insisting they treat her as an equal, but she had never had any reason to believe they doubted her integrity. Now she only had to look in the rancher's angry face to know he was ready to believe the worst.

"I'm ashamed of you, Monty Narrows," Myrtle said. "You know Carla would never do anything to hurt anyone in Overlin."

"Then how does she explain why her herd wasn't hit?"

"How do you know it was not hit?" Ivan asked. "Did you see all the cows that were taken?"

"If I'd seen 'em, I'd have stopped 'em," Monty sputtered. "That's what Frank Bass said."

"Did he see them?"

"I don't know."

Ivan didn't let up. "Why would anyone suppose Carla's herd was spared?"

"Ask Frank."

"Is anyone going after the rustlers?"

"They're getting together right now."

"I will go with them. You should go back to the ranch," Ivan said to Carla.

"I'm going, too. Even if my herd wasn't hit, I'm as interested as anyone else in putting a stop to this rustling."

But when she and Ivan caught up with the gathered ranchers, it was clear that not everyone believed her.

"What are you doing here?" Frank Bass asked.

"We're here to go after the rustlers."

"You can't drive your buggy through the Rio Grande."

"I can ride."

"We don't want you. Go home, and watch over your herd. They might decide to come back after it."

"How do you know Carla lost no cows?" Ivan asked.

"Because none of the tracks came from the direction of her ranch. Or from Kesney's for that matter," he said, turning on Kesney who had come up after Carla. "You two got some special deal?"

"Don't be stupid, Frank," Myrtle said. "You know Kesney was hit a couple months ago."

"He got a warning, but we didn't. Now we don't have time for any more jawing. We got to be riding."

"I will go with you," Ivan said.

"We don't need a foreigner to help us take care of our business," Frank said. "You can hold Carla's hand so she won't be scared."

Carla was furious. It was another slap in the face by men who didn't want to think of her as their equal. Her first impulse was to declare that she would ride with them whether they wanted her or not. She would prove she wasn't afraid of danger. Ivan must have sensed what she was thinking.

"We should go back to the ranch," he said. "Something is not right."

"I know that. Rustlers have hit nearly every ranch in the area."

"I think it was planned."

"Of course it was. You don't think—" She stopped when she realized what Ivan meant. "You mean you think Riley has something to do with it?"

"Riley would have stopped it if you hadn't run him off," Frank shouted. "It should have been your herd, not ours."

The clamor of angry voices indicated the other ranchers agreed. "Let's be going," the irate rancher bellowed. "No point in giving them any more time."

It made Carla furious to see the men ride off and leave her behind, but it was painfully clear they didn't want her with them. That hurt, but it hurt even more that they could believe she would have anything to do with rustlers.

"Go check on your herd," Myrtle said to Carla. "Just because Frank didn't find any tracks coming from the direction of your ranch doesn't mean you didn't lose cows."

"That could be true for me, too," Kesney said.

"Both of you might as well go home," Maxwell said. "The way people are feeling, your hanging around will just cause trouble."

Myrtle had a few well-chosen words for Maxwell that sent him scurrying back to his office, but Carla took no pleasure in the rout of that self-important man. Her neighbors and friends thought she was in league with rustlers. She lost half her ranch and fell in love with a man she'd promised to follow to Poland. For a woman who considered herself as capable as any man, she'd stumbled from one disaster to another.

"Take Carla home," Myrtle said to Ivan. "And see if you can give her something else to think about."

By now Carla was too used to Myrtle's provocative comments to be embarrassed, but it amused her to see Ivan squirm under the old woman's penetrating gaze. Kesney rode out of town with them. Since he spent most of the ride worrying about his herd and his daughter, Carla had little chance to say anything to Ivan until Kesney turned off on the trail toward his ranch.

"He hasn't been in Texas long enough to know rustlers don't kidnap daughters," Carla said to Ivan when Kesney rode off.

"He worries about Beth. She is still young."

"So is Danny, but it didn't seem to occur to him that I might be worried that he's off somewhere with Riley. I hope you're wrong about Riley having something to do with the rustling. Danny could be in trouble."

"I doubt Danny is in danger. I believe Riley ran off the cows so he could be a hero by bringing them back. That way no one will ever ask him to leave."

"Frank and the others don't believe that. As soon as they find their cows, they'll start shooting."

"I am sure Riley has thought of a way around that. He is a careful man."

"I wish Danny was at home."

Carla got her wish sooner than she expected. She walked into the kitchen to find her brother sitting at the table and eating the ham she had planned for supper. Both her joy at seeing Danny and her irritation at him for eating their supper were forgotten when she noticed the bloody bandage around his arm. They both spoke at the same time.

"What happened to you?"

"I thought you'd never get home."

"How did you get hurt?" Ivan asked.

"That's what I came to tell you," Danny said around the piece of ham he was chewing. He swallowed, drank some water, and then turned to Ivan. "You were right about Riley. He's a thief. I think he killed a few people, too."

"You're bleeding," Carla said.

"It's just a flesh wound. I owe Bricker a punch in the face for it."

"Let me look at it," Carla said.

"It's not important. You got to listen to what I have to tell you."

The story came out in bits and pieces, but it transpired that Danny had been assigned to the group looking for stolen cows. He wondered why only half the men were riding with him, but he had been told they could find more cows if they split up. Since that meant he might be paid more money, he was content to follow Riley's orders.

"I started thinking something was wrong when I heard Americans were robbing villages. My Spanish isn't great, but I could understand enough to know people were upset about more than cows."

"What did you do?" Ivan asked.

"I went to Riley with what I'd heard. I thought we ought to try to catch the thieves."

"What did he say?"

"He said that was for the army to worry about, that we were to stick with finding stolen herds."

"What changed?"

"It was Bricker. He never wanted me in the group. He pretty much stayed away from me, but after I spoke to Riley, he was everywhere I turned, glaring at me with his sour scowl, complaining that I was too pretty to be any good. I ignored him until I noticed a gold chain around his neck. He didn't have one when I joined because I'd seen him naked to the waist. I didn't have to see it really close to know it was worth a lot more than we made from the herd we brought back."

"You didn't face him down, did you?" his sister asked.

"Do you think I'm a coward?" her brother demanded.

"No, but I don't trust Bricker."

"I don't trust him either, especially after he tried to put a bullet in me."

"How did that happen?" Ivan asked.

"Bricker never rode with us when we went looking for cows so I started to wonder if he might have been the one doing the robbing. When he was gone, I took a look in his tent."

"What did you find?" Carla asked.

"Nothing, but Bricker saw me coming out. We practically killed each other before they pulled us apart. I told Riley what I suspected. He said Bricker had had that chain for a long time but didn't wear it much. There was nothing I could say after that. Bricker threatened to do something terrible to you or Beth if I started telling people he was a thief, but I figured I was wrong, so I told him I was sorry about what I'd done and wouldn't say anything. That would have been the end of it, only the next time we went looking for cows, Bricker rode with us. We found a stolen herd, but there was a little shooting before we got away with the cows. That's when I got shot. The only person close enough was Bricker. I didn't need to see the expression on his face to know he was going to try again. I used the excuse of taking care of my wound to drop back, saying I'd catch up later. Instead I decided to come back here and tell Ivan what I suspected."

"I'm glad you did," Carla said.

"I haven't finished," Danny said. "I haven't told you about Riley."

"What about him?" Carla asked.

"I found him and some of the others with a whole bunch of cows that weren't stolen from Mexico. They were stolen from the ranches around Overlin."

"We know. A dozen men are out looking for them now. Ivan said he thought Riley stole the cows so he could bring them back and be a hero," Carla said.

"He's planning to bring the cows back tomorrow. He said the ranchers will be so thankful they'll let him set up his camp anywhere he wants. Or as many camps as he wants. After that, it would be easy to raid about a dozen more villages in Mexico before moving to a new location."

"So Riley is behind the thefts," Ivan said.

"Not just that. You know those stolen herds I thought he was returning to their owners? He's selling them to anybody who'll pay his price. Looks like he means to make as much money as possible before clearing out."

"How did you hear all of this?" Carla asked.

"I was caught behind a log half the night before it was safe to get away. I came straight here. Now I'm going to Kesney's to warn him about Beth. I'd have gone there first, but Kesney has given his men orders not to let me set foot on his land. You've got to come with me," he said to Ivan. "He won't believe anything I say."

"I'm coming, too," Carla announced, "and you're riding with me in the buggy. You've already put enough strain on that wound."

Danny argued, but when Ivan supported her, he gave in. When he agreed to let her drive, Carla decided his wound was more serious than he was letting on. The old Danny would rather walk the whole way in his boots than let his sister drive him.

"What do you think the sheriff is going to do after I tell him what I know?" Danny asked.

"Maybe you should ask what Maxwell Dodge is going to do," Carla responded. "He's taken to making all the decisions for the town." She glanced at Ivan. "Myrtle says Ivan ought to run for sheriff. After the way he handled the hostage situation and the search, she's sure he'd win."

"That's a great idea," Danny said to Ivan. "Everybody would vote for you. The sheriff never does a thing if he can help it."

"I do not want to be a sheriff," Ivan said.

"Why not? You need money to go back to Poland. You get paid for being sheriff."

"I will not be here long."

"You'd be here long enough to show people what a real sheriff is like." Danny was still trying to convince Ivan to run for sheriff when they reached the turnoff for Kesney's ranch. "You can practice how to convince people to vote for you by convincing Kesney that Riley is a crook. I don't have any proof, so he'll never believe me."

Ivan was outlining all the incriminating circumstances that pointed to Riley's involvement when he suddenly broke off. "There is a horse ahead without a rider." He immediately put his horse into a fast canter.

"Catch up with him," Danny said to Carla. "That could be Beth's horse."

Carla cracked the whip to send her horse into a slow gallop. "It can't be. Her father won't let her use anything but a buggy."

Up ahead, Ivan passed the riderless horse without slowing down. "Why didn't he stop?" Danny asked. "What's he doing?"

"Looking for the rider." There was no sign of a man trying to catch the horse that had thrown him, so the rider must be down. "I think someone's hurt."

She was sure of it when she saw Ivan pull his horse to an abrupt stop and hurriedly dismount. He bent over a dark shape on the ground. She hoped the man wasn't dead. She knew virtually everyone who lived in and around Overlin. It would be like losing a friend. She was relieved when she saw the man sit up.

"That's Kesney." Danny's eyesight had always been better than hers. "Something must have happened to Beth." He jerked the whip from Carla's grasp and cracked it repeatedly over their horse. The frightened animal went into a hard gallop.

"Stop it!" Carla snatched the whip back from Danny. "You won't help anybody by getting us killed or the horse lamed."

"I know something has happened to Beth."

"You don't know any such thing. Kesney rode from town with us. Something could have happened to spook his horse, and it threw him. He's not half the rider Ivan is, and he's a poor judge of horses to boot."

Danny didn't seem convinced, but she was certain
Kesney had not been attacked. She changed her mind
when she got close enough to see the blood on his shirt.
Danny was out of the buggy before she brought it to a
complete stop.

"What happened?" Danny asked.

"We must get him to a doctor quickly." Ivan picked
up Kesney, carried him to the buggy, and settled him
on the seat. "You must hold him in the seat," he said to
Danny. "He is wounded badly."

"Did he tell you what happened?" Carla asked.

"Kesney was stopped by a man who asked his name
then shot him."

"Was it Bricker?" Danny asked. "I know it was Bricker."

"The description fits only one man I know."

"Who?" Danny and Carla asked together.

"Laveau diViere."

Chapter 21

IVAN TRIED TO CONVINCE HIMSELF THE MAN KESNEY had seen couldn't have been Laveau, but ever since the war, Laveau had managed to stay close to at least one of the men he'd betrayed. If he was here, it was because something had gone wrong with the scheme in which Ivan had unwittingly become a part.

"We must get Kesney to the doctor," Ivan said.

Danny objected. "I'm going to see Beth."

"You have no horse, and you are injured," Ivan told him. "Help your sister get Kesney to town. I'll get Beth and take her to her father."

Danny was all set to argue, but Carla told him, "Let Ivan go. You and Beth would probably get so caught up in your reunion you'd forget about her father."

When Carla turned the buggy and started toward town, Danny was still threatening to get down and walk all the way to Kesney's ranch. Ivan watched a few moments before starting his mount down the trail at a slow canter. He needed to think.

What was Laveau doing at Kesney's ranch? Why had he shot Kesney? Except for losing his temper and stabbing Rafe's stepmother, Laveau had always been careful to avoid being caught in any serious crime that might jeopardize his protection by the army and the Texas government. Was the man getting desperate—or angry enough to forget his usual caution? Having one scheme after another foiled by men determined to bring him to justice was probably enough to send his temper spiraling out of control.

Ivan hadn't gone far when he came to a piece of ground where two horses had stopped. Twelve years ago he wouldn't have known what to make of what he saw, but four years in the war and five years on a cattle ranch had taught him to read hoofprints. This must have been where Kesney was shot. There was no cover. Riders on the same trail would have been visible to each other at a great distance, but that was no reason for Laveau to shoot Kesney. He could have ridden by, and Kesney would never have known who he was.

It took only a moment to see that the horse that came from Kesney's ranch had gone back. That made even less sense. Why should Laveau go back to Kesney's house? Whatever the reason, Ivan was certain it was important. Laveau would never have taken such a risk otherwise. The only thing worth such a risk was Beth, but why should Laveau do anything to her? Did he even know she existed?

Kesney's house stood on open ground with nothing around it Ivan could use for cover. Even several hundred yards away, he could see a horse tethered to the rail. At any other time, he would have ridden straight up to the house. Hoping Laveau wouldn't decide to look out a window, he made a wide circle to come up behind the house from the bunkhouse. If he could surprise Laveau, he might have a chance to find out what he was doing here and why he'd shot Kesney.

It took longer than he expected to reach the bunkhouse. No one was inside so he left his horse there and sprinted across the open ground between the two buildings. Kesney's ranch was one of the biggest in south Texas. His house was a large frame building with a porch across the front. From his previous visit, Ivan remembered four rooms on the main floor with additional rooms on the upper level. An extension at the back housed the kitchen and the dining room. He decided to enter there first—after he removed his boots.

The kitchen door was unlocked. Easing it open, he listened for any sound. When he heard none, he entered on stocking feet. On the far side of a butcher table he saw a woman bound and gagged. Wide eyes stared at him in fear. Indicating she should make no sound, Ivan approached her. "I will not hurt you. Has anything happened to Beth?"

After hesitating a moment, the woman nodded her head.

"Do you know who did it?"

Again she nodded.

"I will untie you, and you will tell me." He removed the gag. "Speak softly. Someone is in the main house."

"It was the foreman and a man I do not know," the woman whispered in heavily accented English. "They tied her up and took her away in her own buggy."

"Do you know where they were taking her?"

The woman shook her head.

Ivan took the ropes off her hands and feet. "Tell me about the house."

The woman described each room, its position, and reminded Ivan of the location of the major pieces of furniture. He decided Laveau was probably in the room Kesney used as his study or in his bedroom. What he couldn't understand was why he was here at all. He had to be looking for something he considered extremely important, or there would have been no reason to shoot Kesney.

"Stay here," Ivan told the woman.

Ivan didn't usually carry a gun. He was glad he'd made an exception today. He passed from the kitchen into the dining room without incident, but he was worried about the door leading from the dining room into the main house. If it squeaked, Laveau would know someone was in the house. He was also fearful that his weight would cause the floorboards to creak. It was essential that he surprise Laveau if he was to have any chance of finding out why he was here.

With infinite care, he turned the knob and began to ease the door open. Much to his relief, it didn't make a sound. He found himself in the broad hall that bisected the house with two rooms on either side. Kesney's bedroom was on his left. On his right was the old kitchen, which had been turned into a spare room. The study was at the front of the house on the left; the parlor where he'd had his dance lesson was on the right.

Should he try the bedroom, a closer but less likely place to find Laveau, or should he attempt to cover twenty feet over a squeaky floor that separated him from the study? There was nothing he could do to prevent the floor from creaking. Before he had time to weigh his choices, he heard a muttered curse and a drawer being slammed. Laveau was in the study.

With great care he placed his foot in the center of a floorboard and pressed down. He had brought only a fraction of his weight to bear when he felt the board start to bind against the boards on either side.

He pulled back. What could he do? He couldn't tiptoe over the floor without making enough noise to alert Laveau. He couldn't go around to the front because he'd still have to walk over the floor plus hazard that Laveau wouldn't see him, hear him on the porch, or know when he opened the front door. There was only one thing to do.

He drew his gun, tensed his muscles, then sprinted down the hall as fast as he could. He slid to a stop in the doorway of the study, his gun pointing at a surprised Laveau diViere. A look of pure hatred crossed Laveau's face only to disappear as quickly as it had come. He was seated at Kesney's desk, going through papers. Assuming a languishing pose of disinterest, he gave Ivan a pained smile.

"You must have lost your way." His voice was steeped in the aristocratic condescension with which he spoke to nearly everyone. "This is not the Reece ranch."

"I know whose ranch it is. I also knew you were here."

Laveau's eyebrows rose. "Now I find that hard to believe."

"You should have checked more carefully before leaving Kesney for dead."

Laveau's eyebrows lowered, his expression turned bored. "I don't know who you're talking about."

"Where's Beth?"

"Who?"

"Hardin's daughter. She has been kidnapped."

"Why should I know anything about that?"

"Because you're in his house going through his desk, while his housekeeper is tied up in the kitchen."

Laveau's boredom increased. "I would never sink so

low." His boredom lessened, and his eyes narrowed. "I am curious to know how you came to be here."

"Kesney is alive and on his way to the doctor in Overlin. From his description, I knew you had to be the one who shot him."

"I'm pleased to know I can't be confused with your ordinary citizenry, but there must be at least one person of distinction in that miserable town."

Ivan refused to let Laveau shake his focus. Laveau wasn't wearing a gun, but that didn't mean he wasn't armed. "Ever since I found out Rilcy was stealing cows and robbing villages in Mexico, I knew you were involved."

"If you're expecting me to congratulate you on your cleverness, you'll be disappointed."

"I would rather know what you hope to find in Kesney's desk."

Laveau's expression darkened, and the latent hatred he usually kept hidden practically leapt out at Ivan. "Kesney ruined a very profitable operation of mine. He came into possession of an incriminating piece of paper—that taught me *never* to put anything in writing— which he used to force me to leave Kentucky."

"For that you had to shoot him?"

Laveau had recaptured his habitual reserve. "He deserved to die. Why do you care about him?"

"He has a daughter who needs her father."

"You always were a sentimental fool. Otherwise you wouldn't want to go back to a country that doesn't exist anymore. That girl will marry some worthless cowhand who'll spend her money and cheat on her as soon as she swells up with their first child."

"You have a poor opinion of people."

"After what happened in your country, you should, too." Laveau stood. "All you have to do is mind your own business for the next year, and you can go back to your precious Poland."

"And what will you do?"

"Pluck some fools of things they can't appreciate the way I can. Then in a month or two I'll move on, and you'll never hear of me again. Shall we shake on it?"

Throughout the conversation, Ivan had been expecting Laveau to get up, move about the room, or reach for something to throw, anything that could give him the advantage. It was that unswerving scrutiny that saved him when Laveau stood and extended his hand. Almost as if by magic, a small derringer appeared in Laveau's hand. Ivan threw himself to the side as a bullet crashed into the wall behind where he'd been standing. Firing as he went down, he hit the floor, then threw himself at Laveau's legs, even as Laveau put a second shot through the study floor.

Ivan struck Laveau with the full weight of his body, which caused the lighter man to lose his balance and send his third shot into the ceiling. Rolling onto his feet, Ivan grabbed Laveau by the front of his shirt and hit him as hard as he could. Stunned, Laveau slumped to the floor. "I have waited seven years to do that, you son of a bitch."

Laveau touched his hand to his mouth, which came away bloody. "Why didn't you shoot me when you had the chance? You could have been a hero for stopping a robbery in the house of a man who'd been shot and his daughter kidnapped."

"I want to see you hanged for two attempted murders."

"I'll never hang."

Ivan jerked Laveau to his feet. "I will take you to the sheriff in Overlin. If you try to get away, I will shoot you." He reached for Laveau's right hand. When it was outstretched, it triggered a mechanism which caused a small derringer to appear. "I have heard of such a device, but I had never seen one."

"It's very useful, and not nearly so crude as a holster."

Ivan spun Laveau around and stripped off his coat. Next he removed the mechanism, threw it on the floor, and stomped it into splinters. He picked up the four-barreled gun. "No more bullets. What were you going to do next?"

"I don't know." Laveau's composure didn't falter. "I've never missed before."

Using Laveau's own belt, Ivan tied the man's hands behind him. "I intend to see that you never have reason to miss again." He pushed Laveau out of the study and toward the front door.

"Don't you want to relieve the housekeeper of her worry?" Laveau asked.

"I'm not letting you out of my sight until we get to Overlin."

Ivan didn't like the sound of Laveau's soft laugh as they left the house.

"You're lucky," the doctor said to Kesney. "With that wound, you could have bled to death. You owe this boy your life."

Carla was amused to see Danny blush. He wasn't used to getting praise.

"Carla made me do it," he said. "She said she'd shoot me herself if I got blood all over her buggy and let Kesney die into the bargain."

Carla laughed. "I didn't say any such thing."

"It's what you meant. Are you done poking at me?" The doctor had subjected Danny to a thorough examination.

"I'm through. Just take it easy until your wound has time to heal."

Carla hoped Ivan would arrive soon. It was all she could do to keep Danny from going back to Kesney's house.

"What are you going to do now?" Danny asked when they left the doctor's office. "I'm going to find Beth."

Before Carla could answer, a rider and horse appeared at the end of the street. Rather than walk or trot his horse into town, he galloped down the center of the street. "Riley found the cows," he shouted as he rode by, "and he brought 'em back." He rode to the other side of town before turning back. His shouts brought people out of buildings on both sides of the street. The saloons emptied first, followed by various businesses and offices. A woman being fitted for a dress emerged from Sadie Lowell's shop. In less than a minute, people living on back streets were pouring into the main road. When the first cows appeared at the edge of town, some men shouted and threw their hats into the air. Women clapped while children raced about like playful prairie dogs.

"Ivan said this was going to happen," Carla said to Danny.

"You'll never get them to believe Riley is behind the robberies now."

"Or that he could have had anything to do with Kesney being shot."

"What are you going to do?"

"Wait for Ivan. He'll know what to do."

"There's nothing to do except make sure Beth is okay. I'll take Kesney's horse."

Carla tried to change his mind, but she didn't try to stop him when he walked away. She felt a growing need to talk to someone. Much to her surprise, the person she wanted was Myrtle. It was impossible to cross the street as long as it was filled with cows and jubilant riders. When she saw Frank Bass heading her way, she was tempted to duck inside the closest store.

"Riley had already found the cows when we caught up with him," he shouted to her over the noisy uproar on the street.

"Maybe he didn't *find* them. Maybe he had them all the time."

"Still trying to defend yourself?"

"Not after Danny showed up today. He'd been shot by Bricker because he found out some of Riley's men were stealing from villages while others looked for cows. They threatened to hurt Beth if he said anything. It wasn't an empty threat. We hope nothing has happened to Beth, but Kesney has been shot."

Bass's self-satisfied look was wiped off his face. "Is he dead?"

"No, but he's so badly wounded the doctor said he can't go home for at least a week. He was shot by Laveau diViere, the man who cheated Danny of his half of the ranch. DiViere gave Riley permission to use my land for his base. Ivan warned us all not to trust Riley because of his connection to diViere."

Bass was having trouble holding his position in the

tide of animals flowing through the street. "Where is Ivan?"

"Gone to look for Beth. Danny overheard Riley say they were only going to stay here another month before they moved to a new place. I'm worried they might try to use Beth to keep us from doing anything to stop them."

"Where's Danny?"

"Gone to find Beth and Ivan. I tried to get him to wait, but he wouldn't."

"I find all of this hard to believe."

"I'm not sure I fully believed it until Danny told me what he'd found out."

"Nobody in this town is going to take your word for it. You can see for yourself how they act toward Riley and his men."

"They'd better believe it before another armed posse from Mexico comes looking for the men who stole from their churches and their homes. They're not going to believe we're innocent a second time."

The cows had passed through town, and the streets were beginning to clear. Maxwell Dodge spotted them and headed their way.

"There's the first person you have to convince," Bass said.

"Ivan will do that." Carla had been watching for Ivan ever since she left the doctor's office. She breathed a sigh of relief when she saw him enter town. A man she could only assume was Laveau diViere was by his side. She'd expected to see someone more impressive, more sinister. Next to Ivan he looked like an overdressed snake oil salesman. Considering the circumstances, his air of superiority was a rather pathetic attempt to show his contempt for those he felt were beneath him.

"How is Kesney?" Ivan asked as soon as Carla reached him.

"He's badly wounded, but he'll survive."

"Where is Danny?"

"He took Kesney's horse to go look for you."

Ivan began cursing in Polish again. By now Bass and Maxwell Dodge had caught up with her.

"Did you find Beth?"

"The housekeeper said she was kidnapped by their old foreman and a man who fits Bricker's description. She does not know where they have taken her."

Carla pointed at Laveau. "What about him?"

"I've never set eyes on that girl," Laveau declared.

"Then why do you have him tied up?" Maxwell Dodge asked.

"Because I found him going through Kesney's study." Ivan took a derringer out of his pocket and tossed it to Maxwell. "When I tried to stop him, he shot at me with this. You can find three bullets in Kesney's house. I expect you can find the fourth in Kesney. This man must go to jail. Where is the sheriff? "

"Off with the men returning the stolen cows," Bass said. "He won't be back for hours."

"I'll take care of this for you," Maxwell said.

Ivan didn't look pleased. He didn't look any happier when he locked diViere's cell and handed the key to Maxwell.

"That is an extremely dangerous man," he said to Maxwell. "Be very careful around him."

Maxwell appeared affronted. "I think I can handle the situation."

"I hope so. Evil follows this man closer than a calf follows a cow."

Carla was relieved to leave the sheriff's office. DiViere might not look impressive, but such deep hatred burned in his black eyes, he looked almost reptilian.

"Is Riley really behind all this trouble?" Bass asked Ivan.

"Yes. Laveau diViere came here to set up a camp so he could pillage Mexican towns. It was only after he learned where Danny's ranch was located that he decided to play cards with him. He offered me the land after a year because he thought I wanted to go back to Poland so much I would turn a blind eye to anything I might see."

"How do you know all this?"

"Laveau told me. He's a brilliant man who wants everyone to appreciate his talents."

Carla looked worried. "We've got to stop Danny."

"I saw him going into the saloon when I rode by," Bass said.

"I've got to stop him before he does something stupid."

But when they reached the saloon, Danny wasn't there.

"Have you seen Danny today?" Carla asked the bartender.

"He came in a short while ago and started threatening a couple of Riley's men," the bartender said. "I told him to take it outside. Do you know what that's about? Can't have been Riley's men causing trouble. They were busy bringing back the stolen cows."

"Where did they go?" Ivan asked.

"Out back. One of them said something about getting their horses. You just missed him by a few minutes. Is everything okay?"

"We just need to find Danny," Carla said. Once back on the boardwalk, she asked Ivan, "What do we do now?"

"They wanted to get him alone," Ivan said. "They may not have known about the kidnapping, but they know about the stealing and the fake rustling."

"Their horses were tired," Carla said. "Maybe they went to the livery stable for fresh ones."

When they reached the livery, a stable hand told them, "Yeah, they was here. I saddled up two nice horses. Boss said not to charge them, they being Riley's men."

"Do you know where they were going?" Ivan asked.

"Nope, but they went off in the direction of Mr. Dodge's place. It's over—"

"I know where it is," Carla said.

The man grinned. "I sorta thought you might."

Ivan was tempted to plant a fist in the man's face, but they had to catch up with Danny before Riley's men got him back to their camp. "Saddle your best horse for Miss Reece. I want it ready when I return with my horse."

If Danny had told the men about the shooting and kidnapping—and Ivan was certain he had—then Danny was in serious trouble. So was Beth. By now Danny could name everyone in the gang. Beth would certainly know her kidnappers. The young people were a threat to the gang's freedom. Without Beth or Danny, Riley's gang could vanish without a problem. Ivan brought the rifle and extra ammunition from Carla's buggy.

Carla's horse was ready when he returned. Her concern deepened when she saw the rifle and ammunition, but she didn't say anything until they were mounted up and riding out of town.

"What do you think they're going to do?"

"Do not worry. We will catch up with them soon."

Carla was fretting before they'd gone a mile.

"How far is it to Maxwell's ranch?" Ivan asked.

"About five miles."

"We have plenty of time."

"Shouldn't we go faster?"

"We need to save our horses until we sight them." *Always save something for the last push* had been their motto during the war. It was one reason they had virtually no losses until Laveau's betrayal.

They had covered about half the distance to Maxwell's ranch when Ivan spotted where three horses had left the trail. "Something is wrong," Ivan said. "They are galloping."

"We've got to catch them. If they take Danny to their camp, they'll kill him."

Just then they heard the sound of distant gunfire. Putting their horses into a hard gallop, it wasn't long before they sighted two men firing at a target that was out of sight.

"Danny must be in that arroyo," Carla said. "He has no protection. We've got to hurry."

"Wait." Ivan pulled his horse to a halt, took out his rifle, and aimed very carefully before squeezing off his shot. A second later one of the men jerked and dropped his rifle. The second man turned in their direction and fired a shot that went wild. Rather than continue the fight, he turned and rode away, leaving his companion to follow as best he could.

"That was incredible," Carla marveled as they started their horses forward. "I've never seen anyone shoot like that."

"In Poland, every man shoots. A prince must be better than anyone else."

"We shoot in Texas, too, but not like that."

By the time they reached Danny, he'd climbed out of the arroyo and caught up his horse. "You don't have to tell me what I did was stupid," he said before either spoke. "I was too worried about Beth to think straight."

"She's been kidnapped," Ivan told him. "Do you know how to find the new camp?"

"I sure do."

"Before we go after them, we need a plan," Ivan said. "Once we have it, we have to follow it."

"We have to leave now," Danny insisted. "No telling what Bricker has done to Beth."

"He wouldn't dare," Carla said. "The town would lynch him."

Danny had several objections to the plan Ivan worked out, but Carla silenced him by saying Ivan's four years of experience during the war was better than Danny's none at all.

"I don't see why we have to wait until dark," Danny objected.

"We are outnumbered. We either use the cover of night or go back to town for reinforcements and hope they do not escape before we return."

"The way the town feels about Riley right now, they'd be more likely to come after us," Carla said.

Chapter 22

IVAN HAD NO DIFFICULTY FINDING A SPOT IN THE trees from which to observe the camp. Despite Carla's demand they leave her land, they weren't far from their original spot.

"I don't see Beth," Danny said.

"Why didn't you tell me Riley never left our land?" Carla asked her brother.

Ivan hushed the pair. "Speak only when necessary. Our only chance of success is to take them by surprise."

The camp was in an uproar with everyone preparing to leave. Men shouted at each other. Occasionally blows were exchanged.

"You should have shot the little bastard as soon as you got him out of town," one man yelled at another.

"Riley shouldn't have taken him on," the man shouted back. "Locals always have more loyalty to someone else."

"Shut up," Riley yelled at both of them. "If you're not loaded up by the time I'm done, I'll leave you behind."

"Stay here and keep an eye on Riley," Ivan said to Carla. "Danny, come with me."

"I've got to find Beth."

"Let's see if we can reduce their numbers first." When Danny looked like he would argue, Ivan grabbed him by the collar. "Follow orders, or go back to Overlin now."

"You agreed Ivan would make all the decisions," Carla hissed at her brother. "For once in your life, shut up and do what you're told."

"What are we going to do?" Danny asked in voice that wasn't noticeably chastened.

"I want to eliminate some of the men when they go to their horses."

"There are several I'm itching to eliminate."

The horses were in a rope corral about fifty yards from the main camp. It was dark under the trees, but a bright half moon cast a pale light over the open plain. Ivan hushed Danny. One man approached the herd, but his horse was too far from where Ivan and Danny hid. He tied his bedroll to his saddle and returned to camp.

"There's nowhere to hide," Danny complained.

But Ivan wasn't listening. Keeping low, he sprinted across the short distance between the trees and the rope corral. Several horses shied nervously, but sensing the mood of the camp, all the horses were restless. Crouching low to the ground, Ivan watched from between the horses' legs as a second man approached. The man dropped his saddlebags on the ground and scooted under the rope to catch his mount. Ivan waited until the man had selected his horse and was working his way back through the herd. Coming to his feet swiftly, Ivan ran the short distance between him and the man. Instinct, or the movement of the horses, must have warned the man. He started to turn but was too late. A blow from the butt of Ivan's gun sent him tumbling to the ground.

"What are we going to do with him?" Danny asked when Ivan had dragged the unconscious man into the cover of the trees.

"Tie him up and gag him. See if you can get his saddlebags. I want Riley to think he deserted."

Danny moved quickly to catch the man's horse and retrieve his saddlebags.

Over the next quarter of an hour, Ivan dragged two more men into the grove to be tied and gagged. Danny might have been caught when he went after the second man's bedroll and saddlebags if Ivan hadn't let loose a howl that sounded so much like a wolf the horses milled about the corral in fear.

"I learned to do that in Poland," Ivan explained. "It makes the deer run from cover."

An empty-handed man approached the herd. Instead of going for a horse, he started calling names.

"He's looking for the men we tied up," Danny whispered to Ivan.

After searching through the herd, the man started cussing.

"Their horses are gone," he growled. "The bastards have cut and run."

"What do we do now?" Danny asked.

"We find where they have Beth. Once we do that, we decide what to do next."

When the man turned back to camp, Ivan and Danny ran across the open ground to the few trees that surrounded the camp. It didn't take long to come up behind the row of tents. Over the noise of the men arguing about what to do now that three of them were gone, Ivan caught the sound of a female voice. He motioned for Danny to follow him. They hadn't gone far before it was clear Beth was being held in one of the tents, and she was arguing with Bricker. Ivan grabbed hold of Danny when he attempted to run past him. "Try going off on your own once more," he said in a fierce whisper, "and I will gag *you* and tie *you* to a tree."

"But Bricker has Beth."

"Do you want him to ride out of here using Beth as a shield?"

"No, but—"

"Then stay behind me. I *will* tie you up. Knock you out if necessary. I will not have Beth put in more danger because you are too infatuated to use common sense."

Danny opened his mouth to argue, took a good look at Ivan's expression, and then backed down. "What do we do?"

"We locate the tent."

The escalating argument between Beth and Bricker led them to a tent set up a distance from the others.

"My father will kill you for this!" Beth shouted at Bricker. "He'll put a bullet right through your heart."

"Your father will never find you." Bricker's voice sounded confident.

"He will. And so will Danny." Beth didn't sound as confident, but she didn't back down. "He'll grind you into the dust and feed your heart to the pigeons."

Bricker laughed. "You're not in Kentucky, little girl. We don't have pigeons in Texas."

"You have buzzards," Beth said. "They'll tear your eyes out."

"I always did like a woman with spirit."

"No woman would have you, especially a woman with spirit."

Bricker mumbled a curse.

"Let go of me," Beth cried.

Ivan put his hand on Danny's shoulder. "Not yet," he whispered.

"I said let go of me!" Beth repeated.

"Riley says we're to let you go after we leave, but I'm thinking I'd like to keep you."

"I said *let go*!"

Bricker let out a howl. "You crazy bitch! You bit me!"

"Touch me again, and I'll do worse."

"Not once I—"

"Didn't you hear Riley calling you?" a voice at the front of the tent asked. "If he comes after you, he'll do worse than that girl."

Bricker uttered another curse. "I'll be back. Then I'll settle with you."

Ivan had pulled out his knife and opened it. He snuck up to the back of Bricker's tent and began cutting a hole through the canvas. "Beth," he whispered. "It's Ivan, and I'm here with Danny. Just stay quiet, and we will get you out."

Not certain Beth could control her excitement, Ivan cut through the tent as quickly as possible. All the while he listened for any sound of Bricker coming back. Once he had an opening large enough, Danny crawled through. Beth threw herself into his arms in a dramatic gesture worthy of a bad melodrama.

"I knew you would find me," she cried.

"Hush!" Ivan said. "Bricker will be down on us before we can get away."

Danny managed to quiet Beth and guide her through the hole in the tent. Ivan knew it would be better if Beth stayed with him, but it would be useless to try to separate the two youngsters. "Stay out of sight back in the trees," he told Beth. "If any one of the men finds you, we'll all be in trouble."

"I want to help. I can shoot."

"Maybe, but—"

"Papa taught me how to shoot." Beth reached for one of Danny's guns. "I'm going to make Bricker sorry he ever lived."

Ivan gripped Beth by both shoulders and shoved his face forward until their noses were practically touching. "You are going to stay back in the trees because if you don't Danny may get killed. Do you want to be responsible for that?"

"No, but—"

"One of those men shot your father. He's going to be okay, but they won't hesitate to shoot any one of us. Do you understand?"

Beth blinked then suddenly seemed to focus. She nodded.

"You will stay hidden until one of us comes for you?"

She nodded again.

"Danny will show you where to hide. Be quick. Bricker will be back soon."

When Danny and Beth disappeared, Ivan cut the ropes supporting Bricker's tent. It gave him a feeling of great satisfaction to see it collapse. He wanted to fell as many tents as possible. It would deprive the men of cover and slow them down in getting their rifles. He dropped two more tents before one of Riley's men noticed. As the man came running toward him, Ivan saw a tent several yards away go down. Danny was back.

A pistol shot rent the air. The battle was on.

Ivan jumped to his feet and put a bullet in the ground

at the feet of the man running toward him. The man stopped so abruptly he lost his balance and fell down.

"Do not move," Ivan called out.

When the man turned to run away, he came into the line of fire from Carla and Danny. The thieves were hampered by being blinded by their campfire, but they fired into the darkness. Two men tried to break through. Ivan shot one in the leg. Carla hit the second man in the pelvis, and he went down screaming. The other men froze.

"Put down your guns," Ivan ordered.

"And let you shoot us like fish in a barrel?" Bricker shouted.

"No one will be hurt unless he tries to escape."

"What do you want?" Riley called out.

"Put down your weapons."

For a moment no one moved. Then one man dropped his gun. He was followed by another.

"Are you all fools?" Bricker shouted. "That crazy foreigner is going to kill all of us."

"Put down your gun," Riley said. "He can't prove we've done anything wrong." When Riley let his pistol fall to ground, the rest followed suit except Bricker.

"Bricker kidnapped that girl," one of the men said. "They can hang all of us for that."

"He did that on his own," Riley said. "I'll swear to it."

Bricker turned on Riley. "You son of a bitch! I'll see you all in hell before I let you leave me to hang." He shot Riley at point blank range.

Before he could get off another shot, Ivan shot him.

The first thing they did on reaching town was deliver the wounded men to the doctor. All three, including Riley, were going to live, but the man shot in the pelvis was in for a long recovery. They left Bricker's body at the camp along with the rest of the thieves, all securely tied and waiting for the sheriff to pick them up. Danny took Beth to her father, who was staying with Myrtle so she could take care of him.

"Where is Laveau?" Ivan asked when he found the jail cell empty.

"Who?" the sheriff asked.

"Laveau diViere. I brought him in for trying to kill Kesney. I turned him over to Maxwell Dodge."

"There was nobody here when I got back," the sheriff said. "I haven't seen Maxwell, either."

When they got to Maxwell's office, they found it empty.

"Cleaned out," the sheriff said. "It's like he was never here."

"Where would he go?" Ivan asked.

"He has a room here in town."

But that, too, was empty. "If he was tied up with this diViere character like you think," the sheriff said to Ivan, "I guess he's made a run for it. He's probably half way to San Antonio by now."

"Maybe not," Carla said. "He has a house about five miles from here. He can't pack everything on a single horse. He'll need a wagon."

"I've got nothing to hold him on," the sheriff said, "except your say so. That diViere fella, either."

"You can't let them get away," Carla protested.

"I've got my hands full with this bunch you've got

hog-tied the hell and gone from here," the sheriff complained. "People in town are going to want my scalp when they find out you're wanting me to put them in jail. The way they see it, Riley and his men found the stolen herds."

"They *found* them because they *stole* them," Ivan said. "It was all part of their cover for going into Mexico to steal whatever they could."

"That's something else," the sheriff said. "Where's all this stuff you say they stole? You said it wasn't at the camp. It sure ain't in Maxwell's office or rooms. Where did they hide it?"

"At Maxwell's house," Ivan and Carla said in unison.

"Well, you can go on a wild goose chase if you want," the sheriff said, "but I'm going after Riley's men. I still don't know what I'm going to tell people when they wake up in the morning."

"Tell them Riley made fools of all of us," Carla said. "He pretended to be protecting us when all along he was robbing villages in Mexico, which put everyone in town at risk."

"You bring back some evidence, and I'll be glad to say anything you want," the sheriff said. "Without it, I'm liable to put the two of you in jail for shooting three innocent men."

"At least he can't say Bricker was innocent," Carla said when she and Ivan were on their way to Maxwell's ranch. "Beth will make sure everybody knows what he did."

Ivan was more concerned with Laveau's escape. It was now clear that Maxwell Dodge was involved in Laveau's scheme, had probably been in on it from the beginning. Maxwell had no idea of the danger he was in. Laveau would hesitate at nothing to achieve his ends. His shooting of Kesney proved that.

Ivan and Carla didn't talk much. There wasn't much to say, and they were tired. After the shootout at Riley's camp, it was hard to work up enthusiasm for another confrontation. Ivan had had his fill of killing in the war. Carla had never shot anyone. It was a lot to absorb, especially on top of everything else that had happened.

Ivan had never been to Maxwell's house, so he let Carla take the lead until he saw something in the distance that looked like a flame. "How far is Maxwell's house from here?"

"Not far. Why?"

Ivan pointed. "Something over there looks like a fire."

"That's where Maxwell's house is." Carla whipped her horse into a hard gallop. "Can you tell if it's the house or a fire outside?" Carla asked when Ivan caught up with her.

"Not from here."

In the several minutes it took them to reach the house, it became clear that the fire had been set only moments earlier. Once caught, however, the flames were spreading rapidly to the rest of the house. The wooden structure, dried in the searing heat of numerous Texas summers, was perfect tinder.

"Why would Maxwell set fire to his own house?" Carla asked as they drew near.

"He would not, but Laveau would."

"Why?"

"To hide something."

"What?"

"Maybe Maxwell's body. Hold my horse," Ivan said to Carla as he slid from the saddle. "I must see if Maxwell is in the house."

The horses, fear of fire bred into them over centuries, sidled nervously. "You can't go in there," Carla protested. "The whole house is on fire."

"I see something in the doorway that looks like a body."

The heat hit Ivan with a powerful blast, but he was certain there was a body in the doorway. He didn't know if the man was alive, but he had scant seconds to get him out. Ignoring the feeling that he was entering an inferno, he staggered up the steps and reached for the man. Taking a firm grip on his hands, Ivan pulled him across the porch, down the steps, and into the yard. As soon as he was out of the reach of the flames, he scooped up handfuls of dirt to smoother the fire that was burning the man's clothes. Once the fire was out, he turned him over.

"It's Maxwell." Carla's voice was infused with horror at seeing the smoldering remains of a man she'd known. His hands and face had been burned so badly he was almost beyond recognition.

"He's been shot. He's badly burned, but he's still alive," Ivan said.

"We have to get him to a doctor," Carla said.

"Get diViere," Maxwell murmured. "He stole everything."

"We'll get you to a doctor," Ivan said.

"No!" The word seemed to exhaust Maxwell. He struggled for breath. "Do you think I want to live looking like this?" he asked, his voice a faint thread. "Get diViere. I won't care if I die as long as you get diViere."

"Where did he go?" Ivan asked.

"Follow the wagon tracks." His strength gone, Maxwell slumped back.

"Do what you can for him," Ivan said to Carla. "I'm going after Laveau."

———⁓———

The cloudless sky was filled with a million flickering stars, but the pale light from a half moon turned the flat and endless plain into a soundless study in silver and grey. The sandy soil under Ivan's horse's hooves shone a white silver. The silence was broken only by the pounding of his horse's hooves, the squeak of leather, the clink of metal. The feeling of isolation, the sense that he was the only living soul on a plain that stretched endlessly in all directions, gave rise to spectral images in his imagination. The sparse grass, dark and withered, made him think of silver-grey fingers, twisted by arthritis, thrusting out of an inhospitable earth. Twin dots of ruby red—the eyes of cows that followed his passage— glowed like the eyes of horned demons. The course of a dry arroyo gaped before him like the menacing entrance to a black abyss. Even the cactus and sage took on the appearance of a scattered army of lilliputian avengers.

Shaking his head to dislodge these fantasies, Ivan concentrated on following the tracks. He'd learned a lot about tracking during his five years in Texas, but in the dim moonlight, it was virtually impossible to tell if Laveau had made the tracks, or if they'd been made by someone else at an earlier date. He was reassured by the knowledge that few people had a reason to drive a buggy across the open plain at any time. He was less assured of his mount's ability to catch up with a fresh horse, even one pulling a buggy loaded with the pillage from several raids.

He debated whether it was more important to capture Laveau or reclaim the stolen treasure. He was certain Laveau would abandon the treasure rather than allow himself to be captured. He had to know that in shooting Kesney and Maxwell, he'd stepped outside the safety net provided by the Reconstruction government. It might be difficult to convince a Texas judge to attach much importance to a stabbing that had taken place in California, especially since the woman had recovered, but no judge could ignore two attempted murders in his own jurisdiction.

Ivan worried whether his horse had enough strength left to catch up with Laveau. From the time Ivan left Carla's ranch that morning, he rode the animal hard all day. His stride had lost its spring, his breathing was not without effort, and Ivan didn't know how much farther he had to go before he caught sight of Laveau. The man always seemed to be just out of sight, just out of reach. If Ivan had been a person to take the dimmest view of everything, that could be seen as a metaphor for the surviving Night Riders' attempts to capture and bring to justice the man who'd betrayed them.

The situation was even more frustrating because rather than disappear, Laveau seemed to be baiting them, circling along the periphery of their lives long enough to disrupt them, then vanishing before anyone could lay hands on him. The protection afforded him by the Reconstruction government, a regime as corrupt as it was onerous, was particularly galling.

A movement in the distance caught Ivan's attention. He held his breath in anticipation, fearful his imagination was playing tricks on him. However, a few moments later he was sure. There was a horse and buggy ahead. A saddled horse was tethered behind. Ivan had every reason to believe Laveau was the driver. With great reluctance, Ivan urged his horse into a fast canter.

His horse stumbled, nearly went to his knees. He recovered quickly, but Ivan knew he couldn't continue this chase much longer. If he didn't catch Laveau soon, he wouldn't catch him at all. He leaned forward, putting as much of his weight as possible over the withers, where it was easier to carry. He had drawn close enough to make out some of Laveau's distinguishing features before Laveau realized he was being followed. He took a single glance behind him then applied the whip to his horse.

The plain appeared flat, but there were enough rocks, shallow depressions, and obstructing plants, living and dead, to make driving a buggy across it challenging. Attempting it at a gallop was foolhardy. The buggy bounced and lurched so violently Laveau was tossed about like a puppet on a string. At one particularly bad bump, a pair of saddlebags Ivan assumed were filled with some of the stolen treasure were thrown from the buggy. Moments later a second pair followed. The look of naked rage on Laveau's face as he glanced back told Ivan that Laveau was aware of what was happening but knew he couldn't stop. Ivan wondered how much more was in the buggy. Laveau struck his horse with several vicious lashes of the whip, but the frightened animal couldn't pull the careening buggy any faster.

Ivan's horse was slowing. He couldn't drive the animal any harder without doing serious damage, possibly life-threatening injury, but he couldn't just give up and let Laveau get away. He knew it was difficult to hit a target while on horseback, especially one that was bouncing about as much as Laveau, but he pulled his rifle from its holster, took aim, and fired.

He missed. Probably because the moment he fired, the buggy lurched violently, and the left wheel came off. It flew about twenty feet through the air, hit the ground, bounced about five feet, before landing on the ground again and rolling about fifteen feet before coming to a stop.

Meanwhile, Laveau jumped from his seat. When he reached inside the buggy, presumably to grab what stolen property was still there, Ivan fired another shot at him. That missed as well, but it served its purpose. Laveau abandoned his effort to salvage any of the treasure. He mounted his horse and rode off at a fast gallop.

Ivan pulled his exhausted horse to a stop. Dismounting the animal, which trembled badly from his exertions, he knew he would only get one shot at Laveau's rapidly vanishing figure. Steadying the rifle on his shoulder, he took careful aim then squeezed the trigger.

He could see Laveau lurch to one side just before he and his horse disappeared in the distance. He had hit Laveau, but he hadn't brought him down.

Damn!

"Kesney said I could be his foreman," Danny said to Carla and Ivan. "He said if I was going to marry his daughter, he wanted to make sure I was smart enough to run the ranch and take care of her."

Beth pouted. "I think it's wonderful Papa is giving Danny a job, but he's forcing us to wait two years to get married. Do you think that's fair?"

"It's not a long time, and you *are* rather young," Carla said.

"But I love Danny. I always will," Beth insisted.

The four of them were sitting in Myrtle's parlor. Danny had endured a long interview with Kesney, while his daughter waited nervously for her chance to talk to her father. Danny seemed relieved and happy. Beth's pretty smile was marred by a trace of petulance. Carla thought it was good Kesney was requiring Beth and Danny to wait two years. It would give Danny time to discover if his infatuation was really love. And she hoped it would give Beth time to mature into a young woman who didn't always think of herself first. It would also give her a chance to learn the difference between what was expected of a young wife as opposed to that which would be tolerated in a spoiled daughter.

"If you love him that much, you won't mind waiting," Carla said. "Besides, you'll see him every day. It'll be practically the same as being married."

Beth didn't look convinced, but Carla was content to leave that to Danny and Kesney. She had a much bigger worry. She had to talk to Ivan, and he wasn't going to like what she had to say. She didn't like it either, but after having gone over it again and again in her mind, she couldn't make any other decision.

Myrtle entered the parlor. "Time for you to scram," she said to Danny. "Your father is sleeping," she said to Beth. "I think you should be here to sit with him when he wakes up. So if you want some time with your young man, you'd better get it now."

Danny and Beth wasted no time in leaving.

"They'll get over this silly infatuation inside a month," Myrtle said. "After that they'll have a chance to see if they can love each other enough to get married."

"Don't be so cynical," Carla said.

"I've been married twice. I know how it works."

"Were you in love?" Carla immediately regretted asking.

"Yes, but not with either of my husbands." Myrtle's gaze focused on Carla. "That's a mistake I hope you're smart enough not to make. Now," she said, turning to Ivan, "what are you going to do about running for sheriff? And don't tell me again that you're going to Poland and taking Carla with you."

Despite Ivan bringing in the stolen items, the citizens of Overlin might never have believed Riley and his men were behind the thefts if Maxwell Dodge hadn't lived long enough to divulge the whole scheme, which had been conceived and set in motion by Laveau diViere. The joy of the Mexicans when they came to retrieve their cherished gold and silver deepened the citizens' guilt for having been so badly duped. When it turned out that the gold chain Bricker had been wearing was the only stolen item that wasn't in the saddlebags Ivan brought back, even the most reluctant doubters were convinced.

Under Ivan's supervision, all the disputes about ownership of various items had been worked out satisfactorily, and he went from being a local hero to a virtual demigod. They would have made him sheriff on the spot, even though the old one hadn't resigned. Others wanted him to take over Maxwell's position. Ivan's response had been to retreat to the safety of Myrtle's parlor.

"Ivan and I need a few minutes to ourselves," Carla said to Myrtle.

"Take all the time you need," Myrtle said. "I have more than enough to do in the kitchen."

Knowing what she had to say, Carla found it almost impossible to look Ivan in the eye. He was everything a woman could want in a husband—handsome, kind, strong, thoughtful, smart, and respected. There didn't seem to be anything he couldn't do. He had enough charm for two people, and his smile was practically a lethal weapon. Most important of all, he loved her and wanted to marry her. How could she tell him she couldn't go with him to Poland—that she couldn't marry him?

Ivan looked at her with a sweet smile that melted her heart. It was filled with compassion and understanding, but no sadness. "I know what you feel you must say."

"You probably do," Carla replied, "but I have to be the one to say it. I love you more than I thought I could love any man, but I can't go to Poland with you. I thought I could, but I can't. I *want* to go, but I can't. I keep telling myself if I loved you enough I could do anything, but deep down inside I know I would end up making both of us miserable."

"When did you decide?"

"I've changed my mind at least a dozen times a day, but yesterday I finally knew for certain. I was with you when we found Kesney. I rode with you to free Beth and capture the thieves. I rode with you to find Maxwell. It wasn't so much what I did but that we did it together. Since you've been here, we've done *everything* together. I will always want to do everything with you."

She could feel the tears welling up in her eyes. She tried to hold them back, but they poured from her eyes and streamed down her cheeks. She started to wipe them away with the back of her hand, but Ivan used his bandana to dry her cheeks.

"I don't know how to live any other way. I would try, but I would end up miserable and making you miserable. If you tried to give me only half the freedom I have here, it would be impossible for either of us to be accepted in your society. I would be a misfit, and you would be blamed for marrying a woman who was unfit by birth and station to be a princess. I can't let you be cut off from your family. Poland is your country, your heritage. I could never be happy knowing I had purchased my happiness at your expense."

She knew what she had to say next. She also knew she should face Ivan when she said it, but she couldn't. Looking into his eyes, knowing the happiness she was giving up, would make it impossible for her to form the words. She dropped her gaze to her hands, which twisted in her lap, and uttered the words that would end any chance of happiness.

"You have to go back to Poland without me."

Chapter 23

IVAN HAD KNOWN FOR SEVERAL DAYS THIS MOMENT WAS coming. It had only been a question of who would say the words first. He had been a fool to think Carla could be happy outside of Texas. He'd been an even bigger fool to think she could have been anything but utterly miserable in Poland. She would have tried to be the kind of wife his family expected. Even if she had succeeded— and he doubted that was possible—the role she would have been expected to play would have squeezed the life out of her. He didn't know if he would have been more heartsick watching this happen or leaving Texas without her. But that didn't really matter because he knew both of these options were impossible for him. There was only one choice he could make.

He looked at Carla, her head down, her hands clenched and twisting in her lap, and his heart went out to her. She had been willing to twist herself into a knot for him only to realize it was impossible. And now she was sacrificing her chance at happiness for him. Knowing that in this moment of her greatest unhappiness she still thought of him first caused him to love her even more. What kind of man would give up such a woman for the sake of a title, even if that title had come with an enormous estate and great power? He knew many such men who would. Ten years ago he would have been one of them, but near poverty, four years of a brutal war, and five years as an ordinary Texas cowhand had changed him.

Nothing could diminish his pride in his family and its contributions to Poland's history, but he deserved no special honors or privileges because of what others had accomplished. Even more important, he realized he wasn't the one to carry that heritage into the future. That required a man whose heart and soul were firmly anchored in Poland. How could he be that man when his heart would forever be in Texas? No one and nothing would ever be as important to him as the woman who sat beside him, this wonderful, unbelievable woman, who was determined to put his happiness before her own. She was stronger and braver than he because he couldn't have done it.

He claimed her agitated hands and calmed them with his own. They were roughened and chapped by work, but he wouldn't have had it any other way. That's who she was, this exceptional woman who'd chosen to love him despite so many reasons to wish he'd never been born. She didn't need a title, wealth, or social position to affirm her nobility. It was bred into her. It was as much a part of her as the color of her hair and the tilt of her chin, the firmness of her principles, or the depth of her love for him. She was his princess, the only one he ever wanted. If necessary, he would spend the rest of his life making her believe that.

"I have known this was coming," he said. "It was foolish to—"

Carla didn't let him finish. "I would try." She looked up at him with tears in her eyes. "You *know* I would try, but it wouldn't work. Everyone would hate me and

blame you for marrying me and forcing them to pretend
to like me." She laid out her entire reasoning process.
"It wouldn't work," she said when she'd finished, her
gaze downcast once more, "no matter how much both
of us tried."

"That is why neither of us is going to try."

She looked up, her expression bleak. "I've been trying to tell myself I had to let you go, that I had to be
ready to say good-bye, but I can't stand even thinking
about it. It would be bad enough if you left right now.
Today. No matter who buys your half of the ranch, it
will kill me if you wait until your year is up."

Ivan put his finger to her lips to silence her. "Even
when you said you would go to Poland with me, I
knew it was impossible. I was so desperate to marry
you I tried to tell myself we could find a way to make
it work, but I realized it could not be. Yet I knew it was
impossible to leave you. That's why I'm going to stay
and run for sheriff. And if you'll let me, we can run *our*
ranch together."

For a moment, Carla stared at him as though she
hadn't understood what he'd said. Then she started as
though stabbed by something sharp.

"But your family is depending on you. You can't
abandon your position as prince. You said your family
has always been important to Poland."

Ivan laughed. "My family has been taking care of
itself for ten years without my help. I have two nephews
who appear only too eager to step into my position."

"But they can't be the prince because you're still alive."

"My sisters will not care. All they want is the position
as head of the family."

"But they can't be the head of the family. You are. You—"

"I've never heard such nonsense in my life."

Both turned to see Myrtle standing in the doorway, looking like a schoolmistress facing two very unsatisfactory students.

"If Ivan wants to stay here, you have no right to try to send him back to Poland," she said to Carla. "He'll do a lot more good here as sheriff than he will parading around a drafty castle wearing clothes that would shame a proper man."

"But he has duties to his country and responsibilities for his family."

Looking thoroughly disgusted, Myrtle turned to Ivan. "Can't you do something to shut her up?"

Ivan thought of several possibilities but chose the one that appealed to him most. He kissed Carla. He kept on kissing her when she tried to talk. He kissed her when she tried to push him away. And he kissed her when she gave in and kissed him back.

"It's good to know some men know how to put an end to female nonsense," Myrtle said. "I'll be in the kitchen in case she has a relapse."

Ivan decided Myrtle's departure was no reason to stop doing something he was enjoying so much so he kept right on kissing Carla. She tried to talk, but failing in that, she gave up and concentrated on kissing Ivan as thoroughly as he was kissing her. In that way they passed a thoroughly satisfactory quarter of an hour.

"Are you sure?" she asked when he finally broke their kiss.

"As sure as I have ever been about anything."

"But what about your family?"

"My going back would make them more uncomfortable than my staying here. I have changed. They have not."

Carla's frown was replaced by a dawning smile. "You really mean it? You *want* to stay here more than you want to go back to Poland?"

Ivan kissed the end of her nose. "I love you. I want to marry you. If that means I have to stay in Texas, then that is where I want to be."

Carla threw herself at Ivan with such force he was knocked flat on the sofa. She covered his face with kisses.

"I understand your enthusiasm," Myrtle said from the doorway, "but I won't have any of that carrying on in my house."

Carla sat up, surprise mingled with chagrin in her expression. "It's not what you think. I was—"

Myrtle's sudden smile was stunning in its intensity. "After what that man just did for you, if you *didn't* kiss him hard enough to drive him half out of his senses, I'd be heartily ashamed of you. Just be glad I'm not thirty years younger. You wouldn't have a chance. Now I *am* going to the kitchen. Be as outrageous as you dare."

Carla smoothed some wrinkles in her dress. "Do you think she's really gone to the kitchen?"

Ivan glanced at the empty doorway and laughed. "What do you think?"

"I think if we don't want her dragging a preacher here so we can be married within the hour, we'd better lock her in the kitchen."

"I heard that."

Carla burst out laughing, but Ivan didn't think that was such a bad idea. It was impossible for Carla to become his wife too soon.

———————

Five years later

"... Anika is finally content with her son's engagement to the only daughter of a wealthy count. Ludmila's husband's ascent to his great uncle's title and fortune means the family can now take its rightful place in society, but that does not mean we do not miss you, my son. I cannot understand why you insist on farming cows. If that is what you must do, we have plenty of cows in Poland. They are much nicer than any cows you have to chase with a rope, though I cannot imagine why you must chase anything with a rope. You should have your servants bring them to you.

I remind you again that you are still Prince Poniatowski. No one can take your place, especially now that you have two sons. I must come to America and that place you call Texas. It must be a very strange place, indeed, if boys who grow up there have no desire to be a prince."

Your loving mother,
Krystina Stanislas
Princess Poniatowski

Coming Soon…

Heart of a Texan

A Night Riders Romance

Available November 2012 from Sourcebooks Casablanca

"I WON'T HAVE HIM IN MY HOUSE," SAID ROBERTA. *The lying, back-stabbing, barn-burning, livestock-killing traitor.*

Nate Dolan had been the only rancher she thought might have had some sympathy for her father. He'd advised him against building the dam, against trying to farm in such dry country, and against making enemies of some of the most powerful men in the area, but he'd always defended her father's right to do what he wanted with his land, no matter how stupid he thought it was.

She would never have believed that Nate would help the other ranchers destroy her father's farm if she hadn't seen him galloping down the drive with her own eyes.

How could the townsfolk even think she'd allow one of the attackers into her house? It would be too much to ask of the most forgiving woman.

"Can't you take him to town?" the sheriff asked.

"He's hurt too badly," said Dr. Danforth.

"I don't care if he dies," Roberta said. That wasn't really how she felt, but she couldn't face the idea of having Nate in her house.

"Well I care, young woman," the doctor stated. "I've seen too many men die, and I don't intend to see this one follow the rest if I can help it. I'll put him in a bed if you have one. I'll put him on the floor if you don't, but he'd going to stay in his house until he's well enough to travel. Then you can tell the sheriff of your suspicions."

For a moment she was speechless with shock and rage.

"It's the only practical solution," the sheriff said.

"I don't care if it's the *only* solution, I won't have that man in my house." She had barely launched into a list of reasons why it was inhuman to ask this of her when four men carrying Nate Dolan's unconscious body walked through the doorway. "Where do we put him?"

"Through there," the sheriff directed.

Roberta thought at first she would position herself in front of her father's bedroom door and dare anyone to enter, but she could tell from the sheriff's attitude that he wouldn't hesitate to remove her bodily. There didn't seem to be anyone to whom she could appeal for support. This was Texas cow country, and people had had little sympathy for her father's stand.

It looked like she didn't have much choice, but she didn't intend to have anything to do with Nate Dolan. Let the doctor see to him. "What are you going to do with him?"

"I'm going to patch him up as best I can. Then I'm going to leave some medicine in case he develops a fever or gets an infection."

"And who's going to feed him and look after him?"

"You are."

"What do you need me to do?" she asked the doctor. She hadn't thought the sight of blood bothered her, but seeing it smeared over Nate's chest made her stomach feel nauseated. She resolutely fought the feeling. She expected she'd see more blood before she saw the last of Nate Dolan.

"I need you to help me extract the bullet," the doctor said.

She took the pan of water, dipped a cloth in it, and started to clean the blood from Nate's chest. A little oozed out of the wound, but it didn't take long before he was clean.

Much against her will, she became aware of his chest in a way that was unsettling. It was almost bare except for a little hair around his nipples and a trail that led to... She quickly averted her eyes. His broad shoulders tapered down to a slim waist. Even in repose, it was easy to see the muscles that enabled him to wrestle full-grown steers to the ground. Like every Texas cowman, his face and neck were deeply tanned, but his chest was pale. No self-respecting Texan would be caught outside his bedroom without a shirt. Some even took a bath in their long underwear when they were on a trail drive.

Nate wasn't wearing any long underwear. In fact, he wasn't wearing anything. The doctor had undressed him while she was gone.

Knowing she was in the room with a naked man was something of a shock. It didn't matter that he was unconscious. He was naked, he was a man, and he was in her house. He wasn't her father, her husband, her brother, or a relative. He was a stranger, a man she knew mostly by reputation. She was nearly certain the doctor wouldn't dress him before he left.

"Pay attention."

She directed her thoughts to the wound, which the doctor's probing had caused to start bleeding again.

"That's better," the doctor said when she'd wiped away the blood. "You're not going to faint on me, are you?"

"No."

"Ah! I think I found it." Seconds later the doctor extracted a bullet. He held it up, squinting at the blood-covered bit of grey metal. "That didn't come from a rifle. He was shot with a pistol."

Roberta's stomach clenched. She remembered standing over her father's body, holding his pistol while tears of grief spilled from her eyes. When she heard the sound of hooves she hadn't hesitated. She'd pulled the trigger. *She* had shot Nate.

"He ought to be okay now," the doctor said, "but you're going to have to watch him. I wouldn't be surprised if he develops a fever. You better hope he didn't get a concussion when he fell out of the saddle. We don't need the biggest rancher in the area suffering from brain damage."

"What do I feed him? How do I feed him?"

"Don't try to feed him anything until he wakes up, or you'll probably drown him. After that, a clear broth for a day or two. Vegetable broth will do, but beef or chicken would be better."

"I don't have any beef, and the chickens were scattered."

"Once everybody hears he's here, you'll probably have every unmarried woman in town above the age of fourteen offering food," the doctor said. "A man like Nate Dolan won't lack for nurses."

"How long do you think he'll be here?" Roberta asked as the doctor was putting the last touches on the bandage.

"It's hard to say. A week if things go well. Maybe two if they don't."

"What do you mean *if things don't go well*?"

"Fever or infection. Some people heal slowly, but he looks like the kind of healthy young man who can bounce back quickly if you take good care of him. You probably ought to sit up with him tonight. If he comes through the next day okay, you ought to be able to relax after that."

"How can I relax with a sick man in my house for at least a week?"

The doctor looked at Nate's unmoving body. "I don't think he'll be getting in your way."

"He's in my way just by being here."

"Well he can't be moved just yet, so you'll have to get used to it. Now I have to go. Mrs. Millican's baby has jaundice, and Mrs. Grady's third boy broke his arm… *again*. Good thing I never had a hankering to be a rich man. This town would be in a mess of trouble." The doctor gathered up his equipment, stuffed everything into one oversized bag, and walked out the door.

"Buck up," he called over his shoulder. "At least your patient is young and handsome. Be glad it's not old Mr. Grunwald. I can't find a nurse who can last half a day without wanting to suffocate him."

How did he know she didn't want to suffocate Nate Dolan? Just because he hadn't shot her father didn't mean he wasn't as responsible as every one of those masked cowards for her father's death.

What was she going to do about the farm? Her father was not a rich man. They depended on their crops to survive. She didn't know what could be saved, but she was certain it wouldn't be enough to put the farm back on its feet. And she was determined to do that even though she didn't intend to stay in Texas. She would not let the ranchers win. The farm would thrive once again. *Then* she would go back to Virginia.

Nate wasn't sure whether he'd simply woken up or regained consciousness. It probably didn't matter. His mind was fuzzy, his vision was blurred, his body hurt, and he had no idea where he was. The last thing he could remember was seeing a fire. He must have gone to help. A fire often meant people lost everything they owned and had nowhere to live. But try as hard as he could, he couldn't remember whether he'd found the fire, or what he'd done after he got there.

A feeling of exhaustion gripped his entire body. He felt incapable of lifting his arm, even turning his head, but that was ridiculous. He was thirty-one years old and was supposed to be in the prime of his life. He'd just spent two weeks in the saddle trying to cross the trail of Laveau diViere. He couldn't be incapable of sitting up.

But he was. He did manage to turn his head. He even lifted one arm, but he couldn't sit up.

What had happened, and why did his chest feel like it was in a vise?

He turned his head to the left and then the right. He was in a small but well-furnished bedroom. It appeared to be a man's bedroom, but it wasn't his or one he recognized.

He listened intently, but he couldn't hear any sound. As much as the mystery of where he was and why he was there unsettled him, he felt safe. Whatever had happened, someone was taking care of him. Unable to move and mentally exhausted, he gave up looking for answers just now. He needed to rest more. Maybe then he could sit up.

—w—

Her father had always said that after a productive day, he felt great even if he was so tired he could hardly stand up. Roberta figured he must have hidden some whiskey in the barn for his brain to be that fuddled. She was exhausted after spending all day cleaning up and trying to save some of the crops. She was too tired to think. She was even too tired to be hungry. After she'd checked on Nate to make sure he was okay, it had taken what remained of her energy to clean up and drag herself to a rocking chair on the front porch. Now all she wanted to do was soak up the cool of the evening until she could summon the energy to drag her tired body to bed.

The sun had set, but it would be light for about another hour. Swallows darted through the air on their erratic flight to catch insects. She suspected a few of the airborne predators might be bats. Just thinking of them made her shiver, but she welcomed any critter that would devour the insects that fed on her crops. They were certainly more welcome than the man driving a buckboard she saw approaching. She recognized Nate's foreman long before he reached the house. If Nate was said to be built along the lines of a greyhound, then Russ McCoy was modeled after a bulldog. There wasn't a man in three counties with shoulders that wide or a neck so thick.

"What do you want?" she asked when Russ brought the buckboard to a stop.

"I've come to take Nate home."

"What took you so long?"

"I didn't know he was here. Hell, I didn't even know he had come back until Gill Pender told me his wife had taken some beef broth to you for him."

"If you know that much, you know the doctor said he can't be moved."

Russ had gotten down from the buckboard and come up to the porch. He was probably an inch or two shorter that Nate, but his bulk made him look bigger. Roberta suspected he could wrestle a steer to the ground without taking a deep breath.

"Taking him home can't be half as dangerous as leaving him here with no one but you to look after him. Hell, I wouldn't put it past you to poison him. If I thought you could hit the broad side of a barn, I'd swear you were the one who shot him."

"If I had, it would have been no more than he deserved for being one of those cowards who murdered my father."

"Nate thought your father was a fool for rebuilding that dam—I heard him say that to your father's face— but he would never have any part in what happened here last night. I don't know how he even came to be here."

"The doctor will tell you when you can take your boss home. As much as I'd like to see everyone involved in the attack hang, I'll do everything I can to make sure your boss survives his stay here. After that, I intended to see every single one of those men punished."

"I heard they were all masked. How can you know who they were?"

"I'll find out." She didn't know how, but she didn't intend to give up until she did.

"I'm not leaving until I see the boss."

"He's sleeping."

"How can I know that without seeing for myself?"

Roberta wasn't sure she could summon the energy to get to her feet, but somehow she managed. "Okay, one look. Then I want you out of my house and off my land."

An agitated voice was heard from inside the house. "Russ, get your butt in here before that woman kills me."

Sins of the Highlander

by Connie Mason with Mia Marlowe

—◦◦◦—

ABDUCTION

Never had Elspeth Stewart imagined her wedding would be interrupted by a dark-haired stranger charging in on a black stallion, scooping her into his arms, and carrying her off across the wild Scottish highlands. Pressed against his hard chest and nestled between his strong thighs, she ought to have feared for her life. But her captor silenced all protests with a soul-searing kiss, giving Elspeth a glimpse of the pain behind his passion—a pain only she could ease.

OBSESSION

"Mad Rob" MacLaren thought stealing his rival's bride-to-be was the perfect revenge. But Rob never reckoned that this beautiful, innocent lass would awaken the part of him he thought dead and buried with his wife. Against all reason, he longed to introduce the luscious Elspeth to the pleasures of the flesh, to make her his, and only his, forever.

—◦◦◦—

"Ms. Mason always provides a hot romance." —*RT Book Reviews*

www.sourcebooks.com

Dylan

by C.H. Admirand

There was nothing he couldn't tame…

Dylan Garahan might be an old hand at lassoing fillies, but one night at the Lucky Star club, and he ends up wrapping his rope around someone that even his formidable strength can't tame. She's wily and beautiful, and she's his new boss. Dylan's had his heart broken before, but even an honest cowpoke has to wrestle with temptation…

Until he got his lasso around her…

Ronnie DelVecchio might be fresh off the bus from New Jersey, but she's a hard-edged business woman and has had her fill of men she can't trust—although she might consider getting off her high horse for that big, handsome rancher with a Texas drawl.

Praise for **Tyler***:*

"Full of witty banter, romance, cowboys, and sweet sensuality…This story will melt your heart." —*My Book Addiction and More*

"Fresh and exciting…an interesting, potent, provocative love-story." —*Red Room*

www.sourcebooks.com

Tall, Dark and Cowboy

by Joanne Kennedy

———

She's looking for an old friend…

In the wake of a nasty divorce, Lacey Bradford heads for Wyoming where she's sure her old friend will take her in. But her high school pal Chase Caldwell is no longer the gangly boy who would follow her anywhere. For one thing, he's now incredibly buff and handsome, but that's not all that's changed…

What she finds is one hot cowboy…

Chase has been through tough times and is less than thrilled to see the girl who once broke his heart. But try as he might to resist her, while Lacey's putting her life back together, he's finding new ways to be part of it.

———

Praise for Cowboy Fever:

"HOT, HOT, HOT…with more twists and turns than a buckin' bull at a world class rodeo, lots of sizzlin' sex, and characters so real you'll swear they live down the road!" —Carolyn Brown, *New York Times* and *USA Today* bestselling author of *Red's Hot Cowboy*

www.sourcebooks.com

Wildest Dreams

by Rosanne Bittner

⚬⚬⚬

*With more than 7 million books in print,
RT Book Reviews Career Achievement Award–
winning author Rosanne Bittner is beloved by
fans for her powerful, epic historical romances.*

Lettie McBride knew that joining a wagon train heading West was her chance to begin anew, far from the devastating memories of the night that had changed her forever. She didn't believe she could escape the pain of innocence lost, or feel desire for any man…until she meets Luke Fontaine.

Haunted by his own secrets, Luke could never blame Lettie for what had happened in the past. One glance at the pretty red-haired lass was enough to fill the handsome, hard-driving pioneer with a savage hunger.

Against relentless snows, murderous desperadoes, and raiding Sioux, Luke and Lettie will face a heart-rending choice: abandon a lawless land before it destroys them, or fight for their…Wildest Dreams.

⚬⚬⚬

"Extraordinary for the depth of
emotion." —*Publishers Weekly*

www.sourcebooks.com

Nell

by Jeanette Baker

—⁓—

The Love of a Lifetime

He came upon her in the light of the silver moon and knew instantly she was the one. It was right, he thought, that they should meet without the trappings of wealth, family, and formality. For in the end, in the sweetly scented darkness, it would be just the two of them. Donal O'Flaherty didn't see English versus Irish. He saw only Nell, and that was enough.

But Fate had another plan. Soon Nell is swept away to the treacherous Tudor court. Yet through the centuries and across generations, she would prove that neither prison bars nor the hands of time could stop the power of a love meant to be…

—⁓—

For more Jeanette Baker books, visit:

www.sourcebooks.com

Cowboy Fever

by Joanne Kennedy

—◊◊◊—

She thought she had it all...

A modeling contract with Wrangler got this Miss Rodeo Wyoming a first-class ticket out of town, but somewhere along the way Jodi Brand lost her soul. When she gets back to her hometown, her childhood friend Teague Treadwell's rugged cowboy charm hits her like a ton of bricks...

He believed he wasn't good enough...

Teague is convinced Jodi's success lifted her out of his reach. Now he's got to shed his bad boy image to be worthy of the girl next door...

But whoever heard of a beauty queen settling for a down and dirty cowboy...

—◊◊◊—

Praise for Joanne Kennedy:

"Bring on the hunky cowboys."—Linda Lael Miller, *New York Times* bestselling author of *McKettrick's Choice*

"A delightful read full of heart and passion."—Jodi Thomas, *New York Times* and *USA Today* bestselling author of *Somewhere Along the Way*

Tyler

by C.H. Admirand

—⁓—

Desperate times call for desperate measures...

When Tyler Garahan said he'd do anything to save his family's ranch, he never thought that would include taking a job as a stripper at a local ladies' club. But the club's fiery redheaded bookkeeper captures Tyler's attention, and for her, he'll swallow his pride...

And one good turn deserves another...

Emily Langley feels for the gorgeous cowboy. It's obvious that he's the real deal and wouldn't be caught dead in a ladies' revue if he wasn't in big trouble. And when he looks at her like that, she'll do anything to help...

Working days on the ranch and nights at the ladies' club, Tyler is plumb exhausted. But could it be that his beautiful boss needs him just as much as he needs her...

—⁓—

Praise for C.H. Admirand:

"Admirand's second frontier romance features clever and well-crafted plot lines." —*Publishers Weekly*

For more C.H. Admirand, visit:

www.sourcebooks.com

One Hot Cowboy Wedding

by Carolyn Brown

———◆———

A marriage made in Vegas...

Hunky cowboy Ace Riley wasn't planning on settling down, but his family had other plans for him...The only way to save his hide, and his playboy lifestyle, is to discreetly marry his best friend, Jasmine King.

Can't possibly last...

Feisty city-girl Jasmine was just helping out her friend—that is, until their first kiss stirs up a whole mess of trouble, and suddenly discretion is thrown to wind.

One hot cowboy, one riled up woman... And they'll be married for a year, like it or not!

———◆———

Praise for Carolyn Brown's Spikes & Spurs series:

"An old-fashioned love story told well... A delight." —*RT Book Reviews*, 4 Stars

"Plenty of twists, turns, and hot cowboys, and a story line that's got to be continued." —*Long and Short Reviews*

For more Carolyn Brown, visit:

www.sourcebooks.com

Red's Hot Cowboy

by Carolyn Brown

—⋙⋘—

He wasn't looking for trouble...

But when the cops are knocking on your door, trouble's definitely found you. And this is where Wil Marshall finds himself after checking in to the Longhorn Inn. It could all be a big mistake, but Wil's not getting much sleep. Then the motel owner—who is drop dead gorgeous and feisty to boot—saves him from an even worse night behind bars. Now he owes her one, big time...

But Trouble comes in all shapes and sizes...

Pearl never wanted that run-down motel, but her aunt didn't leave her much choice. And then this steaming hot cowboy shows up looking for a place to rest. Next thing she knows, she wants to offer him more than just room service. But if he calls her Red one more time, he won't be the only one accused of murder...

Sparks are definitely flying and before long, the Do Not Disturb sign might be swinging from the door...

—⋙⋘—

Praise for **Love Drunk Cowboy***:*

"Brown revitalizes the Western romance."—*Booklist*

www.sourcebooks.com